# In the Eyes of the Son

## A Novel by

# Hans Brinckmann

Savant Books
Honolulu, HI, USA
2014

Published in the USA by Savant Books and Publications
2630 Kapiolani Blvd #1601
Honolulu, HI 96826
http://www.savantbooksandpublications.com

Printed in the USA

Edited by Sabrina Favors
Cover Photo by Hans Brinckmann
Cover Design by Daniel S. Janik

13 digit ISBN: 9780991562206

# Acknowledgements

During the long gestation period of this novel, I received encouragement and ideas from friends and family. I am most grateful for their unfailing support.

I wish to acknowledge especially the valuable advice and specific suggestions offered by my writing partner and translator, Hiromi Mizoguchi, who helped me greatly in shaping the narrative as it now lies before you.

Finally, thanks and appreciation is due my publisher, Daniel S. Janik, for taking on the book, and my editor, Sabrina Favors, for her proven deep interest in the novel's story and her effective professional advice in editing the manuscript.

Hans Brinckmann

In the Eyes of the Son

# Preface

In fiction, where does the author's own experience end and invention begin? It's a perennial question that can never be satisfactorily answered.

Some readers of my two collections of short stories have urged me to reveal where the border runs between the real and the fictional. They wanted clarity, clear demarcation. In some cases there is such a line, but in the writing, I prefer to leave the border areas undefined and allow the story to acquire a life of its own, and the fictional characters to become credible, flesh-and-blood people. The purpose of literary fiction is not to report facts. It's to help both author and reader to avoid the trivial and focus on the essential, thereby making sense of the complexities of life. If it also manages to entertain, and, in the process, causes the author or reader to smile or shed a tear or two, then it is more than serving its purpose.

The book you are holding is a product of *both* imagination and memories. Many of the chapters and some of the characters were lifted, at least to some extent, from remembered experience, especially the chapters dealing with the protagonist's childhood in Holland, his banking career, and the social conditions in Chicago and New York in the 1970s and '80s. The book's main thread—postponement of an inner passion until later in life, and the disharmony this can wreak upon one's life—is not unknown to me either. In my case, the issue was not photography, and I was fortunate to have the support and understanding of my wife.

The characters in this book have already become like real people to me. But let there be no doubt: This is—and must be read as—a work of fiction.

1

# Part One

*Amsterdam 1953-1954*

In the Eyes of the Son

# Chapter 1

*The Desks.* Their mute, innate hostility.

He had barely entered and already they rejected him. He should have walked right out. He didn't.

That was his first mistake.

He confronted them from just inside the entrance to the great pillared banking hall. Closed ranks of stolid conformity. Rubber-stamped smugness.

He was only seventeen, new to the world, and unsure what was expected of him.

In the light of the desk lamps, the pale, bloated faces sprouted from their dark suits like cauliflower. When he appeared in the doorway, they had tilted a fraction; the eyes two fractions. Row upon row of dully interrogating stares.

Like all future leaders, he needed tutors first. Here, beyond this gloomy portal, he would be receiving instruction from the very legions he would, in time, command. Well, not he alone—there were twelve others like him hired for the executive program. But they were elsewhere. They had preceded him by more than two weeks and had already been dispersed over the bank's different departments.

"This is Peter van Doorn, our newest management trainee," his minder announced to the hall. There was no reaction, but he sensed a suspicion, a low-level, unarticulated aversion. It was as if, through the mists of their compromised lives, they decided, not by reasoning but by raw instinct, that there was an enemy at the door, and that it was him. He felt them make a collective vow: *We will emasculate you. We will break your spirit.* A long shudder rose up from his loins through the pit of his stomach to the roots of his dark blond hair before settling with a sense of defeat. The last spasms before surrendering to the inevitable. He was here at the insistence of his father, who had decided that he join a bank.

The personnel assistant took him around to introduce him to some of the Desks. Reluctantly, the solid front opened a crack.

The desks in this hall stood eight across, six deep, forty-eight in all. His desk was the forty-ninth. Two dour men in overalls carried it in. Fitting it in properly would have meant a complete rearrangement comparable to the redesigning of the Stars and Stripes to accommodate Alaska. But that was evidently too much trouble. Instead, they placed his desk to the side, between two pillars. He felt self-conscious and superfluous—the unwanted star in the field.

In the months that followed, Peter and the other twelve young recruits would be given on-the-job training in some of the basics of international banking by a succession of unmemorable tutors. These sessions took place in the afternoons, the mornings being taken up by classroom work. The training would last a year, at the end of which they would be sent out to work in the bank's Asian branches.

His first task was to compose "second reminder" letters to overseas banks requesting a reply to earlier reminders that in turn requested a reply to the original letters—which he was not permitted to see. He didn't remember the name or face of the man who supervised his work. What he did remember was the man's yellowing teeth, his depressing pants, doubtless concealing third-day underwear, and the way he furtively locked his desk—against snooping—when he went to the toilet.

Peter soon learned that all clerks snoop. To glean by stealth snippets of the kind of life they had bartered away for security, he supposed. He never forgot the smirks on their faces when they discovered a tart's photo, a condom, and a bank statement with a fat balance in the drawer of a colleague. Of course their discoveries were always "accidental." Their outward demeanor was controlled and respectful. Decorum must be maintained at all times—another early lesson.

No one was allowed to smoke at their desks until four o'clock and conversation was to be kept to a minimum. The sub-director frequently cruised around the aisles, sometimes swooping down from behind a pillar to catch slackers and nose-pickers and, in the agonizing last minutes before the hour of relief, the addicts trying to beat the clock by a few puffs. When caught, they claimed the office timepiece was slow. Grown men!

Peter wasn't transferred to one of the other floors of the building like his co-trainees, perhaps because he had arrived two weeks later than the others. He stayed in the main hall, at his desk between the pillars, which to him confirmed his status as an outsider. But his duties changed every week, following a training schedule in the possession of the department chief but not known to him. He met the chief only once, on the first day.

"Remember one thing, young man," the chief said sternly from his creaking armchair, while keeping his underling standing at the rim of his weathered desk. "You know nothing. For that is a fact: *You know nothing!* Self-knowledge rooted in humility is the key to building sound character, and that in turn is what makes good leaders. *If* you have what it takes, of course. Which, at this point, must be considered highly doubtful. Any questions?"

The arched severity of his raised eyebrows, together with the parsimony of his lips and bony chin, precluded any affirmative response to this apparent overture.

"No, sir," Peter said.

"I thought so," the chief said, and passed him on to a subordinate.

Gradually, his work became more interesting. By the second month, he was checking bills of exchange and shipping documents presented by export customers against the terms and conditions of foreign letters of credit. He was told to take special care with punctuation.

"The Indians are the worst," explained his instructor-of-the-week. "One lousy comma too many, and they refuse to pay. They send you a little note on cheap, funny-smelling paper with a text I know by heart: 'Invoice not in accordance with credit terms. We are awaiting our client's authority to pay'."

The man intoned this in a fake Indian accent that drew laughs from the juniors and cutting glances from the old sourpusses. "Pure chicanery!" he continued in a lowered voice. "What they want is a discount, the cheapskates. The Africans are rotten too, all the way down to the Cape. Except the Boers, they're okay, good Protestant stock who know they can't screw around with their relatives!"

The candor was a relief. For the first time since Peter entered the bank, he found himself smiling.

Though growing ever more "important," his burdens were never heavy, and he found plenty of time to observe his co-workers as they went about their daily routines.

What struck him was their curious lack of spirit and ambition. After some time he concluded, with the lingering depth-plumbing habit of his high school days, that their mediocrity must be caused by a determination to avoid risk. That's why these types were content to be clerks in banks and government offices, he thought, to escape the necessity of practicing self-reliance. But wait! Maybe it was this refusal, this cowardly search for protection, that was the cornerstone of capitalism! As Peter went to fetch a fresh load of documents, he formulated Capitalist Lesson Number One: Exploit the Employee's Attachment to Stability and Security.

*Hah*, he thought. *These gray mice are content to run the treadmill in their safe little cages, and I'm outside watching them.*

This cheery insight came to him just before smoking time, and he felt a seditious urge to flaunt the rules and light a fag right then and there. But he resisted, not wanting to play into the sub-director's heavy hand. Instead, he amused himself with the thought that his understanding of capitalism's secret methods made him immune to them.

Just then the sub-director tapped a pile of paper on the desk of an elderly document-checker near Peter and said, loud enough for half the hall to hear, "I see you're still on the same bunch as this morning, Paulonius!"

"I know, I…I was busy with something else…"

"Something *else*? Your task in this bank is to check documents. Don't tire your head with other concerns. We have qualified people for that. Understood?"

"Yes, sir. I'm sorry, sir."

"That's all right, Paulonius. You're a good man otherwise."

*Brilliant*, thought Peter. *The boss exacts the apology as the price for providing security, satisfying the needs of both parties. The boss's contempt rises in proportion to the employee's willingness to suffer indignities, which is potentially limitless, as long as they are delivered with firm authority.*

This line of thinking might well constitute another Capitalist Lesson, but its text still needed refining.

The clock struck four. Peter lit up and leaned back in thought. You can't intimidate someone who is willing to take risks, any risk—even the risk of death—in order to know life.

Was he willing to risk death in order to know life?

The question stumped him. Perhaps the argument was getting too grandiose for an apprentice banker.

He placed his cigarette momentarily on the edge of his desk, and with both hands moved a new stack of documents in front of him. The voice of the sub-director made him start.

"You're burning a mark in the wood, young man!" Had he been watching from behind the pillar?

"Oh, no, sir, I'm not. I just…" He picked up the offending fag and held it under the desk.

"You're contradicting me?"

"Well, sir, I mean, I was just…" The Desks had stopped to watch the public execution.

"I said: Are you contradicting me?"

"No, sir, I mean, well…"

"How old are you?"

"Eighteen, sir."

"Eighteen, eh?"

"I mean seventeen. Almost eighteen. I'm…I'm sorry, sir. I didn't mean to…uh…"

"What? Speak up!"

"I didn't mean to…uh…contradict you, sir."

"That's better. You're planning a long career with the bank, aren't you? What's your name again?"

"Van Doorn, sir. I hope so, sir."

"Good! We need promising young men like you!" The sub-director smiled benevolently and continued his inspection, hands clasped behind his back, chest filled out.

Peter brought his cigarette up and took a puff. It tasted foul and he stubbed it out. He was aware of an intense silence around him, and took a guarded, sideways look. The Desks promptly got back to work, eyes averting, throats clearing, mouth corners drooping with obscene satisfaction.

He couldn't believe what he had done. He had behaved like one of them! Nothing in his attitude distinguished him from these sycophants. Yet he knew he was different. Not having had the guts to turn around and march right out on that first day didn't make him one of them. *All right*, he thought, *I might occasionally behave like one of them, if it suits me. But my thoughts are my own even when my mouth strays. What's wrong with that?*

He failed to silence the suspicion that he had, in fact, joined the ranks of the tethered and the timid without sharing their convictions. He was a fraud, a traitor to himself. Without so much as a struggle, he had bartered away his real calling for the tepid comforts and dubious worth of career security. For a Desk.

And *that*, he knew, was his greatest, his truly unforgivable mistake.

# Chapter 2

The calling that Peter had betrayed for a banking career was photography, a passion that had sustained him throughout high school. He had had every intention to make it his life's work.

Although his father, Eduard, worked for a while as a press photographer, Peter had discovered photography on his own. Once Eduard noticed his son's interest in taking pictures, he had encouraged him actively in that direction, until the day he changed his mind for reasons that irreversibly affected the relationship between father and son, and clouded Peter's future.

Eduard had been a left-wing political journalist before the war. He lost his job when Holland was occupied by the Germans in 1940 and was soon sought by the Nazis, who considered him a dissident. Leaving his wife and two children in the care of a cousin on a farm near Gorinchem, among the fat cattle of the Rhine Delta, he went into hiding. Whenever he could, he paid brief visits to his family, under cover of darkness. Finally, in 1943, he managed to escape via Spain and Gibraltar to England, leaving his pregnant wife to give birth, the following year, to their second daughter, Pauline.

Once in Britain, he turned to freelance war photography. He covered the last phase of the war for several British papers and magazines, from the V-2 rocket attacks on London and the battle of Arnhem to the German surrender. When the war was over, he locked away his camera, collected his family, and returned to his old newspaper job in Amsterdam, never to take another picture.

Peter, on the other hand, had enrolled in a photography class through his school when he was twelve. His photos, taken first with a Kodak box, then with an old, temperamental Rolleicord swapped at a school fair for two pairs of boots he had grown out of, were judged "above average," occasionally even "showing promise." On his fourteenth birthday—the year was 1949—his father paid him an unforgettable compliment: He entrusted him with his old Leica III, the camera he had used on the front. Peter remembered the exact words his father had spoken as he placed it in his hands. "If you really love photography, Son, this camera will become your third eye, and nothing else in life will matter." Peter was gripped and did all he could to merit this precious gift.

He took photographs of everything in sight: old trees, churches, dogs, neighbors. Gradually, he gravitated toward street scenes. Whores soliciting. Old men pushing carts. The sun rising behind piled-up trash. He was in that unsettled phase when he still worried about everything that was wrong with the world.

He always had his Leica with him, dangling from his neck. The only time he put it away was in class. He refused to steal shots his classmates urged him to take.

His pictures were composed and atmospheric, made more with an eye to the aesthetic than as proof of daring or confrontation. When photographing people, he took pains to remain undetected. He wasn't interested in recording expressions of anger if that anger was directed at him, or threatened to embroil him.

This approach did not stem from meekness or hypocrisy. It was a logical consequence of the image he had of himself, that of a cool and impartial observer, a seeker of meaning and truth. This principle precluded any action that might interfere with the natural flow of life—with the action he was photographing. It demanded an outsider role.

Or so he thought. Until that fatal event which exposed his guiding philosophy as a charade and changed his life forever. But that wasn't until a year later.

Eduard was always working against deadlines and couldn't spare much time for his son. When he did look at Peter's photographs, his reaction was a typical "Mmm, not bad." Action shots of football matches or racing ambulances or police cars on the chase elicited a higher "Good!" rating.

Only once did a photograph really impress him. It was a dramatic shot of an acrobat falling from the high trapeze at Hagenbeck's Circus—mouth and eyes wide open in terror, arms flailing, fingers spread—into the safety net, which was not visible in the picture. "That's a great shot, Peter!" he exclaimed, adding with a wry wink, "Pity about the net, eh?" The comment shocked Peter, but he laughed sheepishly, taking it as a joke.

The next day Eduard asked a local handyman to build a darkroom for his son in the attic. He found time to help get it going, positioning the enlarger, developing the first few rolls. As a wartime news photographer, he had little darkroom experience himself, sending the undeveloped rolls back home. He was almost as thrilled as Peter to see the images come to life in the developer, like ghosts materializing through the walls of a haunted house.

Somehow, he now managed to give his son the attention that he had always denied him. Together they experimented with sepia and silver gelatin emulsions to get the warm period feel. They discovered ways to correct the light balance, and used filters for dramatic results. They had great fun creating a montage out of a shot Peter had taken of his mother jumping off a low wall and another of a farmer scooping manure from a cesspool.

They were sweating together like real chums in that narrow space, peering over each shot, cropping unwanted details, highlighting a face, a hand, a single horse in a field of racers. They were unselfconsciously intimate, sometimes touching each other with an arm, a leg, a bent shoulder, even brushing cheeks. The lustrous scent of his father's mop of unruly, dark brown hair would still linger faintly in Peter's nostrils many years later, the sweet strength of pipe tobacco mingling with hints of caramel and graphite-and-wood pencil shavings.

Peter was deliriously happy. Neither the bond he felt with his father then, nor the excitement of witnessing the photographs come into being under the glow of the infrared lamp, lost any of its power over the years. The two experiences remained inextricably linked, even long after he had come to realize that his father's interest in his photography had been tinged with unreasonable expectation.

Peter's success grew steadily. He exhibited at school shows, entered competitions, won prizes in the "Urban Beauty" and "Human Interest" categories. He was even elected "Junior Photographer of the Year" by a new photography magazine for a melancholy shot of a teenage girl, a Jewish orphan leaning gloomily over an Amsterdam canal bridge on a dark, wintry day. It was then that he told his father that he wanted to become a photographer.

"We'll see," was Eduard's reaction.

Despite this non-committal response, Peter remained determined to make photography his career. But his hopes were dealt an unexpected and decisive blow the day after his sixteenth birthday. On that day, he witnessed death first-hand.

A man carrying a complete take-out meal for four from a Chinese restaurant was hit by a loose plank that dropped five stories from the scaffolding of a building under construction. The man was walking with his head bent forward, holding the packaged food with outstretched hands, like an offering. Peter had been watching the construction gang at work, hoping for a good shot, when he noticed the plank drop vertically. He shouted a frantic warning but the man didn't seem to hear. He was hit smartly in the neck and died instantly. The food dropped, splayed all over the pavement like hot vomit.

Peter heard the startled reaction of a woman in a blue dress who happened to be passing the stricken man but was unharmed. She had heard the yell and glanced in Peter's direction as he dashed towards the scene. The next moment, the man was hit, and she shrieked. For an instant Peter's eyes caught hers, suspended in horrified incomprehension, as she kneeled by the dead man, unable to utter a word. Her face mirrored Peter's shock at the grotesque arbitrariness of death.

He ran all the way home in a state of panic and just made it through the kitchen door, blurting out what had happened in staccato phrases.

"He was dead…but the food…was still steaming!"

Those were his last words before he fainted.

He came to through layers of coolness, lying on the floor. His mother was holding a cold towel to his brow. His father towered over him, concerned and grim-faced.

"Feeling better, boy?"

14

"Yes…I think so…" He drank some water and smiled up at both of them. "I'm all right now."

"Good, good. Then tell me…" his father began.

"Wait a bit!" said his mother. "Give him time to recover!"

But Peter wanted to talk. "You know, Dad, there was this woman, she was just passing him on the sidewalk, and after he was…hit, she kneeled down to help him. She was wearing a light blue, silky kind of dress with a wide skirt, and the skirt was billowing up in the sunlight. It was very…beautiful right next to that man, who had been alive just a moment before… Do you understand what I'm saying?"

His father had an eager look in his eyes.

"Yes, that was quite a scene. You managed to get some good shots?"

Peter hadn't thought of his camera until that moment and didn't answer.

"Did you?"

"No, I…I didn't think of it. I tried to warn the man…"

His father didn't say anything. His face reddened and he left the room. But he was back in seconds, agitated.

"You hear that?" he said in clipped tones, addressing his wife. "Your son had a once-in-a-lifetime chance to take a truly spectacular shot, a shot of a man at the very instant of death, an unexpected, violent death at that, and he flunks it. He flunks it and comes home crying."

Peter's mother made soothing supplications, but he was unrelenting.

"And then he faints." He glared at his son. "If he'd acted like the professional he claims he wants to be, he'd have gone berserk and used up every last frame he had. But what does this boy of yours do? He forgets to use his camera." His tone of derision didn't hurt Peter as much as the use of the third person in his presence—the implied disavowal that he was his son.

"He forgets and he faints." Eduard gave him a long look of contempt and then abruptly left the house, not to return until late afternoon.

His father's words and behavior would haunt Peter for years. They signalled a point of no return, the definitive end of his childhood, of the happy, intimate darkroom days.

This was the event that settled Eduard's mind about his son's future. In his judgment, Peter lacked the mettle to be a war photographer. It was useless to argue that the war was over, and that in any case his interest was in quite a different type of photography. To Eduard, war photography was the only kind that counted. The only kind of photography worthy of a man. Even in peacetime. Not that he ever discussed this with his son or explained why he had given up photography when the war ended. He never talked about the war, or about his political beliefs.

It was his columns that gave him away. "There is no such thing as peace," he once wrote. "What we call peace is no more than a prolonged cease-fire, the temporary absence of war. The next battle is already brewing. It will involve us all."

Peter couldn't grasp this line of thinking. To him, the world was essentially good and beautiful. As long as people showed compassion for fellow human beings, and worked diligently at overcoming disease and social injustice, there was no reason why there couldn't be peace forever.

His father's loss of interest in Peter's photographic work dented his own enthusiasm. But he hadn't given up his dream. So when he had successfully passed his final exams, albeit with indifferent marks, he appealed once again for his father's support to see him through Art Academy—its creative photography department.

His father lowered the newspaper he was reading, told him to sit down, and gave him a hard look. "You already know how to hold a camera, Son. You don't need any art school to teach you that. What you need is the school of hard knocks." He was sucking his pipe, which no longer emitted the spicy caramel smells that Peter remembered. It stank.

"Dad, I can't get a job as a photographer unless I have a diploma."

"Son, I'm not talking photography. What I have in mind is finding you a job with an international company, one with overseas branches. The Far East maybe. Or Canada. There's a real country with a future. Or America."

"But, Dad, I don't want to."

"This is not a country to stay in, Son. Europe is tired and exhausted, and there's going to be another war. Better get out while you can."

"I don't want to go into business. Business is so…soul-destroying." His father laughed strangely and stared out of the window. A ragtag bunch of loudly shouting neighborhood boys were fiercely kicking a ball in the quiet street, their heaped-up coats serving as goal posts. They looked disheveled and steamy. One of the goalies lunged sideways to stop a ball, and landed on the rough street. He clambered up painfully but went right on, pointing forward and shouting, "Watch left!" His knee was bleeding.

"Why are you not out there? Huh?"

"Aw, I don't know. Don't care much for football."

His father's face flushed. "Damn it! Where's your spunk? Are you my son or aren't you? When I was your age, I was the school champion of wrestling *and* high jump!"

"I know, Dad. But I'm not you. Why can't you accept that?"

His father seemed disheartened. The weathered, dark-haired hand he passed slowly over his face looked veined and ancient. Peter felt a wave of sadness engulfing him. He thought of how close they had been in those darkroom days that seemed long ago now—how much alike they were then. Now he could only see his father's disappointment and loneliness, and it put a distance between them that he hadn't noticed before.

His father took his hand from his face and smiled wanly. Peter realized his father was also aware of their growing distance.

"You're right, Son. Sorry. I shouldn't have said that. But I still think you should leave. I tell you what." Suddenly, he sounded upbeat, as if trying hard to be encouraging. "Why don't you go into banking? Suits your temperament."

"My *temperament*? Why?" It wasn't what he meant to ask, but it was what he said.

"You know, international connections, the life abroad. It'll make a man out of you. I don't have any special connections with banks myself, of course, but I have a friend who can probably get you into the Holland International Bank. They've got branches all over Asia."

"Life abroad?"

"Try it for five or six years, I believe that's the usual contract. If you don't like it, you'll still be young enough to make a switch. But I bet you'll love it!"

Peter nodded gravely and promised to think about it. Embarrassed, his father grabbed him by the shoulders and hugged him clumsily, briefly.

"Good!" he said. "Good." And he returned to his paper.

Without telling him or anyone else, Peter made the rounds of the Amsterdam newspapers and glossy magazines seeking a job as a junior photographer. They all turned him down on the grounds of his young age and inexperience. When he pointed to his portfolios that proved otherwise, they said very nice but that wasn't professional work, and in any case, he lacked formal qualifications.

Next, he visited both the Art Academy's and the School of Journalism's photography departments to ask about scholarships. They both said they didn't have any.

A week later, having found all potential roads to a photographic career blocked, he told his father that he was willing to follow his advice.

# Chapter 3

Before the week was out, Peter went for an interview his father had set up for him with the Holland International Bank through his friend, a professor in Asian studies. To his astonishment, he was promptly taken on for their annual elite in-house management development program which had already started two weeks earlier with a group of twelve young men. The bank was willing to hire him as the thirteenth. "We could make space for you," they said, "as you seem to fit our requirements." He was to enter their private training institute, a boarding school located in Villa Weltevreden in Bloemendaal, a posh suburb in the dunes twenty kilometers west of Amsterdam.

Peter was in a daze. His resistance broken, he yielded to the stream of events that was overtaking him. He couldn't imagine what working in a bank would be like. Still less did he have any concept of living in a faraway country, separated from family and friends. None of this actually scared him—he thought that he might well lack the imagination to feel scared.

Villa Weltevreden, located on Bloemendaal's leafy Duinweg, a meandering hilly road featuring large opulent properties, turned out to be an elaborate late nineteenth century architectural monstrosity grown quaint by the passage of time. It was built by a Dutch plantation owner returned rich from Java, its extravagant design and lavish amenities meant no doubt to ease the prospect of his retirement in the less than salubrious climate of his soggy home country.

The bank had acquired the place shortly after the war, as part of a bankruptcy settlement with the planter's grandson who had managed to squander the family fortune in disastrous stock speculations. The bank's president had personally decided to use the house as a staff training center, a long-cherished dream. To him, the villa's decorative style perfectly matched his concept of what constituted a just and sane world order. And so did its name, which meant "well-contented." It was taken from the official residence of the Dutch Governor General in Batavia, which after the war had been renamed Djakarta.

Weltevreden's director was a retired officer of the Dutch colonial army, a spry, tallish man without regimental moustache but with the kind of scarlet spider-veined cheeks and bushy eyebrows common to the archetype. His name was Captain Lemmerink and he lived with his second wife, who was much younger and had a reputation for sauciness. The boys soon began to refer to her as Lady L.

Between his "Far East experience" and his contribution to the war as military attaché in Canberra, and *her* background in affluent Dutch suburban bridge-playing society—which, rumor had it, had grand-slammed their way through the war with minimal disruption—the couple was deemed eminently qualified to prepare the young men for their important tasks in life.

On the very first evening, over cocktails, the good captain spelled out his priorities: punctuality, an unflagging positive attitude, and correct social behavior, in that order. He then laid out the program awaiting the young men during their year at the villa. At dinner, they would be taught the table manners and social graces that would make them feel at ease in polite society everywhere. Two evenings a week, an outside speaker would come to instruct them after dinner about such subjects as the dangers confronting bachelors in the East, the rising unrest in Indonesia and other remaining Western colonies, and how to handle the native clerical staff. On Friday nights, Lady L. would give lessons in contract bridge or the captain would inform them about wines of the world. On special occasions, there might be a house concert or a dance or cocktail party to which the boys could each bring a "young lady." As there would be no functions on the weekends, the boys were free to spend them with their own families.

"And now," he announced in English, "let us repair to the dining room!"

The young men, not quite knowing what to make of the word "repair," made a show of finding their seats at the large dining table with the help of place-cards fetchingly held aloft by little silver figurines of Javanese servant boys.

They pulled back their chairs but the captain motioned them to hold off lowering their philistine asses until his wife had taken her place. She did so daintily, with the clumsy help of her table partner, a hunk called Harry with whom she had been whispering as they filed in.

The captain took his place opposite his wife and asked for silence. He then said grace, audibly, simply and inter-denominationally, and wished everyone bon appétit to which Lady L. smiled beatifically and invited them to unfold their napkins and start on the soup, which by now was half cold.

"And boys," she continued, "as you will have noticed, I have allowed handsome Harry to choose me as his table partner for this week. That's why I sit to his right. He's not only helping me with my chair but he's going to be a real gallant, aren't you, Harry?" She grabbed Harry's nearest hand and brought it slowly to her lips across the cloven mound of her deep neckline, while looking him straight in the eye. Harry grunted something, blushing massively.

"Oh, you poor dear," she said releasing his hand and patting it lightly. "I'm only talking *dinner*!" Loud laughter.

As for Peter, he was struggling with his own napkin which had got its laundry mark caught in his belt buckle. His persistent activity below table level caught the attention of Lady L., who could be relied on to take advantage of any ambiguous opportunity. A few boys had noticed, too.

"You need help with that, Peter?" Tentative titters.

"No, thank you. I'm just, you know…it got caught." Everybody cracked up. "No, no," he countered tensely, "I mean…this!" The napkin disengaged, and he held it up in sharp rebuke. He felt put upon, unable to laugh with them. He drowned himself in the soup.

"Away from you," he heard Lady L. say in the distance. "Always away from you, Peter!" Her voice startled him.

"Yes?"

"Move the spoon away from you, like this. And you may tilt the plate a little at the end."

Peter did as he was told. "That's much better!" Lady L. said, but this time he didn't smile or look up. *What's all this fuss about manners*, he thought angrily. *I know how to behave, but such matters are never discussed where I come from. We have better things to talk about. Is it just these people, or have I actually entered that cartoon-like world where it doesn't matter what you do or say, as long as your manners are "beyond reproach"* (another of the captain's favorite phrases)? *Good thing I'm not her table partner tonight. I don't think I could be her "gallant" just yet.*

"No, just let Suraya take it away," Lady L. was admonishing Tobias, the oldest member of the group, who had fought in the Indonesian independence war (on the Dutch side) and was trying to make amends by handing the Javanese maid his dirty plate. "And Suraya, remember, always serve from the left, and take away from the right. Clever girl!"

Mornings were spent in class, afternoons in their assigned department in the bank, for hands-on training.

The classes were given in a room in a seventeenth century canal house adjacent to the bank. The subjects ranged wide, from double-entry bookkeeping to Indonesian, English and French language lessons, from typing to practicing "formal address in writing and speech." More etiquette!

Although they were now working in a bank, receiving a small salary even during their year of training, several of Peter's course mates behaved like overweening pests. They performed tribal dances behind one lecturer's back while he was writing on the blackboard, reacted to another tutor's minor witticisms with rude peals of laughter or exaggerated applause, and confused a third one with nonsensical but cleverly phrased questions. Once, they even placed little firecrackers under the steel legs of the lecturer's desk and then set about provoking the speaker of the day to the point where he banged the desk in anger, thereby setting off the firecrackers.

This outrageous behavior on the part of the under-twenty segment of the group was a kind of coming-of-age ritual, a token protest against the career strictures they had embraced, willingly or otherwise. It petered out little more than a month after Peter's arrival, and was followed by a surrender so complete and unquestioning that it embarrassed Peter almost as much as the adolescent antics it replaced.

This same group also behaved most peculiarly in the case of actress Silvana Mangano's double. Silvana's most famous film, *Bitter Rice*, was already some years old, but it still stood as a monument to her smoldering sexuality. Her double-glazed Dutch look-alike, who from the very first day was on view across the light well behind their classroom, soon became the object of Peter's most ardent desires. She was a typist working for another firm whose offices abutted the bank, and her resemblance to the real thing was indeed striking.

Peter's dreams about her were quite shameless, and not a little presumptuous. Her armless office chair was a throne, her black Underwood a mysterious instrument rendered magical by the touch of her angelic fingers.

Peter was not the only one to come under her spell. When she leaned back to stretch, her slender hands smoothing her flowing black hair, the boys howled like a pack of hungry wolves.

Distancing himself a few meters from this crass bunch, Peter threw separate gazes across the light well, which his idol acknowledged with amused forbearance. While she merely laughed openly at the wild animal antics of his classmates, she reserved a soft smile for *him*. It felt like a spring shower, a life-giving benediction. Could it be, he thought, that she reciprocates my feelings? Is she attracted to me?

He couldn't believe it. He was a pale drip, she a goddess. They lived in different worlds. Two sets of windows separated them. He hadn't even heard the sound of her voice. For all her aching proximity, she was a chimera, as remote as the real Silvana.

"Silvana! We love your silvas!" someone shouted, gesturing obscenely to imitate the heavenly bulges of her stunning breasts. The gesture was copied by half the horde. Silvana laughed derisively (of course!) at such banality, throwing back her head and thrusting forward her ripe bosom in stern and definitive rebuke (served them right!).

Then she suddenly straightened up, turned to Peter who, as usual, was standing a little to one side, formed a round kiss with her full mouth, and (could this be true?) touched a finger from her lips to the glass. Then she got up and slowly walked away, taking her chair with her. They all saw her talk to a man at a large desk. He glanced through the double glazing, nodded, and assigned her another place out of sight of the window. The randy chorus wailed with hilarious disappointment and then forgot.

Peter withered away slowly. The kiss lingered. From across the abyss, Silvana had given him a sign.

But he didn't make an effort to catch her coming out of her office. He never saw her again. She did not reappear at the window, not even to make faces at the rowdies. She had vanished.

At eighteen, Peter had already suffered two defeats. Two doors with big, flashing "This Way!" signs above them had fallen shut in front of him, because he hadn't had the spunk to push his way in, no matter what.

That, at any rate, is what he thought at the time. As for the girl, she faded into sweet insignificance. But his failure to force himself through the other door would grow in painful stature as time passed.

# Chapter 4

The sleeping arrangements at Weltevreden were dormitory-like. The top floor of the villa had been converted into a warren of interconnecting spaces, separated not by doors, but by partitions open to one side. Each of these semi-private corners was equipped with a clothes cupboard, a small chest of drawers, and a straight-backed chair by the bed. Books could be placed on a shelf above the bed, and under the bed there were two drawers for personal belongings.

Peter had agonized over what to bring along. He knew he had to leave behind his photo magazines and most of his books. He hesitated over the 200-piece plywood jigsaw puzzle of Esperanto Utopia. That solid jigsaw, with its view of a futuristic city featuring Zeppelins and monorails and skyscrapers with cantilevered apartments and rooftop helipads, had inspired many a youthful dream in him and for a short while convinced him that he would be an architect. He left it behind.

Everything he could not take, he packed in cardboard boxes and left in the attic of his home. In the end, he only brought his camera equipment, several portfolios of his work, and as many books—photo manuals and dictionaries in the main—as would fit on the shelf and in the drawers under the bed.

Peter felt in turn intrigued and depressed by what he learned and heard in his new life. The goings-on at Weltevreden baffled him. He was constantly at pains to catch on, to follow what everybody was talking about. There were always little groups here and there exchanging news and jokes casually, with the matter-of-factness of insiders. They didn't deliberately exclude him, but not being clued in to their confidences was tantamount to not knowing the code, and thus being left out. That's the position he continually found himself in: outsider.

One time, when he didn't understand a joke, Philip, an architect's son who'd flunked the Naval Academy admission tests and had chosen banking as the next best thing, shot out: "God, you are slow, van Doorn! Have you ever got a joke in your life?"

Before Peter could react someone replied, mimicking him: "Oh, yes, once. But I didn't think it was funny!"

Even Peter had to laugh at this, and he managed a rejoinder of sorts: "Some of you fellows' jokes are so dense they require a user's manual!" which saved him from further leg-pulling.

But the incident lingered. He was clearly teetering on the brink of exclusion, of being found too serious and obtuse, not a spoilsport perhaps, but someone who couldn't belong.

The only chap he felt something of a bond with was Gerard Maetsuicker. He was five or six years older, had done his military service, then entered university only to break off his studies to become a banker. He occupied the next cubicle in the warren, and they often sat around talking before lights out. Peter showed him his portfolios. "Damn good work," Gerard commented. That's all. No questions about why Peter didn't pursue photography instead of joining a bank. Damn good work. He sounded as if he meant it, too.

At Weltevreden, two half-days each week were devoted to sport. Apart from fencing ("to learn how to keep the competition at bay"), there were classes in riding ("how to control your subordinates"), swimming ("how to stay afloat") and tennis ("how to give and take"). The choice of sports and their supposed symbolism reflected the personal philosophy of the bank's dictatorial president who had reached the top job before he turned thirty and stayed there ever since.

On the day of their first class at an Amsterdam fencing school, the boys were each assigned a locker.

"We're short of lockers. You're sharing with Baron Dix," said the fencing instructor tersely.

Peter hung up his gear, a little self-consciously, next to the baron's, which looked well used. Dix was a famous family in Amsterdam, but that wasn't the reason for Peter's diffidence. There was a story attached to this aristocrat's name, something an aunt of his had told him. It seems her husband, Peter's uncle and an electrical engineer, had done work for Baron Dix on a few occasions. Then, during the war, the baron had asked him a favor. His mansion on the Amstel had been requisitioned by the Germans, and he asked the uncle to move his art collection to an underground shelter belonging to a friend of his.

The uncle's van had been confiscated by the Germans, and all he had left now was a carrier tricycle. It was a heavy job, hauling the loaded vehicle up and down the bridges. He had brought a young cousin to help him, but he had to do most of the pushing. The baron showed his appreciation by giving him a Rembrandt etching for his trouble.

The exertion, and sufferings of the war, had been too much for the uncle. He took ill and shortly after the end of the war, his wife decided to sell the etching to help pay for the medical expenses. She took it to an auctioneer who gave it a quick look and declared it worthless.

"I'm sorry having to tell you this," he said, "but it's not even by the *School* of Rembrandt. It's a cheap reprint." The uncle never recovered from the disappointment. He felt humiliated and abused. His health took a turn for the worse, and he passed away not long thereafter.

Peter didn't ask for another locker. Instead, he decided to learn to live with this disreputable ghost from the past, and curse it every time he opened the locker. And so he did, for a whole year. Each Thursday when he stowed his gear next to the baron's he whispered, "You have killed my uncle. My curse is on you."

His curse had been little more than a prank, not meant seriously, but it worked. The baron died the following year in a car crash. The news shocked Peter.

The bank's president, now in his mid-sixties, had a very English name, Goodyear, the origins of which lay hidden in the mists of late eighteenth century history, when the British briefly meddled in pre-Napoleon Dutch politics. Among his subordinates he was known as Old Rubberneck, more on account of his peculiar habit to frequently look sideways during conversation than because of any suspected family relation to the tire company.

Rumor had it that Old Rubberneck never mixed with businessmen or other bankers—that he was a recluse pontificating to his parrot and his long-suffering wife about the ills and follies of the country, the banking industry and mankind in general. Virtually the only people admitted to his sanctum on the bank's top floor were Dr. Carstens—his executive secretary who was also his personal lawyer—and the bank's four managing directors, who headed the bank's main divisions.

Peter learned all this during his first few weeks in the bank, mostly at night in the dormitory from his colleagues, some of whom displayed a surprising knack for eliciting gossip from the surly, supposedly antagonistic Desks.

He also learned that there was one other category of mortals Old Rubberneck deigned to receive: the boys from Weltevreden. The call might come at any time and without warning, and answering it promptly was mandatory. The first to be called was, again, gallant Harry, alone, about a month after the start of their training arrival. His name was apparently drawn from a hat. In the train on the way home, he gave a report.

"There was nothing to it. The old man was funny, yeah, but friendly." Pressed for more detail, he added, "Oh, he explained the bank's policies to me but he said it was confidential, so don't ask any questions, okay?"

"You can tell us," someone said. "What the old man means is don't talk outside the bank."

"You think so? Well…" He looked around, making sure there were no eavesdroppers. "We're going to consolidate. No new offices or increase in business. Just making the best of what we've got."

"No new business? You must have misunderstood."

"That's what he said. But I haven't breathed a word. Okay?"

Ten days later, it was Peter's turn.

A uniformed porter took him up in the small, rickety lift, and led the way down a mahogany-paneled corridor to the office of Dr. Carstens.

Dr. Carstens was an impressive gentleman with a pince-nez and a noble stoop which, as Peter surmised the moment he was presented to Mr. Goodyear, must have resulted from a sustained effort to appear insignificant in the presence of his shorter superior.

"The young man answers to the name van Doorn. His file is on your desk in case you require it." Peter noticed that he didn't add "sir."

"That's all right, Carstens, we'll manage, right, van Doorn? Eh, what?" He gave Peter an uncalled-for wink which Carstens pretended not to see as he closed the door behind him.

Mr. Goodyear turned out to be a nervous, rather swarthy man who made up for his slight stature with a strangely exuberant, almost Italianate manner. With his springy energy and unexpected movements, he filled his large, antique-studded office like a circling bee.

"Van Doorn, eh? Very good, very good, do sit, no here, in the middle, on this chair, it was my father's, when he was governor of Surinam. See the crest? Right, very good, so I can get around you, you see? Ha ha! Are we treating you well, eh? Eh?" He stopped six paces from his visitor, blocking the sun that slanted in through the leaded windows. His pose was awkward, with his head turned as if he was trying to peer through a keyhole. "Are we, eh? Eh?"

"Yes, sir, of course, very well, thank you."

"What is it your father does? Eh? It tells things, you know, ha ha. Eh?" He had moved around and was now standing behind Peter.

"He's a journalist, sir, political editor at one of the dailies."

"Very important work, journalism, as long as they don't let us down, that is! Happens you know, journalists writing the wrong things about us. Not your father, I hope? Eh?"

"No, sir, of course not, sir. He writes about…the government."

"Ah! Is he for or against?"

"Sir?"

"Those socialists. They won't last, I tell you."

"Uh, my father tries to be…objective."

Goodyear moved around and was now facing Peter again. "Did you say *objective*? But there is no such thing, you know. You've got to know where you stand, right, van Doorn? And you may tell your father that from me."

"Yes, sir."

"Here at HIB we stand for continuity, not for violent change. You got that? Those preposterous ideas about remaking the world! What did you say your father's name was?"

"Eduard van Doorn, sir."

"Ah, but then I know him. Wasn't he in London during the war?"

"That's him, all right!" Peter couldn't help feeling proud.

"And he writes for Het Parool?"

"That's right."

Goodyear stiffened and reddened. "Your father is…is a radical! He's got it all wrong. You understand? About the Soviets and Sukarno and about America being the enemy. Objective? You'd better not follow his lead, young man, or… or…" He had to take a drink of water before he could continue. "Your father's ideas are…heretical. Not about the coming third world war, he's damn right about that, but about whose side we should be on. There's no choice, you understand! Eh? Eh? Do you want to dirty your own nest? Do you…" Again, he seemed to choke on his own words.

"Sir, please, can I help you?" Peter got up to assist him, but he was waved away.

"No, no, thank you. Very kind. But let me tell you this. You are young. You're with us now, and we'll survive. But we must act wisely. There is another war coming. I'm not investing. I'm consolidating. No new branches, no business expansion. Just doing what we know best: short-term trade finance. We'll ride out the crisis, if we are prepared to make sacrifices! You understand? Eh? Eh?"

"What sacrifices, sir?"

"Very good question, van Doorn!" He stopped in his tracks and bent over, bringing his face close to Peter's. "What sacrifices you ask? Whatever I ask of you. You can start with practicing soberness. Salary demands would be quite out of place in this crisis climate, don't you agree? When our profits can't grow, expenses must be held down. Right? Eh?" Peter was beginning to see what the man was after. For the first time he understood the expression "confidence trick."

"Why, sir…" But the president was walking away, showing his back.

"There're lean years ahead, van Doorn. We need strong men who can weather the storm with us. Loyal men. And loyalty will be rewarded."

"You mean there will be a pension plan?" The question had just popped out, and Goodyear let it hang in the air for his underling to feel thoroughly ashamed about. "I mean," Peter stammered, "I know it may be premature, but..." The president coughed importantly, and, legs straightened and well parted, raised himself on his toes, thumbs tucked in the small pockets of his vest.

"You are eighteen and already worrying about your *pension*? While your whole career is still ahead of you? I'll tell you this: Loyally serve your employer, and you will be looked after. And I never want to hear the word pension again in my presence! You understand?" He almost doubled over to stare Peter in the face again. "Or don't you trust me, eh? Eh?"

"I'm sorry... Actually, it doesn't really mean that much to me, the pension plan," which was the truth. He frantically wondered how to make up for his gaffe. "Sir, is it all right if I ask another question?"

"One then," Goodyear answered curtly, looking at the watch he had pulled out of his vest.

"If Holland is, uh, invaded by, let's say the Russians, how can the bank... how can we survive then? I mean..."

"I understand. Very perceptive, van Doorn. That's really a highly confidential matter, so don't tell your father. Let's just say, we've had some experience during the last war. We moved our legal seat to America then... Now you must leave. I count on you, van Doorn, and remember: Keep the faith, and you will be well rewarded! You understand, eh? Eh?"

Peter said he understood, but the encounter left him wondering about the president's true character. Was he an eccentric doing a pretty good job steering the bank through difficult times? Or a mean old despot trying to get maximum use out of his underpaid workers? Peter wanted to believe the former, but most of the other fellows loudly proclaimed the man to be a tyrant and a skinflint. All the same, they seemed to have few scruples about working for him.

The exception was Gerard. Peter had come to see eye to eye with him on many things. His casual ways had put him off at first. Gerard never took issue with anything he was told by bank functionaries. He applauded speakers generously, rewarded the silliest joke with a ready laugh, and accepted the bank's policies at face value. Yet Peter discovered that far from being shallow, Gerard was merely keeping his opinions to himself.

What sealed his respect for him was something Gerard said the night after Peter's visit to Goodyear. Five or six of them were taking a late walk before turning in. The crickets already sounded feeble, scattered. The full moon was exceptionally bright. But the little group's mood was anything but poetic. They were pumping Peter for details of his audience, and he obliged as best he could. The reactions were predictable:

"You don't believe that for a minute, do you? That he'll take care of us?"

"He's as slithery as an eel in a bucket of sperm."

Gerard didn't take part in this cheap chatter. But when it cooled, he said his piece.

"If you ask me, I think he's pretty much the way he sounds: tough, severe even, a little potty maybe, but fair, provided you don't cross him. An old-school paternalist."

"You can't be serious!" someone sneered. "Old Rubberneck *fair*? He doesn't know what the word means."

"Oh, I'm serious," said Gerard. "I don't rate the man either virtuous or evil. He may have his limitations. But I don't think he's devious."

"He's trying to keep the bank going," Peter added.

"Precisely," said Gerard. "In his rather peculiar way, that is. But you always have to watch out for your own interests. Blind faith is a fool's trap."

"So you agree then," someone summed up, "that you can't trust the old bastard any further than you can throw him."

"That's not what I said," said Gerard. "Not at all."

Their life at Weltevreden and the bank had settled into a routine. After breakfast, they biked to the station to catch the eight-fifteen train. As the thirteen of them cycled along in a long ribbon of cocky virility, they could be heard shouting banalities over their shoulders. Slackers were kidded into pedaling harder. Sweater girls glimpsed on the way rated a ripple of wolf whistles. After leaving their bikes with Crazy Willy in the station lock-up, they ran up the steps to the platform.

Their minds were already somewhere east of Suez, but on the train they kept their voices down in deference to the frowning stockbrokers and lawyers buried in their morning papers.

The classroom work proved unexciting. Accounting, documentary credits, loan analysis—that kind of thing. Peter could hardly sit still through it all. Fortunately, there were also the language classes, history, and ethics—which seemed to boil down to a system of "them and us." This subject was taught by Dr. Carstens.

"Us," they learned, were not only the Dutch bankers in Asia and elsewhere, but all European bankers everywhere. Bankers from north-western Europe, to be precise. Italy and Spain and Greece were not in the same league, and there was no need to worry about them since they would first have to "clean up their mess at home" before they could turn into viable competitors.

As for the north-western European banks, there was an unwritten rule that "we don't snatch each other's customers away." This, Carstens said, is an example of banking ethics. Peter asked what their attitude should be to American banks. Everybody laughed. He was told that there were practically no American banks in the Far East, or anywhere in Europe for that matter, except for small branches serving the U.S. Armed Forces stationed abroad. "The Americans are isolationists," Carstens explained. "They don't understand the world, the Far East least of all, so they won't bother us. But if they do, well, they are a special case. Americans may have European blood, but they follow their own code. They like a good fight, even when there's no war on. But they attack from the front. They are fair warriors. That's how they won the war for us, with some help from the British and the Canadians. We owe them a great debt of gratitude. But we don't need to spare them if we meet them on the field of competition. They wouldn't understand if we did."

So much for "us."

"'Them' on the other hand," said Carstens, "are the people we will never be—never *want* to be—such as the bank's local clerks in Asia. The senior ones among them are of great value to the bank and should always be treated with tact and consideration. For the first few months these Chinese, Indian, Japanese, and Indonesian chief clerks will introduce the newly arrived Dutch staff members to the local practices and rules. But the tutoring phase should be kept brief, and as they are not expected to take on management positions they should never be left in any doubt as to who calls the shots.

"'Them' are also the local Asian banks. They are competitors, but we shouldn't have any qualms about going after their customers, if they have any customers worth going after. 'Them,' furthermore, are the local dignitaries who must be approached courteously. That's what they expect, and they are easily offended. What they lack in real power they make up with long family lineage and elaborate ritual. We should show polite interest in their language and traditions, but there's no need to study either in depth. Non-white people everywhere have long ago learned to align their behavior with ours. Deep in their hearts they covet our culture; it's the reason why the wealthy among them send their children to our universities.

"'Them', finally and crucially, are the indigenous people in general, and young women in particular. Fraternizing with them might affect our judgment and is therefore discouraged. How could we impartially analyze a loan request if we are in the habit of playing Saturday night bridge with their ilk? How could we properly supervise local staff if we visited the bars with them after work?

"Most important of all, we should never get seriously involved with local girls of whatever class. Any Dutch employee found to be engaged in a love affair or seen socially with a local woman is subject to immediate transfer or dismissal. Marriage requires the prior approval of the bank's president, and will not be granted if the bride is non-white, even if she is from a good background. This is not because of racial prejudice, but for our own protection. The woman would not fit in and both parties would suffer from discrimination and cultural confusion.

"Of course, the local night clubs and brothels are quite another matter. Unmarried men can hardly avoid them. It is an acceptable way to solve the problem of loneliness and carnal need. But we should watch out for VD and other sexually transmitted diseases. For that reason," Carstens announced, "a tropical doctor would shortly come over to Weltevreden for an after-dinner talk on this subject 'which will include some practical advice'." In conclusion, Carstens admonished the class not to lose sight of the distinction between them and us, and between acceptable and unacceptable behavior.

He ended with this advice: "I urge you to practice caution and self-discipline, particularly in your relations with the opposite sex."

"Is it me, or did you hear the same thing?" Gerard asked Peter moments after Carstens had left.

"What?"

"The good girls are for them, the whores are for us."

Peter felt a little thrill at hearing Carstens' objectionable message neatly summed up like that. "Sounds like Old Rubberneck's philosophy of life in a nutshell: Keep a clean front, never mind what you're up to after dark."

"Are you coming?" somebody called. "We'll miss the train."

"You go ahead," Gerard answered. Then to Peter, "It's all about avoiding risk, isn't it?" He said it matter-of-factly, almost literally echoing Peter's own thoughts on the day he was caught with his cigarette on the desk. "I mean the terrible risk of going against the grain. It's fear, the hallmark of the bourgeoisie. You didn't expect anything else, did you?"

"Not really. But I'm still surprised."

"I'm not," said Gerard. "I decided long ago to just accept things as they are. You waste less energy that way."

Peter knew that Gerard had studied philosophy for three years before joining the bank, but he didn't look old enough to be talking about long ago.

"What are you looking at me like that for?" Gerard wanted to know.

"Why did you give up your studies?"

"Oh, I got bored. I realized I was better suited to the real life. Ha!" His derisive laugh didn't sound genuine.

"Banking is the real life?"

Gerard didn't need to think long for an answer. "It will be. It should, because international banking is about people and travel and money. I've decided I like money more than all the fashionable theories telling me to despise it."

"But the price…don't you think it's a high price to pay?"

"Listen, van Doorn. There always is a price. In my case, the price for the privilege of smelling Schopenhauer's farts was to be deprived of a life of comfort and excitement. I didn't want to pay that price. Money can buy you the real life. Slices of it, anyway."

Peter turned to face him. "You mean you joined the bank for the money?"

"Why else? Don't tell me you joined out of idealism!"

"Of course not."

"Well then."

Peter racked his brain for a reason why he had entered the bank, other than "my father made me," which wasn't a reason, just an excuse, and one he wouldn't even confess to Gerard. But Gerard wasn't waiting for a reaction. The matter was self-evident. Intelligent people don't work for banks except for the money.

# Chapter 5

It was the twentieth of December, and Peter was home for the holidays. The girls refused to let him help decorate the tree that father got from the nursery. They wanted it to be a "surprise" for their brother, the way mother used to surprise the three of them on the morning of the twenty-fifth. When the kids stole into the still-dark living room at the crack of dawn, feet stuck into cold little slippers, there it was, the beautiful Christmas tree all hung with angels and colored balls and gleaming lights, and with a pile of red-ribboned packages under it, arranged on a white sheet draped around the base. Now the girls had taken over, and Mother let them do it.

From their behavior, he sensed that he was turning into something of a celebrity with his sisters. To Fran, aged twelve, he was the future, the exotic real world. She couldn't deal with it yet, so she just gaped and giggled. Peter hadn't exchanged a normal word with her since he joined the bank. I've lost her, he thought, and when I return home, six years from now, she'll have grown into a woman in my absence and without any help from me.

He felt he was doing better with his younger sister, Pauline, who, at age nine, was a nimble nymph dancing through life. She was still playing with dolls, treating them like equals, talking to them as she moved from room to room. Peter was grateful for her cheerful touch, which he felt was much needed in the house. She was growing into a free spirit, finding inspiration in everyday events and solutions for small challenges, without depending on like-minded friends.

As his departure drew closer, his parents seemed to grow more remote.

His mother was her usual self-effacing self, preparing the meals, cleaning up after the girls, anticipating father. Yet something had changed. It was as if she had already written her son out of the script of her life, and felt better for the peace it gave her. One less man to cope with.

But his father was the real enigma. He acted more jovially to Peter than before, yet seemed ill at ease with him. Each weekend Peter went home with high hopes and an open mind, and each time he felt disappointed. Like his mother, Eduard too seemed to have taken a step away from his son.

Christmas day, before dinner, Eduard offered Peter little cigars and whisky-and-sodas and sat down with him for a "good talk." But his behavior lacked naturalness. Peter sensed an undertow of tension and unhappiness, even resentment, below the surface waves of bonhomie.

He seemed uninterested in his son's new life. He did make an effort by enquiring about it, but could barely bring himself to hear out the replies. Peter wondered if his father knew what Goodyear thought of his politics. At least he must know that the bank (like all banks, no doubt) was anti-Communist and anti-Socialist, pro-colonial and pro-capital. Then why did he arrange a job for his son there? he asked.

"Because only the best is good enough for my son!"

"Seriously, Dad."

"Listen, Peter. I've landed you a plum job. Make something out of it. Impress me, okay? Let's drink to that!" He lifted his glass. Peter didn't join him.

"I don't understand. You write about the evils of capitalism, and you make me work for a *bank*?"

"You don't need to understand. It's a matter of resigning oneself to the unalterable. Also known as making a virtue out of deprivation. Ha ha!" He chuckled and acted drunk, though they'd only had two whiskeys each.

Peter felt his unease turn to anger. "Deprivation? Who is depriving whom? Of what?"

Eduard waved the question away with a tired gesture. "How can I expect you to understand? What do you know about war? About men fighting, killing and dying for their hopes and ideals? About dreams turned sour? You're an innocent, you want to improve the world with good intentions and good

38

works." He raised his glass again. "Well, good luck. I mean it, good luck!" He threw back his drink.

Peter's anger melted into bewilderment. Was Eduard saying good-bye to his son? Washing his hands of him? Why was his smile freezing in his graying beard? Why was the floor sinking? What have they done to the walls: padded them to absorb their laughs, their jokes, their good times of the past? Where are they now, those infrared days of intimacy and excitement over images coming to life?

"Dad, I had a dream of my own!" Peter knew he was reaching out to his father, begging him to understand. To reassure him that his alien future didn't need to be his final destination. That there would be another chance. But his voice sounded muffled, inconsequential, like a timid stranger asking directions. Eduard didn't react. Peter waited. Behind him, the Christmas lights twinkled mindlessly. The father had nothing more to say to his son. He didn't take back or explain that dreadful word: deprivation. He said nothing.

He burped.

Two weeks later, Peter spent a Saturday night weekend alone at Weltevreden. He didn't feel like going home and confronting his father again. As he walked around the nearby dunes, still snow-covered but sunlit, his mind strayed back to the dream he had forsaken.

"The decisive moment is the recognition, in a fraction of a second, of the significance of an event." These were the words of Cartier-Bresson, that great French master of street photography, and they had become Peter's dictum. When he scoured the city as a boy, Leica in hand, in search of good shots, he had instinctively observed that principle, even before he had read about it. He didn't shoot like a news photographer, blindly running the motor drive in the hope there would be some gold among the dross. No, he waited for the right moment, which was exactly that: a moment. With the next breath, it was gone. And that was its beauty. The ephemeral made timeless by the act of arresting it through photography.

The scene itself, the subject, had to be worth the effort. That's something that couldn't be learned, only known intuitively.

All good photography, whether arranged or spontaneous, requires unusual gifts of perception, combined with the technical skills needed for superior execution. That's what makes photography a form of art. And like all good art, good photography has the power to change. It can elevate, move, enrich, disturb. It is never neutral.

Peter wasn't sure how much of this he understood when he was young. He didn't need to. All he had to do then to sense the magic of photography was to hold the unsheathed camera in his two hands. The feel of the cool black body, the deep clear wells of its lenses, the never-failing movements of its intricate mechanics, the soft shush of the film being wound—it all formed part of a mystique that had never ceased to thrill him.

He had never used his camera in the three months he had been at Weltevreden. On impulse, he now rushed back to the house, ran up to his cubicle in the dormitory and lifted the camera bag out of the deep drawer under his bed. He took out the Leica and handled it like he used to, pointing it at something, measuring the light with the exposure meter, selecting the shutter speed, the right F-stop, adjusting the focus, pressing the shutter. He replaced the standard lens with a 300mm telephoto, pointed it through the window at a tree with some bird activity, repeated the procedure, pressed the shutter.

There was no film in the camera, but it made no difference. As he went through the motions of taking shots, a cool realization took hold of him: that he couldn't have taken any real, worthwhile photographs, if the camera had been loaded. It wasn't the lack of suitable subject matter, it was his own condition that held him back. He had lost the commitment, the intimacy and state of mind needed to create good photos. As he put his camera back, he whispered, "You don't belong here. You can't serve me where I'm at now." And then he added: "You will wait. You will always be there for me when I need you, when I'm ready for you again, as long as I don't neglect you." It was a consolation amid the harsh reality that was taking hold of him.

From then on, he took the camera out every so often, at least once a month on average, feeling its weight, turning the aperture and shutter speed rings between his fingers, cleaning the filters, cocking the shutter, pressing the release.

He never loaded it with film.

# Chapter 6

Spring colored the dunes a delicate green. There was a sharp snap in the morning air, enough to chill the breath of horse and man into short-lived clouds. It had been a cold night. The moss crackled underfoot. Little birds shot away from the corner of the riders' eyes. A pale crescent was holding out against the fierce sunlight, as if it too wished to savor this fresh day for a little while before surrendering to the overpowering might of the arching blue.

The horses, stiff as their riders, lumbered up the hill in a long, irritable column. They ignored the little ill-aimed kicks in their flanks, knowing these impatient brats didn't have the wherewithal to make them do anything they didn't feel like doing. They recognized these boys for what they were: rank beginners with barely half a dozen lessons behind them, little better than the day-tripping folk that rode the horses around the lake on summer Sundays.

Over the hill, the pace quickened a little, not on account of suddenly improving riding skills, but because the horses wanted it. It was easier downhill, and they did need the exercise.

Peter van Doorn was bringing up the rear on Nelly, a small white mare looking like a cross between a Shetland and an Arab. She had a fierce temper which showed in the way she lashed her tail to and fro as she trudged along in the wake of the tall chestnut in front of her bearing Gerard. Peter liked this stubborn horse, the way she showed her grit, her disagreement with the fate imposed on her, while doing her duty nonetheless. The other chaps steered clear of her, preferring more predictable temperaments.

Erect and firmly in the saddle, his body warmth contrasting agreeably with the cold air, Peter was almost happy. For the first time since joining the bank, he was suffused with a contentment, a glow, that he didn't remember feeling since the death of the man in the street had put an end to his youth. This outing was no doubt part of the reason. But there was something else.

It had to do with his changing attitude to the bank. Whatever excuses he had been using in the past for finding himself where he was, he now accepted that he had in fact embarked on a career in banking. That was new, and the realization had eased his daily burden of living, of questioning his own sanity and wisdom every hour of the day.

But it wasn't a simple surrender. He hadn't given up his dream. He had merely deferred it, buried it like a treasure, to be dug up some day and given its rightful place in his life. Meanwhile, he had to belong somewhere, and this bank wasn't all bad. He was learning things, meeting new people, and soon he would be living in another culture. This was no time to be depressed.

But he disagreed with Gerard: He wasn't in it "for" the money. For a living, yes, but more for the experience. For getting to know the world. As for idealism, as Gerard called it, Peter nurtured his own private version of it, though he would never have thought of calling it by such an overblown name. "Idealism" to him smacked of unattainable goals, of seeing the world dreamily, unrealistically. Peter believed in human decency and dedication. He believed in the sort of social values his father wrote about. The right stuff. Even in a bank.

Without them, life wouldn't make sense.

They had come to an open heath without marked trails. The riders were fanning out, some spurring on their mounts into a fast trot. On the left, far ahead, he made out Harry galloping away, coattails flying. Peter too nudged his horse, first with his knees, then with little pokes of his boot heels. But Nelly, though alone now, kept on walking with a kind of obstinacy that to Peter seemed a trifle self-pitying. He patted the animal on the neck.

"I know, old girl, life is hard. But why don't we enjoy ourselves a little on this lovely morning? What do you say, eh? Giddy up, horse!" And he gave her a smart kick between the ribs.

Nelly reacted with a fierce swish of her tail and an indignant snort but didn't obey. By now, Peter's horse was the only one still walking. He had fallen back sixty or seventy meters.

"Come on, you spoilsport!" Nelly was no longer his favorite mount. "Get moving!" He kicked her sides angrily. Nelly bucked like a rodeo horse, throwing Peter clear into the rough gorse. Peter's surprised cry reached three or four pairs of ears, and within seconds he was surrounded by jeering blokes on panting horses that seemed enormous from where he lay. He recognized the chestnut directly ahead of him, Gerard doubled up with laughter on top. Between the horse's legs he spied Nelly, briskly trotting away without so much as a glance back.

"The bloody cheek!" he shouted, touching his own cheek which, as it happened, was bleeding. "Damn stupid half-breed!"

"That's what you get for bullying her!" shouted somebody.

"I wasn't, the damn horse just won't listen!" The boys kept on laughing. But they weren't malicious, and Peter gave up and laughed too.

Gerard had dismounted and was helping Peter to his feet and handed him a handkerchief for his bruise.

"Some horses don't like people. Next time try a happy horse."

"A happy horse?" Peter said. "You mean a docile one. A horse that doesn't fight his fate every damn day of his life?"

"Same thing," said Gerard.

With less than two weeks to go until their departure, the training was brought to an end, and they spent their last day at Weltevreden packing and going for walks in twos and threes.

That night, the colonel and his wife gave a farewell party in the villa's small ballroom, which at other times had been their lecture hall. There was a swing trio, and all the boys had brought a girl. Peter's date was Sybille, the classmate he'd been more or less in love with since he was fifteen, but whose feelings for him had never progressed beyond what she called "intimate friendship," an epithet designed no doubt to keep him interested without giving an inch.

It turned out much better than he had expected. The food was predictable —an Indonesian buffet, every middle class Dutch family's last resort—but it was of excellent quality, and very stylish, with Javanese waiters in sarong and batik headbands serving them. After dinner, some of the boys put on a little cabaret about the bank and their year at Weltevreden. Peter had written a song on the theme of "Our unknown future among the bananas and the coconuts," which he sang to Gerard's piano accompaniment. It went over well, and everybody joined in the catchy refrain. There were sketches and more songs, and Berend put on a magic show, in which nearly every trick failed, making it far more entertaining than it would have been otherwise.

Sybille looked ravishing in her blue princess dress and silver high heels, and Peter suffered terribly as he held her warm, pliant body close to his, dancing slowly to the sounds of Stan Kenton's *The Lonely Road*. Never had she seemed more remote, more unattainable, more desirable.

At eleven o'clock the band struck up with *Goodnight, Irene*, and Lady L. dimmed a few more lights for the final, very slow shuffle around the floor. Peter managed to kiss Sybille on the mouth, but her response was limp and he realized once again that she did not share his feelings.

Then they took their girls home to their quarters for the night, a little hotel in the village where they were to share twin rooms. They stood talking and smooching in the doorway and around the front garden with its goldfish pond and china dwarfs until the proprietor told the girls to come in and the boys to get lost.

The party had taken some of the sting out of one gripe shared by every one of the group: that they still didn't know their final destinations. All they knew was that they would be traveling to the East by sea, in two groups, on separate ships. In accordance with bank policy each member's individual assignment wouldn't be announced until well into the voyage, probably after passing through the Suez Canal. The announcements would be made by radio telegram.

The reason given for this peculiar procedure was that there were bound to be last-minute changes in the branch network's requirements, and that the bank didn't want to disappoint anyone with an unexpected switch. The real reason, the boys knew, was that almost everyone was hoping for a posting outside Indonesia, because in Indonesia the pay was reputed to be poor and the political situation worrisome. But only five or six would be that lucky, and the bank's management wanted to avoid the fracas bound to follow the announcements.

The final days with his parents and sisters confirmed to Peter that in the span of one year, relations with his family had subtly changed from inclusive to exclusive. No one was openly cool, of course, let alone unfriendly. It was rather a case of swift adjustment to a looming loss: he was leaving, but their life had to go on. He was going his way and the family had quickly closed ranks. It had covered up its injury like a tree mending its bark around the wound of a severed limb.

The only one whose attitude hadn't changed was Pauline. It wasn't her age, it was her character. She was her usual independent self, wrapped up in her own world, a little quirky sometimes, not making light of Peter leaving her, but not investing it with intolerable moment either. He knew then that their closeness would survive the long separation that lay ahead—that they would always be best friends.

In the Eyes of the Son

# Part Two

*Singapore 1954-1960*

In the Eyes of the Son

# Chapter 7

The ocean liner slowly approached her moorings in Singapore Harbor, guided by two tugs. As the distance between the ship's vertical steel wall and the dock narrowed to a dark canyon, the ship let out three bone-chilling whistle bursts, grossly overdone at such close quarters, as if protesting her forced passivity with a show of unseemly vigor.

Of the seven young men at the railing of the second class deck, scanning the waiting crowd for a likely face, only Peter van Doorn was ill at ease. Like the other six, he was wearing a white shirt and striped tie under his light gray, tropical business suit.

His colleagues, aged between eighteen and twenty-four, seemed quite happy in their getup. Harry Slaker, six foot two, with the square-cut body of a longshoreman and the mentality of a friendly dog, stood like a statue, legs spread, coal-shuffling hands clasped before him. Joop Geesterman, quietly efficient, with a kindly side that belied his inner toughness, hung back a little. Three others, dedicated career chasers with whom Peter still found as little to talk about as on his first day in the bank, were slightly bending forward, hands on the railing, taking in the exotic scene unfolding before them with irritating calm.

Gerard Maetsuicker, Peter's best friend, the philosopher who took nothing seriously, was the only one hanging over the railing, confidently and irreverently looking over the faces on the quay with amused curiosity.

As for Peter, he couldn't believe he had actually arrived in the fabulous

East. He had another acute attack of ambivalence about his choice of employment, and he seriously believed that he was overdressed for the occasion. He said so to the others, who agreed and took off their jackets without an argument, Gerard first, casually, then Harry, laboriously, then Joop, neatly, and finally the other three as a group, indifferently. But Peter had second thoughts, explaining that carrying a jacket around with you in the tropics was even sillier than wearing one. The others ignored his indecision. Peter, not wanting to appear fickle, had kept his jacket on.

He felt unreal, detached, not in his own skin. He had often felt that way back in Amsterdam, but the sea journey had temporarily wiped his self-consciousness away. It had been an exhilarating experience, life among the chimneys and high-polished timber decks, the fabulous food, the constant pitch and roll, the tang in the air.

He loved the ports, Southampton and Genoa and particularly Port Said where bearded men in burnooses were selling dirty pictures, and a conjurer who boarded their ship had wrapped up the pound-note Gerard had lent him and then thrown it overboard, only to retrieve it moments later from behind someone's ear.

And there had been other excitements, like when they were hit by a terrific storm in the Gulf of Aden, right in the middle of a bridge tournament they were all taking part in. The ship rolled so badly that the lounge chairs toppled over and one heavy sofa crashed through the windows. Everybody was seasick—even the ship's doctor looked ashen. But the next day, the sun was back, and the telegram they had been waiting for ever since leaving Port Said finally came through. Their orders!

The telegram was addressed to Gerard, the eldest among them, and he gathered them around him in the bar, and read the message out loud.

"Slaker and Geesterman, to Singapore! De Groot and Filius, Jakarta. Siliakus to Surabaya. Maetsuicker to Tokyo. And additionally to Singapore, van Doorn!"

Peter was puzzled by the apparent afterthought that had decided his Singapore posting, but he felt immensely relieved that it wasn't Indonesia and only mildly disappointed that it wasn't China or Japan. Everybody joined in a round of congratulation and commiseration, clinking their gin-and-tonics and buying expensive cigars.

"Surabaya? Good luck!"

"Tokyo? Reserve me a geisha!"

"Singapore, yeah. I'd wanted Bangkok. Better pay."

"*You're* complaining? Look at me: Jakarta!"

"Same here. Damn!"

"Singapore."

"You too? Well, could be worse."

The telegram said that all except those traveling on to Indonesia were to disembark in Singapore, and that they would be met on arrival by Mr. A. Volker of the Singapore branch, who would escort them to their quarters.

"Volker is my cousin," said Harry. "Sort of. When I was a kid, I once spent a holiday in his parents' house in Gelderland. He was prematurely bald and had a big mouth."

"That's him," said Gerard. He didn't elaborate and nobody asked.

The ship shuddered along her whole great length as she sidled up to the quay, and minutes later, the gangways were lowered, separate ones for first class, second class, third class, and steerage.

Peter watched the Chinese contract laborers that made up the steerage complement start disembarking immediately, as if they were getting off a train, carrying their own bags and bundles. From another door emerged the missionaries and nuns, blinking at the sun as they clambered out of their third class depths. Up the steep plank they walked, with hesitant gait and weak smiles, their faith an indispensable crutch to their unaccustomed bodies.

A band in braided white uniforms and pith helmets played welcome marches without regard to creed or color, though their platform was positioned directly opposite the first class gangway.

"Look there!" shouted Harry. "Near the band. That's Volker! The bald one with the tie. You see, van Doorn, no jacket. What now?"

"You know Volker?" Peter asked Gerard, ignoring Harry.

"Met him once," said Gerard. "At my uncle's, just before the war, when they were both on home leave from the same branch somewhere in Borneo. My

51

uncle was the branch manager, and the Japs caught him hiding the money and chopped his head off. Volker was smarter. He got away before the Japs arrived and escaped to Australia. Of course, he suffered daily on Bondi beach, riven by war guilt."

Everybody fixed their stares on the famous man who, seeing that he had been recognized, waved a long arm at them, not in greeting but to tell them to get the hell off the ship.

"His first name is Adriaan," said Gerard, "but everybody calls him Volker. I'm told he's okay, though a bit neurotic."

Their bags were already taken ashore by sinewy porters who were now lined up on the quay by the baggage of the hundred or so second class passengers getting off here, waiting for a tip they knew would be small but certain, precisely calculated in accordance with the purser's guidelines. Further along, the first class passengers were noisily disembarking down their own red-carpeted gangway, the men slipping last-minute stingy or excessive gratuities into groveling brown hands, the women pretending ignorance of all money matters and fussing over their children and their nannies.

Gerard walked straight up to Volker. "Gerard Maetsuicker. You might remember me from the evening at my uncle's, maybe fifteen years ago."

"Should I? Remind me to think about it. Let's see, you're in transit, right?"

"Supposed to catch a plane to Tokyo tomorrow."

"Right. And who are these?"

Gerard introduced his colleagues one by one.

"We're expecting Geesterman and Slaker for Singapore," Volker said, "and we know that De Groot and Siliakus and Filius are bound for Indonesia. But we have no word about van Doorn. Where's he going? Bangkok?"

"No, Singapore," said Peter.

"We know nothing about that," said Volker. "You have your orders?"

"Here," said Gerard. He showed Volker the telegram.

"Hmm, yes. Well, if that's what Head Office wants…we'll find him something to do." Then, turning to Peter: "You might start by taking that jacket off, van Doorn. You only wear jackets here when you're invited to a polite dinner, and that day is a long way off." Everybody laughed.

Peter remembered his first day in Amsterdam, when he had to sit at a desk that didn't form part of the established pattern. He seemed destined not to fit in. Here he wasn't even *expected.*

The new arrivals for the Singapore branch were allowed one free day to get acquainted with the city and register at the consulate, and another to make the rounds of the major Dutch companies to introduce themselves. Some of this time Peter spent with Gerard. They bought trinkets in Change Alley and grandly sipped a gin tonic at the Raffles. Then Peter saw his friend off at Kallang Airport.

"I'll try to write," said Peter.

"I don't make any promises," said Gerard with an affectionate smirk. "But you're always welcome to stay with me! Always." He waved once, emphatically, and disappeared through the barrier.

The feeling of being stranded on an isolated beach wouldn't leave Peter for days. They had never exchanged personal confidences but Gerard was the closest thing to a friend he had known. Gerard was the only person who had never judged him, the only person who let him be. Besides his little sister Pauline, that is.

On the third day, the "Singapore three" received their assignments in the large, hot office, under ceiling fans that kept the paperwork in constant motion. The older Chinese, Portuguese and Indian clerks and managers smiled indulgently as this new crop of pale know-nothings was paraded around by the ubiquitous Volker, his manner at once patronizing and conniving, as if to say: "We all know they've shipped us another load of nitwits, but it's up to you blokes to show them the ropes. And give it your best shot. You know damn well that soon enough they'll be your bosses!"

Three of the bank's single Dutchmen lived in the dormitory on the top floor of the bank building, one to a room. To their dismay, the new arrivals had to share the one remaining vacant bedroom among the three of them. It was furnished with an iron bed, a straight chair and a wooden locker for each of them. Nothing else.

The official explanation for this army-barracks type accommodation was that they were still apprentice bankers, not rating full pay, and therefore unable to support a better lifestyle, let alone a family. Indeed, marriage was forbidden during the first three years of their assignment (as they had been told in Amsterdam), and thereafter it required prior permission from the branch manager and the head office—which could be withheld if the choice of bride was deemed inappropriate, or the employee's income inadequate.

Unofficially, branch management agreed that each staff trainee was entitled to a room of his own, and efforts would be made to realize this objective as soon as possible.

As for sanitary facilities, there were two spacious, bug-ridden showers and two toilets to serve the six men. The two unsmiling Chinese *amahs*, who moved through the permanently darkened rooms like shadows, had their own modest facilities behind the kitchen.

These two overworked coolies, paid for by the bank below, not only kept house for the six sweating Dutchmen with their daily piles of dirty cotton laundry, they also cooked an extensive warm lunch for them and the bank's four senior managers, all married Dutchmen who invaded the bachelors' space every day for an hour or so with their insider talk, expensive fountain pens and billows of cigar smoke.

Peter was struck by the insensitivity of these superiors who only talked among themselves, virtually ignoring the young men whose house they used. They gossiped about people at the head office and complained about the "incompetence" of the local staff, with the notable exception of a few Chinese whose praises they sang *ad nauseam*. They talked about their clubs, their plans for home leave, their standing in bridge and golf. Seldom did they take up the kind of subjects Peter was interested in: the anti-colonial stirrings in the region, Indonesia's recent independence, the longer-term policies of the bank, cultural events in Singapore. They didn't even talk about women!

Once or twice a week Mr. Vreeman, the general manager, would join the lunch. For the others, this meant a shift in topics toward work problems and difficult customers. Volker, the oldest of the bachelors, was particularly deft in airing thorny issues without loss of decorum.

Peter soon realized that Volker was an ambiguous figure in the office. As the oldest of the bachelors, he was unofficially "in charge of" the unmarried young men. He lived in the bachelors' apartment, and often sought their company. His efforts to curry favor with them sometimes seemed pathetic to Peter. Yet as an assistant manager, Volker identified himself politically with branch management.

Volker's share of house expenses was known to be only a fraction of his income, most of which he remitted to a Swiss bank. He smoked his cigarettes through a long, golden holder, and had the latest Garrard pick-up and large hi-fi speakers. But Peter suspected that this veteran of three years' wartime ocean-gazing in Australia was a deeply unhappy man. It would be some time before Peter discovered the cause of the man's unhappiness.

In the Eyes of the Son

# Chapter 8

Peter, assigned to the Cash Department as a junior assistant, introduced himself to a customer, a Dutch merchant, who had approached him from the other side of the counter.

"So, you're new here?" said the customer. "Well, I'll give you a chance to do an old customer a good turn. See that messenger coming this way? No, the one with the turban—he wants to cash a check I gave his boss. You tell him you can't cash his check because it's not correctly made out. Tell him anything, but don't tell him I haven't got enough money in my account."

The big Dutch trader was sweating heavily as he leaned over the counter.

"But," countered Peter, "he'll be back in no time, with his boss, and demand his money!"

"Ah, but you're closing in five minutes, right? Don't worry, I'll cover before he returns in the morning!"

"If I scrutinize this check," said Peter without looking at him, "it's because I always do. We're not an easy-going bank here."

The Dutchman smiled admiringly and gave Peter a sly wink, which he didn't acknowledge.

It was Peter's first encounter with sleazy practices and he was surprised at his cool handling of the situation, without compromising himself. Still, he felt soiled.

"We need cash, sir," said the Chinese assistant cashier. "Mr. Reitsma isn't here. Can you come along?"

"All right," said Peter. He was glad to get out of the place to fill in for

Dick Reitsma, the Assistant Manager in charge of the Cash Department who was his direct boss and lived in the same dormitory. He went to the vault clerk to obtain a release for one of the three handguns kept by the bank.

As one of the bank's three designated escorts of money transports to and from the Central Bank—the others being Reitsma and Harry Slaker—he was licensed to carry a gun for protection during such transports. But on the few occasions he had been asked to fill in for Reitsma—the primary escort—he had felt ridiculous with the gun clenched in his clammy hand, hidden uncomfortably in his pants pocket. Not only didn't he know how to shoot, but the transports took place in the office car (or on foot if the car was otherwise engaged, like taking Mrs. Vreeman shopping), and Peter had serious doubts if he could, or would, do anything to foil a hold-up.

The Chinese didn't seem in the least worried about such a thing happening. "The gun is just for the insurance," Peter was told, so he came to regard these particular chores as outings.

So far, banking had presented an agreeable face to him. His duties in the Cash Department, for example, included checking the fat piles of colorful checks deposited by traders and messengers of every stripe, totting them up, stamping the paying-in books, obtaining Dick Reitsma's signature, and handing the signed book back to the waiting client.

The Indian messengers were the most polite, particularly the young ones whose manner was gentle and almost effeminate, their classic features belying their humble occupation. But their bosses were the worst nit-pickers. When they visited the bank in person you knew it was to complain about some small bank commission or about a deposit credited a day late, resulting in a minute loss of interest.

The Chinese were harder. Unsmiling, business-like, they were too busy making money to worry about a few pennies. By and large, they preferred to do their banking with the local Chinese banks. But the HIB's Chinese business promoter known as the "comprador" had useful contacts in the Chinese community, resulting in a steady stream of business.

Paradoxically, the smaller Dutch company customers were often the most difficult to handle. They played up the skin-and-flag factor for all it was worth.

"We've got to stick together, that's why I bank here. You're not going to drive me into the arms of those tricky Chinese by refusing a perfectly routine service, now are you?" If they saw you hesitate, they would invoke the British bank across the street who "don't blink an eye at this sort of thing, but you know, I prefer to support my own countrymen!" If you still said no, they would call up the branch manager, Mr. Vreeman, and it was arranged, leaving you feeling like a dummy and cursing that weak-kneed boss in his palm-fringed office.

Mr. Vreeman lived with his wife in a fine villa on Holland Road. They had their own tennis court and swimming pool. He was a pink-skinned, smooth-faced, pudgy man wearing rimless spectacles, gold cufflinks and an accountant's smile that was neither convincing nor offensive. He took an early interest in Peter, seemingly based on little else than Peter's quiet ways and decent manners, as they hadn't exchanged more than twenty words since he arrived.

When Vreeman needed a confidential assistant to decode incoming cables on weekends, he sent for Peter, and instructed him personally in the use of the voluminous, leather-bound code books. Peter accepted the assignment as a matter of course, neither treating it as a burden nor as a special honor, but playing it down in front of his sniggering colleagues, some of whom started calling him "the boss's boy." The Sikh night watchman was authorized to admit Peter into the bank's premises outside office hours so that he could collect the cables and decode them, before taking them to the manager's residence on Saturday and Sunday mornings.

Mrs. Vreeman, dressed in a colorful cotton-print, her face covered in powder and bright red lipstick, received him the first time, smilingly gave him a lemonade and then, holding his elbow momentarily, pointed him in the direction of her husband, who could "as usual"—she said in a tone that betrayed both pride-of-status and resentment—be found on the tennis court, at the end of the east garden, beyond the pool. As she watched Peter taking the steps down from the terrace, clutching the day's cables, she called his name.

"You might use this for the cables," she said, holding a little silver tray that she had just picked up in passing from a side table. "It's so much nicer."

"Of course," said Peter, stopping in his tracks, turning half round, feet at different levels. She came down to him and smiled as he took the tray from her. He turned around and through the trees could see two men indolently swinging their racquets, two diminutive white figures against the brick-red trapezium of the court.

"He likes them on the tray, you see," he heard Mrs. Vreeman say. "It must be his upbringing." A ringing laugh underlined this statement. He looked back at her. Was she making fun of her husband in front of a mere underling?

"Of course," said Peter, swallowing hard. Without further hesitation, he descended the steps, a fleet-footed Mercury now on a godly mission, the tray's reflected sun darting flecks of yellow onto the dark-leafed magnolias that lined the path.

That night, in bed, he reflected on his life since arriving in Singapore. He didn't dislike the work, was grateful for the trust the Vreemans placed in him, and felt a growing interest in the local culture, away from the expatriate scene. He didn't mind the occasional night out with fellow Dutchmen, but what he couldn't stand was the forced conviviality of the bachelors' pad above the bank – the drinking, the joke-telling, the coarse games of strip poker with Chinese girls brought home from the clubs. He would have to start looking for another place to live, a place more suited to – how to call it? – the way he wanted to live. With that still unformed resolve in mind, he finally caught sleep.

The urge to move became even more pressing after he and some of his colleagues got involved in two scandalous incidents. The first, in the Singapore docks, had been reported in the Chinese press. The four of them had gone down to the port area and boarded a Dutch freighter, to visit the first engineer, an old friend of Dick Reitsma, who had driven them there in his brand new Studebaker convertible. They were invited for one drink, but stayed for a dozen, with nothing to eat except some peanuts and a large melon to share, which they soaked in whiskey before consuming.

When they left after four hours, Peter's legs buckled under him and he had to be carried down the gangway and into the car where he passed out. Alarmed, Reitsma stepped on the gas, and in his drunken bravura ignored a summons to stop from the security guard at the gate of the bonded area. Peter came to just as they crashed through the red-and-white striped boom, splintering it as if it was a piece of hard candy. Through the rear window, Peter saw the flaming barrels of the guards' pistols being fired in their direction as they fled. He was lucid enough to notice the cops-and-robbers thrill his screaming colleagues were getting out of this nefarious adventure. As for himself, he sank back moaning and vomited copiously onto the floor.

"Ah, you're conscious?" Reitsma enquired. Peter's affirmative groan reassured him, and at the next crossing he ignored the turnoff for the hospital and instead headed straight home, tearing around corners and near-missing every other car on the way. Once safely in front of the bank, he carried Peter up the steps, unaided and ever so gingerly, all the way to his third-floor bed, where he removed his clothing and covered him with a light blanket, his head propped up to help him ward off further attacks of nausea. Peter, only half conscious, smiled a weak thanks at the three men standing over him and mumbled a faint "sorry."

"For what?" Reitsma wanted to know. "For getting sloshed? You've just joined the club. Give it another month or two, and you can take it standing up, like these fellows here. Not that their brains are any less addled. Now get some sleep, but you know the rule: Be at your desk at nine sharp, hung over or not."

For the next eight hours, Peter passed through purgatory, with excruciating shafts of headache and severe attacks of nausea and vertigo vying for control of his limpid body with brief valleys of blissful torpor, cut short each time with yet another demand on his sickened stomach that had nothing left to give but yellow blobs of bitter gall. When he closed his eyes, the room turned into a rollercoaster. When he opened them, the weakest light brought on the migraine.

The alarm woke him from the deep sleep into which he had finally sunk when dawn broke. He somehow managed to get up and take a shower, but he didn't manage to hold down the toast and weak tea one of the amahs had urged on him, and she shook her head in censorious concern.

When Peter showed up gray-faced at his desk at nine sharp, he was welcomed with a round of applause from his drinking pals. He smiled wanly but waved away the misplaced tribute. He couldn't help feeling that the whole episode had been loathsome and shameful. What he didn't notice is that the

61

local staff had reacted to the applause with raised eyebrows and no smiles, in collective condemnation of these disgusting foreigners and their childishly dangerous games. They had read the Chinese papers, and the suspicion that it was their own Dutch staff who had committed the outrage in the docks was now being effectively confirmed. Habitual loyalty and fear of being branded traitor kept them from turning into whistle-blowers, and the offenders were never identified.

The incident redoubled Peter's resolve to find another place to live. But that was easier said than done, and it took another confrontation with the Chinese population, a couple of weeks later, to stir him into action.

This second event occurred in the Carlton Club, where the boys from the bank occasionally did their drinking and girl-hunting. Since the port foray, Peter was automatically included every time a group from his floor decided to paint the town, which was at least once a week. He didn't really enjoy these ribald outings, but his need for companionship, however unsuitable the company, took precedence over his better instincts.

Sometimes they visited one of the "Worlds"—Happy World, New World and the like—huge dance halls where freelance "taxi girls" made themselves available as dance partners at a fixed price per whirl. The boys enjoyed the dancing but didn't think much of the girls, mostly colorless clerks and nurses and bus conductors earning extra cash after work. The girls in the night clubs, by contrast, were classier and prettier, or at least they spoke passable English and had the knack to entertain Westerners.

The boys usually picked a favorite girl and stayed with her the whole evening. Taking them home was another and costlier matter and not always easily arranged or afforded. On their part, the girls had a reputation to protect, and being seen on the streets with a Westerner might lose them their more stable Chinese patrons.

The Carlton was different. It also catered to foreign couples—mostly young Englishmen and their wives or girlfriends—so the hostesses for the single men had to be discrete. They didn't wait around in an "aquarium" as in other clubs. They were out of sight, sitting down at a table only if called for.

That night, the boys from the bank, joined by some other young

Dutchmen working for the shipping company, occupied a large table in the center of the club, by the dance floor. They hadn't called for any girls yet, preferring to survey the scene and do some serious drinking first. The occasion was Volker's birthday and the drinks for the first two rounds were on him.

They had worked late, and their stomachs were empty. They ordered some saté and prawn crisps with their beers and whiskeys, but the alcohol quickly found its way around their hungry bodies. After a few drinks they began to get louder, Dick Reitsma especially, and Peter, always the spoilsport, found himself cautioning his colleagues to keep their voices down. But they laughed at him, calling him nanny and urging him to drink his whiskey pure, to toughen his timid soul.

Some guests near them, Chinese and Europeans alike, were casting critical glances in their direction. One group of young Chinese men in particular, seated at a large table next to theirs, seemed very annoyed. They were all neatly dressed in dark trousers and white shirts with ties, and they had identical hair styles, short-cut and slicked back with grease. Evidently they were a group of employees of a Chinese bank or shipping company, well-educated and relatively free from the taint of living in a British colony.

This proud group of Chinese men, conscious of their superior upbringing and schooling, had been following the antics of the Dutchmen out of the corners of their eyes, and had almost stopped talking among themselves. Their set jaws and cold stares betrayed loathing for these uncouth colonials. When Volker accidentally kicked over a chair, the whole group froze, and one of the Chinese jumped up to fetch the manager who came over instantly to give the unruly foreigners a stern warning.

After that, the Dutch table seemed docile for a while, but then something happened. A Chinese man in his late thirties, impeccably dressed in a dark suit and striped tie, entered the club with a very white, very young blonde girl on his arm. Necks were craning as they were escorted to their assigned table. More even than the fact that they belonged to different races, it was their age difference that attracted attention.

The couple passed the Dutch table within a few yards, the man fondling the girl's shoulder. Suddenly, Reitsma's voice broke the hush like a surprise arrow released from ambush. "Nice going, Wong. Bertha's sister, I presume?"

The reference was to a thirteen-year-old Dutch girl, Bertha Hartogh, who, a few years earlier, had been married to a Malayan teacher from Singapore ten years her senior in a proper Muslim ceremony. The marriage had caused an uproar among English and Dutch residents, and the Singapore High Court in the end had the marriage annulled and the girl returned to her family in Holland. The case had sparked race riots in the streets of Singapore against the "blatantly patronizing attitude" of the colonial regime and had palpably raised tensions in the territory.

At Reitsma's remark, one of the Chinese from the adjoining table shot up like a jack-in-the-box, and confronted Reitsma. "You take that back!"

Reitsma rose too, a perspiring, disheveled figure, shirttail showing, towering over the correctly attired, tense Chinese, a sneering look on his face. Some of the other Dutchmen tried to make him lay off, but he ignored the pleas.

"I'm not taking back anything!" he declared belligerently.

The Chinese was struggling to contain his rage. "You're drunk and disgusting! Why don't you go home? We don't need you here!"

Reitsma reacted with a supercilious smile, saliva flying from his mouth. "You're telling me what to do? Huh? You little, yellow nincompoop!" By now, half the club was following the stand-off with fascinated trepidation, including the couple whose controversial entrance had triggered the outburst.

Still, the Chinese man was trying to keep the altercation civilized. "You westerners…" he brought out in a choking voice, pulling at his shirt collar for air. "You are disrespectful…you trample on our customs!"

"Some customs!" countered Reitsma loudly, conveniently ignoring the distinction between Malay and Chinese, between these middle-class businessmen and the isolated case of the Malayan teacher. "Screwing our little white girls!"

At this, the whole Chinese table exploded into sudden frenzy. They fell upon the Dutch group as one man, attacking with fists and beer bottles and items of cutlery grabbed from the table. Others from neighboring tables, Chinese and European alike, joined the melee. Reitsma smashed a café chair on the floor, breaking off a leg for a weapon. Several followed his example, on both sides, and the fight was on in earnest. The manager could be seen phoning the police, who didn't show up until after a few noses were broken and limbs bruised and arms slashed. One Chinese was nursing a badly bleeding head wound inflicted with a spiked chair-part. An ambulance was called.

The police broke up the fight, and took Reitsma and his Chinese adversary away for questioning. The rest of the Dutch group quickly paid their bill, and made their escape in the wake of the police, to avoid further trouble. Peter, ashamed and agitated, lingered, and once alone went over to the maligned couple at their corner table to offer clumsy apologies "for what has happened," more perhaps to cleanse himself from an intolerable stain than to provide any sort of alibi for Reitsma, for whose behavior he could only feel revulsion.

The man, surprised and smiling condescendingly, called him a "nice boy," and cautioned him to find "better friends" than those "drunken louts." The girl didn't smile, but eyed him keenly. Peter thought her too young even for him. She said "thank you" and offered him her hand. It felt cool and a little clammy. Peter blushed and escaped as fast as he could, repeating his "very sorry" to the manager, who didn't react.

Reitsma and the Chinese were released after questioning. Reitsma, sobered up by his arrest, apologized in writing for his behavior which he admitted had been provocative and aggressive. The Chinese decided not to press charges.

Peter's solo action was roundly condemned by his friends as disloyal and do-goody.

"Sure, we went too far," said Volker, "but that's no reason for you to be so god damned nice to that yellow fat cat! Whose side are you on anyway? After all, we were right. That girl *wasn't* much older than Bertha!"

The conflict kept Peter awake that night. He realized the cowardice of pretending, with mere words, that you didn't belong to a group, while carrying right on sharing their company. One thing he was sure of: The "my-country-right-or-wrong" principle embraced by Reitsma and Volker and some of the others was not for him. He would judge each situation on its merits. But would he have the strength of his convictions if it came to the crunch?

He didn't know the answer. What he did know was that he had to step up his efforts to find another place to live. With this resolve on his mind he finally caught sleep.

The next day being a Saturday, Peter had "cable duty." Mr. Vreeman was on the tennis court as usual, and after Peter had delivered the cables on the little silver tray, Mrs. Vreeman invited him to stay for a cool drink. She instructed a maid servant crisply "to prepare two pitchers of iced lime-and-soda, bring one here for us with two tall glasses, and take the other down to the court for the gentlemen, so they don't need to come back up for their refreshments." She then turned to Peter and asked him about his life in Singapore.

"I suppose you're having a good time, with the other bachelors?"

"Oh, yes, I suppose so."

"No shortage of girls to dance with, I'm sure?"

Peter gave a short laugh to hide his embarrassment.

"Why are you laughing? Did I say something…wrong?"

"Oh, no, it's just that…it isn't that way, for me."

She looked at him unabashedly, with wide eyes. "You don't *dislike* girls, do you?"

This did go far, but he felt reckless. "Oh, no! But I don't like the kind in the nightclubs."

She looked away. "Then you must be very lonely."

Peter felt at once grateful and taken aback by this unexpected attempt at intimacy. It was the first time since he joined the bank that anyone had shown interest in his inner person.

"I'm sorry if I'm prying…" Mrs. Vreeman said softly. "But you're still so young."

Gratitude wiped away his resistance. He wanted to talk but he didn't know how to express his unhappiness without seeming silly—and without saying unkind things about his colleagues which would amount to another betrayal.

"I sometimes miss my family," he said awkwardly, and instantly regretted it, for that was not the point, and not even totally true.

But Mrs. Vreeman took his admission at face value. "That's quite natural, isn't it? And that place above the bank, with all those men…they do drink a lot, I suppose?"

Peter nodded. "To be frank, I don't enjoy that part very much."

"I didn't think you would," said Mrs. Vreeman, her lips smiling at him with a mixture of motherly concern and something else that made him feel aroused and ill at ease. They were sitting at opposite ends of the short sofa, half turned towards each other. He was aware of her perfumed body heat.

The maid servant entered with the lime-and-sodas and they sipped them with audible delight. Peter relaxed a little. Suddenly Mrs. Vreeman got up and said, "Wait, there's something I want to show you." She walked over to the bookcase and took a leather-bound photo album from it. Plopping back down close to Peter, she placed the album over both their laps, opened it and said, affecting a bright and girlish manner, "Here! What do you think of this lovely creature?"

She was pointing at a posed shot of a slim young beauty with shoulder-length dark blonde hair, and slender arms and legs. She was wearing a sleeveless flowery summer frock, her bosom bulging under its thin material.

"Oh…beautiful! Your daughter?"

"You think she resembles me?" Mrs. Vreeman asked.

"Y-yes, although…I don't know," he fumbled.

Seeing his embarrassment, she relented. "It's *me,* you silly! Don't tell me I've changed that much!" He laughed sheepishly.

"It's the hair, it's different." That was his excuse. In fact, there was nothing of the girl that he recognized in the woman.

"No, darling, it's the innocence. That's what's different. It's gone. I was young then, and very, very innocent. Like you now." She placed an arm around his shoulder and smiled.

She hugged him a little, turning toward him as she did so. He didn't resist. Her womanly warmth suffused him with unreasonable, indecent speed, and he knew where this could lead if he only let it.

"I could arrange for you to live with the Permés," she said. He looked at her. Her lipstick, a bright vermilion, transcended the natural boundaries of her already voluptuous lips, like tomato soup spilt carelessly on the plate's rim. It offended his sense of order and propriety. "They have a spare room facing the back garden, and you'd be in a family. They have twin daughters of thirteen. Wouldn't you like that?"

Guillaume Permé was the rather affected deputy manager of the office, the scion of an old Huguenot family who had held on to their French names, and their correct pronunciation, for three centuries, and seemed to view themselves in an aristocratic light.

"Living with them? But I hardly know Mr. Permé."

"Oh, I'm sure they would be delighted to have you. Anyway, your part of the house is quite separate, and you'll have your own entrance, so..." She winked, and added airily, "I promise I'll drop in soon to see how you're doing!" She got up, rang the little bell that was on the desk, and asked the servant to fetch her handbag from the other room.

"Here," Mrs. Vreeman said as she took a little card and a pen out of the bag and scribbled something down. "Take this. It's Héloïse's phone number. You can call her tomorrow. It will all be arranged."

# Chapter 9

Peter had been living with the Permé family for over two months now, and in all that time, he'd only seen Héloïse Permé once, when he arrived.

Mrs. Permé was the kind of woman one would call handsome: tall, with strong, chiseled features, a long neck, and hair done up in a classical bun. She wore no makeup, and her figure was hidden beneath a shapeless white shift. She had given him a starchy welcome, not unfriendly but impersonal, and with no hint of the "delight" Mrs. Vreeman had promised. Peter couldn't help thinking that the room had been made available to him as a matter of obligation, because the house belonged to the bank. As for Mr. Permé, Peter encountered him only in the office, and that was rarely, and without the slightest acknowledgement that they were sleeping under the same roof.

There was no question that he was living "in a family" here. Not only was he not invited to participate in any way in the activities of the house, his room was in reality a small separate building, connected to the main house by a covered veranda, but divorced from it by a short intersecting wall, with a door in it. Peter had soon discovered that not long after dinner the door was locked from the inside. His little house was surrounded on three sides by a small garden with its own gate opening into a back alley. Mrs. Vreeman had been right on that point: He could come and go unnoticed.

The food was good, but he had to eat his meals alone, at a small table on the veranda, where the Permé's Chinese cook brought his dinner to him at the same time as the family was sitting down for theirs, at seven o'clock every night. Breakfast was placed on the same table at an early hour. Peter always found it waiting for him however early he rose, protected by a fly net, and with the coffee in a thermos.

Peter had never lived alone before. At first he couldn't get used to the deep silence at night, the pressure of it on his ear drums. His movements became deliberate, the little sounds they produced resembling brittle objects that he might accidentally step on or drop onto the stone floor. He tried to minimize his movements, make them more economical, to avoid the intrusions their accompanying noises made on the silence that hung about him like a shroud.

The first week he longed desperately for a radio, but apart from not having the money, and suspecting that the family would somehow disapprove, he soon came to rule out bringing such a sound machine into the hallowed void that he now inhabited. He owned only two electric tools, an electric razor and a rotating electric fan, which had cost him more than a week's salary, but which he found indispensable to a healthy rest. Warned that sleeping with a fan trained on your naked body was dangerous, he aimed its wind at the wall, benefiting from the indirect air stream, and turned it off halfway through the night when the heat was more tolerable.

Peter commuted to the office by pedicab, a cheap form of personal transportation that was available at all hours and at every street corner. The fifteen-minute ride transported him literally between two separate worlds, in neither of which he felt at home, and in both of which he could function.

He was making good progress in the bank. Within six months, he was promoted to the bills department, where he had to check shipping documents—presented for "negotiation" by exporters—for their compliance with the terms of the underlying letters of credit. It was the kind of work he had gained some familiarity with in the pillared hall of the head office, but here he didn't think of his co-workers as "Desks." They seemed to have a healthier attitude to life. They weren't mired in the cheerless morass of clerkly grayness that Peter associated from the start with bank employees in Holland.

One night, after his solitary dinner, when the quiet had sunk into him like molten wax and he was in bed trying to read, his thoughts kept turning to the strangeness of his situation: living a solitary life in an alien environment, far from his family and the country of his birth, often lonely, yet not entirely unhappy. He couldn't see the path before him very clearly, but knew that he would have to find his way by his wits, relying on his own resources.

What he did know was one thing: There was life after this, another, truer phase to follow the drabness and compromises of his present existence. There had to be, or life wasn't really worth living. He wasn't sure how realistic his hopes were, but he felt that as long as he could hold on to them, they would sustain him in his present condition.

He reached under his bed, and pulled out the suitcase. He opened it, and took out his camera from under the light sweaters and extra shirts he kept there. For a moment he was struck again by its black-and-steel beauty, which seemed to have grown more lustrous since he last set eyes on it, right after he arrived in Singapore.

For the first time since he joined the bank, he loaded the camera with one of the rolls of black and white Kodak film he had brought along but never used. He screwed on the 300mm telephoto lens, went out and pointed the camera randomly at a corner of the moon-lit garden, then another, then at the street outside, focusing the lens at an illuminated door or window, at the pool of light under a street lantern. He felt a need to capture something uplifting, a moment of meaning. The night was unusually bright, the oversized full moon just clearing the rooftops, throwing down long, angled shadows.

A door opened across the street, the shape of an old woman slowly emerged. She took a few careful, deliberate steps. Once out in the light, she stopped and lifted her face to the moon's disk. Through his viewfinder, Peter saw her weathered face breaking into an open-mouthed half-smile, or perhaps it was only an expression of awe or veneration at the secret energy of the night's guardian that made plants and trees grow and regulated the rhythms of the oceans and our lives.

She stood there for a long moment, her pallid, wizened face gazing at the face of the moon as if she was scrutinizing the face of a trusted friend.

*She must be very lonely*, thought Peter. *Yet she doesn't seem unhappy*. He kept looking at her. And then he understood, and for a fleeting moment his expression was not so very different from the old woman's. She was beyond such emotions; she was at peace. When he clicked the shutter, it felt as if he had snatched something personal and precious from the old woman, but his desperate need for it—for that visible proof that inner harmony could be found —somehow justified the theft.

When he had his film developed, this was the only shot he had enlarged and framed. It conveyed precisely what he had seen, and it gave him hope.

A few weeks after he moved to the Permé house, Mrs. Vreeman finally made good on her promise to visit him. Thinking of that occasion still made him squirm.

She had come in through the back gate, apparently without first announcing herself to Mrs. Permé. She caught him unawares, after his dinner, while he was reading in his lazy wicker chair, his torso bared. Suddenly she stood there in the doorway, in a white linen two-piece suit, smiling, carrying a package in both hands. He hadn't even heard the gate. Her curly hair, permed and neck-length, was the same golden color as her high heels.

She laughed at his discomfiture as he jumped up and grabbed a shirt and ran a hand through his hair.

"Mrs. Vreeman…why, you…such a surprise!"

"I know. I wanted to call, but you don't have a phone here, do you? You don't mind?"

"Oh, no, only…I can't offer you…"

"Nonsense, just offer me a chair!" She closed the door behind her.

"Of course, here you are…"

"Thank you. Here, I brought you this." She placed the package on the table. "Open it."

It was an Oxford anthology of English poetry in three volumes."Oh, that's fantastic! But really…how did you know that I wanted this?"

"I just knew…" They both laughed. He stroked the books without opening them.

"Thank you, thank you." Without hesitation, he kissed her on the cheek, placing a hand lightly on her upper arm as he did so, and, feeling her yield slightly, kissed her again more slowly. He knew that second kiss exceeded the boundaries of politeness, and that he lingered an instant after planting it ever so cunningly close to her mouth. He took a deep breath as he pulled away, luxuriating in her perfume that seemed at least seven parts her own. He let his hand slide down limply.

"That was nice," she said huskily as she caught his falling hand, and then released it.

"I-I…" he said, taken aback by the effect of his little advance, "I want to show you something." His camera. It was the only thing he could think of.

Mrs. Vreeman sat down self-consciously in the wicker chair he had pulled up for her, and watched Peter pull the suitcase out from under his bed and unwrap his treasure.

"Nobody knows about this," he said as he lovingly lifted the camera out of its swaddling clothes. The telephoto lens was still screwed onto it, a potent, enquiring extension of the camera's neutral self.

"Ah, your secret hobby?" she said lightly.

"No, my alter ego," he said, instantly regretting the pretentiousness of the term.

"You mean you like that more than…poetry?" She was waving a forlorn hand in the direction of the unopened books.

"It's not like that." How could he explain? "It's not a matter of one or the other."

"Oh, yes, it is. It always is in life," she said, suddenly firm. "We can't avoid choosing. We've got to take life by the horns. To seize the moment." She pulled him towards her, camera and all. He perched on her arm rest. She caressed the gleaming beauty with both hands and in doing so rested her lower arms on his knee. "So you want to be a photographer. It's your deepest desire in life, right?"

Right this moment Peter wasn't so sure if there wasn't something else he desired even more, but he answered simply, "Yes."

"Then why resist it?" Mrs Vreeman looked straight up at him, a half-smile playing around her lips.

His parents had never talked that way. What Mrs. Vreeman was saying he had been waiting to hear all his life. Yet now that he heard it, it sounded facile, irresponsible even, as if giving in to desire was the supreme good. Her words, their message, disturbed him. He took the camera from her hands and got up from his perch.

"Actually it's not a desire. It's something in my nature. It will find its way out when the time is ripe." It sounded prim. But it was the truth. He gave a small, embarrassed laugh.

Mrs. Vreeman said nothing. He filled the silence by fussing over the rewrapping of the camera and putting it back in the suitcase. A cat shrieked in the back alley. He closed the lid firmly. Behind him, he heard the hush of Mrs. Vreeman's nylons rubbing against each other. He pushed the suitcase back into its dark space.

"Fulfillment won't wait, my boy," she said softly. "The clock ticks." She looked at her watch. "I must go. Mr. Vreeman must be wondering what's keeping me." Her laugh had a hollow ring.

"Of course," Peter said. The slight breeze from the opening door was a relief. "And thank you again for the books. You're so kind."

"Read something to me, sometime. When you've found your way in them." She pointed at the books, and gave him a quick peck on the cheek, like his mother used to when she had to go somewhere. Under her makeup Mrs. Vreeman's skin was a web of tiny cracks.

"I'd be happy to," he said. He wasn't sure if he meant it. He lightly brushed her freckled arm as he saw her off.

"Good night."

"Good night."

Under the lamplight he watched her chauffeur open the door of her car.

# Chapter 10

A few weeks later, Peter was invited to a dinner party at the manager's house. The invitation came in the mail, a heavy, gold-edged card with rounded corners and a cursive, embossed printed text, with his name, "Mr. Peter van Doorn" expertly calligraphed in the open space. He opened it as he was getting ready for bed.

Two words printed in smaller type in the lower left corner gave him a jolt. "Black tie" they said and they catapulted Peter into that part of life in the tropics he had so far largely managed to avoid: the formal entertainment circuit.

The invitation puzzled Peter. He felt that he and Mrs. Vreeman had a personal relationship the nature of which didn't square with this kind of invitation.

*She's throwing me over*, thought Peter, *because I've turned her down. That's why she includes me with anonymous others.*

Yet he knew better than to decline the invitation. That was "not done" for an underling. Besides, he didn't want to give Mrs. Vreeman the satisfaction of seeing him defeated. No, he would be there, and he would impress her and the other guests with his poise and conversation which—he felt immodestly certain —would help lift the whole shallow business to a more acceptable level. Young or not, he would show them that you could be a banker *and* plumb life's depths.

Then, although it was past midnight, he sat down at his table and carefully composed his acceptance, using the phrases he had learned in Amsterdam for precisely this kind of occasion.

He finally lay down, taking a volume of Mrs. Vreeman's gift with him. He leafed through it, but found most of the poetry incomprehensible. Soon he tired of trying, and fell into a deep sleep.

One night, a few days later, over whisky-and-sodas on the terrace of the Holland Club, Volker told Peter that he was displeased with his attitude.

"You're keeping aloof. Everybody notices. Maybe you're getting too close to the boss and his wife."

Peter blushed, but it was too dark where they sat for Volker to notice. "I'm only doing my duty. Can I help it that I've got to take the damn cables to his house?"

"Sure, that's fine. But it's giving you ideas above your station, so I've…"

"What do you mean, above my station?" Peter interjected, not liking the turn the conversation was taking.

Volker ignored the interruption. "So I've decided to assign Joop to cable-duty from next month."

"*You've* decided? I thought the boss did that himself."

"That's what I mean, thinking you have a special line to the boss. You were selected on my recommendation, of course."

Peter was tempted to say something rude, but he controlled himself, and chose another tack. "Well, but she has…they've invited me to a formal dinner." Instantly, he regretted his peevish, defensive remark.

Volker gave him a quick look and said nothing. He took a packet of Senior Service from his breast pocket, and expertly tapped up a cigarette, which he lit with a flourish using a gold Zippo taken from the same pocket. He put both items back in the pocket while crossing his legs, took a deep, audible draw that made the cigarette glow fiercely and, his head slightly askew and looking Peter straight in the eye, said, "Are you screwing her?"

Peter gazed at Volker in astonishment, quite at a loss for an answer.

"Are you?"

Peter took a sip of his drink to steady his tongue before responding. "How can you say such a thing! You must be joking."

"I'm not joking. I'm asking you a question."

"Of course not. What a ridiculous idea."

"There are rumors. She's visited you in your room at night, right?"

"Yes, but…"

"And you hang around her house on Sundays while the boss is playing tennis, right?"

"Listen, Volker, she's nice to me. She talks to me."

"When married women are nice to young boys it means they want them in bed."

Peter chose to act indignant. "Why do you have to profane a simple innocent interest into something lewd and scheming? Why can't I just be like a…a son to her? The son she never had?"

"Because," said Volker, moving to the edge of his chair, and poking a finger into Peter's chest, "the son as lover is every sensual woman's dream. And because you wouldn't be the first. Yes, that's right. Of course you're incredulous. You're young and unusually naïve. That's why I'm warning you. This nice Mrs. Vreeman has a penchant for young men from the bank. She's very discreet, and therefore all the more effective. I'll tell you a secret on condition that you will never tell anyone I told you. Understood?"

"Understood."

Volker took another puff and sucked the smoke audibly into his lungs. He fixed Peter with an unblinking stare.

"The reason why you were assigned to Singapore at the last moment, and not to some rat-hole in Indonesia, is because we had to send one of our young Dutch trainees back to Holland on short notice. He arrived the year before you, and within months got himself romantically involved with Mrs. Vreeman. He was fucking her at lunchtime, on a regular basis as we found out. Her husband didn't seem to know. He…well, let's say he adores her, and we didn't want to break his heart because we like and respect him. So we couldn't tell Head Office the real reason either. Just made up a story, the young man couldn't adjust to life in the tropics, blah, blah, blah. They made him resign, of course. I'll spare you the details—that would be gossip. And I don't want this to go further. Why am I telling you all this? As a warning. If you value your career, and I think you should because it seems you've got some rudimentary brains, I advise you to stay away from the nice Mrs. Vreeman."

Peter had been listening with bowed head, not out of contrition, more to absorb the stream of information he was receiving. He felt he was aging rapidly, at least ten years in the past ten minutes. Now he lifted his head.

"I've already accepted the dinner invitation."

"That's not the point. Of course you should go. Just don't make a fool of yourself."

"Don't worry," said Peter. "Actually," he added, in an effort to keep a certain distance from Volker, whom he still didn't fully trust or like, "I'd already decided to steer clear of Mrs. Vreeman anyway. She was getting too sticky."

"Now listen, young man. Don't get cocky about Mrs. Vreeman. She's your boss's wife, and she deserves your respect. Are we clear about that?"

Peter was aghast at this double standard, and he wondered if this was an instance of the "hypocrisy of the bourgeoisie" he had read about. It fleetingly occurred to him that his own behavior could equally be laid at hypocrisy's door: to indulge Mrs. Vreeman and cooperate in her gradual seduction of him, and then abandon her the moment his conduct is called into question. Perhaps he was already resorting unconsciously to the age-old stratagem of associating guilt with the *discovery* of an unpardonable deed, and innocence with its successful concealment.

But he kept these thoughts to himself and simply answered with an affirmative grunt.

"Good," said Volker, as he got up to leave, "and remember, keep your trap shut."

# Chapter 11

There were two large tables set for dinner, one in the main dining room, the other in Mr. Vreeman's study, which for this occasion was referred to as the "library."

The seating plan was displayed under a glass plate on a small rosewood table in the entrance hall, and was studied intently by each arriving guest even before they had stepped into the drawing room to be greeted by their hosts. The male guests remained stoic or raised an almost imperceptible eyebrow on discovering their allotted places. The ladies covered their disappointment charmingly by expressing their delight at "being together" in the library with so-and-so, or, alternatively, letting out a small cry of joy when they found their seat was at the main table in the dining room. Peter bristled inwardly at this advance announcement of the pecking order, while at the same time finding it oddly comforting to know beforehand where he had been positioned— surprisingly in the main dining room, albeit at the very center of the table, farthest away from the head and foot command posts.

The Vreemans welcomed their guests with broad, impersonal smiles and a handshake or an obligatory peck on the cheek. He was relieved when Mrs. Vreeman didn't kiss him, seeing this omission as a mark of distinction rather than a snub, the more so as she emphasized what a pleasure it gave her to welcome "one of the bank's most promising young men" to her house and making a point of introducing him to a lean-framed, bespectacled man of uncertain age with longish hair and thin lips who was hovering nearby, before greeting her next guest.

"André, come here, meet Peter van Doorn. Talk to him. I'm sure you have lots in common. Peter, this is André de Montigny. But don't let the name frighten you!"

They shook hands. The distinguished, rather mournful face lit up with a smile and a twinkle. "Hello."

"Hello," said Peter as they moved on into the interior. "Huguenot, no doubt?"

"I'm afraid so. We all have our crosses to bear."

"It sounds beautiful to me, you know, melodious."

"Ah! Yes, but imagine having to identify yourself in Holland at summer camp or army roll call with a name like that! I can tell you, it guarantees a good hazing. Or ostracism, which is worse. I envy your plain Dutch name."

"Can't you, uh, change it then?" asked Peter.

"I suppose I could, on the grounds of discrimination. But you see the discrimination works the other way, too. Besides, I rather like it."

"I can imagine. I would fall for the name before I'd met the bloke!"

"Oh!" drooled André with mock-affectation. They laughed. "Actually," continued André, "I pump my name for all it's worth. It's my sole asset. Trouble is, it hasn't actually got me very far."

André said he was the tutor to the three children of the British governor, and lived alone in an apartment in an old house not far from the Singapore Swimming Club.

"Sounds interesting enough. Don't you enjoy your work?"

"Why? Am I that obvious?" He gave a roguish smile and threw a quick glance around him. "Actually, I hate children, especially mine. Insufferable brats." Peter laughed, and André continued. "But that's all right. I mean, the job buys me the freedom to do what I please."

"Like what?" Peter wanted to know.

"I'll tell you another time. Too risky here," said André. "By the way, what's your cover?"

"Cover? Oh, uh, banking. But in reality…"

"Don't tell me now. Come to my apartment Friday night, and we'll exchange confidences. Shall we say eight? Now we better join the others, or you'll be branded asocial, and that's death for a budding banker."

Peter worked his way around the room, introducing himself first to the men, all much older, mostly solid management types drawn from the resident Dutch and British business community, who were standing around in little groups. They feigned a brief interest in him before resuming their conversations.

Next, he went over to a group of women standing nearby. In some ways, they were like the men, ruddy types with fat arms and smokers' voices talking loudly, who responded to Peter's approach with a laugh and a non-committal question or two and then paid no further attention to him.

He turned around and moved toward the veranda, where other women had formed a group around the flowery rattan furniture. Peter watched them from the entrance.

They invited Peter to sit down with them, and started questioning him in a tone of amused concern about his background, his life in Singapore and whether he had a girlfriend. One of these ladies wanted to know about the "practical side" of a bachelor's life. "I mean, how do you manage, all by yourself?"

"Oh, I don't do a thing," Peter answered, surprising himself with his glibness. "It all somehow happens, from the meals to the cleaning to the pressing of my trousers."

"You poor boy!" chirped another. "So young, and already spoiled rotten!"

"Oh, no more spoiled than your husbands, I imagine," Peter rejoined, to a ripple of laughter.

"Our husbands are quite beyond the pale," said a third, a refined-looking lady in a simple gray, sleeveless silk dress, and lots of gold jewelry. "Not to mention ourselves, right, Diane? I mean, how ever are *you* going to manage back in Rotterdam without your Suni and your Achmad and their half dozen underlings? Or is it a dozen?"

"*Rotterdam?*" answered the striking blonde lady in the ruffled soft yellow outfit addressed as Diane with a theatrical gesture. "What makes you think I'm going back *there*? I *know* I couldn't manage, so I'm staying put. With or without you-know-who."

"You can't be serious!" exclaimed the gray dress. "You'd let Paul go back alone? How's the poor man going to cope?"

"Oh, I'm sure he won't have to worry," said Diane. "There're always selfless little souls like you around who will jump at the chance to fry a man's eggs and darn his socks—in exchange for a little badly needed attention. Nothing personal, of course."

Peter noticed that some of the women had stayed on the sidelines of the bitchy talk, smiling indulgently on the proceedings. One of them, a young woman with a pony tail wearing a striped blue-and-white dress and white shoes with girlish straps, reacted to this last bit of venom with a little sniff. She was perched on the arm of a chair with her nose puckered up and one leg over the other. She said nothing.

Before the grey dress could think of a decisive put-down, Mrs. Vreeman stepped out on the veranda. "So that's where you all are! Discovering my young friend's artistic talents?"

The ladies looked from Peter to her and back to Peter. One of them asked, "What on earth are you referring to, Suzanne?" It was the first time Peter had heard someone call Mrs. Vreeman by her first name. Even her own husband always referred to her as "Mrs. Vreeman" or "my wife" and addressed her as "darling."

"Oh, you didn't know? It's his modesty, I'm sure. Peter is a photographer. Makes the most exquisite photos. You must ask him about it, and about art and life and all that. He has some very interesting ideas! Don't you, darling?" She tweaked his cheek which had turned crimson. "Go on," she urged the group, "ask him!"

Suddenly Peter was besieged with questions. Before he had even attempted to answer the first, he saw Mrs. Vreeman leave the veranda, back into the house. He couldn't believe what she had done to him, and he felt his feelings for her, already bruised, turn to ice.

"Do you do portraits?"

"I love photography! It's so much more revealing than paintings!"

"You can say that again! But is it art?"

"When could we see your work?"

Peter mumbled a few answers but soon excused himself. He escaped down the garden steps. From the corner of his eye he saw the young woman with the pony tail slide down from her perch and follow him. She caught up with him in the garden.

"Going for a walk?"

"Need a breath of fresh air after that," said Peter.

"Me too," answered the young woman. "Phew. That was very unfair to you." He didn't answer. "The problem is, they're bored stiff. They're leading a very unnatural life."

"You don't feel that way?" Peter asked.

"I work for a living. American Consulate. Hi, I'm Sally Turner."

"Oh, so you're Sally. I think we're sitting together."

"Great! I was afraid I might be paired with some old bore."

"Ah, you're American! Which part?"

"Milwaukee, Wisconsin. Been there?"

"No, oh, no. I've never been to the States. And I can't say I feel attracted to it. Too materialistic."

"I know. But you should visit it anyway. Try and live there for a while. I bet you'll love it. All that space. It makes the people generous. Sounds funny, I guess, for an American to be talking like this. But I've been away five years, and I think I can judge it better now."

Peter was intrigued, both by what Sally said and by her perky little nose which was surrounded by a shower of tiny freckles. "What do you mean, generous?"

"It's their minds. I think Americans have healthier thoughts, most of them. None of this…you know," and she made a quick deprecatory gesture in the direction of the veranda. "I mean, we have a lighter touch. We kid around more, instead of this deadly innuendo, this heavy old-worldly bitchiness. By the way, I like photography, too. Especially the darkroom work."

Peter's face lit up. "You have a darkroom here in Singapore?"

"Sure. Photography helps me get through this tropical assignment. Don't you agree?"

Until now Peter hadn't thought of "the tropics" as something objectionable per se. But now, this very moment, he did. "I don't know," he said. "I've hardly taken any shots since I got here."

"I do nothing but. Every weekend. Just to stay in practice. And sane!" Peter stole a sideways glance at Sally. There was something natural about her that he liked. She was unpretentious and got right to the point. "I shoot everything in sight, people praying at the temples, smiling street vendors, Indian women in sarongs, kids at play, anything bright and happy. It's a good balance for my weekday work."

"Maybe you're right about the tropics. I hadn't realized it. I think it's the colonial lifestyle, all this empty show of superiority. I just can't feel part of it."

"That's just it," said Sally. "I thought it's because I'm American. But you feel the same?"

"It's as if...I don't belong here. That's why..." Suddenly he stopped.

She completed his sentence. "...you haven't taken any photographs here?"

Peter looked her straight in the eyes. "Yes! But that's not the only reason." Sally waited, but he didn't elaborate. His true reason—not knowing how to combine his photography with being a banker—was something he felt she might not understand.

"Hey," she said, "why don't you join me one weekend for a photo shoot in Johor Baru, across the causeway? I'd like that!"

Peter was speechless. He'd been here barely an hour, and already he had two invitations and both from people he liked. And it all had nothing to do with Mrs. Vreeman.

"Hello!" Sally was waving two hands in front of his face.

"Oh, sorry, I was just thinking. You hardly know me, and already..." She looked at him with wide eyes. She wasn't beautiful like those American movie stars he'd always found both intimidating and too sugary. But he thought her sexy, in a tight, intelligent sort of way.

"You don't have to if you don't want to. But you seem an okay kind of guy, and I thought maybe we could have some fun together. What do you say?"

"Sure, thanks. Well, why not?"

"Great. I'll tell you what. Next week I'm in K.L., and later this month I'm due for home leave, so it may have to wait a while. But if you give me your phone number, I'll call you once I'm back from the States, so we can fix a date. Okay?"

"Sure," he said. "Here's my card."

The gong sounded. Dinner was being served. Everyone made their way to their pre-assigned seats.

"Oh, there he is! Our elusive cameraman!" It was his table partner on the right, one of the veranda ladies, the blonde one with the yellow dress, and she was waiting for Peter to help her with her chair.

"Thank you. You are a gentleman. Now tell me, I want to know all about your camera work. First of all..." And she proceeded to shower him with a barrage of little questions and comments, but Peter discerned no real interest on her part, and he felt that his answers were as platitudinous as her observations. When she had exhausted the topic, she turned to make sport of her other neighbor, leaving Peter free to talk to Sally on his left, who was being ignored by her table partner.

They continued to talk even at the end of the meal, when everybody around them had fallen quiet, prompting Mr. Vreeman, who was standing at the head of the table, to call Peter to order. "Van Doorn, I'm sure you have many a tale to tell, but may I have your attention for a moment?"

Mr. Vreeman proceeded to make a speech which sounded to Peter like another collection of platitudes, but even Sally—and André who could be seen through the open doors at the table in the library—laughed and applauded heartily when he finished. Peter thought he must have missed something and looked enviously at Sally, his new-found freckled chum who before his eyes had metamorphosed into a woman of the world, a match for any of these colonial matrons. He felt left out, but the quick smile she darted him while applauding restored his self-confidence and he joined in belatedly, having in fact the last clap.

Mr. Vreeman proposed a vacuous toast to "all of us" and sat down, giving a sign to his wife, who promptly rose and invited the ladies to "join me upstairs." On her way out, she passed behind Peter's chair and, leaning over to Sally, said in a whisper too loud to be missed by those nearby, "You'll be careful with my young photographer, won't you, Sally dear? He's not had much *exposure,* you know!" She gave Peter a wink and a lingering little squeeze in the neck and disappeared, dragging Sally along with her.

The men from the library drifted over and took the vacated seats at the main table. Mr. Vreeman snapped his fingers. Two Chinese waiters instantly appeared carrying trays loaded with a choice of cigars and bottles of cognac and Armagnac and a supply of snifters, properly pre-warmed according to the conventions of another climate. With forced half-smiles, the waiters went around the table, and each guest pointed at the smoke and the digestive of his preference. Here, life was as good as ever, and Old Rubberneck's ominous warnings about hard times and impending war seemed far away indeed.

Peter was still digesting Mrs. Vreeman's remark to Sally, the third this evening from the Vreeman couple to embarrass him. He watched the cigar waiter clip a cigar selected by one of the guests, then hold it in the flame of a burning strip of thin-cut wood, lit from a candle, until it glowed red. *What a demeaning job*, thought Peter, *serving the white man like a slave*. When it was his turn to choose, Peter smiled at the waiter, to make common cause with him. But the waiter pressed him, his face an impatient grimace. "You choose, I light," he said, and Peter quickly took a panatella and had it lit for him like everybody else.

From behind his guilty cloud of smoke, leaning back into his chair, he heard André hold forth about the burdens of…what?

"…no fun at all! It's thorny, and there are no sirens along the way to cheer you along."

"Then why bother?" a red-necked gentleman, owner of a department store, wanted to know. "I'd go fishing instead!" Laughter, and a few cries of "hear, hear!" greeted this statement.

"That's what I do," said André, with an enigmatic smile.

"What?"

"Go fishing. Off the jetty. Best way to contemplate the state of the world."

"Best way to catch your supper without having to pay for it, I reckon!" said the redneck amid general chuckling.

"So you're a fisherman, too?" said André, emphasizing the last word. The man threw him a sharp look.

"Strictly deep-sea," he said pompously. "Keep a thirty-footer with a crew of two at the ready. Like I used to in India."

"Ah, of course," mused André. "Things are not what they used to be there, I suppose? Since independence?"

The redneck, whose name Peter now remembered as George White, glared again at his inquisitor.

"Right! And if we've got anything to do with it, *things* won't get out of hand that way here in the Straits, right, Justin?" He turned abruptly away from André to face his host. But André pursued him.

"I don't know India, but in my experience, the Singapore Chinese are very capable managers. They already practically run our businesses for us here anyway, don't they?"

Vreeman, seeing White's eyes flash, intervened. "Now, hold it, André, I'm afraid you're misinformed, and in your position you can hardly speak of personal experience. The Chinese *advise* us on local matters. *We* run the business."

"I respect your opinion," said André courteously. "Mine is based merely on my experience as a customer and client of Western-owned enterprises here in Singapore. I get invariably the most concise answers and the best professional service from the Chinese staff. I go to the British or the Dutch only for cultural comfort."

White got up in a huff, a big man with a large belly that had ash all over his pleated, formal shirt. His jacket hung open. He was pointing his cigar at André. "You're damn right about your cultural comfort. Europeans have made this place what it is. Every damn building worthy of the name here is our work, every decent street, every green park, the port, the causeway to Johor. The Chinese carried the bricks, we told them where to put them. Hand the place over to them, and it will all crumble. Like China itself, it will collapse. Without the white man's whip, the cleverness of the Chinese is just good enough for selling peanuts on the street. You'd better remember that when you contemplate the state of the world on your lonely jetty!"

Scattered applause greeted White's speech. A few frowns, too. White motioned to one of the waiters to bring him another brandy.

87

"I will remember," said André dryly as he looked away, "that a Chinese boatman would guarantee me a larger catch than the miserable small fry I land on my own."

"Yes, van Doorn?" Peter had been trying to get a word in, and now Vreeman gave him the chance.

"Oh, I just wanted to say, I think André is quite right about the competence of the Chinese. I know I haven't been here that long, but I find them knowledgeable and trustworthy and they make few mistakes. I learned most of what I know from Liem and Chong and the others at the office."

"But are they running the show?" White asked without looking at Peter.

"No," said Peter, "clearly not."

"There!" said White triumphantly, showing Vreeman an open hand as emphasis.

"But only because we don't let them," continued Peter. "I'm sure they could manage if given the chance. Eventually."

"Good thing you added that last word, van Doorn," said Vreeman. "You had me worried there for a moment!" Laughter. "Now let's join the ladies. They must be thinking we're up to something!"

"Wish we were," mumbled André, but nobody heard him except Peter. "The smugness in the air is suffocating! What we need is a good, healthy revolution."

Peter was thrilled to hear anyone talk that way, and at a social gathering at that, and he wanted to say something in reply.

But André had already gone ahead into the library where the ladies were waiting for the men, and Peter saw him hook an arm around Mrs. Vreeman's and declare in a clear voice: "Suzanne, Suzanne, I've missed you. I never know what to do when you're not around!" Peter had never called her that and doubted if he ever would. He headed straight for Sally, but she was in a deep discussion with one of the women, and he found himself standing alone in a corner by the open window.

Away from the hubbub, he was suddenly aware of the sharp, deafening chorus of cicadas in the darkened garden. Or were they tree frogs? He looked out and saw the dark shadow of a waiter pass under the trees. A large foraging bat flapped swiftly by, its umbrella-like wings momentarily catching the insect-ridden glare coming from some spotlight that he couldn't see. Peter thought what a good, almost abstract shot it would have made if he had been able to capture the bat on film.

Sally's hand on his elbow gave him a start. "Sorry, I disturbed your reverie?"

He smiled. "It's all right, I was just thinking…about my camera." He laughed sheepishly.

"Poor you, so smitten, and then having to earn a living in an office! We must do something about that." She gave him a quick peck on the cheek that felt nicely moist. "I've got to go. I'll call you when I'm back!"

It was close to midnight when Peter said goodbye to Mrs. Vreeman. She leaned into him and offered him her face which he kissed self-consciously somewhere near her nose. Her body was limp against his, and he felt her arms around him. He kissed her a second time, closer to the mouth. She kissed him back, quickly, on the mouth. For a moment, he forgave her everything and only savored the intimacy between them.

"Good night, Mrs. Vreeman."

"Good night, Peter. See you tomorrow?" she said sweetly, as she released him, and turned to the next guest. Peter made a quick stop at the lavatory, and as he came out he saw Mrs. Vreeman repeat her intimate farewells with André, kissing him on the lips and whispering something in his ear.

# Chapter 12

Peter was twenty minutes late for his appointment with André, as the pedicab driver had trouble finding the address.

The door was opened by a well-groomed, Chinese house-boy who offered him a limp hand. "My name is David. André is expecting you." He followed David up the stairs of the old Victorian house. The house-boy was walking self-consciously, slightly swaying his hips, and leaving a faint trail of delicate perfume.

The living area, two spacious connecting rooms, was sparsely furnished with rattan tables and chairs, a few large Chinese cabin trunks, and a chaise lounge with flowery cushions. Indian *dhurries* were strewn across the floor. In a corner, with a little clip-on spotlight trained on it, was a meter-high dark brown Buddha, covered with traces of gold leaf. The walls were lined with books of every description. Two lazy ceiling fans churned the air. Behind a slatted half-partition, Peter caught a glimpse of an upright piano with sheet music scattered all over and around it. Nearby, piled up against a wall, was a mountain of colorful cushions.

André was reading on the covered porch. He rose from his large woven bamboo armchair with an "Ah, there you are! I thought you might've disappeared into the house next door. I can't match their kind of hospitality, I'm afraid."

"Oh, why?" asked Peter.

"It's a brothel." André laughed as he motioned Peter to an identical chair facing him across a small coffee table. André was having a gin, lime and soda

91

and asked David to bring another one for Peter. "It's the house drink," he said, "unless you prefer it without the gin?" Peter said no, it's fine, and André pushed a large three-part wooden bowl full of crisps and nuts and olives in his direction after taking a handful himself. He noticed Peter glance around.

"This is my retreat from the world. I hardly let anyone in. You like it?"

"Very much," Peter said truthfully. "It seems to reflect your…character."

André smiled. "That's why I keep it a secret. Fear of exposure of my dark side." They chatted like this for a while, with Peter being more and more at ease with André who, he thought, respected him as an equal. When Peter confided that he often felt isolated, André held up the book he had put down when Peter arrived.

"I'm reading this," he said, "Hermann Hesse's *Steppenwolf*. You know it? No, well, I'll lend it to you. It's required reading for people like us. Most of Hesse in fact. He's my current favorite. Nowhere else will you find life's essential dilemmas summed up like in Hesse. Except maybe in Flaubert or Stendhal."

"I haven't read much."

"Of course not. You haven't had the time. But you will, you will. It will be your sustenance, as it is mine. How else do you think I can stay sane, with three recalcitrant hooligans in my charge, and parents who don't care what their offspring learn as long as they 'dress for company' when ordered to and can say a proper 'good afternoon' and 'good evening' like little monkeys to the anonymous legions of forgettable guests that troop through their salons throughout the 'diplomatic season'? I need a good dose of Proust after a day with them."

Peter fell silent. He found André's stream of words exhilarating, but also intimidating. André noticed and looked serious. "Sorry, I didn't intend to overwhelm you with my predilections. Tell me about yours. I mean, what are you, deep down, below your banker's mask? If you don't mind telling me?" His gaze on Peter was not one of challenge or vulgar curiosity. It was kindly, not intrusive or patronizing.

"What am I, you want to know? Well," he hesitated. "Basically…I'm a camera," he said. He was impressed by the simplicity and forthrightness of his own reply, and the words hung between them in the gathering tropical dusk like a solemn oath. Then he laughed in embarrassment and relief, and André laughed with him.

"That's beautiful…and I'm sure you've never put it like that before."

"No, it was a slip of the tongue, really."

"Ah, but a very revealing one! Identifying yourself with your instrument like that. It's like me saying I'm a pen."

"Oh, you're a writer! That doesn't surprise me, actually. What do you write?" André rose and walked over to one of his bookcases. He took out a file box filled with magazines, and pulled one out. *The New Yorker.* He rifled through the pages. "Here. This sort of stuff." It was a piece entitled "Of sins and wages."

Peter took the magazine from André's hands and stared at it reverentially. His father had sometimes brought home copies of *The New Yorker*, and Peter had enjoyed looking at the covers and the cartoons. The text had been too difficult for him.

"You can borrow it if you wish. I have some more, although they don't publish everything I send them. They're very picky."

"You write in English, then."

"Oh, yes. I was brought up abroad you see, in the States and England, mostly. My father was a diplomat until he was reassigned to The Hague, in '37. That was a shame. I could never get used to the Dutch. I was nineteen and had just finished secondary school in London. I had no affinity with Holland at all. And you'll never guess what happened next."

"You…fell in love?"

"Ha, ha! No, I was promptly drafted into the Dutch army."

"But you'd not even lived there! Did you actually serve?"

"No, I returned the draft notice with the notation: 'Has left the country' and took the first boat back to England. My father was furious. He believed in answering your country's call. I was more interested in an education. In the end, he relented, and agreed to put me through university. In England."

He ordered another round of drinks, and told Peter the rest of his story. He had gone up to Oxford and read English and history. But he couldn't get used to the student rituals and the bland food and the institutionalized stuttering. And to warm beer and hot water bottles and the sniffling pallor of his fellow students. He also found that he preferred French writers to most English. After a year, he dropped out. Cut off from his father's support, he took a job as a private chauffeur to a landed count, who was impressed with his name and family credentials. His duties were to drive the count, the countess and two small kids back and forth between their country manor in Gloucestershire and their Westminster flat. He had intended the job to be temporary, but the count asked him to take on the tutoring of his children. He liked that work, and found time to write, at first little impressions of English life, then "personal accounts" of life in America as he remembered it. Encouraged by an American journalist he had befriended at a Chelsea party, he sent some of his work to *The New Yorker* and to his surprise, they accepted one of his essays.

"So that's where you spent the war years?"

"No, no, in Australia. The count got antsy because of Hitler and the looming war. He decided to move his family to Sydney, and take me along. And that's where I stayed, with that family, until '48, when they returned to England."

"What made you come to Singapore?"

"Oh, a friend of the count, an Aussie diplomat, hired me, and he was posted to Singapore. And one thing led to another, and I ended up with the British governor. Still tutoring kids, believe it or not. And still writing!"

André's story quickened Peter's own hidden ambition, and he felt a surge of affection for his camera and for the photographs that lay wasting in the trunk under his bed. Why couldn't he, too, cut the knot and launch himself on a creative career? What was keeping him? André guessed his thoughts.

"It's not too late, you know." Peter simply looked at his new friend expectantly. "I don't know anything about photography, but I can tell you have a creative mind and an eye for things, and you know, the world needs such people. They're all too rare."

"You think so? But how can I be sure I'll be able to make a living?"

Once again, André looked him straight in the eye. "The concern about feeding and clothing yourself should always take second place to the greater duty of fulfilling your potential. You don't owe the world anything, but you do owe it to yourself to discover your true nature, and to arrange your life accordingly."

"You're right," said Peter. His heart was pounding in his throat. "But something holds me back."

"It's called attachment to security. It's the worst enemy of freedom." Where had Peter heard this before? Ah, of course, it had been his own formulation, right after he joined the bank: "Capitalist lesson number one. Exploit an employee's attachment to life and security." Now he himself was one of those being exploited like those colorless clerks back at the head office, those Desks. He had allowed it to happen to him, and done nothing about it.

David came in to announce that dinner was served. They moved to the adjoining room, where a table was laid for two. It was going to be Chinese. David came in silently, and placed a platter of spring rolls on the table. André picked one up with his chopsticks, and put it on Peter's plate. "Even humdrum Chinese food beats English meat and potatoes, hands down. And this is better than humdrum."

They ate and drank in silence for a few minutes. Peter savored the delicate crispness of the wrapping and noticed how well it contrasted with the succulent chicken and vegetables inside. But his thoughts distracted him. He couldn't understand how André could be both a writer and an employee. Hadn't he bartered away his freedom for security like everybody else? He asked him.

"It's a question of what you make the center of your life," said André. "Writing is my first priority. The job is simply a means of living. We all must eat. Kafka was an insurance clerk. Camus worked in a trading company. But employment was not the axle of their existence. Writing was."

"I find I can't combine it, photography and banking. It's got to be one or the other. That's my dilemma. Because I doubt if I could earn a living as a photo-artist."

David brought in a whole broiled fish that smelled delicious. "My cook could never bake a fish like this if she lay awake wondering if she'd still have a job next month." André parted some of the crisp brown skin with the cutlery provided, revealing the soft white flesh underneath. "Help yourself," he said, "and let your soul enter your chopsticks."

The words hit home. For a few long moments Peter's mind sunk deeply into the heavenly food, and he thought he had never eaten anything so delicious. And it wasn't just the taste of the food that enthralled him, it was the bond he felt with André, who seemed to understand him like nobody ever had. Happiness filled him with a warm glow, and his eyes met André's as they both delved into the luscious sea bass. André lifted his little glass of lao-shu wine, and Peter did the same.

"When you're thirsty, drink," said André, and they both emptied their cups never letting their gazes drop. "That's what the Zen master replied when asked what the nature of the Buddha was. I haven't come across a better answer yet."

Later, troubled by the unease that lingered persistently under the blithe mood of the dining table, Peter returned to the question of priorities. He wanted to know how he could possibly combine photography with work in a bank if that work pulled him inexorably upward, placing ever increasing responsibilities on his shoulders.

"That's the point, my friend," said André. "You can't. You've got to let go of your ambition to leadership and power. That's illusory anyway, if you're in employment. Like Kafka, you must be content to be a clerk, or at best a bookkeeper or translator, some job that doesn't involve your soul, earning just enough to live. Only then can you hope to be free."

"Just enough you say, but you have a boy and a cook!" Peter said, almost defiantly, with a sidelong glance. They were reclining now on the heap of cushions by the piano, twirling the cognac around in their glasses.

"I'm lucky," said André with an easy air. "I'm well paid. And don't forget that Huguenot name! But when I leave the brats, I'm free. I keep strict school hours with them, and I don't carry my work around with me like a yoke. When I'm home, I make music, I eat, I write. Among other things. Tell me," he continued, abruptly changing the subject as he placed a hand on Peter's knee, "do you have a regular girlfriend?"

"Oh. No," said Peter, stiffening slightly under the touch. "I guess I'm rather clumsy at that sort of thing."

"I don't think so. Suzanne tells me you're a good kisser." He took his hand away. "In fact, I think she's yours for the taking." Peter felt the blood jump to his cheeks. He stammered something, and got to his feet. "I'm sorry," said André, "did I shock you?"

Peter looked down at him, struggling to regain his composure. "Well, yes, actually, you did. It's not true that I'm… You mean she talked to you about me?"

"She tells me everything," said André. "We're quite intimate, you know. But in case you wondered, we're not lovers and never will be. Just friends. And you needn't worry. I'm totally discrete."

Peter sat down again and collapsed on the cushions. "You're not telling me she asked you to talk to me, are you? I mean, you're not playing Cupid for her, I hope?"

"What if I were? She wants you, you want her." Peter again half-rose in protest. "Well, don't you? Be honest with yourself. She's not unattractive. And you need have no qualms about her husband. After all, he is a vegetable down there."

Peter reacted with a surprised look.

"You didn't know? Poor man, something that happened in the war, in Sumatra. So he must let Suzanne have what she needs. You might as well take advantage of it."

Peter found this kind of forthright talk very disturbing and incredibly exciting at the same time.

"It will solve your problem, without any cost to you."

"What problem?" Peter asked, his eyes wide.

"Come on, you know what I mean," said André. "Listen, I'm your friend. And let me tell you something. I, too, was still a virgin at your age. Apart from the occasional wanking sessions with school friends, that is. So I understand."

Peter leaned back and closed his eyes. "No," he moaned. "I couldn't. Not with the boss's wife. With anybody's wife. It's not right."

"That's fine. Actually, I'm glad you react that way. But then you must stop leading her on. I've found that there are two things in life we've got to be clear about. One is lovers. The other is the choice between self and security. All the rest is a matter of opinion."

When Peter left, André said, "You're always welcome in my house. I think we have something in common."

Peter walked to the nearest corner where half a dozen pedicabs were waiting along the kerb, their owners smoking and talking in the dark. As he rode home, Peter wondered what exactly it was that André and he had in common.

# Chapter 13

Time passed. Increasing responsibilities and the whirl of his off-duty life conspired to take Peter's mind off his frustrations. He had to admit that he was enjoying his work, and his sense of being an outsider had lost some of its strength.

One day he was called in by Mr. Vreeman and was told that, as Joop Geesterman was being transferred to Hong Kong, Sunday cable duty was reverting back to him.

The following Sunday, resuming his previous routine, he took a pedicab to the office. As before, the cables were awaiting him on the hall table. Among them was a long coded telegram from the Head Office of the "strictly personal" category, which Mr. Vreeman—to Volker's infinite annoyance—nevertheless wanted Peter to decode. He went into Mr. Vreeman's office, opened the steel cabinet with the key he had been entrusted with, and lifted out the heavy code manual.

It took Peter an hour and a half to decode the four-page message. It had to do with the "rapidly deteriorating situation" in Indonesia, and the bank's twenty-five branches there, which the Sukarno government had threatened to nationalize. If Sukarno makes good on his threat, the message continued, the Dutch staff of nearly two hundred men and their families would probably have to be repatriated at short notice, and Singapore would be the logical "concentration point" from where passage back to Europe, by air or ship, could be arranged. Amsterdam instructed Vreeman to make the necessary advance preparations, including the appointment of a senior officer from his staff.

When he reached the Vreeman villa, Peter was told that Mrs. Vreeman was indisposed, but that Mr. Vreeman would see him in the library.

"Do sit down," Mr. Vreeman said affably. "Drink?" Peter hesitated. "You're not going to let me drink alone, are you? Achmad," he said to the house boy, "bring two tonics and ice and the gin bottle and we'll mix them here."

Vreeman read the telegram, nodding repeatedly. Then he put it aside and said, "Bad news, but expected. Sad for all those people... We'll all be busy for a while, if Sukarno has his way. May have a job or two for you as well. Up to it?"

"I think so, yes."

"Thought so. Doing all right, aren't you? No complaints?"

"Not at all. I'm fine. And I'm enjoying my work." A half-truth, he thought.

"Good, good. My wife is not too much of a nuisance, I hope?" He eyed Peter through his rimless glasses, his smooth, reddish face in a little smile, his fingertips forming a five-span arch held up in front of his white, open-necked tennis polo. Peter snapped a mental picture of this man, his superior, who was asking him, a mere underling, about the behavior of his own wife. It would be perverse if it weren't so pathetic.

"Oh, no, on the contrary. She's been very kind. I only wish I could be more helpful to her." Peter was surprised at the cool, self-confident way in which he uttered this statement.

"You could, I'm sure. Just ask her. She likes you, I know. She's sorry she isn't here to greet you this morning. Had too much to drink last night, at a dinner we gave. Then she gets that way. You know." Vreeman raised his hands in a helpless gesture.

The drinks arrived. Vreeman opened the gin bottle and filled his own glass to the brim before pouring half as much into Peter's. He lifted his glass. "Hair of the dog!"

They continued their conversation for a while longer, exchanging platitudes, and as nothing much of substance followed, Peter finished his drink and excused himself.

Two weeks later, on a Sunday night, he had trouble catching sleep. He was watching a little pale lizard diagonally traverse the low ceiling of his bedroom, across the wide expanse of featureless plaster, to an uncertain destination.

"Why bother?" Peter said aloud. "There's nothing there."

Just then the lizard stopped and made a sound. "*Tjitjak,*" it said.

"How d'you do? I'm Peter." The tjitjak, for that's what the locals called these things, continued on its way, picked up speed, and then suddenly dropped onto the bed. Peter retrieved it from the sheet's folds. It felt like something made of soft white rubber, without any bone to it, limp and cool to the touch. He put it on the window sill, and the creature instantly disappeared behind the shutter.

The tjitjak had distracted him from his heavy thoughts, and now he sighed, confronted once again with recent events in his life. First there had been the intimate evening with André, who seemed to understand him better than anyone he had yet met. Then that Sunday morning when Mr. Vreeman had probed him over a drink about his relations with his wife, followed a few days later by his announcement that the Head Office had officially promoted him to the rank of Assistant Manager, with authority to sign. Peter had felt a surge of pride and gratitude at this proof of trust, and for once he wasn't thinking of his camera as he thanked Mr. Vreeman for the good news. Only later, in bed, did the reality of his situation come home to him. He was now well and truly embarked on a career in international banking. What was it that André had said? You've got to choose between self and security. He was right, of course. But the self would have to wait a while.

André's message was a radical one: Follow your star, if you have one. Peter knew he had one. He reached under his bed and touched the suitcase. He felt very tired, but his mind was wide awake. He resolved that one day soon he would leave the bank and follow his star. But perhaps he should first give Sally's way a try, combining work and photography, to warm up and find out how good he was.

But wasn't Sally's way the path of compromise and accommodation? Of selling out? Or could it be that its followers were totally in good faith and had nothing to explain, because they simply weren't aware of any dichotomy? Sally had chosen a career, and seemed quite content in it. And taking photographs was her hobby, that's all. What on earth was wrong with that? Why couldn't he be the same?

He didn't know. All he knew, with all the conviction that was in him, was that he wasn't like that and could never be. "Damn!" he shouted as he threw himself once again onto his other side. "Damn! Damn! Damn!" He pounded his pillow mindlessly. The reverberations made the tjitjak drop again from the ceiling, right into the pillow. "Stupid you! Can't you see it's leading nowhere? Stupid! Stupid!" But he lifted the soft, cringing thing gingerly from the linen and returned it to the ceiling. "There, since you insist!" It instantly resumed its journey in the direction it had been heading.

He wasn't sure why he was so restless. He wasn't faced with some crucial decision that couldn't wait another day. Then he realized that his agitation wasn't mental, it was physical. It had to do with what had happened to his body the night before.

Volker had invited Peter and all the other single Dutchmen from the bank to a housewarming party at his new apartment, and afterwards the men decided to go dancing at the New World Dance Hall before heading home. They got a nice table together at the hall, with girls known to them from earlier visits.

Peter's girl was a taxi dancer he had met once before. He liked her. She was a tall Chinese-Malayan, quite slim, with a shy manner which he found particularly appealing. When they danced, she let her body slump against his, hip bones touching, yielding completely to his lead, her face partly obscured by her chin-length hair. She didn't say much, but she smiled at everything he said, her beautiful white teeth gleaming through her hair. Her name was Amanda, and she said she worked as a clerk in a shipping company by day, her night job as a taxi dancer serving to help support her grandparents.

The girls were unusually friendly, and when the club closed at midnight, four of them agreed, amid a lot of giggling and frowning, to come home with the rather drunk but still well-behaved Dutchmen. One of the boys floated the idea to go up to their apartment above the office to play strip poker and use the beds on turn. But once the girls understood what they were being set up for, they got angry and threatened to go home. Reitsma told them not to worry, they wouldn't be forced to do anything they didn't like, but they seemed unconvinced.

Peter had been quietly chatting up his own girl, and he was afraid she, too, might change her mind. But he managed to hoist her into a pedicab and make his escape, to the jeers of the other men, who called him a spoilsport. He felt a little drunk and reckless, and was determined to make Amanda "happy" as he repeatedly put it, to her pleased protestations.

Once home, however, he had felt limp and tired, a feeling even a hot shower could not dispel. Amanda showered after him, and when she came into his room, partly wrapped in a bath towel, Peter was surprised how thin and knuckle-kneed she was. She smiled shyly, the rounding peaks of her bob almost meeting at her mouth as she inclined her head downward in a characteristic pose.

"You want me?" she asked, her knobby feet pigeon-toed on the stone floor, and he felt a surge of affection that bordered on pity. He opened the bedclothes with a smiled "of course," and she dropped the towel and slid in beside him, rubbing the full length of her lanky body against his, instead of—as he had unreasonably expected—cuddling up in his arms like the forlorn kitten she seemed to be. Her breasts were tiny and the prickle of her hard pubic hairs distracted him, but her practiced, eager lips found his and in their kissing, he could transcend for a moment the gaping distance between them.

It disturbed him that the fragrance of her oiled hair was soured by hints of smoke and beer, that her hips felt oddly hard and angular for someone so pliant, that there was no language between them to enhance their lovemaking. She sensed his disappointment and whispered in his ear that she wanted him inside her. But his arousal remained localized and mechanical, a far cry from the loving, sweeping fusion of bodies he had hoped for. His fatigue returned, and when at last he mounted her, overcome with sleep, it felt as if he was pushing a loaded cart uphill, always pushing, hoping to reach a destination, to find relief, which finally came, barely sensed.

He rolled over, spent, beyond caring if he had made Amanda "happy," and promptly fell into a deep sleep. When he awoke in the morning, she was gone. On her pillow was a red hibiscus flower she had evidently plucked from the bush outside his front door.

The recollection now, alone in bed, made him feel sad and inadequate. He

103

had finally lost his virginity, but the act had turned out to be a disappointment, a non-event. Wasn't there anything he did that he didn't regret afterwards? Would he ever stop doubting every move he made? Even at this hour the air was oppressive. He got up to switch on the fan, taking care to point it away from his body. Soon, the sweat on his body turned cold and clammy. He covered himself with the bed sheet, and tried to relax. He glanced up at the ceiling, searched its borders for the tjitjak, found it at rest high up on the wall. "Lucky you," said Peter. "You're there!"

When he finally succumbed, his sleep was fitful and unrewarding, and when his alarm clock went off, he was relieved that his office duties were awaiting him.

# Chapter 14

Eduard wrote Peter a short letter to congratulate him on his promotion. It was perhaps the fifth or sixth letter from his parents in two and a half years, each one written in reply to a letter of his own. It was always his father who did the writing, his mother limiting herself to a few clumsy lines to fill any space left on the paper.

Since his arrival in Singapore, Peter's thoughts of his family had become increasingly abstract to the point where he sometimes found it difficult to put faces to the names of his sisters and parents. His family was becoming an unreal and sacred part of his existence. He missed them with the kind of intensity he imagined deeply religious people longed for God, as an unattainable but never-to-be-forsaken ideal.

That's why he had stopped writing Sybille, and why he never wrote any of his former high school classmates or his Weltevreden colleagues. He'd rather not write at all than send letters full of disembodied half-truths about himself.

To his family he did write, albeit only once every few months. From their infrequent answers he gathered that the picture he projected of himself was a heroic one, that of a staunch, hardworking expatriate, making the best of exceedingly difficult if not hostile conditions, trying to save a sinking ship, all this at the expense of personal pleasure and recreation, which had to wait until better times. Not a word about Sally or André or Mrs. Vreeman, or about his still latent photographic ambitions. His letters were all about dutiful activity and survival in the perilous East. Reading them you would be convinced—as indeed his father appeared to be—that their writer was a well-adjusted young man, embarked on exactly the right career.

Sally had gone back to the States for her two months' home-leave, but it wasn't until three months after her return that she finally called Peter to suggest a date for their planned day trip to Johor. "I'm so sorry for the delay, but I was preoccupied with work and visiting friends and whatnot. I hope you still want to join me?"

But Peter had lost interest in the project. His long-felt uneasiness about the incompatibility of their approach to photography wouldn't go away, and he finally decided that by being true to himself, he would also avoid deceiving her. Instead of hurting her feelings with a full confession, he simply told her that due to his heavy work load and lack of "mental space" he was unable to find time for pursuing photography the way he wanted. She responded cheerily not to worry, and that he was welcome to call her anytime he felt like it.

One day, André called him. "Come over for drinks. Something I want to show you."

It had been several months since they last met, and Peter's heart was pounding as he entered the house. David greeted him like an old friend, lightly touching his arm as he preceded him to the lounge. André was stretched out on the floor, lying on his back on one of his Indian rugs, eyes closed. "He's meditating," David whispered as he motioned Peter to a chair. The prostrate figure seemed not to notice him, started breathing heavily, then moaning and writhing, the head twisting back and forth, the arms and legs making jerky movements, like someone in an epileptic fit. Peter couldn't keep his eyes off him, not taking his friend's behavior as an affront but unsure what to make of it. David sneaked back in with a glass of the house drink. "It will soon be over," he whispered.

Peter didn't touch his drink, his eyes were glued to André's, caught them the moment they opened, steadying on Peter in a peaceful gaze. Slowly, André turned on his side, raised himself on an elbow.

"I do this whenever I'm tense or out of sorts..." He paused, recovering his wits. "To restore my inner harmony." He patted his chest, yawned repeatedly like someone who had just woken from a coma. "You see," he continued as he struggled to his feet, "someone tempted me last week with a lucrative offer, the

106

headmastership of a new international school in Kuala Lumpur. I knew it would be the ruin of my writing and my freedom. But greed and the dangerous appeal of status made me give it serious consideration. Then I got a stomach pain and heart palpitations, so I put myself into this routine which I learned from a friend in London. I'd been neglecting it but I do it every evening now, mostly standing up. It helps you see things lucidly, to focus on what really matters. To eliminate the mental poisons. And you know, it works. Slowly, the broken pieces inside me are coming together again."

Peter shifted uncomfortably in his chair. He was allergic to any form of esoteric religion or cult and wondered how a bright and intelligent man could blindly submit to the dark forces unleashed by some obscure mystic. "So you've decided," he tried, wishing to bring the conversation back to the rational, "not to take the job?"

"That's the signal I keep getting in these meditations. It would be unwise to go against it, don't you think?"

Peter was anxious to change the subject. "You said you wanted to, uh, show me something?"

"I think I just did," said André, with a dead-pan face. "Don't you think it was a rare experience?"

"You mean this was…a show?"

"Oh, no, I'm just teasing. I just happened to be in it when you arrived and decided to let it run its course. Thought that it might help your problem, too. You know. That you might want to try it."

"I don't understand why…" Peter objected, but André interrupted.

"Actually, there was something else. This." He walked over to his bookcase and took a small carton box from an upper shelf. Inside was an old camera, a Graflex foldable that opened up to reveal bellows and took four by five inch sheet film. André handed Peter the opened camera. "What do you think?"

Peter didn't let on that he had never seen a camera like this. "Oh, it's splendid. You have to be a real blockhead not to get sharp definition with a negative this size. But can you get the film for it?"

"You'd have to find out."

"You want me to? You're going to use it?"

"Not me. An uncle left it to me when he died, and it's been languishing in dark cupboards ever since. Thought perhaps you might find a use for it."

Peter felt a mixture of gratitude and resistance. He sensed that André wanted to haul him over to his side, inspire him to make the right decisions. He knew his friend was right, that this was exactly what he should be doing, breaking the shackles of security, to make room for genuine things. He yearned for the strength, the resolve to do just that.

But he emptied his glass and rose and said, "Thank you, you're very kind, but I couldn't accept such a great gift if I wasn't sure I could actually put it to work. I must…think about it."

"Oh, take it. It's not such a great gift, just an old thing that nobody will miss. Who knows, it might inspire you, and," he added with a wink and a hand on Peter's arm, "maybe make you think of me sometimes!"

Peter cringed. André's innuendo felt like a heavy stone on his heart. "No," he said firmly now. "I can't accept it. I'm not ready for any of this. I…need time. You must allow me time." It sounded pathetic, but he was suffocating and fled to the street, to the open air that might not be his space but at least wasn't somebody else's.

# Part Three

*Chicago 1967-1975*

# In the Eyes of the Son

# Chapter 15

After thirteen years in the Far East, the job offer in Chicago came unexpectedly.

Chicago! Hard-working, self-important city of extremes. Severe winters, sweltering summers, spring skipped, fall the only bearable season. Glorying in the great architectural legacy of Louis Sullivan, Mies van der Rohe and Frank Lloyd Wright. Impotently landlocked half the year, tenuously tethered to the North Atlantic by the Saint Lawrence Seaway's umbilical cord the other half. Midway between greatness and the everlasting plains. Capital of the Midwest, hovering indecisively between time zones, between the clear-cut alternatives of the old-worldly East Coast and the still beckoning West.

And the wind! Nowhere in metropolitan existence does the wintry wind cut as it does on the Chicago lakefront, a primal scythe intent on felling everything in living sight, and nearly succeeding. Freezing temperatures doubled by its mighty chill, reinforced by the icy wastes of the frozen lake, one-and-a-half times the size of the Netherlands. A turbo-charged glacial vapor making a mockery of mere winter coats, reducing sturdy men to triple-layered defensive bundles festooned with mufflers, furry hats, padded mittens, and earmuffs.

A hard place to live, Peter felt at first.

After Singapore, where he rose to Volker's old position as the third in command, he had spent three years in Hong Kong as manager of the new Kowloon Sub-Branch, Old Rubberneck's only concession to his no-growth policy. That was followed by a stint at the large Hong Kong Main Branch, as

Deputy General Manager, a post he held for four years.

The Chicago offer was made after the Holland International Bank was taken over by the biggest bank in the Netherlands, a purely domestic bank, which had got the idea into its head to go international. Mr. Goodyear, sent into sulking retirement, was still reported to be pontificating to all and sundry about the impending world crisis and the need to consolidate. Most of the other senior directors had been kept on. As "international experts," they were valuable to the new owners.

Because of his track record, Amsterdam had selected Peter to join the team dispatched from the new head office to take charge of the bank's first acquisition in the United States: the medium-sized Dearborn Bank, a dignified but troubled Chicago bank that could be had cheaply and provide the purchaser a flying entry into a highly important region of the huge American market.

Highly important, yes, but as Peter soon was to find out, intensely parochial and with an ingrown system of double standards. Liquor orders from the dry suburbs wrapped in plain brown bags were delivered in unmarked vans by the booze stores on the edge of the city, neatly circumventing the prohibitionist traditions of those pious neighborhoods. Minorities were kept firmly in their place, the solid white front being cracked only, and mealy-mouthed at that, when Federal affirmative action laws forced employers' hands. The churches were powerful, intrusive, exacting tithes, keeping everyone on their Sunday-best behavior, while stifling change and restraining the rising forces of social equality and participation.

No bank from outside the city was allowed to set up branches in this American heartland, and that included foreign banks, whose increasing visiting forays into the Chicago banks' backyard drew reactions of sarcasm and ridicule. "We can do without suitcase bankers here," was a typical comment. "Sears got all the suitcases we need."

So the Dutch bank's move, officially sanctioned by the authorities to save the tottering Dearborn without cost to U.S. taxpayers, was watched with keen interest and subjected to a wad of special conditions reflecting the industry's protective instincts. The Dutch were made to promise to respect "local traditions" and the "illustrious history" of the bank, keep on management and staff, retain the name, and refrain from disrupting the market.

But nothing prevented them from making "additions." So the name was changed to Amsterdam Dearborn Bank, the bank's president, Bud Maynard, suddenly found he had a Dutch chairman above him, and the Management Committee of four Americans was fleshed out with a brace of three dour functionaries from Holland, plus Peter, the only member of management with international experience. Even the new Dutch chairman, Boudewijn De Rooy, lacked overseas exposure apart from a stint as a trainee at one of New York's major banks when he was a student.

The parent bank's new president in Amsterdam, a former economics professor and finance minister, had personally informed Peter of the Chicago assignment when he was called back to the head office from Hong Kong to receive new orders. But it was Old Rubberneck, during a courtesy call Peter felt moved to pay him, who had provided the more memorable advice.

The old man was "out for a walk in the park" when Peter called, and he tracked him down enjoying the sunshine on a bench. "So, it's Chicago this time for you, is it, eh?" he said with his customary facial animation, although he remained seated this time. "Well, let me tell you this, van Doorn. Repeat for us in Chicago what you've done in Singapore and Hong Kong. Show the locals respect without ever leaving any doubt who's in charge. Teach them our ways without showing them your hand. Understand? Eh? Eh?" Sidelined or not, he was still giving sermons. Still talking about them and us.

At first, Peter didn't understand what the old man meant by "not showing them your hand." He'd been discreet, but never deliberately withheld information to enhance his own position.

He had seen people do that, Guillaume Permé in Singapore came to mind. That man never told you anything, and when he did, it was grudgingly. The last thing Peter heard, he had left banking and gone to Africa as a missionary. "To withhold the Gospel from the natives," said Volker. It was the only time Volker had ever said something funny. Maybe he was happy being called back from limbo in Colombo and given Permé's position.

Before flying to Chicago, Peter had spent four months at the Amsterdam head office to prepare himself for his new duties. But despite these preparations, his first five or six months in Chicago had been stressful, with nobody on the Management Committee agreeing with anything he said or did. The three head office people despised this "glamor boy" from the former colonies—all ex-colonies having become a trendy embarrassment.

What pulled him through was Boudewijn de Rooy's crucial backing. Peter soon discovered that what Boudewijn lacked in field experience he made up for in foxy tact. He disconcerted his American associates with his sudden bursts of sly laughter, as if he was enjoying some private joke, but never forgot to consult them before taking a decision. He seemed without vanity and preferred one-on-one contacts to the plenary team meetings, which he was happy to let Bud Maynard, the American president, chair.

For Peter, this arrangement had its drawbacks, as he experienced in June 1968, when he was reprimanded by Maynard for being late for a meeting on the morning of Robert Kennedy's assassination. His excuse that "the outrage" had upset him met with a cold stare and the comment that "we're here to discuss bank policy, not politics."

But Boudewijn's divide-and-rule method made him a force to reckon with, as he never showed anyone the full picture, not even Maynard, whom he kept guessing about Amsterdam's intentions. All the same, he didn't interfere with Maynard's status as the bank's spokesman, and he built a personal relationship with him over golf and private dinners with the wives. *Brilliant*, thought Peter, finally grasping Old Rubberneck's advice, though he doubted if he could ever apply it himself.

Boudewijn kept in frequent touch with Peter. At first, he consulted him only on routine international banking matters—Peter's area of responsibility—but before long he was also using him as a kind of confidential sidekick, particularly in dealing with Amsterdam.

"The Three Musketeers are too busy sorting out the books," he would say, narrowing his eyes. "I prefer you handle this." He didn't need to add "confidentially, of course." That was understood.

Before the year was out, Peter had adjusted comfortably to his new life, grateful for the opportunity to settle down in an environment that was, after all, more congenial to him than either Singapore or Hong Kong. Not long thereafter, he found a wife.

In the Eyes of the Son

# Chapter 16

Life with Clara, a Vassar art history graduate, had added further to Peter's newfound sense of stability and purpose. They had met at the garden party given by Bud Maynard for a broad spectrum of Chicago business and society figures to mark the first anniversary of the bank's change of ownership. Clara attended the event with her parents, and Peter, hovering near the entrance to help welcome the guests, had spotted her instantly and introduced himself.

They had drifted off together, two slim people at a function dominated by sated business types. Peter was struck by her tall, dark-eyed intelligence, the way she held her head in a slight downward tilt. With her mid-length auburn hair and quiet manner, she seemed almost European to him.

After that first meeting, they had started to date, and it soon became clear to them that the interest was mutual and growing. To Peter, Clara combined an understated perspicacity with feminine warmth and beauty. And he believed that she felt attracted to—or at least intrigued by—the half-hidden, non-banking side of his character.

Whatever it was, they fell in love. They met whenever they could, cuddled and kissed in cars and cinemas, in parks and at parties, at his place and hers. They didn't go all the way. Rather surprising for a Vassar girl (he thought), Clara restrained his advances, telling him softly but firmly that "the bed should wait."

But not long after that, Clara had suddenly proposed marriage, a subject she had avoided until then. Elated, Peter had accepted instantly, and they started discussing dates and venues and invitation lists. But Clara continued to refuse sleeping together, which she claimed was a step they were not ready for.

Peter *was* ready, but he wanted to start his life with her on a harmonious footing, without forcing anything. He knew her reluctance had less to do with a lack of desire than with the need for her to convince her parents that Peter was the right man for her. She had said as much.

"The problem is Pa and Ma. They aren't so sure I should marry you. I don't want to upset them, you know. So we'll have to win them over. Convince them that your Dutch bank is safe and respectable—that *you* are respectable, and clever, even though you didn't attend university. That you're here to stay, that you're ambitious and civilized and responsible, and that you'll go to the top. That I wouldn't be marrying *down*. In fact, I agree with them on that score."

Peter had difficulty falling in line with the kind of thinking that placed greater faith in "safe and respectable careers" than in character and personality. Banking was safe and respectable, apparently. Peter had never thought about his own line of work in such terms, perhaps because he had grown up in a family where left-wing, anti-establishment principles prevailed.

But he lived in America now, and he was in love.

"I understand," he said. "I'll do my best to convince them that I'm... worthy of you, even though I've no inherited money of my own. All I can bring to the marriage is my salary, *new* money. You think they will accept that?"

"Oh, Peter...of course you are worthy of me!"

"Well, but the fact is that your family has *old* money, you know, the kind of money that no longer reeks of the deeds committed to create it. Money that wasn't made by anyone alive but already there."

"It was made on a railroad, I think," Clara said.

"You *think*?" Peter laughed. "And I thought only British old money was coy about its origins."

At that, Clara managed to be more precise. "The line creeping up north along the lake to Racine and Green Bay, I seem to remember. Great-great-grandfather was an early investor and his gamble paid off. What we've got isn't enormous," she had to admit, "but enough to get by. Pa doesn't really have to work. But of course he does."

Mr. Addams was a prominent corporate lawyer. He was also chairman of the board of the Art Institute and a board member of the Law Society. He and his wife moved in Chicago's very best circles. He had planned to marry his only daughter off to a scion of one of the city's great families. But after meeting Peter a few times and seeing how serious Clara was about him, he eventually relented on condition there would be no grand wedding and no expectations regarding the family fortune. Peter and Clara would have to make it on their own. Clara's brother Andrew, younger by three years and a polo-playing, stock-manipulating business graduate of Northwestern, was to inherit all.

"Nothing personal, of course," Mr. Addams told Peter almost jovially. "You're a fine fellow and a gentleman, and I expect you'll take good care of our Clara. But you must know we have a family tradition here, and we like to keep it that way. That's mighty important to Agnes and myself. I'm sure you can understand that."

Peter had felt a huge relief. He wanted to marry Clara, not her fortune. The prospect of being beholden to her famous father had intimidated him, and seeing how strenuously Clara had advertised her Dutch fiancé's qualifications to her parents in order to overcome their resistance, he had almost broken off the engagement. Having no "background" himself, he found the spectacle of dynastic positioning hard to understand and not a little reprehensible.

Clara had been furious at her father's harsh conditions, which her mother had tacitly supported, but she quickly recovered when she saw Peter's eagerness. Her newly disinherited status made her more desirable to him. An ex-heiress, he had joked with her, how very erotic! Far from feeling insulted, Peter's pride was restored, and he noticed that in her eyes he had suddenly grown in stature and manliness.

"We'll build our own life," she agreed. "It's wonderful to start from scratch." Peter had the tact not to remind her that they would have a flying start: his by no means inconsequential salary.

While they were dating, Clara had told Peter that she was a firm supporter of women's rights. She had no intention of pursuing these in a strident, feminist way, which she felt wouldn't square with leading an orderly married life and consolidating their—*her*—place in Chicago society. She merely believed that in every given situation the battle of wits and wisdom, the struggle for control, had to be fought entirely on the basis of the quality of minds, without regard to gender.

She had felt embarrassed by the simplicity of her creed, but there it was, her own personal attempt to counter the discrimination she saw all around her. The patronizing attitudes, the crude jokes, the infuriating innuendo about women's need for male protection. Hardest to take, she said, were the suggestions of women's "delicate nature," which rendered them unfit to do a man's job. Any man's job. The prejudice proved to be worst in her parents' circle, where she had least expected it. After all, what else was wealth good for if it didn't make you more liberal and broad-minded, more *modern*?

That prejudice was noticeably present at a dinner given by George and Betty Graham, shortly before their engagement. A proper affair it was, in their luxury apartment on East Goethe Street. The walls were covered with priceless art, from Gainsborough to Braque. George, a stockbroker, came from a long line of Michigan landowners who he said traced their origins back to the Mayflower. Betty's family part-owned the Marshall Field stores.

After dinner, Peter and Clara were studying one of the paintings, a late Cézanne, and up walked George Graham. He turned to Peter.

"You lucky devil," he said. "Is it too early to congratulate you?"

"Well, no, or actually yes…" waffled Peter, blushing.

"That's what I thought! So here's to you both! You'll make a fine pair. And let me say this, Peter, you chose well. A beautiful young lady of fine family background who didn't waste her time studying law or economics or something dreary like that! Bad enough we fellows have to suffer that stuff!"

Clara smiled sweetly at her host. "You're so right, George," she said. "Business, finance, law, all quite inappropriate for us self-respecting young ladies. After all, we have a reputation to uphold!" George flinched ever so briefly at this ambiguous comment, and excused himself. "Male chauvinist pig," Clara whispered to Peter as George joined another guest.

Her father was something of a patronizing bully, too, she said. Hardly better than George Graham, really. She'd show him she didn't need his money —that she could make her own, separate from the railroad money or her family name. By forming a partnership with Peter, opportunities would certainly arise.

She thought they would make a swell team. She knew nothing about business, of course, but somehow Peter's talk about new ventures and corporate mergers excited her more than discussing the influence of the Post-Impressionists on Cubism. Or, for that matter, listening to Peter's recurrent sighs of regret about the photographic career he sacrificed when he became a banker. Peter was brilliant, but his intelligence was of the short-term, managing kind. His mind was orderly, logical. He worked best within a framework. To her, business was visceral, not only the money part of it, but the dynamics, the power she sensed behind the big deals that the Chicago Tribune was always writing about.

And the buildings! She found it thrilling to watch the skyscrapers rise out of the cavernous sites along South LaSalle Street and Michigan Avenue. Who conceived these buildings, she wondered? What kind of men hired the architects, the contractors, the bankers?

If she, with Peter's help, could one day control one such building, or own a couple of those Mies van der Rohe high-rise apartment blocks along Lake Shore Drive…well, that was further down the road. But she could start with buying up and converting a derelict townhouse or two in resurgent Old Town, and rent the apartments to up-and-coming Board of Trade jobbers and young graphic designers. It shouldn't be too hard. She would show her parents that she was no pushover. That she could build her own fortune, with her husband's professional help. She would show them that they were wrong in not placing their bets on Peter.

Their wedding, fifteen months after his arrival in Chicago, was a simple affair in a local church, followed by a small reception at her parents' lakefront home in Highland Park. Nobody from Holland attended. Peter had explained to his parents that he thought they would feel "lost" in Chicago, and that he would bring Clara home to meet the family, "as soon as I can get away."

As it turned out, Mr. Addams surprised his daughter on her wedding day with a handsome six-figure check, which Clara, to Peter's delight, placed on a term deposit with the Amsterdam Dearborn Bank, albeit under her sole signature.

They bought a house in Wilmette, a lakeside community half an hour's commute north of Chicago and slowly settled down. A year after their wedding Clara gave birth to a son, whom they named Diedrich, after the fictitious "Dutch historian" created by Washington Irving. Theirs was a typical American suburban life revolving around Peter's work routine, Diedrich's growing needs, and community affairs. Peter enjoyed the distractions of garden barbecues and days on the beach, but the cold season was a different matter.

He found the winter Sundays hardest to get through and he suspected Clara thought the same, though they avoided complaining about it. Dark and rainy days were bad because you couldn't go out, but freezing, sunny days were worse. The bright winter air beckoned and the bones craved exercise, but the wind would be biting and the daylight short-lived, and there wasn't all that much to do for a suburban couple with a four-year-old child. So the promise of radiant Sunday mornings was seldom fulfilled, and the day all too often ended in a mood of irritation over opportunities missed, time wasted, and life generally being stagnant, lacking direction and meaning.

To Peter, Mondays mornings were a blessing, weekend headaches miraculously swept away by anticipation of mail, strategy meetings, the energy of the competitive environment. What he called the attractive side of corporate life. He had never identified with the nasty part: the endless jockeying for position, the bad-mouthing, the blatant flattery, the cooking of statistics to support a dubious scheme, the withholding of negative information to get a plan approved. Yet from his safely elevated position Peter found even that spectacle curiously intriguing, confirming as it did his skeptical view of the typical banking mentality.

So for one reason or another the office, maligned all Sunday and most weekday evenings, at Monday's breakfast suddenly loomed all-important, an excuse for gobbling down his buns and coffee, for impatience with his son's incessant questions. Clara had learned to accept these mood swings as part of the realities of married life.

Though she had no job to go to and could drop off Diedrich as late as eleven, she always got up to make breakfast. Peter felt grateful for this. Her sharing of his moment of professional preparation, offering moral support for the work ahead which, despite its financial rewards and fleeting satisfactions, he still saw as "fundamentally averse" to his character and temperament as when he first entered banking twenty years ago. He knew this to be a sensitive issue with Clara, something she was getting tired of hearing, because in her view "the evidence" was clearly in conflict with this claim.

In the early months of their marriage, Peter's tales of his youthful successes in photography had been entertaining and endearing to her. She sympathized with the frustration he had felt at being denied an artistic career by an unreasonable and overprotective father. She accepted and understood his reluctance to be "just an ordinary banker," finding this side of him rather attractive. It distinguished him from the run-of-the-mill Chicago businessman who had few interests outside their work besides football and golf.

But his never-ending diatribes about the "despicable character of bankers" and the longing he betrayed from time to time for "a more meaningful" kind of life were getting to her. He sometimes looked at her in an irritable, almost contemptuous way. Once, when she asked why he couldn't practice photography on the side, as a hobby, he had snapped at her. "How can you expect me to do creative work when I'm stuck in this bourgeois rut?"

Stung by the implied condemnation of her values she had replied angrily, "It seems you resent not only being a banker, but having me for a wife."

He had apologized and assured her that he would never want to lose her.

Clara said she might have understood his attitude better if his banking career had stagnated. But the fact was that his career so far had been impressive, certainly for someone with no more than a high school diploma. She credited his intelligence and practical nature, as well as his broad interests, which he said he had fed assiduously over the years with self-study and unstructured readings in everything he could lay his hands on, from monetarist economics and exchange rate mechanisms to Russell's philosophy and Confucian social doctrine. He had borrowed books from André in Singapore before getting into the book-buying habit himself, and for most of his years in Asia he had subscribed to the London *Economist* and *The New Yorker* magazine. What's more, he had distinguished himself in every banking assignment, and as a result been given promotion after promotion. And hadn't he told her that he enjoyed his life in Hong Kong so much that he had paid scant attention to the Vietnam conflict that was building up to a major war a mere six hundred miles to the south?

That was one aspect of Peter's past she had difficulty comprehending. How could he have been so unconcerned? He said that his Hong Kong circle had referred to the conflict as an "American war" and "distant thunder" and shrugged his shoulders when she had asked him whether America had done the right thing in getting so deeply involved.

"It didn't affect our life," he had said. "And it didn't seem that close. Most of the news about it reached us *via* the States."

"I'm talking about the *morality* of the war," she had persisted. "I mean, you were living right at the edge of the conflict area."

"I don't think the morality of it was much of an issue in the early phases, even here in the States. It became a hot topic, didn't it, once the body bags were coming home by the hundreds and thousands? But since you ask," he continued, "I always thought America has been woefully underestimating the national distinctions between Asian countries. I still think so. The domino theory is a simplification of what was and is essentially a series of separate social revolutions in countries with distinctly different national identities."

She had accepted his viewpoint, which strengthened her own opposition to American involvement in the war. And it had confirmed her positive opinion about Peter's intelligence, and, paradoxically, her irritation over his insistence on wasting it with his moaning about "what might have been." Damn it, the bank had picked him for the Chicago job because of his ability. Why couldn't he be satisfied with that and build his life around this great opportunity?

# Chapter 17

"Sorry I'm late," said Peter as he took the chair opposite Clara's in The Bakery, one of his favourite Chicago restaurants. "Boudewijn called an after-hours meeting."

Clara looked at him fondly, stroking her glass. "Nothing serious, I hope?"

He didn't answer. "How's that wine?" he asked. He had to unwind first. "How's Diedrich's cold?"

The waiter recited the entire menu from memory. This was the only restaurant they knew where there was no printed or written menu, not even a blackboard. You had to prick up your ears and make mental notes as the actor-waiter went through his impressive mnemonic trick. And Peter liked the long heavy curtains around the little entrance hall, to keep out the cutting wind when the door opened.

"No big problems," said Peter at last, sipping his Meursault, the same as Clara's. "Just the usual head office hogwash. You know: You're falling short of the agreed goals and objectives. You are to reduce costs by ten percent, never mind how. They don't understand we're in a recession here, and in a foreign market!"

Clara smiled and took his hand. "Shouldn't you explain to them that this isn't a foreign market at all, but a domestic one? That this is an American bank developing an American business base?"

"They don't want to know. They throw us on a heap with Colombo and Hong Kong and Volendam. Sometimes I hate this job!"

The first course had arrived. Deep-fried whitebait for Clara, shad roe for

Peter. They tasted each other's dish. The delicious food failed to derail Peter's thought train.

"I think I'll take out citizenship, so I'll be free to quit when I feel like it."

"Quit? To do what?" Clara tried to sound casual.

"Oh, I don't know. Something different. Totally different."

"Like what?" said Clara, holding up two whitebaits on her fork, their silvery skins shining through the crisp coating.

Peter methodically, unnecessarily, separated the orange roe from its thin membrane. He didn't answer.

"You're not still nursing that old dream of yours, are you?" Her eyes were on him, his on his plate. "I mean, as a hobby, fine. But as a profession?"

Peter stiffened visibly. "Well, you can't deny that it's a more honorable line of work than flogging loans," he said, still obstinately looking at the food.

"Flogging loans?" she said icily. "What in the world do you mean?"

"That's all we do, basically. You know that! Trying to get companies to borrow our money. They can get all they need from their own bankers, but we offer it cheaper, easier. We undercut. We flog. To gain market share. It's disgusting, dishonorable."

Clara stopped eating. She had learned to cope with her husband's normal job stress, his need to unburden himself when he came home. But this went beyond that. This was serious.

"I didn't know you hated your job that much," she said tentatively. "Poor you. You want to quit the rat race, is that it?" Slowly, she raised another little fish to her lips.

"It's not the rat race. I'm not ambitious enough for that," he said. He started cutting up the remainder of the shad roe mindlessly. "It's that I simply can't stand the whole atmosphere of this bank. Of banking. I mean, what values does banking have? None that I can think of. We lend to the makers of Agent Orange. We finance Latin American dictators and our own nuclear power industry. We make huge loans to polluters, speculators, fast-food chains. Banking is a conspiracy of mediocrity where original thought is suspect, and social conscience is mistaken for a disease. It's a stagnant pool where the same old ideas are slowly stirred around, and merit is measured by how you hold the ladle. It's the graveyard of the human spirit, the final solution for talent and spontaneity. It's a non-career." Throughout this monologue he hadn't looked at her, and he still wasn't doing so now. Quickly, he stuffed his mouth and took a gulp of wine.

"I know how you feel, darling," Clara tried tentatively. "Banking and business are hardly meant to edify the soul." She waited for him to absorb this expression of sympathy before continuing. "But, you know, I'm sure you wouldn't talk this way if you were the boss. If you were the one that called the shots." Peter didn't react. "Right?"

Peter held his breath as the waiter took the plates away.

"That's not the point, Clara. Besides, that scenario is years away. I'm not even close."

"Oh, I wouldn't say that. Boudewijn is sixty-two. Bud is already retired except in name. The Three Musketeers have dwindled to one. Boudewijn thinks the world of you. You're his heir, anointed or not."

"It doesn't work that way. They'll send a new man from Amsterdam. And anyway, even if I *am* the boss, I'll still be little more than a stooge for the big boys back home. And I still won't change my thinking about banking."

"Just give it time. Three years. In three years, you'll be on Mount Olympus. Head of Dearborn counts for something here, you know. Never mind Amsterdam. What do they know anyway? You'll be setting the agenda."

At last, Peter looked at his wife, and what he saw gave him a jolt of pride and affection. The confidence she had in him! She was radiant with loving confidence, with an unshakable faith that he could do anything he set his mind to. He marveled at her gift to lift him out of the deepest gloom, and felt his doubts of only moments before shrivel into irrelevance. How could his feeble hankering after some childhood mirage stand up to the reality and potential of the life she and he now inhabited?

They had a handsome house in the Northern Suburbs, two cars, an enviable circle of friends, and most important of all, a little cupid of a son, with his mother's dark eyes and his father's blond curls. No, Peter was convinced that nothing on earth could be worth endangering this happiness, and he was resolved to bury his silly old dream once and for all. He smiled and sighed.

Clara smiled back.

"By the way," said Clara, "have you talked to Ralph Storey yet about that derelict property on North Wells?"

They had both ordered the same main course. Stuffed quail. Peter wondered why they always ordered this when it was on the menu. All the fuss with the little bones, and hardly anything to sink your teeth into. He guessed it was the stuffing. Or maybe because it was trendy.

"Have you?" Clara insisted.

"Sorry, yeah, I did, actually. He knows the building. Says it can be saved. It's structurally sound. Just needs complete refurbishment. He thinks you could carve twenty apartments out of it. But, darling, I haven't got the time."

"I have. Just tell me which people I should work with. Some clever builder-developer, isn't that what you call them? But I want somebody who is not going to walk away with the deal."

For the rest of the meal they talked about nothing else. Clara was pumping Peter for all he was worth. Where to get the financing. How to pick an architect. How to keep the builder honest. Which lawyer to use. How to market the units. Peter faked half his answers. Clara noticed and chose to ignore it.

"But, darling," said Peter cautiously. Why did he always call her darling when he was about to put her in her place? "Are you sure you want to get involved in this sort of thing? Don't underestimate the dog-eat-dog realities of the property game."

"I'll manage," she replied, ignoring the innuendo. "Oh, it's going to be fun! I think I'll have a dessert. How about you?" She squeezed his arm and kissed him quickly on the cheek. "Dinner's on me today."

Four months later, purchase completed, work on the North Wells property began. From the start, it was Clara's project. She formed a company, named it Clearwater Projects, Inc. and took sixty percent of its two hundred and fifty thousand share capital, financed by part of the money her father had given her for her wedding. Peter put in for the remaining forty percent but had to give her an option to buy him out at book value whenever it suited her. The art history graduate from Vassar was learning fast.

She found an experienced builder-developer, Jack Drummond, prepared to execute the project for Clearwater on a fifty/fifty profit sharing basis, with Clara retaining a veto over matters of design and marketing. The choice of architect fell on a well-known Chicago figure, Magnus Petersen, a friend of her father's, who had several famous Chicago buildings to his name. This minor conversion he would delegate to an assistant, but the name of the Magnus Petersen bureau on the brochure was a clever move.

The construction of the twenty-two apartments and common areas behind the preserved late nineteenth-century facade took fifteen months. A severe snow storm and a couple of power cuts delayed the work by a few weeks, but they still came in well before the financing deadline.

The pre-sale was a success. A third of the condominium apartments were sold on spec, at only slightly discounted prices, and another seven units attracted buyers once the model apartment had opened for inspection. The rest were sold within two months of completion, and the whole project left a pre-tax profit of almost half a million dollars. The bankers, Harris Trust, were well pleased, and indicated their interest in financing Clearwater's further projects.

During the whole process, Clara tried to stay in the background, going about her daily chores as mother and wife in the usual way. But she managed to keep an eye on things, sometimes turning up unexpectedly at the site. Her name appeared nowhere in the sales literature, but the involvement of Mr. Addams' attractive daughter in the development was well-known, and used to good advantage by the sales staff.

The property was ready for occupancy on the fifteenth of May. Clara resisted the temptation to give a reception and make it a public occasion. Instead, she invited Peter and Jack Drummond and Magnus Petersen and their wives to dinner at the Top of the Rock restaurant with a view of the Chicago shoreline, where she didn't skimp on the wines, and had a souvenir for each of her guests, Peter included: an exquisite, small, silver platter engraved with an emblem featuring a stream pattern and the enigmatic motto, "Clearwater runs deep."

Peter was happy for her success but couldn't help feeling uneasy about Clara's determined efforts to carve out her own place in society. Was she preparing for independence? And what was this nonsense about clear water running deep? What was his wife trying to prove?

# Part Four

*Amsterdam 1977*

# In the Eyes of the Son

# Chapter 18

The years passed. Their life had settled into a predictable routine, Peter shouldering his increasing responsibilities at the bank with apparent confidence, and Clara steadily deepening her involvement in Chicago property development. Yet paradoxically, as Peter's success grew, so did his long-suppressed doubts about the career he had embraced. He tried, and usually succeeded, to keep his thoughts to himself, thus maintaining a semblance of harmony on the home front.

Shielding Diedrich from any domestic discord was perhaps Peter's chief concern. The boy, their pride and joy, had been growing up without serious problems, and impressed them with his bright character and inquisitive mind.

In the spring of 1977, they took a two-week vacation in Holland, to finally get Clara to meet his family, and show off the now eight-year-old Diedrich.

Peter had been back on business many times since their marriage but never brought Clara as he had promised, and she hadn't pressured him to take her. He thought she would be uncomfortable—with his folks, their house, the city, the country. It was all a far cry from the grand, windswept spaces of the Midwest, from the elegance of their Chicago life. He didn't really feel much at home in Holland anymore himself.

This time, too, it was business that required his presence in Holland, a three-day conference of the senior managers of the bank's foreign branches and subsidiaries. Boudewijn couldn't make it due to his wife's serious illness, and Peter was asked to go in his place. The holiday was to be tacked on to, or rather precede, the business meetings.

They arrived at Schiphol on a radiant mid-week April morning. Peter rented a car. He wanted to show Clara the chromatic glories of the bulb fields before confronting her with the sober interior of his parental home. And Diedrich might enjoy the trip, too, if he could stay awake long enough.

They wound their way through the narrow country roads south of Haarlem until they hit the narrow strip of mixed sand-and-peat in which the bulbs thrive. The season was at its best; the German license plates of tourists were much in evidence.

Clara was captivated by the rectangles of color slapped down like giant tiles on a vast kitchen floor—red and white and yellow and orange and near-black tulips, blue and pink and white hyacinths, yellow and white daffodils. Complex, hybrid shades, too. But always one color to a field, which always had even measurements. Diedrich didn't last beyond the third slab of red (he did like red best), but Clara was ecstatic.

"What I like is the clarity of it all, the refusal to compromise. I didn't know that was a Dutch trait..."

*Well, is it?* Peter wondered. He had always been ambivalent about the bulb fields, finding their arrangement and bright coloration too simplistic. "I think it just makes commercial sense to grow them like that."

"Well, then at least it shows that the Dutch have a clear head for business."

Peter took a detour to show Clara the mansion where he had begun his banking life, Weltevreden. It was still there, with a different name and different owners. He decided to spare his wife the details of that memorable year, and she didn't ask.

The sightseeing over, they headed for Amsterdam.

Peter's father was retired now, but they were still living in the old house in Amsterdam. Peter and Clara were to sleep in Peter's former room, a prospect Clara "simply loved," but which presented certain emotions for Peter that he could not understand and decided not to face just yet. Diedrich's bed was in Fran's old room.

The visit began well. Peter found an old, large jigsaw puzzle on an upper shelf in his room, which his mother had kept there all those years, "because it was Peter's favorite." The puzzle showed the center of an imaginary modern city where everyone spoke Esperanto, Zamenhof's new language that he believed "would unify the world." He showed it to Diedrich, who couldn't wait to get to work on it.

Clara was fascinated with everything and everybody, and exuded the kind of inquisitive charm and deliberate consideration that Peter had come to associate with well-bred, young, American women. From the start, she professed a keen interest in "all things van Doorn"—and Dutch. Sometimes her enthusiasm seemed to overwhelm Peter's parents, making them turn inward and defensive, as if to hide from a sun too bright. But Clara, sensing this, would adjust her approach, pulling back just enough to allow the others some breathing space, before resuming her questioning about Dutch traditions or history or art, or the van Doorns' memory of the German occupation.

On this latter subject, Clara found Mr. Van Doorn alternately effusive and reticent. When she asked him whether his flight to England in the middle of the war had caused him pangs of conscience, his answer came easily. "Of course, it was a hard decision to leave my family behind. But I would only have become a burden to them. I was being hunted, you know, so if I had stayed on, I'd have to go into hiding and be dependent on them for feeding me and keeping my morale up. That would have been a heavy task for them, and besides, I'm not the type for that."

Clara nodded. "And the other aspect of it," she persisted, "the escape from facing up to the Germans. Didn't that bother you? Didn't you feel sometimes that you should perhaps have stayed on, regardless of the risks?"

Eduard didn't answer. He looked at his daughter-in-law as if she had just stolen his coat, then at his son who was sitting next to her, and back to Clara, who added quickly, "Please don't think that I'm being judgmental. I'm just wondering what war does to a person's value system." This only made matters worse. Eduard seemed to shrink into spiky, hedgehog-like self-protectiveness. Peter wondered if he should intervene.

Then, in a changed voice, his father said, "What do you Americans know about our values? Our sufferings, our inner depths? You've never had to face a foreign invasion."

"I didn't mean to…" Clara said, clearly shocked. "I'm very sorry. I was trying to learn, to understand."

"That's all right," said Eduard unsmiling. "But you can save yourself the trouble. There's nothing to understand. If you aren't part of it, you will never understand. So I prefer not to discuss the matter." He got up, managed a wry smile, and offered them another drink.

Two days later, on the Sunday after their arrival, Peter finally got Clara to meet Pauline, Fran and Fran's family. They all gathered for a welcome dinner prepared by Mrs. van Doorn, now called "Mom" by Clara, too. She couldn't bring herself to call Mr. van Doorn "Dad" quite yet.

Pauline, just back from a business trip to France, and Fran and her husband Herman and their two small children, and Diedrich of course, filled the house with noise and laughter and much running around, which Mrs. van Doorn complained she was no longer used to. But she smiled as she said this, and busily returned to the kitchen to finish the meal she had been working on all day. Her knowledge of English was rudimentary, and she seemed quite happy to have other things to do while the rest of the family talked to "the children from America."

Mr. van Doorn's English was quite fluent, an odd mixture of Dutch accents and British self-deprecation. Peter thought he looked old for his sixty-eight years and wondered if he had been unable to accept that Holland's rising prosperity had been achieved without revolution, without the aid of state socialism. It must have made his career as a leftist political writer seem wasted in retrospect.

But deep inside Peter lurked another explanation for his father's decline: that it was he, Peter, who was to blame. Perhaps the old man had never recovered from his disappointment at finding, in the days of Peter's early flings with photography, that his son was fundamentally different from him. He knew his father considered him over-sensitive, lacking the guts to carve out his own place in the world, ready to fight, to suffer for a cause, a principle. Or even to know what he wanted and pursue it unequivocally. Instead, he had compromised. Like Faust, he had traded his soul for a life of comfort and wealth. He had committed the ultimate sin: to be untrue to himself.

Peter cringed to think that this might be his father's opinion of him, but he managed to suppress the thought, which in any case his father had never expressed.

But if Eduard van Doorn was an unhappy man, he did his best not to show it. Apart from the brief run-in with Clara, he had been an exemplary host right from the moment of their arrival, opening good bottles of wine, showing Clara his books on European history and the family photo albums, and insisting on taking Clara and Diedrich on a canal trip while Peter went for a walk with his mother.

There were moments when Peter noticed something worrisome in his father's behavior, like when he caught him staring out of the window, or slumping in a chair, brooding. Once or twice he thought his father threw him a dark, cold look, but Eduard averted his eyes so quickly that Peter couldn't be sure. He felt agitated under the strain, sensing premonitions of disaster.

There were no such complications with Pauline or Fran. At thirty-three, Pauline had grown into a strikingly beautiful woman, of medium height, with large blue eyes, a chiseled, porcelain face, and golden hair, smartly cut in the pageboy style. She wouldn't have been out of place at a flapper ball in the Roaring Twenties, Clara later told Peter in bed.

Pauline's pronounced tastes and opinions on many subjects made a lot of sense, and were relieved by the same light touch that she had as a child. She hadn't become an artist as everyone expected, though she had studied drawing and sculpture for three years at the Lyon Art Academy. While primly boarding there with a French schoolmaster's family, she had managed to also get a good taste of another kind of life: that of the cafés and cheap nightclubs where most of her fellow students hung out.

When she realized that her talent was too small to make a go of a professional creative career, she had turned her growing love of wine into a professional skill, honed through countless trips to the nearby Bourgogne, and serious courses in wine tasting right there in Lyon. Back in Holland it hadn't taken her long to find work as a taster and promoter of French wines.

At the Sunday family party, Mrs. van Doorn gently nagged Pauline to find a decent man to settle down with "before it's too late."

"Pff," was Pauline's inconsiderate answer. "Who wants the shackles of marriage? I don't ever want to get trapped into such an impossible arrangement, which equates free expression with disloyalty and repression with virtue." This rather pompous statement was made in Dutch, but Peter translated it for the benefit of his wife, who laughed, with a sidelong glance at Mrs. van Doorn, who pretended not to have heard her daughter's disparaging remark.

"You don't need to marry," offered Clara, trying to be helpful. "Why not just live together?"

"Cohabitation? But that's worse. It's got all of the drawbacks and none of the few advantages of marriage, such as security and a stable breeding ground for children, if you want children, which I don't. No, I just have lovers, thank you, *when* I have them."

"I don't know what it is with men," she confided to Clara later, "but after a while they all become lazy and possessive. They all want to retire to some kind of predictable routine. Are men that insecure?"

Clara smiled. She wasn't sure if she wanted to reveal the inner workings of her relationship with Peter. "My experience is limited," she said. "But I don't think all men are alike. Some seem to think constantly about new challenges. The paradoxical quest for security may be their way to control that inner urge for adventure and freedom. That's the way men are brought up, Pauline. They are brought up to suppress their hunting instincts and settle down to domesticity, not to deal with independent women like us!"

She had made common cause with her sister-in-law and wondered why. She couldn't accept Pauline's philosophy of life and hoped her view of men would mature, that time would make her see reason. "Otherwise she'll end up a very unhappy woman," she said later to Peter.

Peter didn't know what to say to that. He felt some affinity to Pauline's way of thinking. Yet he knew Clara was right in questioning Pauline's values, unless of course his sister would prove strong enough to arrange her life without the need for men. Which he doubted.

"She'll end up with some writer or artist twice her age," was what he finally came up with, half-facetiously. "Someone well-traveled and witty, who can give her the long rope she needs."

Clara nodded. "And she'll forego children. Which she'll live to regret, too."

As for the continuity of the race, Fran and her husband Herman, a devout, church-going welfare worker, were seeing to that. They already had produced two children, a third was on its way. They had barely taken part in the conversation. Fran was helping her mother, self-consciously navigating her distended belly around the house like a trophy of fecundity. Herman kept an eye on the children who were fascinated with Diedrich's strange language and funny-looking American clothes.

Herman was a very decent and intelligent chap, despite his droopy mustard-colored moustache, perennial tweed jacket with elbow patches and corduroy trousers. He had sound opinions about the Dutch welfare system, which he said had recently been tightened to prevent abuse. "Like not paying child benefits when the family isn't even living in Holland. Or making sure that somebody isn't sponging off the government if he's actually holding down a black-market job, cash under the table, you know."

Clara wanted to know how the social benefits were paid.

"Ah," said Herman, a toothy smile curling his pale lips, slightly flattening the arch of his sagging mustache. "That's easy. Once the paperwork is approved, we credit their bank or postal account every month for as long as they are entitled to receiving the payments."

Clara showed surprise at the leniency of Dutch arrangements. "In the States, we're not so generous. People on unemployment have to queue up every week for their welfare check. You can see the long lines at City Hall. Young and old alike. That's the reality of life, I guess." She sighed.

"That's barbarous!" interjected Eduard. "Our system is much more civilized, don't you think?"

Clara was stung. "Well, our way is a little humiliating, perhaps, but barbarous? After all, we're talking about people who are supported by tax payers. There's no harm in making them aware of that!" Mr. van Doorn abruptly got up from his chair and angrily stalked out of the room. Clara mutely threw up her hands with a questioning look at Peter.

"It's all right," he said. "He'll get over it. You touched his old socialist nerve." He tried to make it sound convincing, while his heart was skipping beats.

Fran's call to dinner mercifully changed the mood. Eduard was the last to sit down. Clara was sitting to his right, and before he raised his glass in a toast, he leaned over and whispered a few words of apology to her. Clara's grateful smile seemed to mollify him completely. He said, "You may call me Dad if you wish," and managed a most gracious and eloquent little welcome speech.

# Chapter 19

Soon after dinner Fran and Herman left, their two exhausted kids slung over the father's shoulders like bags of grain. Diedrich had grown silent, too, and he didn't object when Clara took him to his room and put him to bed, next to the half-finished jigsaw on the floor.

Pauline started yawning, and announced that she too was calling it a day. But she lingered, making dibs and dabs at conversation, and helping Mother, along with Peter and Clara, with the dishes. When she finally did go, she turned around in the doorway.

"Why don't you three come over to my place in the next day or two for a spot of dinner, French slapdash style," she said, "so we can get down to some serious gossip?"

With his daughters gone and his wife announcing that she was going to soak herself in an herbal bath, Eduard brought out the cognac and cigars, but Clara excused herself, pleading a slight headache, and the two men were left by themselves.

"Quite a lady, that Clara of yours," Eduard began, as he lit his cigar with a wooden match.

"Yes... You think so?"

Eduard took his time with the cigar before answering. "Oh, yes, quite your type. Well-mannered, beautiful, charming. And rich. What more could you want? I toast your discerning eye!" He lifted his glass and took a sip. Then, looking away, he added, "Simplified your life, hasn't it?"

"What do you mean, Dad?"

"You know damn well what I mean. Some people have ideals. Others want to live well. You made sure you could live well. Oh," he quickly added with the emphasis of a raised open hand and a lowered head, "nothing wrong with that, of course. It's the way water flows. I'm happy for you!"

Peter felt the color drain from his face, but he wasn't ready to join battle.

"Well, thank you. But you're wrong, Dad, Clara is not rich. She was disinherited, as you well know." Even saying this much was an effort. For years, he had wanted to thrash out the old unspoken conflict with his father, but now that the opportunity was there, he didn't have the stomach for it, the energy.

"What?" said his father with unmasked sarcasm. "You're not even a confirmed gold digger? Now you're really disappointing me! If you have to opt for the good life, you might as well go all out. Marry a rich bitch instead of someone just pretending to be one."

Peter slammed down his glass.

"You take that back! Clara pretends nothing. We don't need her family's money, thank you very much. We're doing just fine as we are." His father looked out of the window, into the night sky whitened by the lamp of a full moon. When he spoke again it was in a small voice.

"You're right. I shouldn't have said that. Clara is a lady, and real ladies don't pose. As for you," he said, returning his gaze to Peter, "You're being irritatingly naïve about the whole thing. Her father is a famous and wealthy man. You told me so yourself. His daughter will get a slice of the pie, somehow. He'll change his will or settle a royal sum on her during his lifetime, mark my word. Fathers can't help being sweet to their daughters."

Peter wasn't appeased. "The point is, Dad, I didn't marry her for money. Put that out of your head."

His father smiled skeptically from above his snifter. "Either way, you've settled for security. By supporting capitalism through both career and marriage, you have insured yourself against financial calamity *and* against the necessity to question the meaning of human existence. You have achieved peace of mind without even a hint of personal struggle. It's quite an achievement. Bravo!" Again, he lifted his glass in mock salute and took a gulp of his brandy.

Peter swallowed hard, trying to contain his fury. "What would you know about my private doubts? How can you say with such cynical certainty that I have peace of mind? You don't know me any better now than when you declared that I was unfit to be a photographer! You were wrong then, and you are wrong now."

"No, no, no. *You* are the one that's mistaken. A man's character is judged by his actions. You have the mind of a banker because you *are* a banker. You knew how to click a shutter all right, but you didn't have the *passion* to be a *good* photographer."

"You wouldn't let me. You blocked my way."

"So what if I did? True passion always will out. A reluctant father should have been the least of your obstacles. I wish to God that you had proved me wrong, that you'd stood up to me and told me straight to my face: I don't care what you say, Dad, I'm going ahead, because that's what I want to be! It didn't even matter *what* it was you wanted to be, as long as you wanted it with everything you had in you. But you didn't. Goddamnit!" He rose, faced Peter. "You didn't fight. You meekly accepted what I offered you. I thought you were a man but you…you…" He choked on his words, started coughing, persisted. "You didn't have the *guts* to be anything more than a 'good employee'. A bearer of bricks for the castle of capitalism." He coughed some more, managed a crooked smile. "I like that…don't you? A bearer of…" Peter, wounded, aghast, flew at him, trembling with rage and sorrow.

"Stop that! Stop it!"

"A bearer of bricks…" taunted his father.

"I always knew it! That's what you thought of me!"

"…for the castle…"

"Still do! You wanted me to have your cruelty, your killer mentality!"

"…of capitalism!"

"You left no room for who I was!"

"How's that for a ready-made epitaph? Eh?" His father had another coughing fit, worse than the first. He stood bent over his armchair, convulsed, retching. Peter watched and waited. The pause calmed him, but his calm was icy, unfeeling. The coughing subsided. His father made as if to say something

143

conciliatory. But Peter wouldn't let him.

"How can you stand there mocking me, while you yourself for thirty years and more could think of nothing more original to do than parroting the utopian balderdash of Marx and Engels and their bankrupt socialist running-dogs, stuff that is a thousand times worse than the most exploitative form of capitalism? When all you could do with your life was scribbling one impotent editorial after another declaiming the virtues of collectivism while—totally oblivious to your pious manifestos—the rest of the country went about the business of creating jobs, infrastructure, a decent society, largely through the efforts of ordinary people doing their duty in a free and open society? Do you really think you have the right to criticize *me*?"

As Peter spoke, his father's face had slowly fallen, and he was now slumped in his chair, his glass limply held between loosely pleated fingers, his chin touching his sternum. Peter, surprised by his own outburst, plumped down in his chair, and stuck his nose in his snifter. The silence between the men was punctuated by the distant screech of a braking bicycle, someone shouting "Stop it, stop it!" in the street, the clatter of a metal trash can on the pavement. Eduard raised his eyes, his earlier smile back around his lips.

"The difference is that *I* know how it feels to believe passionately in an ideal and to throw oneself body and soul into the fight to attain it. The outcome, you see, is less important than the struggle. The thrill, the fulfilment, is in the striving. Once you've experienced that, you know your life has been worth living."

"I know," said Peter. He sighed. "You think I don't, but I know. I understand. Don't you think I envy you for that? I always have. You were my hero, you know. Until…"

"Until the day an innocent man got killed by a stray timber."

"Isn't that always the way innocence is killed?" Peter said. "By accident?"

"Or by the ugly face of reality. If you can keep danger and the real world at bay, there's no reason you can't go on dreaming forever."

"Dreaming forever?"

"Isn't that what you wanted? To go on dreaming?" Eduard looked intently at his son.

"About what?"

The irritation was back in his father's face. "You mean you still don't know?"

"What, Dad?"

"For God's sake! That your dream was an illusion! That you wouldn't have made the grade as a photographer! I mean a top-notch one, because anything less is not worth the trouble. A lens man possessed: unflinching, unsentimental, and utterly devoted to his craft. Another Robert Capa. That's what we're talking about, or not?"

Peter had no answer. His clarity of mind was gone. He felt surrounded by a fog. Looking at his father, he felt uneasy, but he could feel no hatred. Rather puzzlement at being so misunderstood, and so loved at the same time. He was certain now that his father would never understand him. But he felt compelled to explain himself anyway.

"I...I've never given up my ideal." He'd said it in a flat, unemotional voice. "Despite my banking career, despite Clara and Diedrich, despite the good life and all the trappings of status and success. Get this, Dad," his voice lowered now, emphatic. "There is nothing that I want more in life than to express my deepest feelings through photography." He rose abruptly. "What I want is to add something to life that wasn't there before. A way of looking, a visual whisper that might give hope to someone, or insight, or a sense of beauty. An enrichment... That's my goal. And I intend to reach it. Someday I will prove it to you."

His father, the cynicism drained from him, regarded his son feelingly. Peter's eyes met his. It was the first time for as long as he could remember that his father had looked at him that way. He felt the tears well up.

"If only you could have loved *banking* that much," said his father. "I so much wish for you to be *happy,* you know. You believe that, don't you? But how can you have happiness if you don't have inner harmony?" There was a perceptible change of tone. "You're wasting precious time with that two-track thinking. A man's life isn't meant to be frittered away with idle imaginings. You've got to *choose,* and then get on with it."

"Right," said Peter, pulling himself together. "At least we're agreed on that." He roughly dried his eyes with the back of his hand and got to his feet. "Of course I believe what you say, Dad. Always have. It's just that I can't understand how you could ever have turned out to be my father."

Back in his room, he found Clara sound asleep, with Diedrich in her arms. His son had moved from his own room to theirs, seeking the comfort of his mother in the double bed. Peter gave them a long, fond look, wondering at the mystery of their presence in the very same room where he had dreamed his adolescent dreams. "This is my family." He mouthed the inaudible words. "My wife, my son. They matter more to me than anything else. I will never forsake them." But he felt his pulse quicken guiltily as he repeated his solitary vow. Where did this agitation come from?

Then he knew. He wasn't at ease with Clara and Diedrich in his old room. The ghosts of his youth were asserting themselves. They were unleashing a long-stifled storm in him, a conflict that he had not wanted to face but that he knew he had to resolve before much longer.

# Chapter 20

"This is what I mean," said Peter, pointing at a Kertesz picture of a *Melancholy Tulip*. "The fusion of photography and art. Photography *as* art. Observe how he identifies with his subject, the single, sad, drooping tulip in the little glass vase. The emotion of it. The tragedy." Clara nodded.

They were in Naarden, half an hour's drive from Amsterdam, for the annual photography fair. Peter's mother was looking after Diedrich.

Clara felt awkward to be alone with her husband. It had been a long time, a year or more, since they had been together without others present, except in bed. They were used to having their son or some third party filter their comments, soften them or subtly change their direction like a billiard ball caromed off the sides of the circumscribed space. She realized how rarely Peter and she had really talked since Diedrich was born, other than the daily gossip, Peter's from the bank, Clara's about Diedrich and the house, and sometimes about her building projects. But that kind of talk was simply an extension of their separate lives, monologues delivered to an audience of one. No response was expected, just applause, commiseration, a tear or two perhaps.

Here, though, they were naked once more, like in the early days of their courtship and marriage, but instead of a caress, every word now seemed a potential weapon, a missile capable of wounding. Of course they still cared for each other. But somehow their expressions of affection were less convincing than they could be. Than they had been.

The days of blind devotion were definitely over. Direct exposure now meant danger, the danger of criticism and irritation, of being found wanting, of getting hurt. She was grateful for Diedrich, though she suspected that his very arrival had widened the distance between her and Peter.

Clara thought the Grote Kerk, the church dominating the medieval village from its elevated position and the main venue for the fair, was too cavernous for the display. Peter disagreed. "The light is what counts. And most of the pictures have been enlarged to the right size for the space. I love this building." He told her that the Saint Matthew's Passion was sung here every Easter to packed pews. "The only time the church isn't empty."

They walked over to the section with works of young Dutch photographers. Clara didn't think much of what she saw there. "Too thematic, too much evidence of examination tests."

"What's wrong with a theme?" Peter countered. "A theme can concentrate the mind. I like working with a theme."

"Fine," said Clara. "Did you bring your camera?"

"You have it," Peter answered. "You already took some shots with Diedrich."

"I mean your Leica. I thought you might have brought it."

"You know I can't do any serious work with it when…you know."

"When I'm around. I know. But you seem so keen these days on everything photographic, I thought perhaps you wanted to try. Just a thought. Forget it."

But Peter couldn't. He hadn't told Clara about his talk with his father, other than to say that they'd had a long-overdue chat, "about everything and nothing." But Clara's casual remark laid bare the still-open wound his father had inflicted on him.

"You still don't understand, do you?" he said with a sarcasm that he didn't intend but was unable to control. "I can't combine my present way of life with any kind of creative work. The two are mutually exclusive, as I've told you time and again. They're…two different worlds."

"All right, point taken. But then the least you can do is not rub your frustrations in my face by dragging me to exhibitions which in your opinion I'm unable to appreciate."

"What? *You're* the one that suggested we come here! Who's dragging who?"

"*Whom.* Because I knew you wanted to go. I was only thinking of you." She squeezed his arm. "You're still upset about your father, I know."

Peter said nothing. He patted Clara's hand and slowly walked away to look at some more young Dutch photographs. When she caught up with him, in front of a large surrealist photo collage of a nude muscular man being attacked in the neck by an oversized open-mouthed herring in full flight, he said, "Yes, I'm sorry. I'm upset. You know what he said? That I lack the *guts* to be a real photographer. My own father!"

"Only fathers know how to be cruel," Clara said. "It's their way of expressing love, of giving direction." Peter looked at her in amazement.

"Ah, so you agree with him? You're on his side!"

Clara placed both hands on Peter's arm. "Peter! It's not a matter of choosing sides! It's a question of…of accepting reality, of…growing up! Of leaving youthful things behind where they belong. Can't you see that?"

Peter abruptly disengaged himself from her grip. "Why is everybody so worried about my mental age, I wonder?"

"Because we're all concerned about…" Clara started, but Peter didn't let her finish.

"You think you can fit me out with some sort of synthetic banker's soul, don't you? By nagging me to death…"

"Peter, please!" Clara was throwing glances at the other visitors around them who were eavesdropping on their row.

"…about my supposedly juvenile cravings, and shaming me into putting up and shutting up? Is that how you want me to be? Huh?"

"Peter, stop it!"

But Peter, vaguely aware that he was behaving just like his father had, couldn't stop. He ignored the staring strangers and Clara's pleading gestures. "The over-sensitive man who underwent a delicate operation to remove the source of his weakness? Would that suit you?"

"Peter, I'm warning you!" Clara had given up pleading with her husband. She was now confronting him, head lowered, gaze menacing. This only encouraged Peter.

"*You* are warning *me?* I have a surprise for you. Nobody, not my father nor you nor God himself, is going to cow me into becoming something I am not. I am what I am and I'm going to stay that way. Only more so. You hear me? I'm not going to change to suit your requirements. Take it or leave it!"

All at once, Clara froze, as if he had led her across an invisible barrier into some white frigid space. She felt her jaw stiffen, and all her tender, placating instincts shriveled up into something disposable, unwanted, like young plants killed in a ground frost. She stretched herself to maximum height, turned on her heels and without another word walked away from him.

Peter, uncomprehending, saw her erect figure recede and then leave through the church portal. He noticed how the sun struck her white linen summer dress and made it light up the moment she stepped onto the pavement, as if she entered another existence that didn't include him. He saw all this, yet the scene seemed utterly unreal, like a well-acted drama put on for him alone, a drama he could choose to feel contempt for, or tolerate, or ignore.

He began to tremble, like he sometimes did when his stomach was empty. He stifled his urge to run after her and instead continued his inspection of the photographic display. He was now in a section of Dutch war photography, but the images failed to register. He took two or three deep breaths. The trembling ebbed away as he reconnected with reality. He expected Clara to return, and gave a quick sharp glance at the church door, fully anticipating her entrance at that very moment. But she was not there, nor could he catch sight of her in the glare of the street beyond.

He kept guard for a minute or two, staring fixedly at the door not to miss her entry, convinced he only had the timing wrong, not the inevitability of her return. But the framed white space in which her figure would soon materialize like a divine apparition remained empty, like a promise unkept.

The full impact of what had happened now hit home. The drama was real, the actor himself. She had shaken herself loose, had actually walked out on him.

Panic seized hold of him. Trying to stay calm, he took a look at the "Historic Scenes" section, focusing on a particular frontline action shot. It showed an Allied paratrooper being bayoneted by a German soldier during the battle of Arnhem, the surprise and anguish on the young paratrooper's face juxtaposed with the German's fiendish determination, which nevertheless betrayed another kind of fear and, it seemed to Peter, self-disgust at the enormity of his deed.

"Arnhem 1944..." he mumbled, reading the caption. And then "Eduard van Doorn, born Amsterdam 1909." Peter felt a jolt. "Eduard van Doorn," he repeated. Abruptly, the powerful combat image assumed another kind of aggression, one directed at him. "No!" he told himself, forbidding the horrible, self-pitying impulse to unfold into a full-blown thought.

Looking again, assuming the cool gaze of the critic, he realized how close his father had been to the action. No doubt he had used a telephoto lens, but nothing bigger than 125 mm, which put him at a mere seven or eight meters away. He probably cropped the picture, but even so, ten meters? Twelve tops.

A group of high school students led by a teacher surrounded him. The teacher, a woman in her mid-thirties, gave him a quick smile and said, "Sorry." He smiled back, easing himself a few steps further to the rear, behind the children.

"Here we have a good example... Nick, Rennie, may I have your attention? A good example of what I've been trying to say, that war photography isn't art." She spoke with a conviction that seemed wasted on most of her unruly, distracted mob. She was wearing old blue jeans, a faded yellow T-shirt and beaten-up sneakers. Her hair was tied in a neat ponytail. Over her left arm she carried a worn leather jacket, far too heavy for the balmy spring weather. Peter noticed her poverty, but he was also aware of a fierce, unfettered spirit in her, a love of work and life that belied her economic plight.

Peter looked at her, faintly envious, eager to hear what she had to say. "War photography is a window on life in all its cruelty and horror," continued the teacher. "The photographer isn't creating anything. He is a reporter, and his task is to inform. To inform us of what is really going on in the world, so that we may make the world better."

"Miss," said a strapping, freckle-faced youth of at most fifteen. "Why didn't he just throw his camera at the bloody German? He could have saved a life." A chorus of approval supported his view.

"Well, he could have, perhaps. But don't forget, his task was to record, not to participate. If he hadn't taken this shot, we wouldn't have this view of the inhumanity of war, would we now?"

"But it cost a life," persisted the youth. "Is this picture worth a life?" A shocked tension had gripped the group, betraying bafflement at the terrible choices that awaited them in adulthood. One of them, a perky dark-skinned girl with eyes that broadcast untainted confidence and vigor, rebutted him.

"If he had done what you say, *he* would have been killed by the German. And then we wouldn't have *any* of his pictures!"

"So?" countered the youth, belligerently. "Do I give a shit?"

The group broke into tittering relief, and the teacher, hoisting up her heavy jacket, let it go for a few seconds, before calling her flock to order and telling them to cut out the foul language.

The group dispersed like dogs unleashed, heading generally towards the exit, the teacher trailing behind, left with Peter.

"Sorry to have crowded you," she said briskly, transferring her jacket to the other arm. "Forcing you to listen to that kid stuff."

"No, no," said Peter. "It was very…illuminating. What you said. You see, I'm…very interested in the subject. I mean, professionally." He felt like a fraud.

"Oh, you are a photographer yourself? What do you do?"

"Uh, social realism, you might say. Candid stuff."

Her face lit up. "My field, too! We've got to talk." She reached into a pocket of her jacket and brought out a card. "Here," she said. "Give me a call when you feel like it. I do freelance work on the side. When school is out. Doesn't pay, but it's good for the soul. Excuse me, got to mind my herd! I'm Laura. What's your name?"

"Peter. Peter van Doorn," he said, unthinking. But Laura didn't make the connection. She hurried after her children through the church door and out into the street. He saw her bend forward between two girls, her arms around their shoulders, the leather jacket clutched clumsily alongside the smallest of the girls. And then he lost sight of her in the blaze of summer light.

Meeting Laura had momentarily taken Peter's mind off his predicament, but now, once again, he was aware of a void in the pit of his stomach. He was perplexed at Clara's behavior, her actually leaving him stranded, without explanation. A sickening shaft of guilt rent his insides. How could he have carried on like that, make those accusations? She was right to dump him. He was worthless, a spineless wastrel. Just as his father said.

He wandered into the village and roamed the streets for over an hour, in the forlorn hope of finding her. At last he sat down on the terrace of a small restaurant, where he ordered a Grolsch and a large apple-and-syrup pancake. The traditional Dutch dish, dismissed by Clara as "incurably childish," revived his confidence. He felt certain that Clara had merely wanted to make a point, and that all would be well the moment he returned home.

The prospect put wings on his feet. But when he turned the key in the door of his parents' house, Clara and Diedrich were not there. His mother was sitting on the sofa, peeling potatoes, her face mired in gloom.

"They've gone to a hotel, by taxi," she said, her voice a tangle of incomprehension. "She just packed her suitcase and went off. Said something I couldn't understand. About you. And that she'd call later."

"Where's Father?"

"In town. To the book market, I think. He's been gone for hours. Wasn't here when…" She seemed to suppress her tears. "Peter, what's wrong? You can confide in your mother. I'm so worried."

"I don't know, Mother. I wish I knew, but I don't." That wasn't the truth, but for now it was all he could say. He sat down next to his mother and let her caress his hair. At his moment of unhappiness his presence alone seemed enough to her. And hers for him.

The phone call came at half past seven, just as they were finishing dinner.

"Where are you?"

"At the Hotel de l'Europe. I've bought tickets for tomorrow's flight to Chicago. I'm leaving, Peter."

"Don't you owe me an explanation?"

"I don't think I *owe* you anything. But I was going to suggest that you come over tonight, after I've put Diedrich to bed, so we can talk. But let me tell you now, Peter, my mind is made up. Just remember that when you come here. Okay?"

153

"How can you? What do you mean?"

"We'll talk tonight. Come around nine. Room twenty-five."

After dinner, mother went to the kitchen, leaving Eduard and Peter alone to talk.

Eduard said he "understood" Clara's decision. "It's now up to you," he added. "It's your affair, Peter. You must live your life, just as I had to live mine."

Peter told him he had seen the Arnhem photograph.

"Oh, that one. Yes, things were clearer in those days."

"Why did you never show me that shot, Dad?"

"I was afraid you might faint," said his father, laughing roughly. But he apologized instantly. "Just joking. What I mean is, you were too young then."

"That's half a life ago, Dad. I've been back umpteen times since. You never showed me those photos, the real ones."

"You never asked me."

# Chapter 21

He biked over to the hotel on his father's bicycle, alternately pedaling hard and freewheeling to the rise and fall of the arched bridges. It was still light, and everywhere the sidewalk cafés were crowded with young people in jeans or shorts lounging lazily behind a drink.

The canals were filled with revelers in little boats, savoring the warm spring evening with beer and laughter. But Peter was unable to lose himself like that. He was not a joiner. That was one thing he and Clara had in common. They disdained social clubs and never watched team sports. Tennis was as far as they got in organized recreation. Clara was an advanced player, twice champion of the women's division of the club they belonged to. Peter's problem was his weak forehand, aggravated by recurrent bouts of tennis elbow.

Why was he thinking about tennis? Here he was on his way to confront his wife who was about to fly home without him, and all he could think about was his weak forehand.

The Hotel de l'Europe was familiar to him. The bank usually booked him in there on his head office visits. He was never sure if he liked it, what with its cramped and creaky bedrooms and its pretentious waterside restaurant where frock-coated waiters checked your every move for pedigree and poise.

The night porter looked over his half-spectacles and greeted Peter with a little forced smile. "Madame and the young gentleman are in their room, I believe. Room twenty-five, of course." he said. "Is there anything you wish me to send up for you, sir?"

Peter said "no thanks" and leaped up the two long flights of stairs, welcoming the resulting accelerated heartbeat for the alibi it provided for his agitation as he knocked on the door.

There was no response, and the silence was so deep that Peter wondered if they were there. At length he knocked again. He now heard a shuffling sound and the rattle of the night lock being disengaged.

"Sorry, I was in with Diedrich, making sure he's asleep," Clara said matter-of-factly as she walked back from the door, her footfall absorbed by the thick carpet. "He's in there. Go and give him a hug." She motioned towards another door at the end of the smallish double bedroom.

Peter was grateful for Clara's casualness, the way she moved about the room, as if there was nothing unusual about the situation, as if they were both staying there. "Take your time," she said with a little wave as she disappeared into the bathroom.

Peter stretched out beside his son on the narrow bed and cuddled him fondly. The boy moaned in his sleep and for a moment seemed startled at the intrusion into his woolly world. "No! No!" he said loudly, pushing Peter firmly away. "Don't. Don't touch me!" Then he sat up straight and threw a confused look at his father. "Wha…wha… Oh, Daddy…" Reassured, he collapsed laughing. "Daddy, I think I dreamt… Big bear, big bad bear…" He puckered his nose and grinned and shook his head. And off he was again, safely nestled in his father's arms.

To Peter there was, at that moment, nothing more precious and sweet than his son's face. The long, dark brown lashes. The light pink cheeks, still full and creamy and unblemished. The small nose, already holding promise of elegant elongation, to emulate his mother's classic lines. The swirl of the well-shaped ears—which Clara said resembled his—translucent against the light flooding in from the other room, revealing a tracery of tiny blood vessels. The mouth was an original, neither Clara's nor his, full of character in its purposeful intensity. Peter studied the strong double curve of the fleshy upper lip, one curve slightly higher than the other. Lips for kissing, thought Peter. He'd be a heartbreaker when he was older. But lips for battle, too, for launching arguments and winning them. The moderate lower lip was the perfect match for its dominating mate, sensitively drawn with a fetching little dent in the middle, not the typical

Dutch, heavy, sensual lower lip that Peter had inherited from his father and grandfather, but not as thin either as Clara's, which bordered on the severe.

And framing this adorable face were the curls, broadly sculpted like waves on an unruly sea, true blond in color, without a trace of straw, not silken but springy and firm, making the curls stand away from the scalp like the rays of the stylized sun he had seen on ancient Roman temples.

Being with his son calmed him and readied him for facing his wife, whom he now saw coming out of the bathroom and throwing a glance in their direction. Peter allowed himself another few minutes with his son before slowly disentangling and giving him a final fond hug. Then he stepped confidently into the bedroom.

Clara was waiting with a half-full bottle of wine and two glasses, one of which had a residue of the red wine in it.

"Want a sip? It's passable Macon Villages."

"Thanks, yes…" He thought how normal everything seemed, how unlike the row they had in Naarden. There was nothing to fear, their life together would go on. All that was needed were some words of kindness and contrition, a gesture.

He sat down in silence opposite Clara. She filled their glasses. He raised his, fixing her with a slight smile. "Clara, I can't tell you how sorry…"

"Don't," she interrupted firmly, brandishing her free hand, palm open. "You were simply stating the truth, Peter. No need to apologize for that." She took a quick sip and put her glass down.

"The truth?" Peter asked. "Taking my frustrations out on you? What's that got to do with the truth?"

"Everything. You spoke your mind. Clearly, unequivocally. You mapped out your course. And mine. You could've picked a better place, and chosen less offensive words perhaps. But that's nitpicking. Besides, I provoked you. What's important is the message, and that came across loud and clear." She picked up her glass again and slowly swished the dark liquid around, following the flow with her eyes. Her heavy eyelids and the dark hair falling across her cheeks made her incredibly beautiful to Peter.

"Clara, please…" he began, but she cut him short with the simple act of raising those lustrous eyelids and gazing at him. He thought he saw the glistening of tiny tears, but her voice betrayed no weakness.

"How could we have made such a mistake?" She said it at once firmly and softly, like a footprint in the snow. Peter could not believe her words.

"You know you don't mean that! We were in love, remember? Still are, aren't we? I know I am, madly! Nothing has happened that can't be undone."

Clara's fond little smile, her head atilt, seemed to pity him, like his father's. He knew he wasn't being mocked, the glow in her eye was too affectionate for that, but this only confused him. "You and me and Diedrich… my family…it's the most important thing in my life! Can't you believe that?"

"Peter, please…this isn't about what *happened*. This is about what's *there*, what's been there all along, but I was too blind to see. It's about you keeping a secret mistress, and I won't have it."

"What are you saying? You're accusing me of… What's gotten into you, Clara?" Her eyes were twinkling now, amused to have caught him out.

"What else is that black beauty of yours, that girl named Leica?" Peter's grimace was sheepish, relieved. But Clara pressed on, her manner now serious. "She's been tucked away for too long, Peter. Don't you think it's time to acknowledge her for what she is? Your true passion? Make her respectable?"

"Nonsense! That's just a…a boyish dream. Nothing more. You've said so yourself. Why are you suddenly taking it so seriously?" Clara slid forward on her chair, wielding her wine glass like a drunkard spoiling for a fight.

"Because you keep thrusting her into my face, reminding me of her qualities, of how much better a life you could have with her than with me. How you've missed your chance in life by not marrying *her*, and how one day you will do right by her, and make up for all the lost time. That's why, Peter."

"I was talking about my *career*, Clara. Not my personal life! Don't mix things up, for God's sake. My dilemma is between banking and photography. God, do I have to explain all that again?"

"No, you don't. Because you are mistaken. Let *me* explain something to *you*." She rose, motioning him to stay put. "I like passion in people. Commitment. When I met you, you seemed a committed banker to me. You talked in those terms, you see. You were not only charming and handsome, but you were convincing. You seemed the kind of man who stood behind what he was doing. Not a fraud. The genuine thing. You may not have realized it but when you married me, you married that belief in your integrity. It was… implicit in my willingness to marry you."

"That's not fair. I've been upfront with you. I told you all about my photographic past."

"Like a boy telling me about his old toys, yes. Come on, Peter, we're talking adult stuff here. Spare me your feeble excuses."

"Okay, so what have I done wrong to deserve this lecture? What are you trying to tell me, Clara? Come right out with it!"

"All right, I'll tell you. I'm leaving you, Peter. I love you, God knows I love you. But I must leave you, because…" Peter was trying to embrace her. "No, let me finish, Peter, let me finish! I must leave you because I cannot bear taking second place to another passion with its own secret system of values. You see, I never minded your late work, your travels, entertaining your customers, your colleagues, because that sort of thing doesn't threaten my position, *my* values. It's just a matter of organizing one's time. I'm the perfect corporate wife, really. But I no longer want to fight that rival force in my marriage, that brooding other self of yours that has its own incomprehensible agenda in which I have no place. I'm tired of battling a phantom."

"Okay, I understand. You are right. I will kill the phantom. It's high time anyway. I want to keep my family together."

"A noble sentiment, Peter. But we're mismatched. You've got to be true to yourself. Live your dream."

"No, no, Clara! I don't want to lose you. Don't do anything rash, please. Think it over. I'll do anything…"

"Too late, Peter. I've been living with this thing for too long. I've *had* it. And your moaning only strengthens my resolve. Damn it, can't you be a man about it? You've been indoctrinating me all these years about the nobility of your ambition, the mistake you made in becoming a banker. Well, I accept it! I understand! And I say, marry your camera! Conquer the world! Impress me, for once."

"And you and Diedrich? What will you do?"

Clara smiled a thin smile. "Yes, Diedrich. Of course there's Diedrich to take care of, isn't there? I'll do that. Don't worry, I'm up to the task. It'll be hard on him at first. You must do what you can to see him, write him, phone him. Show him that you love him. Make it appear you're not abandoning him."

"Wait a moment…who's abandoning who, huh?"

"We're discussing the child, Peter, not the parents. You've already let him go."

"That's a lie! I want to…I will… How can you be so callous? How can you expect me to…to…"

"Precisely. I hadn't expected otherwise. But that's all right. Really. You've got to have a free hand."

Peter fell silent, dumbstruck by the implications of what Clara was telling him. Was he really incapable of decisive action? Of accepting his duties as a parent? True, all the major decisions in his life had been made for him by others. His banking career, his coming to America, his marrying Clara. It had all been the initiative of other people. *She* had proposed to *him.* Even the decision to have a child had not been his. And now this, his wife's decision to leave him and to take the child with her. Wasn't there anything worthwhile in his life that *he* had initiated? Nothing at all?

Perhaps not. But there was one thing he *could* do. The one step in his life that no one could take for him, and that would demonstrate beyond question that he was not a coward. So far he had failed to take that step, and it was this failure, his sickly vacillation, that had finally cooled Clara's feelings for him. All the talk without action. She was right. He was despicable. What was he to do? He couldn't focus his thoughts.

"And the house, what about all our stuff? Do you want the house?"

"That's up to you, Peter. I'm the one who's leaving, so you have first rights to the house."

Were they actually discussing separation, divorce?

"But what about you, Clara? What are you going to do?"

Clara turned around and walked away from him. "Oh, don't worry about me. I'll manage. I've got Clearwater, remember?"

Yes, he remembered. He recalled her successful projects, four so far, each more profitable than the former, and all in partnership with Jack Drummond, the builder, and Magnus Petersen, the architect. He remembered, not without bitterness, how his own role in these projects had become progressively smaller, ostensibly because of potential "conflicts of interest" with his banking position, but really because Clara wanted Clearwater to be her own show. But right now his thoughts weren't about money.

"I mean, you alone…"

"Oh, that! Well, I'm hoping that it may be easier living without you than it ever was living with you!"

"Has it been that bad?" was Peter's crestfallen response.

"Aw, Peter, where's your sense of humor? Come here, I do want us to part on friendly terms."

She pulled him towards her and kissed him on the cheek. But when he kissed her back it was on the mouth. She pushed him away. "You've got to go back," she said.

"I'm in no hurry…" He had moved behind her and was caressing her well-shaped shoulders. He wanted to reach around and touch her breasts, but didn't dare to.

"I didn't move to a hotel for nothing," she said, but he thought he felt her weaken in his embrace.

"Why *did* you move to a hotel?" he wanted to know.

"To draw a line," she said. She turned around to face him, and looking him straight in the eye, she slowly ran a finger across his chest. "A clear and unmistakable line, Peter. A line of demarcation."

"Yes," he nodded, comprehending at last. He felt a brief stirring of the opportunities that opened before him. "It will all be different now, won't it? For both of us…"

"For Diedrich too," she said, her voice husky now and unsteady. "You will spare us a thought sometimes, won't you?"

He was seized by acute grief and held her close. His tears flowed freely, and at last she let go too, her cries of sorrow mingling with his sobs as they clasped at each other in a last hopeless rite, an affirmation of their impossible love for each other.

"You understand, then?" Clara said after a while in a small voice.

"Yes, yes. I *understand*. Mentally. But how can I *accept* it? How can you? How could anyone?"

"We'll learn to accept it when we realize it saved us from growing to hate each other."

"I could never hate you."

"I don't think hate is an emotion that you can choose or deny, Peter. When it comes it will overpower you, take possession of you. It's a fearful thing."

"You hate me already?"

"No. But I recognize the early signs. And I don't ever want to be in its grip. I want to remember you…lovingly."

She looked up at him, her eyes filling again. They embraced and stood quietly, swaying slightly, their bodies pressed together, as if the warmth of this last act of intimacy could protect them from the coming chill, a chill that had already entered their lives and changed them irretrievably.

# Chapter 22

Clara and Diedrich left the following day, two days before the end of their two-week holiday and the beginning of Peter's three-day conference with his banking colleagues, somewhere in a castle retreat southeast of Amsterdam.

Ignoring Clara's objections, Peter accompanied them to the airport in a taxi. On the way, they stopped at his parents' place. He told the taxi to wait while the three of them went in to say goodbye.

Diedrich got permission to rush up to the attic to find some old comic books of Peter's, and Clara perched briefly on a chair opposite Eduard, who sat down on the sofa, his wife at his side. Peter had urged her not to mention "the subject," to leave things vague, also in the interest of Diedrich.

Clara disagreed. "They have the right to know."

Peter relented. "Then you'd better do the talking."

"I'm sorry to cause you distress," Clara said, looking from one parent to the other, "but I think you can understand. I just can't live any longer with a man who doesn't know his own mind. Who can't *choose*. I do love him, but I *must* leave him, before it starts affecting my sanity."

Eduard took Clara's hands.

"I understand. It's always been his problem. Always. I'm sorry, I'm sorry..." He released her hands, stood up roughly and walked away. Never once did he look at his son, or even acknowledge his presence in the room.

"What a pity, what a pity!" said Peter's mother in Dutch, not quite knowing what to do next. "And the child! The poor child!"

Peter assured her that Diedrich—who was just returning carrying a pile of old Asterix magazines—would get all the loving attention he needed. That he would see to that.

"Really?" said his mother doubtfully. "The poor child…"

"Mom, look!" Diedrich said, holding up the comics triumphantly. "May I borrow them, Dad?"

"Sure, and you may keep them! Take them back to Chicago if you want."

"Wow! Really? Thanks, Dad." He embraced his father, who thought this a good moment for all to say their final goodbyes.

Eduard, somewhat recovered, quickly hugged his son. "I know it's tough. Just remember what I said before. If you don't end that division inside you, your life will fall apart. Remember that."

The trip to the airport passed in painful silence. Diedrich was immersed in his comic books, while Clara studied the dreary scenery. Peter's conversational openings were stranded in dispirited grunts.

The diversion of unloading the bags and checking in brought temporary relief, but Clara said they'd "better go through" right away, "for Diedrich, you know," thus averting further awkwardness.

They kissed briefly. Diedrich, too absorbed as he was in his newfound treasure, gave his father only a quick peck on the cheek, then made up by waving frantically as he and his mother disappeared through the barrier.

Clara, elegant, brainy, faithful Clara, the ex-heiress from America's heartland, who'd just ended her nine-year marriage to the distraught Dutch banker she left behind, Clara Addams, as she had already started calling herself again, President of Clearwater Incorporated and chairperson-elect of the Vassar Alumni Club, didn't look back.

# Chapter 23

It was still before noon when Peter left for the Hooge Vuursche Castle, a wing of which the bank had rented for the duration of the conference. He wanted to get away from the accusatory atmosphere at home and give himself a few hours' breathing space before plunging into the forced camaraderie of the thirty-odd senior international managers expected to filter in during the course of the afternoon and evening, with the conference due to open the following morning.

He was the first to check in. Good. That left him free to carry out his little plan to go riding on the nearby heath. There was a stable where they rented gear and horses, and he was keenly looking forward to a long ride on the heath.

The clerk handed him a message, "just received," to call his Chicago boss, Boudewijn De Rooy, not in Chicago, but at an Amsterdam hotel. Puzzled, Peter dialed the number, and was put right through. Boudewijn said his wife had passed her crisis and was on the mend, and he had decided to join the conference after all.

"There's some important business on the agenda," he confided. "We've got to talk, you and I. The conference doesn't start till morning, so let's have dinner tonight. I know a good place in Bussum."

"Fine," said Peter. "I'm glad you're here, Boudewijn. Actually," he added, his heart thumping, "I want to talk to you, too."

He hung up, staggered by the force of events. His father's admonishments, Clara's leaving, Boudewijn's unexpected arrival. To talk? About what? He'd have to tell *him* something.

165

The thoughts and emotions jostled for position in his head as he made his way to the stable. He was grateful for the chore of saddling the dapper chestnut with the endearing white patch on her muzzle the stable manager had recommended for someone "experienced, but a little out of practice." A mild-mannered mare, he had called her, without tricks, but with "enough oomph to scare the rabbits."

The horse's name was Shannon. She had belonged to an Irish lady married to a Dutch oil man.

Peter followed the narrow, sandy path along the edge of the wood, mostly oak and some pine, from where he had a good shaded view of the heath. He walked Shannon for ten minutes before easing her into a trot. The air was mellow and dry, the spring sun warm on his skin. There wasn't a soul around.

He couldn't help thinking about his future. He tried to visualize his life as a photographer, but based where? Chicago, of course, it had to be Chicago, for Diedrich. He'd have to rent a small apartment somewhere in the city's Near North. Clara should stay on in the house with Diedrich.

A panic gripped him. About money. He did have savings, but could he live on the income? Could he afford to travel, buy equipment, materials, take Diedrich on holidays? Probably, if he lived frugally. What kind of work would he do? No newsy journalism or advertising, that much he knew. No fashion. Nothing really commercial. Portraits, perhaps. Art? Photography as art and social commentary. The human story. Nature, yes. And cities, buildings. The essence of things. But above all, people. Conflict, loneliness, ecstasy. Laughter. Sadness. The waste. The unfulfilled dreams. The *meaning* of it all. But how to start?

He felt a chill. The sun had slipped behind a cloud. He spurred Shannon into a trot, then a spirited canter. Passion, that's what was needed. Why didn't he *feel* it, then? Why, after all those years of yearning, wasn't he wild with excitement now that his hour had come at last? Why the hesitation?

Shannon was protesting, her front legs stiffening, her head rocking back and forth. Peter had reined her in a little at a fork, but confused her about the direction he wished to go. "Okay, old girl, I'm sorry." He shifted his weight demonstratively to the right, with a matching tug on the reins. Shannon took the command, shaking her head as if to say, "No need to *overdo* it!"

That evening, at the restaurant, Boudewijn explained the important business he had alluded to. It was the bank's plan to buy up a medium-sized British bank. He had just been briefed on the plans by the Head of International Banking.

"And they want you to run it, almost," he added. "Together with a couple of bean counters from Headquarters, of course, and alongside the present English managing director, chap by the name of Donaldson. Ian Donaldson. Nice guy. Mid-forties."

"What, you've met him already?"

"He's here, joining us for the conference. Part of it, anyway."

Peter swallowed hard. "I...I don't think I want to go. I can't. I...I'm not accepting." He had intended this to come out calmly, but doubted if it did. Boudewijn raised his eyes slowly without making a reply, his silence respectful, even affectionate, Peter thought. More understanding than his father.

"Actually," Peter continued, gravely, "I've decided to leave the bank. I wanted you to be the first to know."

Boudewijn leaned back incredulously. "You're not telling me you got a better offer, are you?" Instantly adding, "No, no, that can't be. That's not your style."

Peter assured him it was nothing like that. "It's purely personal," was all he would say. "It's got nothing to do with the bank, or with you. I just want to quit...banking."

"Quit banking," Boudewijn repeated in a flat voice. "Quit banking. You must have your reasons for that."

"Yes, I do," Peter said without expanding. He felt bad about his own reticence, but felt an obligation to add, "And there's another thing. I hate having to tell you this, Boudewijn, but Clara and I are splitting up."

Boudewijn's face, already drawn, now seemed to pale in shock. "Oh, that's bad news. On top of everything else. What a sad day this is. But why, Peter, what's happened?"

For a long moment, Peter thought he would tell him all, but he demurred. "It's a long story, Boudewijn. Actually, Clara and I are parting on good terms.

And I'll continue spending a lot of time with Diedrich, of course. It's just that, well, I want to be on my own for some time. A long time. There're things I want to do, by myself."

Boudewijn was listening intently, but it was evident Peter's story didn't satisfy him.

"I know you deserve a better explanation, Boudewijn. But right now, this is all I can say. But please don't worry about me. I'll be all right."

Boudewijn rose, looked away, and gave Peter a half-hearted pat on the shoulder.

"We only have one life to live, my friend. I just hope…" He turned his head and gave Peter a hard stare. "I just hope that you won't ever have to regret how you've lived yours."

The next morning, Peter conveyed his decision personally to the chairman, who was attending the opening meeting to make his announcement about London. He looked astonished. "At least I don't have to stand there looking like a fool." He poked an angry finger at Peter. "You could've told us a little earlier, though."

"I only decided yesterday," Peter replied truthfully. The man gave a hard, derisive laugh. Peter knew that would be the reaction of half the bank.

The chairman gave his speech about the London acquisition and ended by introducing Ian Donaldson. Then, returning abruptly to the rostrum he had just left, he tersely announced Peter's resignation. "Mr. van Doorn has decided to leave us, for reasons that he knows best. I thought you should all be aware of this as you carry on with your meetings."

The chairman's choice of words inevitably set the rumor mills spinning about Peter's motives for quitting. When asked, Peter, blithely ignorant of all the gossip, simply repeated what he had told Boudewijn, which wasn't much. Nobody believed a word of it.

Eduard's reaction to his son's decision to quit the bank had been a stony silence, which was fine with Peter. He would have hated it if the old man had made a demonstration of his revived hopes for his son's redemption. His endemic suspicion of Peter's motives and ability to persevere, of his *guts*, was a mark of Eduard's character, not easily erased by his son's act of midlife rebellion. He needed proof positive. Peter thought he would provide it—in time.

But first there were the doubts to overcome. They stole up on him during the night. They validated his father's skepticism. He wondered if he had the talent for the new road he had chosen, whether he had any worthwhile ideas. His doubts slowly extended to the relevancy of photography as such. What was its role in society anyway? Did it have the power to change people, to be anything more than a peephole for the curious, satisfying their insatiable hunger for evidence of glamor, violence, weirdness, poverty, power? Was it really worth giving up a family and a successful career only to cater to this universal, vulgar need for titillation, entertainment, shock?

Peter had been tossing about for hours. He felt sweaty and nauseated. His stomach was empty, but he had no appetite. He needed a drink of water. He dragged himself out of bed and softly descended the stairs. He found the kitchen tap by the pale white light of the half-moon. Sipping his water, he wandered into his father's study, lit the desk lamp, ran his fingers along the bookshelves. There were many books on politics, history, philosophy and social issues, on language, on the Second World War. But where were the books on photography?

Ah, there they were. *WWII in Photos. The Great War in Pictures. American War Photography.* And photo books about warplanes, Formula One races, parachute jumps. One with the title: *The Camera as Secret Weapon.* Jesus. Wait, there was *Arnhem: A battle too far. A photo reportage.* Peter pulled it out and rifled through the pages looking for "Eduard van Doorn" credits. He didn't find any and consulted the index. Ah, there he was, van Doorn, Eduard. One entry. He went to the page. It was the photo he had seen in the Naarden church, of the German soldier bayoneting the Allied paratrooper. Just this one image, among the hundreds in the book and the thousands Eduard no doubt had taken of the battle. He felt a surge of compassion for his father.

*One image.* In a collection of hundreds.

"Was this shot worth a life?" the boy at the exhibition had asked.

Peter closed the book. He wondered if *photography* was worth a life, *giving up* a life, a career. Or was that something else? One thing was clear: He had burned his bridges. Perhaps he went too far, but the deed was done. The time for doubt was past. Doubts were destructive emotions, gnawing like termites at the roots of the tree he wanted to *liberate* from its humiliating confinement. The inner tree that had always been there, but had never been allowed the light of day.

He went back to bed, nursing the image of the stunted, light-starved living tree finally being given space and air and sunshine. It gave him hope and confidence, and it finally carried him off, at four-thirty in the morning. His sleep was deep and dreamless and nourishing, and when he awoke, the day felt as new to him as it had a right to be.

That morning, Pauline came over to say goodbye. She found Peter in his room, packing his suitcase, though his departure was still two days away. She didn't seem too distraught over her brother's new bachelor status, and was predictably supportive of his decision to become a photographer.

"Now I'll come and visit you," she promised. "I don't think you'll stay long in Chicago, though. Just doesn't sound right for a cosmopolitan photographer!" She smiled affectionately at her brother. "Why can't you come and live closer by somewhere?"

"Because of Diedrich," Peter explained.

"I know," she said somewhat sadly, but with an undertone of "So what?" She had her father's hardness, his ability to sacrifice compassion for passion, or truth, when the crunch came.

Peter's perception of the world lacked their clarity. He didn't understand how anybody could be sure about anything. Wasn't life far too complex for that? The best one could do was bumble along in good conscience, stop frequently to survey the scene, and hope for some wisdom and the luck of the draw.

"The good thing about photography is…you can practice it anywhere," he offered lamely.

"Right," was her instant response. "That's what I mean. You don't need Chicago for it!"

His mother called that the coffee was ready.

Pauline sighed. "Big brother, I'll be watching you!" She waggled a finger at him. "I always thought you'd be famous, remember? I still do."

Peter smiled uncomfortably. Why did his family have to have these expectations of him? First his father, now Pauline. Clara too, in a different sense. And, who knows, Diedrich, in a few years' time. Only Fran and his mother left him alone. He realized they were also the two women he had least in common with.

"Coffee!" It was his mother's voice again from below.

"Coming!"

They were down in seconds, his mother waiting behind a home-baked cherry pie. "Ah, my favorite! Thanks, Ma," Peter exclaimed.

The woman before him smiled, and cut three slices. "It isn't the season yet, but I still had some preserved cherries left. Though they don't taste the same as fresh."

Peter took a bite of his slice. "Mmm. Can't tell the difference. As good as real."

"It's so good to see you two together," said his mother, looking pleased. "It's like old times, isn't it? You were always such good children. Fran too, of course. But especially you two. You got along so well. Still do, don't you?"

Pauline looked at Peter, who looked back. Pauline blushed and nodded emphatically, and Peter looked at his mother and declared solemnly, "Mother, that will never change."

In the Eyes of the Son

# Chapter 24

He dug up the crumpled card that Laura had handed him and called her number. The phone rang many times and Peter was about to give up when she answered it.

"Sorry, I was hanging the laundry. Who's this?"

"Peter. We met at the Naarden photo festival. By the war photographs."

"Peter! Of course. You want to come over? I've got half a bottle of good Vougeot and a veal stew that's in its third day and therefore exactly right."

"I can't. My mother is cooking dinner. Can't I come later? Just for drinks?"

"Any time at all. I'm not going out."

Laura was cropping black-and-white prints on a large hardboard trestle table when Peter arrived. A single Z-lamp illuminated the table and her face, leaving the rest of her bent-over body in the half-dark. She had buzzed him in, shouted "Three flights up!" and left her flat door open.

Laura lived in two rooms on the third floor of a seventeenth century gabled house on Reguliersgracht. It was a long climb up the narrow stairs. He recognized the leather jacket hanging from a hook on the landing. She welcomed him from her stool with a broad sideways smile. She was wearing jeans and a well-washed, navy-colored T-shirt with the words "Own up!" printed in large yellow letters.

"Just chopping some unwanted bits off my social misery collection," she said. "It feels like amputating limbs… As if they need any help with that!" She got off her perch and took Peter's coat, which she hung on the same hook as her leather jacket.

"What good initiative!" she said. "I *thought* I'd hear from you again…"

She showed Peter the enlargements. The shots were all of dark-skinned people, some crippled, most shabbily dressed, in dirty, overcrowded streets. There were close-ups, medium shots and long shots, all remarkably sharp in focus and dramatically lit. "Where's that?" he asked.

"Jamaica. I went there for a week's visit on the cheap. Packed like sardines on the plane. Stayed in youth hostels. Never saw the beaches. Too busy shooting away." She had a fetching way of tossing her ponytail while emitting a bold, inviting kind of laugh.

"Was it…depressing?"

"Not more so than reading the daily world news. But yes, there's a lot of suffering. I expected that, of course. That's why we go, right?"

Peter hesitated. "Laura, there's something I want to tell you before we go on. I'm not a professional photographer. Not yet, anyway."

"I never thought you were." She laughed. "That 'not yet' sounds intriguing though."

She insisted on pouring out her Clos Vougeot 1970 before letting Peter open the Pouillac he had brought.

"Just opened last night. Should still be drinkable."

Why is it, Peter wondered, that artists without money still manage to drink good wine, while well-paid business people drink stuff from the supermarket, except when they're on expense account? André had told him long ago in Singapore, "I'd rather drink water than plonk." And *he* couldn't even be called an artist. The same with food. When artists had cash, they splurged. When they didn't, they subsisted on bread and coffee. What they disdained was the mediocre, the watered-down compromise, the bourgeois preoccupation with stretching a dollar.

"A penny for your thoughts," said Laura as she poured the wine.

"I was thinking," said Peter, raising his glass, "about the relationship between art and quality, between good wine and… inspired photography." It was indeed an exemplary burgundy.

"There's none. I just can't stand cheap wine!"

174

Peter smiled. "Neither can I. But tell me, how do you balance teaching with trips to Jamaica?"

"I teach two days a week. Art appreciation, to the kind of classes you saw. Keeps me on my toes. Those kids take no shit. The rest of the week I work on the shots I've taken on my travels during the school holidays."

She sold her work to whoever would take it: photography publications, newspapers, Sunday magazines, photo agencies. More often than not the work was returned. Occasional exhibitions brought her name to the public's notice, but they didn't seem to help much with her commercial efforts.

"There's no decent living in it, believe me. Not for me, anyway. But it's all I want to do. Simple as that!"

"How did you get into photography?" Peter wanted to know.

"It all started on a visit to New York, seven years ago…" She poured the rest of the wine. He leaned back in the canvas director's chair, feeling very relaxed. There was a naturalness, an absence of pretence that he found refreshing and oddly calming. He had half-expected to be judged and found wanting. But Laura didn't seem to be aware of the existence of a chasm between her world and his, or if she was, it didn't concern her.

"New York fascinated me, the contrasts, the squalor, the ostentation. I wanted to make my own record of it. So I went to 47th Street Photo and blew a whole month's income on a Pentax with all the lenses. I just started shooting, learning new tricks at night from a manual I'd bought. I went everywhere—Staten Island, the South Bronx, Coney Island, Rockefeller Center. After that, I traveled through South America for five months. A friend of mine organized an exhibition for me in his Utrecht gallery after my return. One hundred framed shots, chosen from more than three thousand negatives. Another month's income. I did sell some. But in spite of the good reviews I've failed so far to make the big league."

Peter had been glancing at the photos on the table as she talked.

"It will come. Your work reminds me of Salgado's. Same eye for suffering. Those intense heaps of humanity in distress. Even your technique: the foreshortening, the light. But you're more different than you resemble him." Peter was surprised at how he could speak with such certainty.

"In what sense?" she asked.

"Yours is a woman's view."

Laura, intrigued, cocked her head. She seemed undecided if she should take his remark as a compliment. "Why do you say that?"

"I'm not sure. Maybe because Salgado emphasizes the heroic. A kind of macho Paul Robeson grit pervades his work. Your photos are more... compassionate."

"Mmm," Laura said, without comment. "Tell me, has the shutter bug bitten you, too? Or are you just planning to become a critic?" He looked at her, but there was no sarcasm in her face. At most, mild amusement.

"No, it's got to be hands on. Shall I open this bottle?"

She handed him a corkscrew. She changed the glasses and took them back to the kitchen. Peter looked around. The place was not large but without clutter. It reflected the character of its occupant, he thought: unambiguous, demanding, open. They moved to the "balcony" which was really a little roof area with some well-tended potted plants. They sat down on the small narrow bench. It was chilly but there was no wind, and the half-moon illuminated the surrounding rooftops. They could catch an angled glimpse of the illuminated Westerkerk tower.

Peter felt Laura's body heat where their hips were touching. Neither made an effort to change position. They quietly sipped their wine. Peter said, "Nice little bench," and they laughed, and fell silent.

After a while, she said, "Now tell me about yourself."

Peter tried to stick to the essentials: his photographic youth, the sudden death that he had failed to catch on camera, his father's ire, his banking career, his never-fading love for photography. He also told her about the last few days' events, leaving out the details of his painful, fateful confrontation with his wife in Naarden, minutes before he'd met Laura. But he did say that he and Clara were splitting up.

"Well done," was Laura's comment when he was through. "It seems you escaped in the nick of time."

Peter rose. Her remark bothered him. He found it aggressive. To agree with it was to betray Clara. No, that wasn't it. To agree was to accept Laura's intrusion into his life. Yet he felt exhilarated by her free talk. And he couldn't really disagree with her conclusion. It sounded an incredibly facile thing to say for someone who barely knew him, but it was perceptive.

Peter wondered if he could become part of the world Laura inhabited, the world of people apparently unconcerned with material comforts and social status, of people dealing in essential truths, and willing to exhibit their feelings and state their opinions. Laura's concern seemed to be with people living in far-away slums, people whose language and skin color she didn't share and whose history she barely knew. Was that what's called altruism?

Peter doubted if he could be that way, if he *wanted* to be that way. He had never been convinced that the do-gooders were, by their nature, superior people. He accepted that most of them genuinely believed in what they were doing, and that their selfless work often made a crucial difference to the daily lives of those they helped. But he had always been disturbed by the implied superiority, the cultural arrogance of Western charity and missionary activities in poor countries.

He checked his thoughts. Laura was no charity worker. She was a concerned observer. She observed and reported with striking visual images. Were they having any impact, those images?

"Tell me," he said, his thoughts jumping a few connections, "would you have thrown your camera at that German soldier at the battle of Arnhem?"

"I've no idea," she answered. "How can we know our actions and reactions beforehand? There's too much at stake."

"At stake?"

"Getting the message out. That's the main thing, and I suppose our actions are determined by that fundamental duty. That Arnhem photographer felt he *had* to take that picture, didn't he? He may not have been a warm-blooded person, but he was a hell of a communicator."

"That photographer was my father."

For a moment she was silent. She too got up and leaned against the railing, away from him. Then she turned around.

"Well, congratulations! So it runs in the family!"

"Except that there is a difference," Peter said.

"I know. You told me," said Laura. "But I think you've got that all wrong. I think your father was simply venting his own frustrations on you when he said that you were a disappointment to him. I don't believe that he was really judging you."

"Why do you think that?"

"You told me he's a journalist. Journalists *comment* on history in the making, don't they? They don't *make* it. A very frustrating position to be in, I'm sure, if what you *really* want to do is wring necks or kick ass. Your father was caught between his family responsibilities and his impulse for action. He chose the family. He probably would have been much happier as a politician or a soldier. Like you."

Peter was amazed at this analysis. He and his father alike? "I've never for a moment thought that *I* wanted to be a politician or a soldier."

"Because you have a fixation on your father's denial of you. But who knows? You're also really a man of action."

"Tell me, Laura, how can a photographer know such things? You speak with such…authority." He took a large sip of his long-neglected glass, and so did Laura.

"Let's go in," she said. "I'm getting cold. You didn't ask me what I did before I got into photography. I'll tell you," she said when they were seated in the director's chairs again. She tossed her ponytail around and laughed. "This will surprise you. I was a practicing psycho-analyst, for eight years, here in Amsterdam. I loved the work, until I suddenly lost my taste for it. It was like, waking up one morning next to your lover and realizing you're no longer in love with him. I guess I got tired of the never-ending tales of divorce and sexual frustration, of the wallowing in self-pity and identity crises of my clients. So seven years ago, I sold my practice and used the money for that trip to New York and South America. From psychology to photography. And no regrets."

"So you were leading a double life, too."

"Not at all. I gave up when I got fed up. *Then* I discovered photography. As a means to an end, really."

Peter nodded. Laura's tale somehow reminded him of the "first destroy, then think" logic of the nineteen sixties' anarchists, of the German Rote Armee

Fraktion and the Sekigun-ha, their Japanese counterpart. It was a far-fetched association.

"Do you believe in revolution?" he asked.

"In direct action, certainly," was her prompt answer. He liked it that she showed no surprise at his train of thought. "Revolutions are bloody. It's got to be really bad before I'd pick up a gun. But we may be getting to that point. If big business doesn't change their stripes. Which they won't, of course." She said all this with a smile and in a quiet voice.

Peter thought, she's living on an altogether different plane from me. He had no idea of the dark thoughts living in the minds of the likes of Laura. He sensed layers of passionate idealism below the inoffensive exterior of this strangely alluring woman.

"I represented big business," said Peter. "I don't think we were aware we were doing anything terribly wrong."

"That's the crux of the problem, isn't it?" said Laura. "Ignorance. Isn't that why you've left them, so that you can expose them for what they are? Their utter contempt for the welfare of the people they claim to serve?"

Although he'd been critical of banking, Peter hadn't thought about business in those terms at all, and he felt uneasy hearing it talked about like this.

"That was not my reason for leaving. I'm leaving because I want to be a photographer, and because I've never really liked the atmosphere of banking, the smell of business."

Laura leaned forward, her eyes keenly focused on him. "And where do you think that *atmosphere,* that *smell* comes from, Peter? It's generated by that festering pit of greed, of hunger for larger markets and bigger profits. By disdain for the suffering masses and contempt for social justice. It's the unhealthy atmosphere of growth for its own sake, growth that serves no higher human purpose and doesn't even make economic sense, except to the pockets of the perpetrators. It's the rotten atmosphere of selfishness and exploitation. That's where that stench comes from. Can't you see?"

"Maybe so. But such is the nature of business, isn't it? It's never been otherwise and it never will be."

"Oh, it's tenacious and powerful, all right. That's why we must be clever and committed if we're ever to break its back."

*She's a red-blooded revolutionary,* Peter thought. Quite a contrast to most Western "intellectuals" nowadays, who seemed more interested in the heady and lucrative possibilities of media exposure than in righting social wrongs. This was the dawn of the era of egoism. Altruism and idealism were being thrown on history's rubbish heap. He was aware of all this, and was amazed to find the discredited ideal of social revolution alive and well in this old Amsterdam canal house. He took a slow sip of his wine.

"That's pretty strong stuff, Laura," he said at length. "I'm not sure if I want to follow that line of thinking. You see, I simply want to take photographs."

"Of what, Peter?" Laura was like a bulldog now, unwilling to let go.

"Of…anything that can illustrate our unique place in the universe. Our sufferings and our joys. Our sense of beauty, too."

"And you think that will satisfy you? You, an intelligent man, a manager used to taking action? Will it be enough for you just to observe and *take pictures*?" She spoke in a low, penetrating voice, perfectly calm and controlled. Peter thought she could be a formidable adversary.

"I think so. I won't know until I find out."

She tossed her ponytail and made a little smile. She had large eyes and an intelligent chin. "So you're going to click your shutter aimlessly, without a principle, a message, an *ideology* to guide you? A man of your age. Are you sure you're not going to waste your time?"

Peter was squirming under Laura's relentless questioning. She was touching raw nerves, unexplored territory within him. Her probing was precise. He knew he hadn't thought through his photographic plans. He was relying on the right inspiration and ideas once he was a free man. But he didn't want Laura or anyone else to analyze his motives. She was out of bounds with her provocative interrogation.

"Why should it worry you, Laura, if I waste my time? I am responsible for my own actions, as you are for yours. Not every photographer needs to be an agent of *revolution*!"

"No," she retorted, "but every true artist must be *engagé*, one way or another. Art without moral commitment is useless and unnecessary, because it has no redeeming value." She drank her wine without lowering her eyes. "Or do you still stick to the ghost of that discredited concept of *l'art pour l'art* that died long ago?"

Peter didn't want to continue the discussion. Laura's presence was becoming oppressive. He felt tired and wanted to go home. His heart sank at the thought that he wouldn't find Clara and Diedrich waiting for him.

"Maybe we should leave that discussion for another time," he said as he got up.

"When will that be?" she asked, without getting up, her glass twirling in her hand. "I do think there is hope for you, you know."

He managed a half-smile. "I don't know. I'm leaving tomorrow for the States." This news seemed to startle her.

"You've come to see me the night before you leave? Oh, I feel *honored*!" She rose and came up close to him. Her fingers crept playfully along his chest as she looked up at him, her voice noticeably softened. "But tell me, Mr. Banker, *why* did you come to visit me? In your last precious hours?" Her sudden change in demeanor seemed brazen.

"Oh, let's just say I wanted to find out if...if you were real." No, that didn't do. That didn't do at all.

"Of course I'm real. Did you have any doubts?" She pressed her body against his and threw him a coquettish glance which, like everything else about her changed tack, seemed a put-on. Yet somehow his lust was acting up.

"I wanted to get to know you," he said, disentangling himself. "But I'm not sure that was such a good idea. To tell the truth, I find you rather...lacking in subtlety."

Laura pondered this, her chin resting on clasped hands. "And you, big boy, are talking in riddles. Could you be more specific? Please?" Her sexuality to him was blatant, provocative. He had to be brusque.

"All right, since you ask. I find you brilliant, ruthless, offensive, intolerant and manipulative, and I'm convinced that you'll do anything to get what you want. Anything."

His own words amazed him. They didn't sound quite right, he left something vital out, though he didn't know what.

181

Laura abruptly turned her back on him, then swung round to face him again, her ponytail swooping after her, her breasts heaving.

"*You* wanted to see *me*, remember? And let me tell you why. To cry on my shoulder and have a cheap fuck. The posh banker turned reluctant dropout, engaged in a bit of sexual slumming."

Was that really his *purpose* in coming here? He suddenly wasn't sure.

"And now you're miffed," continued Laura, "because I take the trouble to talk some sense into you, and I turn out to be far from an easy lay. Because I make you think for your pleasure. Really think. So what do you do? You run scared and insult me to cover your retreat. Know what that's called? Cowardice. Well, goodbye, Mr. Coward. Go back to the stench of banking where you belong. I certainly did misjudge *you*."

She handed him his coat and held the door open for him. Peter was groping for something to say.

"Oh, and about all that subversive talk of mine," Laura continued, in a changed voice, "that was just an act. I'm really a pussycat who would *love* to have a more comfortable life." She pulled her mouth into a parody of a sweet smile, and made cat-like movements with her hands. "Won't you stroke my fur, please, Mr. Banker? It's soft…"

His instinct told him to throw her to the floor and tear off her clothes. Instead, he took two steps away from her, onto the landing. He took a deep breath and turned around.

"I didn't mean to insult you. But you confuse me with your wild talk. What are you anyway?"

"You don't know what to believe, do you, darling? Well, I'll help you. I'm having you on. I was dead serious. I meant everything I said. And remember this, when the day of reckoning comes, you'll be on my private hit list. Not because you're a banker. *Were*, excuse me. Although that's reason enough. No, you'll be on my hit list for thinking of me as a common slut. That's always the bottom line, isn't it? Personal revenge. So, in the immortal words of that unreformed pederast Baden-Powell, be prepared! Until then, goodbye!" And she threw the door shut in his face.

As he was groping for the hall light switch in the dark, the door reopened, with Laura's silhouetted, haloed head blocking the light behind her. He could just make out her moving lips. "Of course," she said soothingly, "you can ring my bell any time you decide to continue the discussion. I love a good chat. A persuasive argument turns me on. But if all you can do is insult a girl, then…" For the second time, she slammed the door shut.

He walked down the stairs in a daze. "Crazy bitch," Peter mumbled angrily as he cycled back to his parents' house. His agitation got an extra edge from the hard climbs up the arched bridges as he worked his way across the inner city canal system. "Destructive. Everything she says. Destructive and manipulative." The descends of the bridges mellowed him. "She's a mixed up woman. Mixed up and unhappy. Who knows what kind of suffering made her like that?"

It was past midnight when he unlocked the front door. To his surprise, he found his mother still awake.

"Your father waited up for you. He finally turned in half an hour ago."

They talked for a while about nothing in particular, and she made Peter a mug of herbal tea which he drank gratefully.

"I mix these myself," she explained proudly. "I buy the herbs at the Albert Cuyp market. It's very good for you."

Peter smiled and nodded. How normal everything seemed at home, how peaceful and unthreatening. His encounter with Laura was receding into the gray miasma of all that was disagreeable in the world, and in its place had come a woolly layer of familiar things and trusted feelings and understanding. Of continuity.

"You are not going to accept what Clara is doing to you, are you?" His mother's voice reached him through the herbal mist.

"Well…I can't say. I mean, she has her rights, and she's got a point. We'll have to give it time." He nodded as if to affirm the reasonableness of what he had just said.

"I know your father wouldn't have tolerated it. Imagine I had run off with the children… Can you imagine that?"

"No, Mother, I can't. But these are different times. We'll just have to wait and see. And I think we both need to go to bed." As he got up and headed for the stairs, his mother took his hand.

"You'll always be my boy, you know that. Always. Whatever happens."
He kissed her and patted her on the back, and said good night. As he climbed
the steps, he wondered why he couldn't feel a stronger emotion for his mother
than a kind of distant affection.

He slept fitfully. Sensations of touching Laura's body disturbed him again
and again, and he saw her lips in the darkened doorway whispering the same
words: "Come back, come back." He woke up shouting, "No more words!" His
body felt hot and aroused, and he could not catch sleep again. A desperate act of
self-stimulation finally carried him off into a dreamless sleep that lasted only a
few hours but proved long enough to refresh him, and free him from the
cloying images of Laura and her beckoning message.

# Chapter 25

Breakfast featured two special visits. Both Fran and Pauline dropped by on their way to work to wish Peter a safe journey. They didn't stay long. They just had their cup of tea and one or two slices of brown bread with cheese before giving him a hug with promises of writing soon.

Everybody avoided referring to the painful realities Peter was facing, but Pauline whispered, "Keep your pecker up," in his ear and gave him a smacking kiss on the mouth and then bolted out of the door, followed by the ponderous Fran whose pregnant state had become more evident even in the two weeks Peter had been there.

All through breakfast, Peter's father had said little, but he smiled and nodded a lot. With the girls gone, Peter had expected a change, but Eduard just went on smiling and saying nothing.

"Anything wrong, Dad?" Peter had asked, with the girls still there. "Your good mood is getting to me."

Eduard laughed, the deep sonorous laugh of bygone days.

"I'm happy seeing the harmony back in the family, that's all," he said.

"When my marriage is breaking up and I'm taking a plunge in the dark and I don't know where I'll be living next month? Or where the heck the money will be coming from?"

"Maybe that adds up to more harmony for you."

Peter was tired of listening to all that prattle. Tired of telling others his story. And ashamed of having revealed his dreams and frustrations to so many people.

It was time for action. Maybe Laura was right. Maybe he was, in the final analysis, a man of action. A doer.

He looked at his father. *Maybe that adds up to more harmony for you.* Astounding words. But he was not going to respond. He had enough of words.

He still had most of the day ahead of him before catching an evening flight to Chicago.

Laura's last words were pursuing him. More words! How could he free himself from their tyranny? He felt a powerful urge to poke a hole in Laura's presumptuous opinions. *Banking is a festering pit of greed... Art that's not engagé is worthless... Being an observer is a waste of time.* Worst of all, she had called him a coward! He couldn't leave that unchallenged. He'd have to straighten her out.

He lied to his parents that he had meetings at the bank and left the house. "I'll say goodbye later," he said, pointing at his bags in the hall. "I'll pick them up on the way to the airport."

He didn't call Laura. He took a taxi straight to her house. She was home and buzzed him in.

"Well, if it isn't Mr. Banker himself," she said mockingly, as she opened the door. "Did you forget your umbrella or something?" She was wearing the same jeans as the night before, but her T-shirt was a different one, a plain salmon pink with one word printed on it in large purple letters: DARE!

"I forgot nothing, except to respond to your calling me a coward." He stepped through the door, which she closed softly behind him.

"Well, aren't you?" said Laura. "My definition of a coward is a person who evades the consequences of his own actions."

"There are other definitions I can think of. But I'm not here to trade linguistic niceties, I'm here..." said Peter. He had prepared himself for this speech, and wanted to keep the momentum going, "I'm here to tell you that your view of me is wrong." Laura motioned him to sit down, but he waved the offer away.

"I stand behind the decisions I've taken, and have every intention of becoming a first-rate photographer. Whether my style or subject matter will turn out to fit your norms is of no concern to me. You have no right to call me a coward just because I don't buy your analysis or your values."

"Have you finished?" Laura asked.

"No," said Peter. "There's more."

"Will it wait for the coffee? It should be just about ready."

"Yes, of course." He was being too nice again. "Black, please. No sugar."
*Augh!*

Laura disappeared into the kitchen, and returned with two elegant porcelain cups of coffee. The cups were set on saucers.

"I detest mugs," Laura said. "They remind me of sweaty summer camps and building sites." Peter thought of the stained mugs in the portable cabins at Clara's Chicago construction sites. Clara, too, hated mugs.

"So?" Laura was asking. She sat down and started sipping her coffee.

"The other thing is…" he said, still standing. He moved closer, and now stood squarely before her, legs parted, feet firmly on the floor. He hadn't touched his coffee.

"Yes?" said Laura.

"I did feel attracted to you from the first moment we met, but I didn't come here yesterday with the purpose of seducing you. And I certainly don't consider you an easy lay. I want you to know that."

Laura crossed her legs and smiled self-consciously. For the first time it struck Peter how *neat* she was, how tidy and clean for an artist. She put her coffee down.

"Well, thank you. And what about all those things you called me? Ruthless, intolerant, manipulative, what about that?"

"That stands. I'm not here to change my opinion of you."

Laura nodded. "You think I'll do anything to get what I want?"

"I believe so, yes. Anything." Calling a spade a spade somehow made the spade more dangerous. He knew he should leave her now. After the coffee. Which he still hadn't touched.

Laura rose to her feet. She was half a head shorter than Peter, but this didn't deter her from looking him straight in the eye, chin atilt.

"And that prospect doesn't frighten you?" she asked.

"I think I can handle the fear. In fact, I notice that I'm relishing it," he

187

said, with a faint smile.

"You're not afraid *I* might seduce *you* and have you in my power?"

"I'd pit my strength against yours, and make it an even deal."

"But that wouldn't achieve my purpose, would it?" Laura said this casually, looking away.

"Maybe not. Unless your purpose was simply to seduce me."

"Why would I want to do that?"

"For the sheer pleasure of it. For the achievement."

She met his eyes head-on now. "You have a high opinion of yourself, don't you?"

"No, I'm simply offering a hypothetical proposition. And let me add that I would rate *my* successful seduction of *you* also something of an achievement, because I know you're not turned on by mere physical looks."

Laura laughed. "You're so right. If I was, you wouldn't make the grade, would you? With that pale body."

"Well, then on that score at least we are alike. For me, too, sexual attraction centers around the mind. Your physical attractiveness is an unexpected bonus."

Laura's reaction to this double compliment was to take Peter's face in her hands and cover his mouth with a careful kiss, and then another, lingering one. He kissed her back, in equal measure. Their pulses quickened. She stepped back and looked at him.

"It could work," she said with contrived sangfroid.

"Yes," he agreed, matching her self-control. "We are in equilibrium."

"In equal states of readiness, I'd call it," she said, up close again, her hand feeling his arousal. She sought his ears with her lips. "You know," she whispered, "I'm switching off my brain. I just want to slide into it with all the barriers down."

They knelt on the floor, facing each other, all lips and tongues and fingers, exploring. The groping was both tender and lustful, but the bed was where they finally copulated, a ritual of primordial gravity, a sacrifice as much as an exhilarating, life-giving act. Peter knew in his bones and in the root of his manhood that this was different from all the sex he had known before. The sex he had experienced was either chaste marital lovemaking, with Clara, or plain fucking, with others. Clara never used that word, fucking, which she found vulgar and demeaning, redolent of secret affairs and quick animal couplings. You made love with your wife; you fucked your mistress or a whore.

But what they were doing here was neither. This coupling was in a class of its own, highly charged and sensual yet considerate, and free from pretence and formality. It happened outside the confines of morality or exploitation, in the hot sexual center of the perfect present. These thoughts came to him without pattern, in wisps, as they lifted each other ever higher to the peak of their joint ecstasy.

Afterwards, on her double bed, she said, "Who seduced who?"

"*Whom*." He smiled. "I think it was a classic example of the perfect crime: no clues and no suspects."

"And no motive."

"No motive. Therefore no offense. Case dismissed."

She cuddled up to him and became wistful. "I didn't believe this was possible. I thought there always had to be a motive. Or a price to pay."

"You must have been badly betrayed. Or mistreated."

"It's not that. Although yes, I have. Both. But the point is, lovers' sex always has such strings attached. You always get a bill presented, unless you're the one presenting it. It's never unselfish." She lifted her eyes to his, as if expecting a denial.

But she had made Peter thoughtful. "Perhaps that's because of the ancient expectations surrounding love and courtship. Expectations of marriage and offspring. And property. If we can let go of the expectation of marriage…"

"And of financial rewards, or some other *motive*…"

"…then maybe we can have sex for the sheer beauty and pleasure of it."

Laura sighed. "For the sheer beauty and pleasure of it. That's how it should be, always. But can it be, really?"

"I don't see why not."

"Because you've left something out. Something vital. The emotions. Good sex is always linked to emotions. They mess everything up. Afterwards."

"Not if you let them run their course. And if you are open to each other,

189

you know, non-judgmental…"

Laura fell silent. Peter thought she had dropped off. She hadn't. She spoke to him softly. "Why don't you move to Amsterdam, Peter? You could do your work from here. We could do things together."

Peter shook her off abruptly.

"What's this I hear? A new creed adopted and betrayed all in the span of, what, ten whole minutes? So you had a motive after all!"

She looked shocked at his reaction. "It isn't that simple," she said. "And I did warn you."

"Oh, no, Laura. This isn't fair. We went into this together. Without conditions or expectations. *In equal states of readiness,* remember? Now you're trying to…I don't know what. I won't have any part of it!"

"Hush, I'm just teasing," she whispered as she clung to him. "It's a girl's way of saying that she liked what you did to her."

"It sounds ominous to me," he said, but he felt touched by her soft smile that to him had a tinge of sadness about it, and he took her in his arms again.

She looked up at him and met his eyes. "Don't worry, I may be an old cynic, but I'm not the ogre I made you think I was. I promise to leave you alone. But that's the only promise I make."

"So, I'm still on your hit list? Or have you turned your back on all that now, too?"

"Oh, no, that's unchanged. Except you're now just a class enemy."

"Is that better or worse?" He kissed both her nipples.

"Much better. I can sleep with the enemy. Anytime."

# Part Five

*New York 1980*

In the Eyes of the Son

# Chapter 26

From his loft window on the fourth floor of a former garment factory on Greene Street, Peter looked out at the fire escapes across the street through the slanting ironwork of his own, hoisted-up fire escape—the multiple Z-pattern that characterized many of the century-old buildings in this part of town.

He liked the design: the functional married to the aesthetic, or rather, the functional had become the aesthetic. The cast-iron contraptions, grafted onto the façade of each building like unforgivable afterthoughts, over time had learned to live in harmony with the masonry and windows behind it, which in turn had learned to accept these unsightly barnacles. Now, Peter thought, the fire escapes *defined* these buildings.

The loft was basic, large and functional. It was a rental, but he had been able to secure a ten-year lease, and the landlord had agreed to the "leasehold improvements" on condition that Peter would leave them in place when the lease was up, or if he cancelled it, which he was permitted to do at any time with three months' notice. He had divided the loft into two parts: the rear for living, the front for working. The working part was one large space, but where it abutted the living quarters, he had built a darkroom across a third of the loft's width. Another third was taken up by a file and stockroom.

On the whole, his new home had served him well since he moved in, over two years earlier. The decision to move to New York had come a few months after he rented a small furnished apartment in Chicago, right after his return from Holland. A temporary move, to give him time to think matters through.

It didn't take long for him to conclude that staying in the same city as

Clara and the bank was a bad idea. He kept running into people who wanted to know what happened and what he was up to. What's more, Clara was building a new life for herself. Peter was convinced there was no other man in the picture, but she was a rising factor in Chicago society and in the business and banking community, where her modest success with property development had given her a claim to independent status, increasingly unrelated to her father's.

And then there was the overwhelming importance of New York as the center of the arts in the eastern United States. If he was serious about making his mark in photography, he simply had to be in New York. No other city came close.

What had worried him was Diedrich. He feared becoming alienated from him, and turning him into an emotionally deprived child. Clara had told him how exciting Diedrich found the alternate weekends he spent with his father in Chicago. Peter took him to the museums and they rode the elevators to the top of the Sears Tower and the John Hancock Tower. Sometimes they just stayed home with books or games or to watch baseball on T.V. Peter had never cared much for the game, but Diedrich's enthusiasm infected him. He was amazed how much Diedrich knew about the rules and the players' names, and he was happy to let himself be educated by his son.

When Peter asked Diedrich one day how he would like to see the Yankees play in New York, he practically dropped his cola.

"Oh, Dad, that's great! To New York! To see the Yankees! Wow! When are we going?"

From then on, it was easy. Far from being sad that his father was relocating to New York, Diedrich was all for it. "So I can visit him, and he can take me to the Yankees! And I want to go to the top of the Empire State Building, and ride the ferries around Manhattan. When's he moving?"

It had worked out well. Diedrich flew over once a month, escorted to and from the plane by airline staff to connect with the sending and receiving parents at each end. Father and son ended up spending even more "quality time" together this way than they did in Chicago.

But Peter wasn't kidding himself. It wasn't the same as living together as a family. He missed Clara and Diedrich at the oddest times, like when facing breakfast alone, or when buying his groceries and always choosing small portions, or when cleaning his teeth at bedtime and hearing the sound of brushing lose itself in the loft's desolate emptiness. Sometimes he thought of his early days in Singapore, his first experience of loneliness, though he was better able to cope with it now that there was a clear and compelling motive for living alone.

No, he didn't feel that his move to New York had been a mistake. When he was asked his opinion of life in the city, he had a ready answer: "I love the neighborhoods, the quirky individualism, the vibrant cultural life. I hate the violence and homelessness, the filth in the poor streets, the taxis' broken springs. On balance, it's an experience everybody should have in their lives."

This assessment invariably raised eyebrows.

"But the contrasts between rich and poor, don't they bother you?" asked an artist friend, visiting from Amsterdam. "And the ostentation, the unsavory flaunting of wealth, you find that acceptable?"

"Well, actually, no to both questions. But you can't have the good without the bad. It's a mixed package, dripping both blood and honey. It's life in a nutshell, a *big* nutshell, big enough to fit every type of human ego, every ideology, every creed and color, every…but I'm blathering."

Actually, he didn't like discussing New York with outsiders. They all had their views, usually derogatory, based on nothing but hearsay or fleeting impressions. It was different with New Yorkers. They, too, complained a lot, but that was part of the ritual. It took some of the stress out of living here if you could rave and rant about what a lousy city it was, and how it was going to the dogs.

Once, some years back when he was still working in the bank and visiting New York on business, Peter had ridden through a wet mid-Manhattan in the car of a customer who had insisted on driving him back to his hotel. He was a Jew in his mid-fifties whose parents had brought him from Germany in the late nineteen-thirties. He was driving a battleship of an old Buick, trying to steer it around the potholes of 6th Avenue without scraping the pavement. The long car heaved and pitched, and Peter imagined sparks flying from the exhaust pipe each time it hit a rough patch. It was a hazardous journey, with the driver narrowly missing pedestrians dashing across intersections against the lights, and trying to keep his windscreen clean in the dirty, steaming rain. He was under visible stress, and swore a lot, not only to himself, but at people on the street. He kept rolling his window down to hurl invectives at hapless passersby and rival drivers.

"A hard city to live in, isn't it?" Peter remarked, when they had reached a quieter stretch.

"I tell you something," the man replied. "New York City is a dirty, corrupt, demented, fucked up place. It's mean and violent and the people are all crazy. It's hell on earth!" A pause. "But I love it. Don't ask me why. I just love the goddamn city! I wouldn't want to live anywhere else!"

Peter was beginning to feel like the man in the Buick. Despite its horrors, New York had become a kind of amorphous friend to him, a multi-headed buddy he could rely on for a good time, and a sympathetic ear and kick in the ass when he needed one. He found his buddy everywhere, in the shops around the corner, among people walking their dogs or sipping espresso in a West Broadway café, among visitors to the downtown museums and on the Staten Island Ferry.

Sometimes his buddy took on a more tangible form, when he talked to a stranger, or they to him, usually no more than a few words, but occasionally getting acquainted and exchanging names. In his solitary existence, he never felt excluded. In this way, he had made a few friends with whom he would have a drink or a cup of coffee.

He had also made friends with his upstairs neighbors, Carlo and Tomoko Pavera. Carlo, a first generation Italian-American, was a graphic artist specializing in covers for a number of well-known magazines, and his wife, half Japanese, half Irish-American, a set dresser for off-Broadway theaters. They were a typical downtown New York couple, hard-working and highly motivated and well-paid for what they did, but with only the most basic medical insurance and without any certainty of continued employment. They had two children and juggled their planners to match the kids' school rosters. When they went out in the evening, or when their schedules conflicted, they hired a baby sitter, a luxury that could add up to a quarter of their net monthly incomes.

Carlo said they considered Peter an ideal friend, because he was alone, worked at home, and, like them, was a freelance professional. They enjoyed his stories of the places he had lived and worked. And his son's age was just right, midway between their children's. From the very first time Peter met them, on the landing, they had opened their house to him. They helped each other out when necessary, but respected each other's privacy.

The best thing about New York was that people accepted you without first checking your credentials. They seemed to proceed from the principle that you were okay until proven otherwise. Not so in Europe. There you had to establish your reputation first, before you were let through the front door.

His true inspiration was his work. The start had been slow. He had to re-learn all the routines. For a few weeks, he had consulted a freelance darkroom technician by the name of Gary to bring him up to speed on that side of the profession.

The picture-taking he did alone. He traveled the length and breadth of New York City in search of images. One thing that bothered him about photographing people was the innate *intrusiveness* of taking pictures. He tried different techniques to lessen the problem: telephoto lenses, hidden vantage points, or pretending to shoot in a different direction, then briefly pointing the camera at the real object while clicking the shutter. None of this was satisfactory. He realized that he couldn't avoid intrusion if he wanted to do top-notch "people photography," and that's what he had decided he wanted to do at this stage.

He often thought of Laura. He wished she were nearer, but felt grateful she wasn't. She would have driven him crazy. He needed all his wits to make a success of what he had started. And he doubted if their thrillingly brief affair in Amsterdam could have been stretched into a satisfying relationship.

Besides his old Leica, he also used a technically far more advanced Nikon-F, but because it was a single-lens reflex, its response was slower, as the mechanism had to allow for the mirror to swing out of the way between the clicking of the shutter and the exposure. This made it less suitable for candid shots, for which he continued to use the Leica.

He learned that in supposedly candid photography there was, in fact, a lot of posturing going on. Some people turned into instant actors when they knew they were being watched. The homeless and the down-and-out in the Bronx and the Bowery sometimes became aggressive or covered their faces when a camera was pointed at them. But even among them there were the self-conscious poseurs.

At first, Peter had turned away whenever that happened, a posed picture being beneath his standards. But when he reflected that the *situation* he had found these people in had not changed as a result of his intrusion, and that the brief moment of recognition and attention he offered perhaps restored to them a modicum of self-respect, he changed his mind.

Once he had crossed this line, his work became easier. While he seldom asked their permission beforehand, his demeanor suggested a considerate and flexible attitude, which seldom triggered an aggressive response.

His photo archive had been expanding steadily. He did his own developing and printing and regularly sent the prints around to photo agencies and galleries, and to the small number of surviving photo magazines. But after more than a year, he had made only a few isolated sales, mainly of shots he had taken of the massive anti-nuclear demonstrations in New York in September '79, following the Three Mile Island disaster, when two hundred thousand people had marched and Jane Fonda was among the speakers. His savings were running out, and he knew he wouldn't be able to continue without adequate income for much longer.

# Chapter 27

Peter had moved to New York in 1978. A year and a half after his arrival he had his breakthrough. A downtown photo gallery on his list invited Peter for a meeting to discuss the possibility of a show.

After seeing more of his work, they decided to mount a small solo exhibition for him. They proposed early September, leaving him about five months to prepare for the show. Peter wasn't entirely happy with the date—at the tail end of the summer holidays—but he accepted, excited about the opportunity.

The gallery went along with Peter's suggestion for the show's title, "White Poverty in Black New York." He already had some material dealing with this theme, and the hot season was a good time to gather more. New York's simmering racial tensions tended to come to a boil during the sweltering summers.

The gallery owner, Bernard Devine, liked the provocative title which reflected some of the photos Peter had sent him. One was a shot of two old, white bag ladies chatting on a broken bench in a Harlem playground, surrounded by a whirl of running and frolicking black kids. Another was a profile of a young blonde woman, decent middle-class looking, crouched on a street corner, her hand held up to receive a coin from the outstretched arm of a black woman. One of the most compelling shots was that of a light-skinned teenage boy sitting on the stoop of a tenement building, sneakered feet propped up against a low wall, drooping head propped up by a clenched fist, the elbow supported by his hipbone. He seemed deeply troubled. His forehead was furrowed, and his fleshy mouth drawn in a downward arch that betrayed desperation rather than sorrow. Behind him was the blur of a black girl's arm and laughing face, a girl at play, running past him, oblivious to his despair.

Peter felt these images confirmed what the newspapers had been reporting: that poverty in New York was not confined to blacks and Hispanics, with poverty among whites rising and now constituting almost ten percent. Peter's images also showed that blacks could be as generous as whites and that loneliness and the loss of hope was not the province of any one race. He wondered how he could improve on these shots, and what Bernard meant when he urged Peter to add a few more "really shocking ones."

The following afternoon he loaded a fast black-and-white film into his Leica and hit the streets to see what he could come up with. He was wearing jeans and a navy sweater. It was a partly cloudy day, and although it was already April, it looked quite cold. He had only a couple of hours of good light left. He'd dug up his red woollen ski cap and pulled it over his ears. His mirrored, unshaven reflection made him grin. He looked the part of a harmless street bum.

He took the 5th Avenue Express to Harlem, and started walking. As usual, the street crowd was a motley one. Shopkeepers and housewives and other upright citizens going about their business. Old and crippled and lonely-looking people inching along to nowhere in particular. Crazies of every description and skin color filling the gaps in the neighborhood with their troubled presence, relying on its tolerance and understanding.

Peter stepped into this multitude self-consciously, wondering how he could best make himself inconspicuous. He tried standing aside, half-hidden behind a tree, camera in hand. But this attracted attention and hostile glances. He tried stepping gingerly, heel-to-toe, along the edge of the sidewalk, like someone belonging and slightly deranged. This caused less passing suspicion, but the balancing complicated his handling of the camera. He switched to a third technique: staring mindlessly ahead while smiling spasmodically and advancing very slowly in the middle of the sidewalk. This worked much better. Passersby hardly took notice of him as they parted into two streams.

He began pointing his Leica, the aperture closed down to 22, which gave him ample depth-of-field. The 400 ASA film allowed him to use a relatively fast shutter speed of 1/125th second. This way he was prepared for most situations, and there was no need for constantly checking the settings.

As he continued his slow walk, he pretended to be taking pictures left and right, punctuating each shot with a wide, inane grin. This attracted some attention, but it seemed everybody regarded him a harmless loony. Soon, he started taking real shots of people. *Click*—smile, *click*—smile, he went, aiming casually as he pressed the shutter.

He turned into a side street and was confronted by a bevy of black nurses wearing white caps and gray habits, sisters from a Catholic hospital evidently. With them was a small Caucasian girl of perhaps seven or eight with dirty blonde hair, dirty skin and a bloodied nose. Her faded green flannel dress was torn, and her shoelaces were trailing. She was whimpering, her narrow shoulders shaking pitifully. It seemed the sisters had just happened upon the girl moments earlier, and were trying to comfort or help her. Peter had already taken two shots of the group by the time he came face to face with them, and they split ranks to get around him.

"What happened, sister?" Peter asked one of the nuns just as she was passing him. "Was she beaten?" The sister seemed surprised at the question and smiled shyly.

"Oh, we don't know, really," she answered. "Do we, Sister Stephanie?"

The older nun addressed as Sister Stephanie peered at him from behind her spectacles. "Well, no, not really. Unless our little friend here is now able to tell us."

They had all stopped in the middle of the street, and Sister Stephanie kneeled in front of the girl. "This nice man wants to know what happened. What shall we tell him?"

Peter kneeled too. "Did someone hit you?" he asked. "Or did you fall?" The girl was still sobbing, as she looked anxiously at Sister Stephanie, and at Peter and back again.

"Did someone hit you?" asked the sister.

The girl nodded, tearfully. "He always…hits me…when I'm bad."

"Who?" asked Peter. "Who hits you?" The girl didn't answer. She looked

201

pleadingly at Sister Stephanie, who said, "It's all right. We'll see what we can do for you." She rose and nodded at Peter. "Thank you for your interest. Did you get a good picture?"

Peter smiled awkwardly, and made a deprecating gesture. "Oh, it's nothing... I'm sorry about the girl. If there's anything..."

"Thank you," said Sister Stephanie as she took hold of the girl's little hand. "But I think we can take care of the matter. Can't we, Sister Amanda?" The two nuns nodded at him as the group moved on and turned the corner.

Peter knew that the scene he had captured on film was spot-on, but he felt upset by the little girl's plight. He reminded himself not to get involved each time he observed a touching scene, or he might forget to press the shutter. *Again.*

He walked on, resuming his "dopey act." It surprised him how easily he could switch from one role to another. He laughed. If his Chicago colleagues could see him now! He, Peter van Doorn, *ex*-banking executive, *ex*-husband of *ex*-heiress Clara Addams, scouring the streets of Harlem, tilting his camera at anything that caught his irises. They would surely think he'd gone over the brink. The joke was on them, he thought. A little wave of sadness engulfed him as he continued pointing his Leica, *click* and smile to the left, *click* and smile to the right. It was the absence of someone to share this joke with, *click*, for it *was* a joke, wasn't it? *Click* and smile.

It was beginning to get dark, but he carried on. He caught sight of two black men, quarrelling in front of a kind of boarding house, a crowded, low-rent apartment building. It looked like a turn-of-the-century townhouse, double width, with a stoop in front, and attractive architectural details around the windows and along the roof line. It must have been a stately burgher's mansion once, but now it looked run-down and shabby. It was full of people, human movement filling almost every window. Most of the windows were already lit up. The building itself seemed alive, pulsating and breathing with the multiplicity of sentient life oozing out of its every aperture, like a giant toy house with animated dolls inside.

The two men were shouting and gesturing emphatically. One moment they seemed ready to hit each other's faces, the next they were pulling back, shaking their heads at the other's stupidity. Peter kept pressing the shutter. He knew the scene didn't exactly fit his theme, but he liked the shots and thought he could use them somehow.

Then he noticed the large trash can on the curb, piled high with rubbish. On it someone had daubed, in crude white paint, the words WHITE TRASH and an arrow pointing downward. *Unbelievable*, thought Peter, and forgetting all about his loony pretence, he took a few more shots of the fighting scene, with the trash in the foreground. He positively hummed with satisfaction as he packed up his camera and headed for home.

Back in the loft, he lost no time developing the day's catch. One of the shots of the black sisters with the crying child was sensational: the child glancing up at Sister Stephanie, a gleam in the corner of one eye accentuating the poignancy of her expression of hope and fear. A heart-rending image. And thematically, it was right on target. Peter thought they could use this image for the poster. If they're going to *do* a poster.

The next few months, he frequently returned to Harlem and other racially complex parts of the city.

Slowly, the shape of the exhibition began to emerge. Bernard Devine had wall space for forty standard-framed prints, single file. Partial double hanging would increase that number. The standard frames were sixteen by twenty-four inches though larger and smaller frames could also be mixed in.

Early in July he called Gary, the darkroom technician. "I wonder if you could come over and give me a hand. I've got to do a large number of prints for an exhibition. Yeah, that's right, at the Magazine Gallery. You know it? In September. Great! Thursday is fine, at ten."

They worked together for five days. When Peter said he couldn't afford to keep him any longer, Gary offered another week free of charge, and that proved enough. Peter invited Bernard to the loft to show him his work. He made sure Gary was there too, to impress Bernard that he had an assistant.

Bernard seemed pleased with what he saw. He loved the Harlem shots of the nurses and the girl, and some of the shots from a Queens mixed-race neighborhood. But what intrigued him most were the shots of the two fighting men in front of the tenement apartment house and the rubbish bin with the

"WHITE TRASH" message, only two of which Peter had enlarged to exhibition size.

"Good stuff," Bernard commented. He wanted to see all of the dozen or so shots taken there. When Peter showed him his smaller prints, he noticed that Bernard was paying more attention to the building in the background than to the two men.

He asked for a magnifying glass. "There's something…" he muttered. Methodically, he peered at each print. "There!" he shouted. "In the corner there, that window. Look for yourself. A black guy hitting a woman. A white woman. Right there!"

Peter took the magnifying glass. The window indeed framed a burly dark male attacking a crouching Caucasian woman with what looked like a rolled-up umbrella.

"Can you blow that up, that corner?" Bernard asked.

Gary set to work on it. Peter and Bernard looked on as the image materialized in the bath. It was gritty and not in sharp focus, like a still from a security camera enlarged as court room evidence. But it unquestionably showed a man beating a woman.

"It reminds me of the long shots they took of those terrorists at the Munich Olympic massacre," Peter said.

"Right," exclaimed Bernard, "or the shot from *Blow Up*. Remember that great movie?"

"You think we should include it?" Peter asked.

Bernard looked at him incredulously. "*Of course* we include it. It'll make the show!" When Peter remained silent, he added, "You gotta problem with that?"

"It might prove, uh, too controversial," said Peter. Gary nodded in agreement. "It may trigger protests."

"So?" Bernard said aggressively. "Do we give a shit? Let them protest all they want. It'll be very good for the publicity. And you took it straight from life, right? A scene from everyday New York, right? It's not made up."

"No, but it may not be what it seems to be. It may be just a bit of play-acting or something. Or some harmless domestic quarrel."

"Hey, look again," said Bernard. "Does that look like play-acting to you? See the man's expression? Well, we can't actually see his expression, but his *stance*. That's not the stance of a guy who's just *pretending* to hit someone. And what if it is? You've got enough shots of decent blacks being civil to needy whites to balance this one nasty scene. But this one will bring in the crowds."

"Well," said Peter, tentatively, "as long as we don't use it for the poster."

"Come on, Peter!" said Bernard, raising his voice a little. "What're you afraid of? Pickets from Harlem? A scathing review in the *Times?* Don't forget that *all* publicity is *good* publicity. *Of course* I'm using it for the poster. In fact, I've just decided I'll *do* a poster. 'Cause of this shot. Cheer up! It'll give you your fifteen minutes of fame!"

"I'm not interested in fifteen minutes of fame. I'm interested in building a lasting reputation for integrity. Of solid workmanship."

"Big words. Frankly, I dunno what they mean. Integrity? Workmanship? I'm interested in showing the public shots that hit home. That tell it like it is. Even if it hurts. *Especially* if it hurts."

Peter walked to the window and looked down into the street. On the opposite pavement a black, elderly vagrant was rummaging through a trash can. Another rag-picker, Hispanic by the looks of it, shouldered him out of the way. The man didn't even look up. He walked on, bent-backed, his eyes scanning the pavement for likely flotsam. On the corner, a young white woman in a miniskirt was smoking a cigarette, arms folded, slowly pivoting on her platform shoes, her long blonde hair streaming in the breeze. A dark-skinned, middle-aged man with a short beard, Puerto Rican or Cuban, perhaps, wearing a gray suit, stopped and accosted her briefly, then moved along. Further on, a hefty black man in overalls was unloading boxes from a truck and handing them to a sinewy Asian man who placed them on a pavement elevator. The black was smiling broadly, his forehead shone. The Asian, Vietnamese or Chinese, didn't smile. He shouted something. The black man stopped and listened for a moment, then turned to make an obscene gesture at the Asian, who was just then lowering himself on the elevator to the basement level.

Everywhere and all the time in New York the races were interacting, using and abusing each other. All groups were equally guilty of contemptuous and discriminating behavior—racial, social, personal. The difference was that the comfortable, educated people controlled their contempt, even turning it into something noble like tolerance and respect for different cultures. The untutored poor vented their feelings openly.

Racial difference wasn't the real problem—that was an inescapable fact. The real problem was poverty. It was poverty that bred crime and cruelty and exploitation, not the color of your skin. There was plenty of bad behavior going on among blacks and among whites, without the need to look for a cross-racial cause.

In the white-dominated United States it helped if your skin wasn't dark, but in Peter's opinion, it was ludicrous to maintain, as much of the black lobby and some white, bleeding heart liberals so often did, that it was the blacks in New York who did all the suffering. The objective of Peter's exhibition was simply to redress the balance somewhat, to show that no race had a monopoly on poverty and suffering and abuse.

"Okay," said Peter as he rejoined Bernard and Gary, "I agree. We'll use this shot for the poster, but on one condition: we add a subtitle. Something to emphasize that we're not implying a racial slur."

"How about 'A Balanced View'?" said Gary.

"Yeah," said Bernard. "That sorta thing. But stronger. Something like, 'The Other Face of Deprivation'."

"And hope the typesetters don't misspell it 'depravity'," Gary said. They laughed.

"Mmm," said Peter, "'White Poverty in Black New York—The Other Face of Deprivation'." He repeated the word, "Deprivation." His father had once used that word against him, but he quickly silenced the association as irrelevant. "I like that," he said instead. "And at a stroke we've snuck in a politically correct term for poverty. This should silence at least some finicky critics."

"Don't get your hopes up," said Bernard. "If it isn't a P.C. pervert or screaming fundamentalist trying to sour your life, it's a fucking gay activist or some black rights fanatic of the old school." Peter reflexively leaned away from him and the harsh words. But Bernard continued. "This is New York, and New York is full to bursting with raving maniacs all waiting to remind you that you've just kicked them in their particular set of balls."

Peter looked worried. "And you find that acceptable?"

"No. But have we got a choice? It's a fact of life. I'm used to it. Anyway, maybe we're lucky."

"Maybe we should forget about the poster," Peter ventured.

"Listen, my friend," Bernard said, poking a finger at Peter's chest. "It's either a poster, *this* poster, or no show. Make up your mind. What's it gonna be?"

"Okay, sorry. It's that, um, I'm not yet used to New York realities."

"You've caught some of New York's *realities* on film very competently! Now stand behind your work. Believe me, it's gonna be a great show."

In the Eyes of the Son

# Chapter 28

Ten days later, Peter had a surprise visitor. André de Montigny, his friend from those long-ago Singapore days, was in town and phoned. They hadn't seen each other in twenty years, though they'd managed to stay in touch through Christmas cards.

From a distance, Peter had followed André's successive moves from Singapore to Manila and finally back to England where he had been now for more than three years as a freelance writer and teacher of English to foreigners. He lived in Battersea, on London's south side, in what he had described as "a peculiar Victorian ground-floor flat that's too big for a studio and too small for a dream."

"I thought I'd chance it," André said as he came in, lightweight tan jacket dangling from a crooked finger, taking off his Panama hat. He kissed Peter on the cheek. "I had to be in New York anyway to see my agent, to prove that I actually exist."

"You don't write for *The New Yorker* anymore? I've been looking for your articles."

"Only when I've something to say. Which is rare these days. No, I'm knee-deep in writing fiction. The great make-believe! So much more satisfying. The perfect vehicle for self-adulation. Don't you agree?"

They were standing in the middle of the room. André was still carrying his jacket and holding his hat and leather-trimmed rattan briefcase. Peter took them from him and admired the case.

"It's colonial retro chic," said André. "Knocks 'em dead in publishing land! Oh, I'll keep that." He donned his jacket, coughing briefly. "You've created a polar zone here!"

"Too cold? I can turn down the airco."

"No, no, it's lovely after that warm soup out there. And you used to say that Singapore was too hot for you!" He plopped down in a chair. "But tell me about yourself. How absolutely exciting! Free at last!"

"You were the one that showed me the way," Peter said.

"I didn't. Did I?"

"You don't owe the world a thing, you told me, but you must be true to yourself. That's what you said."

"Did I really? What an irresponsible thing to advise anyone. I'm so sorry." He smiled mischievously.

"Later, I found out you pinched it from *Hamlet*," Peter said. "The idea, anyway."

André laughed. "It's a cheap universal truth."

Peter showed his friend around. But André seemed less interested in the loft's physical dimensions than in Peter's. "You look slim and handsome, I must say. Do you work out? You know, little push-ups and things?"

"Hardly. But I do *walk* a lot, for my work."

"How absolutely wonderful to hear you say those words: *for my work* —and meaning photography and not banking. I can't tell you how happy it makes me that you've cut the umbilical cord with that soul-destroying world of finance. Was it very painful?"

"Not really. And I've never looked back," said Peter. He realized it was the first time he had said this, to anyone. It was the truth. "What did hurt was..." but he couldn't complete the sentence.

André observed a considerate silence. At length, he said, "Your wife and son. Of course. How sad. How absolutely dreadful. But...you don't mind my saying this?"

"What?"

"It was absolutely necessary. Women can be a terrible drag on one's creativity."

Peter didn't answer. "What would you like to drink?" he asked.

"A beer. Because this is New York. I find it's the only thing to drink in New York in summer. Don't you agree?"

Peter returned with two cold tins of beer and two tall glasses and sat down.

André put a hand on his arm. "I am sorry. How indelicate of me. You will forgive me?" He had become more openly gay, less restrained than Peter remembered him. It made him feel vaguely uncomfortable.

"Of course, and you're quite right. It's good to be alone. I seem to be getting inspiration from the experience of loneliness."

"The experience of loneliness... That could be poetic if it weren't so intellectual. Don't you ever just let go?"

"I did once. But I doubt if it will be repeated. It's not really in my character, I suppose. I'm too leery of the consequences. Of the price to pay."

"Nonsense!" André exclaimed. "That's your Calvinist roots acting up. I'm sure in New York you can have it all, like London. Everybody does. There's no social control, no morality police. You can do what you like and get away with it. It's *abstention* that carries the price. The stigma."

"I wasn't referring to the wagging tongues. I was thinking of what my father calls inner harmony. I try to avoid what I might regret later."

"Oh, my, what a dull life you must have! It wouldn't make any difference in *my* life. I seldom regret anything. Except buying shoes that pinch."

"Metaphorically, that amounts to the same."

André laughed. "The difference being, of course, that your feet seem to be more sensitive than mine."

"Maybe. Yet you were the one that needed meditation to sort yourself out."

They continued talking over dinner under the overhanging plants of *Greene Street* restaurant, and again back in the loft.

"Do you have any news from Mrs. Vreeman?" Peter asked.

"Suzanne? Not recently. We did write each other after I'd moved to Manila. Poor Suzanne, she didn't have much luck with men. After you turned her down, she was quiet for a while. Then she turned to Volker. You know

Volker. He'd do anything to increase his self-esteem. He fucked her silly. It was what she needed. Then her husband got posted back to headquarters and she became the most proper, devoted, well-behaved banking matron you could imagine."

André's glibness bothered Peter. He changed the subject to photography, and showed him his pictures for the exhibition.

"Absolutely fab!" said André. "Though the theme seems rather incendiary to me."

"You think so? But it's a very New York subject."

"Oh, the media will love it. They'll come flocking, like bees to honey."

"Or flies to shit," said Peter morosely. "I'm prepared for the worst."

"Don't worry, they won't kill you. They won't torch the gallery. But you're right, you must expect some flak. Heaps of flak. How exciting!"

André yawned and complained that he had to get up early to catch a morning flight back to London.

Peter saw him to the street. They waited for a taxi. He wondered when he would see his friend again. André guessed his thoughts. "If you can manage a stopover in London on the way to Amsterdam. You do go back to Holland a lot, don't you?" he said without waiting for a reply, "Then I'll try to make it to New York every year or so."

"I can put you up."

"That would be lovely. I don't like those cheapy, mid-town hotels. They're so depressing."

Suddenly, the mournful expression Peter remembered from his Singapore days was back on André's face. Gone was the smooth, playful affectation, the polished self-satisfaction of the urbane aesthete. What Peter caught now was a glimpse of a solitary, cocooned soul about to return to its circumscribed existence between frugality and hope. The face of a life half-lived, half-endured, and wholly tentative.

A taxi pulled up. André embraced Peter with a surge of faked vitality. "You'll come and see me soon? You can stay with me, too, of course. If you don't mind the sofa. It's a Molteni, very comfortable. I know. I've slept on it. Done something on it, anyway."

He gave Peter a quick peck on the lips and got in. "Lex and 23rd," he told the driver, a fat Irishman with a green cap and a sideways sneer for the spectacle he had just witnessed, of two men kissing.

It would be a silent ride for André, all the way to the hotel, a ride marked by mutual disdain that was worse than racial.

# In the Eyes of the Son

# Chapter 29

Clara and Peter agreed to skip Diedrich's monthly visit to New York for August, because it was too hot and dirty and crawling with tourists, and Peter was too busy with his show. With Gary's help, he completed all the enlargements, and left them with the framers.

By the twentieth of August the posters were up. The blue-gray hulk of the attacking male and the provocative title in contrasting orange were well-pitched to catch the attention.

The posters were everywhere. On billboards, fences, walls of derelict buildings, in the subway. There were some behind SoHo windows, in cafés. Gary said he'd seen one in the Guggenheim and one in the downtown employment office.

The exhibition was listed in art magazines and some museum publications. The Sunday supplements would follow closer to the date of the opening, which was set for the first Saturday after Labor Day.

A week before the opening a letter of protest arrived at the gallery. It was from the NAACP and it condemned the "overtly racist theme" of the exhibition and demanded that it be canceled and the posters removed "forthwith." But the letter's tone was polite and a touch world-weary, and contained no sanctions for non-compliance.

Bernard replied with an equally polite note, thanking the association for their interest, and encouraging its members to view the exhibition to "convince yourselves that, far from being racist, the photographer has emphasized the universal nature of poverty, and highlighted several instances of generous and concerned behavior by blacks toward troubled white members of our population." No reply was received to his letter.

There were no further signs of trouble brewing. There were some calls, including one from *The Harlem Times*, asking for details of the exhibition. The photography editor of *The New York Times* wanted to know who this Peter van Doorn was. "A Dutch photographer who's recently moved to New York, the son of a well-known Dutch war photographer," was Bernard's answer.

"A foreign correspondent looking for trouble?"

"No, an art photographer," Bernard replied. "Just come and see."

He needn't have added this. They always came to the Magazine Gallery's openings, in droves, the journalists and press photographers and TV news editors. The gallery was famous for its press previews, because of the well-stocked bar and the excellent food that accompanied the booze. Bernard didn't believe in cheap bubbly and stale canapés for journalists. On press nights, he spent money on hard liquor and substantial snacks: cold salmon in aspic, roast chicken legs, a variety of sushi, and large cheese platters with sliced French bread. Such offerings invited serious grazing.

Bernard's largesse usually was rewarded with good press coverage. Not necessarily *favorable* reviews, of course—these were professionals with a reputation to lose. But his shows were reviewed in more publications and in more local TV art and entertainment programs than those of most other New York photo galleries. And the reviews translated into visitors and the visitors into sales. Photographs exhibited at The Magazine were always for sale even when the photographer was already dead. Rule of the house.

Actually, the booze and bites were not an extravagance but an investment, which Bernard normally managed to retrieve from the sales of the photographs—from the artist's share, that is. It was his policy to take fifty percent upfront from gross sales, and to deduct his expenses from the other fifty percent that was payable to the artist. If the sales fell short of the overhead, then the artist owed him the difference, to be settled in cash or kind —photographs, usually.

As a result, Bernard had an enviable collection of photographs by both

216

American and foreign photographers. Its overall value rose with each obituary. Obituaries were essential to the health of his collection. He saw to it that his newspaper friends did not neglect reporting on the death of photographers who had exhibited at his gallery.

Bernard had made all this clear to Peter, and obtained his agreement at the outset of their discussions. Peter recalled Bernard's specific words at the time. "You're an unknown quantity in this city. But I happen to like your work. So I'll take the risk. If we can do it my way." Doing it Bernard's way also meant that there were to be no other guests at the press preview than members of the press. Friends and family had to wait until the following day, the official opening for Bernard's mailing list of collectors and prospects, photographers and artists, professionals and businessmen. Anybody potentially useful. Including names contributed by the exhibiting artist.

They were waiting for the press people to arrive. Peter did a final check of the exhibition with Lunette Springer, the gallery manager. He had personally supervised the hanging, but Lunette's experience and good taste had helped him resolve questions of sequence and overall balance.

Peter realized that he didn't feel happy. Here he was, in the heart of New York, for his first professional exhibition, to be judged by the cream of U.S. photographic critics. Quite extraordinary, when you stopped to think about it, and inconceivable even a year ago. Yet all he could feel was alienation and dissatisfaction. What was he doing here all by himself, he wondered, without family or friends to share this precious moment, his moment of triumph? And *was* it a triumph? Over what? *Of* what? Of will over inertia? Inner harmony over…over what again? What exactly was he proving with his exhibition? Wasn't he simply making an exhibition of *himself*? Of his compulsive need to…to…

He felt faint and sat down on a chair. He asked for a glass of water. He felt hot. It was hot in the gallery.

"Is the airco working?" he asked Lunette.

"You want it cooler?"

"I'll just step out for a minute," he said.

The heat outside hit him like a wall. The air was stagnant. The foliage of the tree opposite was rustling, suggesting a breeze that he didn't feel. He crossed the street. The tarmac was soft and hot under his shoes and he skipped quickly to avoid getting stuck. Under the tree, he caught a whiff of moving air. He turned around, facing the gallery door, to keep an eye on arriving guests.

Then he noticed what looked like an approaching crowd of people. They came up from the left, from the direction of Washington Square. In the shimmering heat, it was hard to identify the individuals. It looked more like a vibration of semi-solids, floating eerily above the scorching asphalt. As it came nearer, the apparition revealed itself more clearly as human beings walking together, some of them carrying banners and signs on poles. It looked like a street demonstration, momentarily disfigured in the trembling, overheated air over the pavement.

The marchers were mostly wearing jeans and T-shirts, but some women wore long white cotton dresses. As they came nearer, Peter saw they were all black, and they clearly formed one group of perhaps thirty or more people, walking in silence.

The first guests arrived in two taxis. They cast a glance toward the demonstrators as they entered the gallery.

Peter could now read the slogans. "Stop white racial backlash!" and "Expose photo-racism!" and "Your lens lies—the facts don't!" Some of the press people, walking towards the marchers, stopped to talk to them. Flash bulbs popped. Then they too went in.

The demonstration came to a halt at the gallery door. There was a conference. Peter crossed the street and entered the gallery, greeting the marchers as he passed. He had to talk to Bernard and decide how to handle this situation.

"There he is!" said Bernard loudly. "We thought you'd joined the protest!"

"That'd be easier than confronting them," Peter joked, as he shook hands with the guests.

"But not nearly as much fun," said one of the journalists. "Were you planning a confrontation?"

"Not unless I'm forced to, no. But I wonder how they got wind of this?"

Laughter. "The city is plastered with posters," someone said. "They do seem to invite attention." More laughter.

Peter smiled indulgently. "I mean, how did the marchers know about the press preview?" He felt like a schoolboy having to explain a silly question.

"Oh," Bernard intervened, "didn't I tell you? They called a few days ago and Lunette gave them the details."

Peter was furious. Telling him now, in front of the assembled press, shaming him.

"Of course," he lied, "it slipped my mind." He glanced through the windows. The group seemed to be readying itself for something. Ignoring them seemed the best policy for now. Peter invited the journalists to view the exhibition, "before it gets too crowded." God, he felt clumsy. "You can see for yourself what all the fuss is about."

"...white backlash! Stop the white backlash!" The demonstration was getting louder and rougher. Each time the door opened, the shards of protest hit the small, swelling crowd of reporters. Peter finally managed to exchange a few words alone with Bernard. "You could've told me," he said, his tone biting.

Bernard shrugged his shoulders. "I thought I'd spare you the aggravation."

"You needn't have worried," he said in a clipped tone. "I think I know how to handle situations like this." He felt a surge of adrenaline and stood a little straighter.

"There's nothing to handle," said Bernard. "They'll stay outside. They'll want to avoid being charged with trespassing."

"Who's talking about trespassing?" Peter asked defiantly. He crossed the gallery from Bernard all the way to the door. The eyes of the press, now numbering over twenty, followed him. He opened the door with a flourish and faced the protesters. The chanting ceased.

"Ladies and gentlemen," Peter said in voice that carried right back into the gallery. "It's too hot to be standing in the sun like that. Why don't you come in for a cool drink and a first-hand look at the photographs? It may help you define the exact nature of your protest."

"Oh, an invitation!" cooed one of the men, wearing a woollen cap and a big smile.

"We got no intention comin' in," said a belligerent-looking woman with short-cropped hair. "We got no mind lookin' at no photographs. We jest want you to take them down!"

"Yeah," chimed an emaciated man with a shaved head and large, crazy-looking eyes. "We don't deal with white trash!"

"But the man is inviting us in, right, man?" said another man making a sweeping gesture.

"That's right. I'm inviting you in," said Peter as he stepped aside to encourage them to enter. "I am the photographer, and right behind me here is the gallery owner, Mr. Bernard Devine. We invite you to come and view the exhibition." He looked hard at Bernard as he said this, and Bernard flashed him a look back that signaled icy solidarity.

"Well," said a well-dressed young man in a light blue, striped baker's suit and tie. "In that case, we'll be happy to continue our protest inside!" He made a step forward and others followed. He clearly was the leader.

Peter raised his hand. "You misunderstand. The invitation is to view the exhibition. Not to carry on a protest demonstration." The man stepped back, and so did the others. "The choice is yours."

There was a brief conference between the leader and some of the demonstrators. Then he stepped forward again. "All right. We accept your terms. But if we don't like your show, we'll resume our demonstration right here on the street. We're not giving up our right to protest!"

Peter waved them in and they trooped past him. The press people made room for the marchers. The leader seemed to know some of them. Peter walked up to him. "I'd be happy to show you around, but you may want to view the pictures on your own."

"That's right," the leader said as he walked away without looking at Peter.

The marchers spread out over the gallery. After a few minutes, some of them began to talk to the reporters.

Bernard began to melt a bit. "You handled that well," he whispered in passing. "But you should've checked with me first."

"An eye for an eye," said Peter. "Besides, I'm paying for the booze." He was thoroughly enjoying himself, and he mixed with the reporters and talked to some of the marchers, who had started drifting toward the bar.

But the leader noticed and called them back. He gathered his flock around him, held a brief muffled conference and asked Bernard if he could make a statement.

"Sure can," said Bernard. He asked for everybody's attention. "Our guest has something on his mind."

"I want to make something clear to you," the leader said in a voice that reminded Peter of a preacher's. "We have come here today to protest an exhibition of photographs which, on the basis of its title, poster and advance publicity, can only be regarded as inflammatory and racist. We have now seen the full collection of photos, and our opinion remains unchanged. The fact that some of the images show black people being kind to white people in no way excuses the damaging effect of the show as a whole, and of some of the more outrageously offensive images in particular. As concerned black citizens of New York, we therefore reject this exhibition as a deliberate attempt to sow racial discord and distort the facts about poverty in New York. We demand that you dismantle the exhibition immediately. We will continue our street protest until you have done so." The others supported his demand with shouts and raised fists. They started to make for the door as Peter halted them.

"Wait," he said with a smile. "I'd like to exercise the right of reply. That is, if Mr. Devine lets me."

Bernard nodded. The marchers' leader crossed his arms in anticipation.

"I haven't lived in New York very long," Peter began. "Two years only. But long enough for me to admit to a real love for this city. What I love most about New York is that it allows people to do what they want, to express what's inside them. New Yorkers are not arrogant or stuffy or pretentious. They *include* you. They've included me, even though I'm a foreigner. Now

221

that's a major virtue. You won't find that in many places in the world. Another thing I love about New York is its fairness. You can get a fair deal and a fair hearing in this city, mostly."

"Fucking white shit!" somebody shouted. "Why do I have to listen to this shit?" It was the man with the wild eyes. The leader lifted his hand to silence the heckler.

"Okay," Peter resumed, "maybe I'm privileged. Maybe I don't have the family memories of hatred and discrimination that so many people in this city have to live with. But I think things have improved, and today you can get a fair hearing if you have a fair complaint.

"So when I started shooting pictures in the streets of New York, I felt carried along by these good things that I love about this city. And all the photographs you see here have been taken from that perspective. They have no intent to hurt. They are not politically motivated. As a foreigner, I don't have the vote, and I wouldn't know what party to vote for if I had!"

Scattered laughter greeted this remark. Someone shouted, "Then what're you doing here?"

Peter ignored it and continued. "The photographs are real images of the New York as I have encountered it. Fair, free, warm-hearted shots of New York life in all its exuberance and sadness and success and failure. And, yes, its violence, too. Black life. White life. No more, no less. Okay?" Indecisive mutterings.

"Now about that title," he continued. "It's true that I have a problem with one-sidedness. I think there has been an under emphasis of the plight of the white poor in this city, perhaps in this country. That's not your fault. You have your own interests to look after. But it's my good right to highlight some of that white poverty in the midst of black New York, just as it is *your* good right to point out black poverty among white America, as you have been doing so competently and sometimes effectively in the past. It's only fair, isn't it? Ask yourself this question: Would you tolerate any kind of protest against a photographer exhibiting shots of black deprivation in the midst of comfortable white neighborhoods? Would you?"

Peter stopped for effect. There was a murmur among the marchers, but no one took up the challenge.

"Of course you wouldn't. Because you wouldn't think it fair. You have an eloquent spokesman. If you disagree with anything I have said, I would welcome a rebuttal. Thank you."

Some members of the press applauded, and some of the marchers seemed ready to put their hands together, too, but they were awaiting a signal from their leader, who now stepped forward.

"We hear what you're saying. We're willing to accept your good intentions. But one serious complaint remains. You've done yourself and us a disservice by picking that provocative photograph for your poster. It sets the tone, and the tone ain't pretty. It's ugly. It's anti-black. And it's false."

Peter threw a glance at Bernard, but Bernard was studying his shoes.

"That photograph," said Peter "was taken by accident. It's a tiny corner of one of the other shots, actually discovered after development. But it's a real scene. Of New York today. And as such, it is as relevant as the other photos on display."

"You hear that, friends?" the leader said, addressing the marchers with studied indignation. "He has taken a tiny little corner of a photograph and blown it right up to poster size. And he took all that trouble because he'd been looking with a magnifying glass for *one* image of supposed black aggression to illustrate his preconceived notions about black behavior. I'd call that *selective racism*." Affirmative murmurs and derisive laughter from the protesters.

"It's normal photographic practice," said Peter, unfazed, bluffing. "Half the prints displayed here are from cropped negatives. Including those showing black generosity. The point is that none of the shots were staged. They reflect actual observed behavior. And they've got nothing at all to do with racism."

The press again broke into applause, and the solidarity of the marchers was clearly crumbling.

"Okay, okay," said their leader, smiling nervously. "I have a proposal. You allow us to quote what you just said in *The Harlem Times*, and we'll call off the protest. What d'ya say?"

"I have no problem with that," Peter said.

"Great!" said a young woman in dreadlocks who had come with the marchers. She stepped up to Peter and introduced herself. "I'm Carmen Roberts, reporter for *The Harlem Times*."

Suddenly, another woman broke away from the marchers and confronted Peter. "No, no!" she shouted. "You ain't sweet talking me! No, sir! Your lens is lying!" She was the one who had declared earlier that she had "no mind to look at no photographs."

Two or three of the marchers supported her with shouts of "yeah, yeah," while others tried to silence her.

"It's jest as mah sign sez, mister. You're the white backlash. You want nothin' but stir up trouble!" Efforts to calm her only encouraged her. "You're lying, mister! Your lens is a two-face. You tell half the story, the white man's half! You're not sweet talking me!"

Two of the other women took her by the arms and tried to escort her out of the gallery. This infuriated the thin young man with the glasses, and he joined the woman's shouts of protest.

"Liar! Blacks are still poor! Nothin' has changed! Death to defamation!"

Some of the men tried to calm him down. The man's shouts mingled with the woman's as they were being led away.

Peter thought the man was deranged, but he felt some sympathy for the woman. He thought her version of New York was just as valid as his and he said so to Carmen who was still standing next to him.

"You mean that?" Carmen said, astonished.

"I do. No single image can tell the whole story, can it? Not even a whole gallery full of images. The truth has more faces than we can name or recognize."

"I like that," she said. "But it's not an American way of looking at things. We like our truths black or white." They both laughed at her unintentional pun.

"I see them in shades of gray," Peter said.

"That's because of the Dutch climate?" she asked.

Peter laughed. "I think more because Holland is a small, crowded country. We can't afford to be confrontational."

"This show is pretty confrontational though," she said. "What's your next project? Race-based again?" She took a small voice recorder from her handbag. "You mind?" Peter pretended he didn't.

"Several projects," he lied. "A series on single parenting, you know, divorced children."

"Divorced children! That's a potent title. Black and white?"

"Color, this time. It's a better medium, I think, when you want to emphasize the positive." He was making all this up.

Carmen smiled. "What I meant was, are the divorced children both black and white?"

"Oh, well, I don't know yet."

"You do consider yourself a race-conscious photographer, of course." A leading question.

"Only in the sense that we should teach our children not to think in terms of race but in terms of character."

"Come on! You're showing us just the opposite here. You're pitting black against white like nothing I've seen in years!"

Peter reflected on this allegation before answering. "This is a racially divided country. I'm simply an observer of that fact. I'm not suggesting a remedy."

"So you're denying your work carries a message?" Carmen insisted.

*You're just like Laura*, Peter thought. He wouldn't let himself be trapped.

"The images carry their own message. I think the viewers are competent enough to recognize it."

The next few days Peter scanned the papers for reviews. They were mixed. There were twelve or thirteen in all. *The New York Times* gushed about the photography, but was strangely dismissive of the confrontation with the protesters. "An unseemly and unnecessary spectacle" was how they referred to it. But it paid Peter a backhanded compliment. It called him "a photographer whose greatest talent may well be political. His manner of disposing of the protest marchers from Harlem was in the best traditions of soap-box oratory."

*The Harlem Times* carried an article covering both the exhibition and the confrontation in about equal measure. It expressed no opinion on the artistic merits of the photographs. It concluded with these words: "Van Doorn declined to be pinned down on his thoughts on race other than to say in effect that he didn't have any. If that's true, we should take his photo reportage seriously. He may help us see ourselves in a more unbiased light, as people of different ability and character, rather than as members of different races."

Reading this, Peter thought they had overstated his innocence. He decided to stay clear of the whole gamut of race relations for a while. He'd have to find another subject.

# Chapter 30

Clara and Diedrich showed up unexpectedly at the opening the following day. Peter had sent them an announcement, but Clara had phoned that she couldn't make it. "The Elm Street conversion is at a critical stage," was her excuse. She'd try to drop in some other day during the exhibition.

But here she was. "Unforeseen delays with Elm Street," she said as she walked in. "Suddenly, I've got all this time!"

Peter kissed Diedrich, his spirits lifting. Clara looked great in her natural linen outfit and the light gray hair band holding back her lustrous dark hair, as always cut to chin length. He could feel her body warmth as they kissed. He had to be careful not to read too much into her visit.

"I'm so glad," he said as he gave Clara a light squeeze. "It was about time, too!"

She smiled evasively and turned for a quick look at the exhibition. "So you've done it! Congratulations, Peter. I'm so happy for you."

"Go take your mum around, Diedrich. You'll recognize the shots you helped me print."

They stayed a little over half an hour. Clara said they had to go and see "a friend," but they could meet later for dinner, "if it's not inconvenient."

"I'm having dinner around the corner with Bernard and Lunette and a few others," Peter said. "Why don't you join us?"

"Oh, no, that's too tiring for Diedrich."

"No, it isn't!" said Diedrich. "I want to go. And I want to stay here. I haven't even seen half the photos!"

"Really better not, darling. I'll tell you what, Peter. What time will you be home?"

"Ten-ish, I'd think. Quarter past."

"We'll be there around ten-thirty. I have the address. Can Diedrich stay over with you? I'm staying at the Drake." The Drake. That's where they used to stay together whenever they visited New York. They both liked the place for its faded gentility.

"Fine. Sure. Ten-thirty then. You're making my day!"

"Stirring stuff, Peter," she said with a sweeping gesture. "Committed. Truthful. Almost passionate."

He tried giving her a grateful kiss on the mouth, but she offered him a cheek. "We'll see you later," she said.

Diedrich followed her, sulking, sending a dispirited wave to his father over his shoulder.

*Committed. Truthful.* Almost *passionate.* The assessment pursued Peter as he chatted with the guests. How could *she* utter those words: almost passionate? She, cool, unimpassioned Clara, the virgin bride with the sensible skirts and the Clearwater values? How could she tell? Committed, truthful, fine. But passionate?

The opening was well attended, considering the weather and the pre-season scheduling. Most visitors headed straight to the bar for a cool drink before viewing the exhibition.

"I came because of the *Times* article," said an elderly man who called himself a collector of images. "And because of the child-and-nurses shot shown with it. That's a great image. Very moving." *Truthful.* "I've asked the lady to reserve one for me."

A couple of high school seniors wanted to know where exactly the shot of the young, homeless woman was taken. They were doing a paper on homelessness and thought they might interview the woman.

A nervous lady in her late thirties wearing a smartly-cut, light blue pants suit, wanted to know how long Peter had been traveling and when he was planning to return to Holland.

Peter laughed. "No, no, I'm not traveling. I live here. This is my city."

*Committed.*

"Really? That's interesting," she said. "But your accent... Oh!" She had spilled some of her drink on her suit. One of the waiters brought her a napkin. "Silly me! Thank you. As I was saying, your accent, you see. It confused me!"

She laughed hysterically, briefly. "The pictures, too. I couldn't imagine somebody with his feet firmly on Manhattan rock, an *insider,* taking pictures like these."

Peter was getting interested. "Why do you say that?"

"Well, you know the Japanese proverb, 'It's dark at the foot of the lighthouse.' I mean, the best view of earth is from outer space, isn't it?" Again that laugh.

"You think my photos have no validity because I'm too close to the scene?"

"Uh, yes, that's what I thought. But then, I don't trust the outsider view either, because he has no stake, no commitment. It's all pretty hopeless, really."

"Hopeless?"

"Yeah, I mean, to find people—writers, photographers, reporters—who can tell it like it is. Who are neither too far nor too close to be credible." This time no laugh but a smile that was more like a grimace. She was looking at him intently.

"And now?" Peter asked. He wanted to hear the rest.

"Now you've got me all confused." Brief hysterical laugh. Fluttering of eyelids.

But she had already lost interest in him. She pretended to see an acquaintance, flashed Peter a neutral smile, said, "Excuse me," and moved on, rotating her hips as she walked away. Twenty minutes later, Peter saw her leave with some man she had evidently picked up.

*New York*, Peter thought. *Crazy town.*

The last guest left close to eight. Bernard was waiting for the servers to pack up so he could close the gallery.

"Good turnout," he said. "Normally, I get five to ten percent of the mailing list, fifteen tops, but that's mid-season. This time…what d'you say, Lunette, twenty?"

"About that, probably," said Lunette.

"But hardly any blacks," said Peter.

"Our mailing list is not exactly pitched at readers of *The Harlem Times,*" said Bernard.

"But some may turn up from tomorrow. I wouldn't be surprised," Lunette said. "Because of their coverage."

"Yeah," said Bernard. "And if they do, it's because of Mr. van Doorn's speech. I'm sure they loved that piece of demagoguery."

"Demagoguery!" Peter was surprised at the vehemence of his reaction. *Almost passionate.* "I said exactly what I felt!"

Bernard smiled slyly. "Whatever it was, it's not hurting sales. Seven red stickers on opening night. Two more and we've covered our costs," Bernard declared. "Thereafter, it's pure profit."

Peter wondered why people were willing to fork over five hundred dollars or more for a framed photograph. It couldn't be for the signature on them. Where was the glamor of owning a van Doorn? He didn't know, and he didn't care to know. He was tired of analysis. He was longing to see Diedrich. And Clara.

But first, dinner with Bernard, Lunette, and two photo editors from the magazine Bernard had invited along.

After the dinner, which was pleasant enough, Peter escaped during coffee and hauled a taxi back to his loft, just in time to welcome Clara and Diedrich. His son was yawning constantly but torpedoed all suggestions that he go to bed with a pointed reminder that "tomorrow is Sunday." He wanted to stay up and do everything the grownups were doing.

It was, after all, Diedrich's day. For the first time in over two years he had his mum and dad together in the same room. It was like old times at last. He could never understand why his father had left. Some of his classmates and friends had divorced parents, but then there always seemed to be another man or woman in the picture. But his parents didn't even seem to be unhappy with each other. They always kissed when they met. Why couldn't they just make up and live together again? He had asked them, more than once, but they hadn't given him a clear answer. They mumbled difficult words like "incompatible" and "fundamentally different," and his mother spoke of his dad's "deep-seated needs" and "unresolved conflicts." He had no idea what they were talking about. All the same, his grief had been made bearable by the special weekends with his dad alone.

"May I take a look in the darkroom?" he asked Peter.

"Okay, but if you want to touch anything, ask me first."

"Sure, Dad."

Clara smiled. "He's always a handful when he comes home from visiting you. Everything is better in New York!"

"Of course it is," said Peter. "Don't you agree?"

"Oh, I like Chicago. You know I do."

"That's hardly what I meant."

"I know. But you're so...settled, Peter. You've found what you've always wanted, haven't you?"

"And lost everything else in the bargain," he said, trying not to sound melodramatic.

Diedrich was making yelping noises from inside the darkroom. Before Peter could go and see what the excitement was about, Diedrich popped his head round the corner. "The shots of me, Dad, they're great! May I show them to Mama?"

"Of course you may. They're still a bit wet." He didn't have to be more specific. His son knew how to handle fresh prints.

"You haven't lost Diedrich," Clara said. She was holding her head in her characteristic way, erect and inclined slightly downward and sideways, her eyes blinking up from under the clearly drawn arch of her eyebrows. It was this pose that had caught Peter's eye when he first met her more than ten years ago. He still found it indescribably alluring.

"I know. But darling..."

"Hush," she said. She touched his knee with her hand. "Don't say it. I know. I *know*. The pain of it. But that's the way it is, isn't it? The eternal triangle."

231

Peter nodded. "You, me, and my black mistress," he said. Diedrich was gingerly carrying a large flat board with some prints on it.

"They're almost dry, Dad. Look, Mama, me on the ferry. And look, me and Lady Liberty. And here, I love this one…on the roller coaster! Look, I'm hanging upside down!"

"It must be a trick print," said Clara. "Your hair is flat on your head." Diedrich looked alarmed and studied the photo closely. Peter smiled knowingly.

"It's *not* a trick print!" said Diedrich. "Look at the other boy. His hair is hanging down like a witch's! Why not my hair, Dad?"

"Because you have curly, sturdy hair that doesn't lose its shape that easily," said Peter.

"And look at this one, Mama. I took it!" It showed an alarmed and unsmiling Peter on the New York Library steps, looking beyond the lens as if he'd just noticed something profoundly unsettling. Clara laughed. "What were you witnessing, Peter? Ed Koch in drag?"

"Worse. Some rowdy spitting on a passerby, an old lady in a yellow chiffon dress."

"Yuck! Why did he do that?"

"No idea. She probably insulted him. Probably with good reason. He seemed the kind that gets in other people's way. Carelessly."

"What do you mean?"

"He was lumbering and obese and he was wearing a green-striped T-shirt," Peter explained.

"Dad called him a striped melon, ha-ha!"

"Sometimes I hate New York," said Clara.

"Sometimes I hate New York, too," said Peter.

"I love New York," said Diedrich. "Not sometimes. Always." Clara and Peter smiled at him, at his youthful enthusiasm. He yawned again.

"Time for bed," said Peter. "Your mum and I want to talk a little."

Diedrich darted a glance from one to the other. "Oh, sure," he said, his face lighting up. "Talk all you want! I promise I won't *disturb* you."

"Don't forget to brush your teeth, wise guy," said Clara. "And give me a shout when you're between the sheets."

"No sheets here…a *quilt*."

"Of course. I forgot, you told me," she said. "Call me when you're ready for the kiss."

"Okay. Goodnight, Dad."

"Goodnight, Son."

Clara was tearful when she returned from kissing Diedrich goodnight. She walked over to the window, turning her back. For a few moments he stayed in his chair, showing respect for whatever it was that had made her cry. Then he rose and put his arms around her. She took his hands and pressed them against her breast.

"It's so hard for him," she said. "He so much wants us to…" She was choking.

"Of course. So do I. So do you. We all want that."

"Then why don't we?" she asked urgently, turning around, suddenly angry. "Why are those pictures of yours so goddamn important that you have to wreck your family, your life, my life, his life? Why?" Her hands were again holding his, clenching them hard.

He lifted her hands to his mouth and kissed them.

"I don't know," he said. "I love you more than I could ever express. I want you back so much that it splits me in two. And yet…"

"I know. You can't give up your mistress. I know! I know! I know!"

"She's not my mistress. I don't sleep with her. She's my…my high priestess, my goddess."

"That's worse."

"A lot worse. I can't dismiss her. She's always there, demanding my worship. It's strange, but when I'm longing for you, when I miss you so much I can hardly bear it, I pick up my camera and hit the road. Or I dive into my darkroom and turn on the red light. And soon I forget my misery. I forget everything. Or maybe all of it, even my love for you, is transmuted into my worship of her, my goddess. I love you, she commands me."

"You are a romantic, you know. A romantic, passionate man."

"*Almost* passionate."

"Yes. You're still holding back. Still clinging to me, to your other life."

"Isn't that what you want?"

"Don't talk that way! What I want is irrelevant. Don't shift the responsibility on to me! Don't be a coward!" Coward. Laura had called him that, too.

"*You* were the one that walked out on *me*, remember?" he said.

"Because you kept confronting me with *her*. Your black beauty with the silver tits." He had to laugh. It was funny, but it didn't sound right out of her mouth. "What are you laughing about? I'm serious! I hate her. I hate all your shots, your enlargements, all the evidence of your prodigious virility with her."

"Aren't you carrying your metaphor a bit far?" he said. "I'm only a photographer, the camera is merely my tool. There's no reason why we couldn't live together again as man and wife, and both do our own thing. You in your office, me in my studio."

Clara plumped down on the sofa, kicked off her shoes, stretched out her legs on the seat. "It wouldn't work," she declared.

"Why not?"

"Because I know you. You can't *create* when I'm around. You sulk and complain and make me feel guilty. You want your independence, your precious, untrammeled freedom. No, I'd only be in your way, slowing you down, forcing compromises on you. You'd be unhappy. Again."

"I'm unhappy now."

"You men! You always want it both ways. The wife *and* the whore."

"She's not a whore!" The absurdity of his defence hung in the space like a verdict by a corrupt jury. "Augh," he erupted in frustration. "The things you make me say!"

"I don't make you say anything that's not already inside you. I'm merely the agent of your truthfulness. You've just confirmed why we split up in the first place. I feel vindicated."

"Vindicated?"

"I'm not the type to be an artist's lover, Peter. Available and rejectable at the master's whim. Muse and mistress. Angel and tramp. Everything but wife. I want to be number one."

"That's unfair. You've always been number one. I've never treated you as a mistress."

"Because you knew how to suppress your true feelings. Except when you let them show."

Peter sat down next to her on the sofa and sighed. He gazed at her, taking in her body with his eyes, his nostrils. She had a natural perfume that spoke perennially of autumn, of fallen leaves and sunlight on moist soil. Their eyes met. She rubbed her bare legs together. The way she did that reminded him of the girl in a Hemingway story set in the Michigan forests. She too had rubbed her naked legs together, and it had been more than the boy could endure. They had made love under the trees.

Peter stroked his wife's legs and she let him. His caresses traveled upwards, and he felt her frisson as his hand reached her inner thigh. She grabbed his head with both hands and pulled him up to her and kissed him on the mouth. Her lips were cool to the touch. He opened her blouse.

There were no words between them now. What they wanted was insulation, however briefly, from the stark facts, from the merciless consequences of truthfulness. A respite.

He fondled her breasts, seeking the nipples.

"On the bed, darling," she whispered between kisses. They glanced into Diedrich's room as they passed it. He was fast asleep, not under but on top of his quilt.

They undressed each other and lay down on the bed. They embraced with the smoothness of touch and sureness of positioning that betrayed years of togetherness. Peter very nearly swooned. It had been too long, too cruelly long. He was greedy, wanting to make up for lost time. His kisses and caresses, his urgent attempts at quenching his pent-up thirst, his whole delirious lovemaking, couldn't fill the void that had grown inside him. He wept as he entered her.

The sweetness of her embrace was overwhelming to him. He knew he would never again find this purity, this guiltless bliss. With Clara, he had never felt lust. She was incapable of lustful, urgent sex in the backseats of cars, under bushes, in train toilets—the kind of situations, imagined or experienced, that fanned his desire like bellows to a smoldering fire. Their lovemaking was untainted by the grime and deceptions of messy affairs and the intrusions of a leering world. It was, Peter had always felt, love of a different order, acted out on a higher plain. It lacked for him the erotic charge of an adulterous tryst, but it was virtuous, wholesome, and serene. The thought of it had often moved him, as it was moving him now.

Two years. It had been two whole years. He drank in her scent and watched in wonder as she undulated under him, admiring her still firm and beautiful body. He never knew what her thoughts were when they made love and he didn't know now. Did she have the kind of lecherous fantasies he often had to enhance his pleasure? In the past, she had often seemed remote, self-possessed, keeping her eyes closed. But today, every part of her was wide open, her lips parted, her eyes moist with desire. She eagerly pulled him into her, her hands encouraging his thrusts. He had never seen her like this, so active, so passionate. He smiled at the word. His Clara, passionate? Why had he never thought of her that way before?

She was riding him now, erect, proud, with style. And with an intensity that surprised and unnerved him. She was the rider and he the stallion. She spurred him on. Was she going after her own pleasure? It excited him, but he wasn't ready for this role reversal. She resisted his attempt to maneuver her under him. They ended up on their sides, face to face, intimately chained.

It was not a comfortable position, but her warm skin and the erotic tension in her body intoxicated him, and she responded to his urgency, his desperate clinging. Their orgasms were almost simultaneous and his was deeply satisfying. Hers, following his, seemed too. She let out a deep sigh.

They didn't move for a long time, allowing the stirred-up emotions to run their course. At last, Clara carefully disengaged herself and went to the bathroom in his robe. Peter waited for her with his arms folded under his head, still glowing with the fullness of his relief.

She smiled when she returned. Peter thought she looked radiant. She carefully draped the robe over the chair and started to put her clothes back on.

"What are you doing?" Peter said. She didn't answer and continued dressing. "Clara, why are you dressing? Aren't you staying over?"

She sat down on the edge of the bed and looked at him. "I want a divorce, Peter," she said softly.

He didn't believe what he had just heard. "What did you say?"

"I want a divorce." Her voice was firmer now. "I think we should divorce as soon as possible."

Peter jumped out of bed and grabbed his robe from the chair where Clara had left it. "You can't be serious. Right after…that?"

"Yes. *Because* it was so good. Too good for comfort. Divorce is the only way to get you out of my system. You know I don't sleep with men I'm not married to."

"Ah! A joke!" he laughed, unnaturally.

She got up and moved over to him. Her hand, its strong, slender fingers spread out, was on his chest. "I don't joke about these things, Peter. This was the last time we made love. Couldn't you feel that? We wanted it to end on a high note, didn't we?" Her eyes were brimming.

"No, darling…this can't be. This is inhuman!"

"It's time, Peter. Time for the wife to make way for the mistress."

"Cut it out, will you? You are being ridiculous. Denying love like that!"

"I'm not going to ask for anything, of course. Not even for Diedrich. I'm even willing to offer you…"

"No! I don't want to listen to this."

"Shall we use my lawyer or yours?" She was drying her eyes with a tissue.

"Clara…"

"Don't tell me you can't handle this. You seduced me. Now be a man and throw me out."

*Be a man…* Inexplicably, her words triggered an image of his father locking away his Leica on his return to Holland in 1945. That willful, unhappy act his father had once told him about, and since then had refused to discuss again. *Be a man and throw me out.* How could he? How could anyone in his right mind?

"Please, Peter," Clara was pleading with him. "There is no going back, you know that." *Banking will make a man out of you.* Those had been his father's words. Had banking failed him then? What did it mean anyway, to be a man?

"You've made your decision. Now you've got to accept the consequences." Laura's words. *A coward is someone who doesn't accept the consequences of his actions.* Was he a coward?

"Tell me to go and I will go. Don't force me to have to decide by myself..." What was this? Giving him the honor? Then Clara said something that he would remember as a turning point in his life.

"If you can't do it, Peter, if you can't bear to leave me, you'll fade into insignificance. And your son will never learn to respect you." She stood by the door, fully dressed.

So that was it! To be a man was to be respected by your own son.

"Yes," Peter said, almost determined now, almost convinced. "Yes. I have to be alone. You must go, and not come back. It breaks my heart, but you must leave me."

All of a sudden, the melodrama got to him. He resented her for making him go through this, for toying with his emotions and trying to lecture him.

"Please go," he said. She had always done that, between the lines. Lecture him. About the virtues of banking, of building a career, a fortune, a place in society. About morality and a regular, orderly life. A life with a minimum of risk-taking. She was superior to him because she was clear-headed and principled. He could never live up to her standards, and the effort had exhausted him. She would never leave him alone, she had to control him. That wasn't her fault. It was her nature. She was beautiful but to him she was poison. Beautiful poison.

She was still standing by the door.

"What are you waiting for?" he said, impatient now. "Don't worry about Diedrich. I'll drop him off at the Drake tomorrow around noon. Is that convenient?"

She nodded emphatically. Again, her eyes had filled. Then she turned and left the bedroom for the living room. In the doorway, she turned back and stopped.

"Goodbye, Peter. I will always cherish the memory of this evening. Please take care of yourself." A moment later, he heard the front door click shut. He recalled the four words she had uttered after seeing the exhibition: Committed. Truthful. Almost passionate.

Put that on my tombstone, thought Peter. He wasn't sure if there was anything left worth living for.

Beautiful poison. The phrase came back to him again and again as he tried to smother his grief in his pillow. How could he have stuck that label on her? She, Clara, poison? He tried to think of other poisons that were beautiful but couldn't come up with a single example.

Then he remembered Diedrich. Of course! He hated himself for his wave of self-pity. He looked in at his son's room. The boy was sleeping fitfully. He seemed older, adolescent, no longer a child. Was he having an unhappy dream? Peter didn't know, but he knew he would try to give Diedrich as much of himself as he could give, and hope that would lessen his unhappiness. His pain.

Respect. Clara was right. If you can love and respect your father, you feel less lonely. Peter had always loved his father. His respect for him had sometimes been sorely tested, but he didn't think he had ever lost it. When he was younger he had even felt fiercely proud of him, for what he had done in the war, though he didn't understand what that was, and for his pipe-smoking depths which had exuded importance and wisdom that other boys' dads could never equal. The "darkroom days," that's how he remembered those good times. Their warmth had survived all subsequent tensions and disappointments, its memory sustaining him whenever he had felt low and alone.

Yet his father had never left his family, except during the war. He had given up photography and come back home and stayed. With his wife and children. That had been *his* choice. Surely that was not the act of a coward.

There was much about his father he didn't understand. Most of all he didn't know whether he had his father's character, as Laura suspected, or its opposite, as he had always believed.

# Chapter 31

From a slow start, attendance at the exhibition gradually increased. Two weeks into its twenty-five day run, eighteen prints had been sold, including three large ones at eight hundred dollars each. The protests from the black community had evaporated. There even had been a letter to the editor of *The Harlem Times* praising "Mr. van Doorn for supporting the black quest for equality by turning the race argument on its head. In highlighting white poverty in black neighborhoods, he removes the stigma of structural black inferiority, and raises the possibility of white folks having to meet, in certain situations, a desirable black standard." It agreed with the paper's rejection of the show's poster as "regrettable, in bad taste," but urged readers to judge the work "on its intrinsic merits, not on its commercial propaganda."

"What did I tell ya?" Bernard exclaimed. "We got the attention we wanted. What hurts, works."

Even if no further prints were sold, Peter's share of the print sales, minus overhead, would exceed three thousand dollars. Not bad for a fledgling, but he had to do a lot better than that to make a living out of photography. He still had some savings, enough to live on modestly for now, provided interest rates didn't plummet or inflation soar. His largest regular outlay apart from the rent was for photo supplies, but one or two exhibitions a year plus a dozen magazine sales should cover most of those costs.

At least he needn't worry about support payments for Diedrich. Clara was taking care of all costs single-handedly. Her parents had evidently released some funds to her now. She was even setting up a special account on which Peter could draw to cover expenses associated with Diedrich's New York visits and "vacations together." He could also make use of it in an emergency for himself. Peter said he didn't need this.

"That's fine," Clara said. "But it will be there just in case. Consider it insurance. Money should never become a factor in the father-son relationship."

A week before the show closed, there was a surprise phone call from Holland. It was his father.

"I've read the reviews you faxed me, and I've decided I want to see the exhibition for myself," he said. "It's time to visit America, anyway. Get to know the enemy." Like many left-wing European journalists, his father had always avoided soiling his socialist purity with exposure to the main source of capitalist evil. But times had changed. Besides, he'd come for a different purpose.

He arrived two days later. Peter met him at Kennedy.

*He looks young*, Peter thought, *slimmer, and with a new spring to his step*.

"Eduard van Doorn. Welcome to America," he said. The deliberate formality of the greeting seemed appropriate to the occasion.

They embraced. *Tobacco and caramel*, thought Peter. It was the old familiar scent, all right, though fainter.

"Had a good flight, Dad?"

"Good enough. I ate and slept, and when I woke up, we were here!" He was carrying a small suitcase and a shoulder bag. Though retired, he still looked the reporter.

They took the bus to Grand Central. Eduard glanced out to catch his first glimpses of America.

"Traffic rolls differently here," he observed. "Less nervously."

Peter had noticed that, too. "Lower speed limits than in Europe. And bigger cars."

"They sure seem less aggressive than the Dutch," said Eduard, laughing at the implied paradox.

"I'm glad you could come, Dad," said Peter. "You look well."

"I feel well."

"Are you hungry?" Peter asked.

"I can eat."

"We'll have a bowl of Manhattan clam chowder at the Oyster Bar. And anything else you like."

They walked through the great hall of Grand Central. Eduard stopped in the middle and looked up and around. "A bit like Victoria Station," he said. "But bigger."

"I have a rule of thumb," said Peter. "If you multiply European dimensions by two and a half, you get the American size. An inch for every centimeter. From refrigerators to beds to elevators."

"And egos?"

"And egos."

They found two seats in the pit of the oyster bar, facing the chefs, who were cooking chowder and frying fish in front of them, at three levels. The top tier was level with a higher part of the station and had a window with a counter where you could eat standing up. While waiting for their clam chowders, they watched a burly, grimy man in overalls, a construction worker perhaps, stop at the window and order half a dozen oysters on the half shell. They were produced instantly, and he ate them with a practiced hand without looking up. Eduard was amazed.

"A laborer eating oysters!"

"That's New York," said Peter. "The ultimate egalitarian society." Eduard's quick glance met a deadpan face trained at the chowders which were just then being set in front of them.

"I won't pick up that gauntlet just yet," said Eduard. "I prefer to enjoy my first American meal free from ideology, but with a little black pepper."

Peter laughed.

The weather was balmy as Eduard set out the next morning for his first walking tour of Manhattan. He wanted to get an impression of the main parts of the city first, and then visit the exhibition. He wanted to do this alone, with the help of a map. "I want to see the city with my own eyes before seeing them through yours."

He walked for three days, covering corners of SoHo, the Village, the East Village, Little Italy, Midtown, Central Park and Brooklyn. He rode the subways and the buses. Each day he returned in the late afternoon, exhausted and satisfied, ready for a pre-dinner nap.

At night, they talked, about everything and nothing. Somehow, the most personal subjects were being avoided: Peter's divorce and relationship with Diedrich, his new life as a photographer, his father's life as a retired man. Over simple dinners in neighborhood eateries they discussed American history and politics, the weather, the technical side of photography, women in general, airports, and of course, the day's sightseeing. Eduard's enthusiasm for New York waxed and waned with the degree of urban suffering he had witnessed on his walkabouts.

"What a terrible city!" he exclaimed the first day as he walked through the door. "All those homeless people in the subway stations! They are everywhere. Nobody looks at them. It's like Dickens but worse. Because we *know* better. So much for 'Send me your huddled masses'. What they really mean is 'Keep them, we don't want them'."

The following day, he was effusive in his praise of almost everything he had seen. Central Park. The Village. Brooklyn Heights. The sour note was provided by Donald Trump. "I saw him, in front of Trump Tower. He was getting out of one of those long cars—what do you call them?"

"Stretch limos. You mean you recognized Donald Trump?"

"Of course. Ridiculous car! With a bar and television on board, and windows with blinds. He had a blonde on his arm."

"Ivana."

"How do you know?"

"You mean you know about Donald Trump and you don't know about Ivana?"

"I don't approve of the dalliances of these American millionaires. I find them disgusting." He was dead serious.

"Oh, Dad, come on. This is New York. Here you have to rise above approval or disapproval. It's Gotham City, where amorality reigns and everybody is a rake or a fool. Besides, she's his wife." They were having a drink before going out to dinner. Peter, leaning back, took a casual sip of his Scotch-and-soda. "This is Fun City, USA, Dad! You either love it or hate it. I love it."

Eduard shifted uncomfortably in his chair.

"You feel right at home in New York, don't you?" he said incredulously.

For the first time since Eduard's arrival in New York, Peter was aware of the old gulf between them. It was still there.

"Yes, I do. It's a great city, a fascinating place to live."

"So you're here for the city. For nothing else."

"What is that supposed to mean?"

"To enjoy yourself, with photography as your alibi."

Peter felt his old rage return. He started counting. That's what he had learned from André. When anger is rising, count to ten before venting it. Six, seven, eight, nine, ten.

"That's unfair," he said calmly. "You've come all the way to New York to condemn me before seeing the evidence?"

Eduard didn't answer. He looked out of the window in his infuriating way, chin up, eyes focused on some faraway detail.

"Dad, answer me!" He found it hard to control his temper in the face of such pig-headedness.

"All right. I reserve my opinion. Shall we go out then?"

"No," Peter answered. "I don't feel like eating right now. Why don't you go ahead? You know your way around New York."

"Fine. I'll go to last night's café. I like the food there. I have the keys." He got up and without another word left the apartment. The door fell in the lock the way it had done when Clara left him.

In five minutes, he had calmed down sufficiently to think of joining his father. "He's reserving his opinion," he reasoned. "It's his *manner* that bugs me."

Ten minutes later, he sat down at his father's table by the window. Eduard had ordered Manhattan clam chowder. "I like it," he said. This mollified his son.

"I'm glad there are some things in New York you like."

245

"Oh, there's a lot I like about it. The women, for example."

"The women?"

"Yes, take this waitress here. Pretty, and very intelligent. She's an actress, between engagements."

"Dad, they're all actors between engagements. In New York, you don't admit to being just a waitress."

"Is that so? You mean she was lying to me?"

"Maybe, maybe not. Which one is it?"

"The one with the black hair and the nice breasts. There."

"Hmm. See what you mean. She probably *is* an actress. Yes. Classical."

He looked at his father and they both burst out laughing.

"You old rogue!" Peter exclaimed. "I didn't know you had that in you."

"I've got it in me, all right. The question is, how do you bring it out? When you're too old to turn a head."

The waitress came round to take Peter's order.

"This is my son Peter I told you about," said Eduard. "The photographer."

"Hi," she said, "I'm Lucille. Your father is a real gentleman. We had a nice chat, didn't we? He thinks the *world* of you." She looked straight at Peter as she said this.

"Sometimes he has a strange way of showing it," said Peter, trying to make it sound light, and patting his dad on the arm to signify his forgiveness.

"Ohh..." she intoned in mock-sympathy. "I'm sure you are a fabulous duo. I'm envious, you know. I really am..." She let this linger just long enough to convince Peter that she meant what she said. "Well, what may I get you?" She *was* very pretty. But this was not the moment to think about that.

Father and son spent a reasonably enjoyable hour together, skirting the subjects that had caused their row. They amused themselves surveying passersby and patrons, guessing what each did for a living, or pretended to be doing. Then they talked about the craziness of New York.

The following day, Thursday, was Eduard's "Harlem day," kept until the last, "to have a sound basis for comparison," as he put it. Peter felt increasingly irritated by his father's deliberate planning, his stepped approach to what he seemed to regard as a momentous event: the viewing of the exhibition.

"You said your exhibition closes Saturday? So I still have two days to see it. I'll go Friday. Or Saturday. It doesn't matter. I want to be well-prepared."

Why, Peter wondered, hadn't Eduard just gone over to the gallery on the first day? If he had done that, they would already have discussed his work in depth by now. What he got instead was a lot of self-conscious posturing, a slow build-up of uncalled-for suspense, as if his father was a juror steeling himself for a high-profile trial. Why couldn't he be more of a father and less of a judge?

In the Eyes of the Son

# Chapter 32

As had become his habit, Eduard left shortly after nine o'clock, to beat the rush on the subways. Also, as usual, he told Peter not to expect him back before five at the earliest, and to get on with whatever he wanted to do in his absence. But Peter, always half-expecting his father to call or come home during the day, hadn't left the loft on his own since Eduard's arrival, except for brief errands. Today, too, he decided to stay home and do some dark-room work.

For dinner, mindful of the day's challenging schedule, and the anti-capitalist diatribe likely to follow, he planned to eat in: a simple dish of fettuccini and freshly made pesto sauce, with a green salad on the side. He would get the ingredients later from a supermarket.

Around three o'clock, after doing the shopping, Peter was on his way back to the loft. It was an overcast, muggy day, and still hot. Carrying his bag of groceries, he decided to have a quick *latte* at the corner café. He sat down at a small table inside. They had the radio on full blast. The local news.

Peter picked up a magazine someone had left, his ear half-cocked to the news bulletin. "Mayor Koch, in an unusual move, has instructed the New York Police Department..."

"One latte?"

"Thanks."

"...and in another development..."

"Do you mind paying now?"

"How much?"

"Three dollars."

"A report has just come in...an elderly man, believed to be a foreign tourist..."

He handed the waiter a five dollar bill.

"...stabbed on a Harlem street in what is believed..." Peter felt a chill.

"You mind your change in quarters? I'm out of..."

"Wait, I want to hear this!"

"...a Dutch national, was taken to Mount Sinai Hospital where he is said to be in critical condition. The police department called this the most serious case of..."

"God! My father!" Peter cried. "Keep the change!" He rushed out and grabbed a taxi. "Mount Sinai!"

"Use the Expressway?"

"Yes, yes!"

"Through town is cheaper."

"Take the fastest way!"

Even so, the ride took an agonizing forty minutes. He should have called first, to ask how his dad was doing. Find out if it *was* his dad. There were so many stabbings in this godforsaken city, why did it have to be Eduard van Doorn of all people? Stabbed... Why? Why would anyone want to kill a harmless tourist in the middle of the day?

The driver was preparing to leave the expressway. "No," Peter commanded, "go on to the next exit, that's quicker."

"Then I gotta backtrack."

"Never mind. Do it!"

"Okay, boss."

Peter was shifting on the seat. Its springs were broken. The shock absorbers were shot, too. The back wheels hit their housings each time the car went through a pothole. His back was hurting. The driver was slowing down each time he approached a light.

"Can't you go faster? Take the yellow lights!"

"You want me to run the lights? You pay fine?"

"No red lights...yellow, I said."

"Okay, boss. I run the lights. You pay fine."

He ran all the lights indiscriminately, red and yellow, just ahead of the crossing traffic. He drove right up to the hospital's main entrance and stopped with screeching brakes. His victorious grin betrayed a mixture of disapproval and excitement. Peter tipped him generously and bolted out.

"Hey, boss!" the driver yelled after him. "Your bag!" His groceries.

"Keep it!" he shouted back, gesturing. "I don't need it!"

Inside the hospital, Peter rushed to the reception desk.

"Van Doorn... Yes, we have a van Doorn. Edward, right? In Emergency. No visitors."

"I'm his son."

"You can go to the Emergency Reception. They handle the emergencies."

At Emergency, Peter encountered a large cluster of people besieging the three receptionists, who seemed unable to cope. They were evasive in their answers and avoided looking anyone in the face. They studied their fake, painted fingernails and the computer screens in turn. It took Peter ten minutes to catch the attention of one of them.

"He's in surgery," she said, her eyes on the monitor.

"Eduard van Doorn? He's in surgery?"

"That's what I'm telling you."

"Where's that? Surgery."

"You can't go there. You'll have to wait."

"How long? When did he go in? I'd like to have some information about his condition. I'm his son."

"You'll have to wait. Check again in half an hour."

The Emergency waiting room was huge. Instead of chairs there were long benches. About half the seats were occupied, mostly by blacks and Hispanics. There was an air of grim expectation, of the familiar, too, as if many of those waiting had been there before and knew the routine. Their way of questioning the receptionists lacked the frantic tone he had used himself. They weren't exactly calm but more patient, accustomed to bureaucratic rebuffs and delays, and the dearth of the kind of considerate treatment the affluent took for granted. It's the poor who do the waiting, he had read somewhere. And who suffer the indignities.

But he had to find out where his father was and what had happened to him. He looked for "Surgery" but there was no separate entrance. Again, he went to Reception. The other end, to try a different person. Five minute wait.

"My father is in surgery. Could you tell me where that is?"

"Didn't she tell you that you can't go there?"

"I know. I just want to know where it is, so I can…"

"It's behind us here. Nobody can go there. You're to come back here for the progress reports. Next!"

His situation, he realized, was no different than that of all the people around him. The ultimate egalitarian society, he had told his father, tongue-in-cheek. Here, it was literally the case. It surprised him. He had always thought Mount Sinai to be one of New York's top hospitals. Meaning, he realized without shame, that people with a certain *background* would be treated with courtesy and priority.

Well, it was good to have this experience, particularly in light of his exhibition theme. He looked around. There were three or four whites among the waiting crowd. They looked solitary and elderly and withdrawn, in contrast to most of the blacks and Hispanics who were there in clusters of twos and threes, some keeping a lively conversation going, spiked with the occasional yelp or high-pitched giggle. A good shot for his exhibition, he thought. Fits the theme.

Two stretchers were rolled in. Human bundles, with bandages and blood showing, nurses running alongside with the oxygen and the drip. Accident victims, by the looks of it. Traffic? Domestic violence? Stabbings?

Peter felt an acute pain in his side and he leaned over to ease it. He tried to imagine what his father was thinking now, if he was conscious. He couldn't. He felt quite unable to put himself in his father's place.

*So that's how it is*, he thought. When they cut you up, when you face pain, surgery, coma, death, you face it alone. Never mind how close you've been all your life to someone, to your family. Never mind if they are nearby, literally. You face it alone, inside yourself. Without the familiar faces and environment to ease you through. Without the context.

Death: an event without context.

Except for those left behind. For them, context is everything. We want our dying loved ones near us. They comfort us in their dying hour, not the other way round. No, that was a selfish thought, though it might be true. He knew he needed his father desperately now. Was his father dying at this moment? All by himself, with his son sitting ten, twenty meters away? What were they doing to him? Did he realize what was happening to him?

Panic seized him. He had to find out. The receptionist, seeing him approach, yelled at him through the throng of leaning, waiting relations. "He's still in there. We'll call you." He looked at his watch. Quarter to four. Almost an hour since he got here. He felt very tired. He closed his eyes for a few moments.

"Van Doorn!" The amplified sound of his name startled him. He felt stiff as he ambled over to the desk.

"Your father's in a room on the third floor."

"Thank you. How is he?"

"Only information I got. Ask the station on the third floor. They'll be able to help you. Okay?" She gave him a sympathetic smile.

One of the nurses at the third floor station asked him to sit down while she called the attending physician. He arrived within minutes, briskly, coattails flapping.

"I'm Dr. Fenstein. What can I do for you?"

"It's about Eduard van Doorn."

"Ah, yes. Your father was brought in here with two deep gashes in his lower abdominal region. Punctured both his large intestine and his ureter. No damage to the kidneys. He'd lost a lot of blood. I don't know the circumstances. We only deal with the medical side. Dr. Samuel has performed emergency surgery. It involved a massive blood transfusion and... just a minute..." He consulted the clipboard the nurse had handed him. "Yes, a colostomy. A passage for the solid body wastes. Temporary measure, we hope. The patient has responded well to the surgery and appears to be resting comfortably."

"A colostomy, that's pretty serious, isn't it? Is he out of danger?"

"That's hard to say at this stage. We'll keep him in intensive care."

"Is he conscious?"

The doctor looked at the nurse.

"He's coming out of sedation now," she said.

"I'd like to see him," Peter said.

"I'm sorry," said the doctor with a practiced smile, "but we can't allow visitors until he has regained some of his strength. I'm sure you understand. It's to protect the patient. If you could call us tomorrow we may be able to tell you more."

"Couldn't I just, uh, see him, let him see me? He's visiting from Holland, you see. It might help his recovery to know that I'm…" He couldn't complete his sentence. He felt the tension break inside him. He turned around not to show his tears.

"Of course, of course. I understand. Why don't you wait over there, and the nurse will let you know if you can go in. I don't promise anything, though, and it may take a while. Half an hour at least. Maybe an hour. Is that all right?"

"Yes, thank you. Sorry…"

"The nurse will get you something to drink." Peter saw the doctor nod to the nurse.

It was an hour and a half before Peter was called. He was allowed to see his father for three minutes. He could talk to him, but the patient was not allowed to speak.

Peter found Eduard flat on his back in a four-bed ward, his head on a low pillow. He was hooked up to tubes and monitors, and strapped down to the bed frame. Evidently the doctor had informed him of his son's visit. He didn't show surprise, but he managed a smile and a nod.

"Thank God you're alive! Dad, what did they do to you? Don't answer, don't talk. I don't know what happened, but I'm going to find out. What a horrible thing. I hope you're not in pain?" Eduard slowly shook his head. "I'm so sorry."

Eduard nodded, and faintly squeezed Peter's hand that had taken his.

Peter sat down on the chair. "I'll be back every day, twice a day if they allow me, until you're recovered."

The nurse signaled that time was up.

"You're in good hands here. This is a fine hospital."

Eduard nodded again. "Bye, Dad. Have a good rest." In the door he had a sudden impulse. He turned around. "The exhibition has been extended by a week," he lied. "So you'll still be able to see it." Eduard smiled and gave him the tiniest of waves with his tied-down hand.

In the Eyes of the Son

# Chapter 33

"Mother? It's Peter. I'm fine, yes. I'm sorry to be calling so late. What time is it there? I woke you up? Oh, good, staying up late, are you? You see, Mother, Dad is doing fine, but, well, he's had a little accident. Yes…no, no! Nothing serious, it seems. Some street robber who tried to steal his money and then, well, beat him up. Yes, rather badly. Some internal injury. But he's in good hands here. They've already performed a little operation on him… I don't know exactly, but he's doing okay. I just went to see him. He sends his love to you. Yes, so don't worry. But I thought you should know. I'll give Pauline a call, too."

He called Pauline and gave her a version closer to the truth.

"You're sure he's going to be all right, Peter?"

"Darling, I don't know. He's very weak, but you know Dad, he's a tough old bird. And his eyes looked bright."

"Oh, that's a hopeful sign. Poor man. And poor Mama. It's so…" Her voice broke. "Sorry, but it's so sad. You and he in New York… Say," she said, more calmly after a few moments now, "you want me to fly over?"

"That would be great, of course. But I don't want to cause a panic. Maybe better wait a day or two."

"I can help you cope. Take turns visiting Dad. And I could see your exhibition in the bargain!" Peter didn't tell her it was closing the following day.

"What about your work? Can you just…"

"Oh, fuck my work. This is about our dad, right? I'll come over. I'll

257

check first thing in the morning about flights, et cetera. I just think I should be with you now, just in case, you know."

"Okay, thanks. Yes, maybe you're right. Will you inform Fran? Break it to her gently, will you? When is the baby due?"

"Not for another month or so. Sure, leave it to me. You better get some rest, too, brother dear. Don't you have someone to, you know, give you some moral support? The neighbors? Clara?"

Peter hadn't thought of Clara since hearing the news of his father's accident on the radio.

"You've just given me all the moral support I need," he said truthfully. "You're a gem!"

Having done his family duty, Peter took a taxi to the Harlem Precinct Police Bureau. The place was a faithful copy of the NYPD television series: A confined space peopled by a cross section of the neighborhood in various states of injury, distress and indignation, the mood precariously balanced between high drama, low humor and tedium.

The duty officer was looking for the file.

"Van Dowren you said? Van his first name?"

"No, Eduard. Last name is van Doorn."

"Spell that for me." Peter complied.

"Ah, van Doorn! I've got it. Edward. Your father, you said?"

"Yes."

"If you can wait there, I'll see if I can find the officer assigned to the case." He disappeared through a door, and a few minutes later returned with a plain-clothed man vaguely resembling Sammy Davis Jr.

"Detective Sergeant Williamson," he introduced himself. "If you care to come over to this side..." He motioned to a wobbly chair in front of a weathered wooden desk, behind which he took a place.

"So you're the son of the victim? Pleasure to meet you. Right. Now, we've got a bad case here, a real bad case. Some scum attacked your father in the street with a sharp object, probably a knife. We have no witnesses. First we heard about the stabbing was by telephone from a shopkeeper near the scene. A passerby found the victim lying in the street, bleeding profusely. She asked the shop to call an ambulance and inform the police. Very decent lady, name of Rose Sparkles. Excuse me, something I haven't had time to check," he said as he swiveled around. "Any of you guys know a Rose Sparkles?"

"Sounds familiar," said a cop sitting nearby. "Sparkles. Sparkles. Didn't we bust a scene there couple of years ago, over on Riverside Drive?"

"That's her," said a third one. "On a tip-off from Smart Leo."

"Yeah. Rose Sparkles. Except she was clean as the driven snow. A school teacher. Pretty, too. No previous record. Just a couple of unsuitable friends."

"You heard it," said Williamson. "The person reporting the crime is believed reliable."

"You questioned her?" Peter asked.

"I did. By phone. She promised to make a deposition but she's yet to appear."

"What other steps did you take to find the attacker?"

"Steps, you say? Problem is, the perpetrator had already fled the scene when the victim was found. So far we've not located any eye-witnesses to the crime."

"When do you intend to question my father?" Peter asked.

"We've already done that."

"You have? When?"

"In the ambulance. On the way to the hospital. He was conscious. Quite bright matter o' fact."

Peter had to absorb this extraordinary feat of official diligence—questioning a victim who was fighting for his life in a speeding ambulance. But he had to admit that it served the cause of justice. "You interviewed him personally then?"

"Yep. It's my case. This here is the transcript of the interview." The officer read out a few passages from the report, the upshot of which was that, according to the victim, the attack had occurred in a quiet side street and that the attacker had tried to kill him. The report added that the victim's money belt had not been taken, and that there were signs of a struggle: a bruised arm and a scratch on the back of one hand. Williamson's provisional conclusion was that the attacker was probably surprised by the resistance encountered, or by the approach of potential witnesses on the scene, and had panicked without completing the murder or the robbery.

"So, for you, this is a case of attempted robbery aggravated by a stabbing?"

"Well, your father believed his attacker's purpose was to kill him, not to steal his money. That's what he said."

"What's your opinion of this theory?"

"We have nothing to substantiate it. Other than the money belt had not been taken. Which fact is duly included in my report, as you heard."

Peter thought it wiser not to pursue the subject. He had strong doubts about his father's claim, but didn't want to be openly disloyal to him.

Williamson said he was holding on to the money belt for the time being, as it might be used as evidence. However, Peter was welcome to its contents: his father's passport, New York house keys and one hundred and eighty-five dollars in cash. He signed a formal complaint, which the police said they needed to stay on the case.

Peter thanked the sergeant who promised to advise him of any developments.

He took a taxi home. The first thing he did when he entered the loft was to call his upstairs neighbors, Carlo and Tomoko. The contact with Pauline had helped, but he had to see someone in the flesh, tell them what happened, get some plain old sympathy.

Thank God they were home. They were just finishing dinner and suggested he come over around nine.

"Fine, great. You're sure I'm not upsetting anything?" They said he wasn't, and that they would have the kids out of the way by then.

The next moment, Peter felt ravenous. A trap door had opened in his stomach. He raided the fridge, wolfing down everything in sight. Half an apple, some sliced ham, leftover Waldorf salad, a fistful of pretzels, a cold chicken leg. Within minutes, his stomach began to hurt. He lay down on the sofa and slowly massaged the sensitive area. He cursed himself for his intemperance. What had come over him? He never behaved like this.

This damn stomach. He lay on his side. The pain eased. He still had an hour. He would just rest a bit…

The phone startled him. He stumbled to answer it, glancing at his watch. Half past nine. It was Carlo. "Thought I'd just let you know that we've bundled the brood off to bed, so if you care to come over…"

He did. Tomoko welcomed him with a kiss and a giggle. Carlo, barefoot in a red T-shirt and shorts, waved him into a deep armchair without getting up. He grinned broadly. Peter liked Carlo, his utter lack of pretence. He was a hotshot designer in the world's most competitive city, but he might as well be a truck driver from Omaha.

"What's up, Peter? How's your father?"

"That's why I needed to see you. Something's happened." He gave them a blow-by-blow account, calling it a foiled mugging. Tomoko recoiled in shock and withdrew to the kitchen. Carlo was silent for a while as the seriousness of the event sank in. "I suppose it was a black guy, the Harlem attacker?" he said at last.

Peter realized that the police hadn't referred to the race of the assailant, and that he hadn't asked them either.

"I don't know. The police didn't say."

"Can't you have your dad moved somewhere closer by?" said Carlo.

"I'll try, once he *can* be moved."

Carlo shook his head in dismay. "He shouldn't have put up resistance. In this city, you should never put up resistance. My principle is, they can have anything they want, as long as I may keep my life and my wife." Tomoko had come back with a cold, damp towel for Peter. "And the children," she said.

"And the children," agreed Carlo. He gave his wife a proprietary pat on the hip as she passed.

"The poor man," said Tomoko. "Will he be all right?"

"I hope so. If there are no complications." He gratefully placed the towel on his forehead, then his neck. "Ah, this feels so good."

"Listen," said Carlo. "I don't know what we can do in concrete terms. But if there's something, just let us know."

Peter told them that his sister Pauline was planning to fly over from Holland in the next few days.

"That's great," Carlo said. "Still, feel free at any time to come over for a chat, to blow off steam, whatever. Okay?"

"We could take care of Diedrich when he comes over next," added Tomoko. "Our kids would love it."

Peter didn't stay long. He embraced them and told them he needed to make some phone calls. He called Clara. She wasn't home. He left a message. Next he called Bernard at the gallery. Bernard sounded upset when he answered the phone. "You want me to call back tomorrow?" Peter asked him, realizing the late hour.

"Naw," Bernard said, "that's okay. I'm pissed because that hotshot photographer with the posh studio on 57th Street just called to tell me he can't make it for next week's opening. Wants me to postpone the opening by ten days, 'cause he's got to go to Paris. The jerk. The invitations are out and the posters have been up for weeks." Peter raised his agnostic eyes to heaven in silent acknowledgment of the inscrutable nature of fate.

"Jesus," he empathized, back on earth. "You mean he won't have his work ready for hanging? Or he can't make it to the opening?"

"Both. So I'll just have to push back the opening and do a second mailing for the invitations. I hate the guy. I'll have to place correction ads all over the place, and turn away any public that shows up regardless."

"Don't do that. Can't you just keep my show going? I could maybe change some of the pictures, give you some new material. Not to disappoint the unwary."

"Maybe I can, maybe not. But that's not the point," Bernard said.

"Not for you, I know," said Peter, "but for me, nothing could be more to the point. You see, the reason I called you..." And he told him what had happened, and what he had told his father about extending the exhibition. "I knew it couldn't be done. But, well, I just had to, you know, give him something to look forward to. To fight for...you understand?"

"Yes, sure. Sure. Stabbed in the belly, you say? That's insane. I suppose it was a black thug, the attacker?"

"That's unclear."

"This goddamn wicked city is getting worse by the day. I think I'm gonna sell up and move out. Somewhere nice. I have a cousin living in the Hamptons. She's been telling me for years to move to her village. Maybe I will. I'm getting tired of fighting all these battles."

"I know," said Peter. He knew Bernard meant every word he said. And would have forgotten them by morning. "You should do that. I'll come and visit you with a bag of pretzels, and give you all the news that's not fit to print. You'll be dying for both!"

Bernard laughed. "Every day you sound more like a true New Yorker."

"What about the exhibition? Can you help me out?"

"Sure, and never mind the extra material. I can just extend you for a week, as is. No problem, as it turns out. You'll have to thank the jerk of 57th Street for that. And take care of your dad. I'm sure he'll recover soon. Reporters are a hardy breed."

In the Eyes of the Son

# Chapter 34

Bernard's optimism, though based on little more than his kind heart, seemed warranted. Eduard was making good progress.

When Peter called Dr. Fenstein the next morning, he was told that his vital signs were almost normal, that he'd had a good night's rest, and that he could now begin to receive visitors, preferably one at a time, for short visits, and not more than two a day.

"We've moved him to a private room," the doctor said. "And we're keeping a close eye on him."

An hour later, Peter was at his father's bedside. What struck him from the moment he caught sight of Eduard was his lively expression, his *eagerness*. He was pale, but his eyes were searching and animated. When he saw Peter, he grinned and said, "There you are!" and motioned him to come and sit down. He was very much in charge.

Peter took the chair, warily. He couldn't account for this unaccustomed exuberance.

"Sorry to put you to all this trouble," said Eduard, and then, "He didn't want my money, you know!"

"Who?"

"The attacker. He wasn't after my cash."

Peter smiled. He hoped the smile wasn't patronizing.

"You hear what I'm saying? He didn't want my money!"

"Of course he wanted your money. Why else would he attack you?"

Eduard stared at him. "You're not listening. Nobody's listening. I'm *telling* you, he just wanted to kill me. He wasn't after the money!"

"Why would anyone... Why are you so sure, Dad?"

"He'd been following me, I'd half noticed him, felt him behind me, like a shadow. Then he was gone. The next moment, I was looking at my street map, he's in front of me, out of nowhere, pointing his knife at me with one hand, and snatching the map away with the other. He throws the map on the street. Then he starts pulling at my clothes with his free hand. My pants, my shirt. I fend him off, kicking him and pushing my fists in his face. And then he stabs me. Deep. I felt the cool steel slide into me. And being pulled out. And a second time. The piercing pain. He tried to kill me, of course, but he made a bad job of it. I'd have done it better!" Eduard started coughing, and he frowned and held his left side. The cough subsided.

"Is it hurting?"

"What d'you think?" Another cough or two. "First the assassin cuts me up, then the surgeon." He leaned back into his pillows, grinning again. "Amateurs," he said mockingly.

"He didn't demand your money?" Peter said incredulously.

"Never said a word. Just wanted to kill me."

"But he was trying to get at your wallet! You just told me."

"I said nothing of the kind. He just pulled my shirt out so he could see where to plunge his knife. I tell you, he's an assassin."

"That's ridiculous, Dad! Who would be out to kill you?"

Eduard gave him a knowing look. "You give that some thought, boy. Remember I'm the father of a controversial photographer!"

This unexpected turn of thought stunned Peter. Surely he couldn't mean that he, Eduard van Doorn, on a private visit to New York, had been a *target?* How would they know him, his connection to his son? They didn't know where he lived. And who were "they" anyway? The Harlem marchers? The face of the thin young man at the press opening came floating up. The crazy one. Could he have? Nonsense. Peter wasn't that important! It was all pure coincidence.

"Was he black?" he asked.

"Couldn't tell. He was wearing gloves and one of those ski masks.

Anyway, that's irrelevant."

This convinced Peter even more that it had been an attempted robbery. Nothing more. He was about to tell his father so. But the eager expression in his father's eyes held him back. He had seen that expression before, long ago. He couldn't remember when, was it back home, in Holland, when he was a schoolboy? In the darkroom days? Yes, that's when it must have been, that expression of strength and hope. Of conviction. It was that same look. The look he had lost long ago.

The look of unshakable faith. His father believed in what he had just suggested: the assassination scenario. And his socialist principles made the color of the assassin's skin irrelevant.

"Can't you see?" his father said. "He followed me all the way from the loft. He was waiting for you. But I came out. So he decided to kill me instead. Pretty nearly succeeded, too!"

The implications of his father's theory were too complex for Peter to handle at this moment. He needed time to think. But Eduard, his face flushed, was pressing him for approval.

"This city is a war zone! You're risking your life here!"

"What you're telling me, Dad, is…well, far-reaching, and you may…"

The nurse interrupted them. "Time's up!" she said brightly.

Peter patted his father on the arm. "I'll be back tomorrow, Dad. With Pauline." The moment he said it he realized how unwise it was to spring a surprise like that on a man in his condition.

Eduard didn't reply. He just stared at his son.

"I'm sorry if I upset you. Thing is, she's never been to New York either and with you in the hospital and my show still on, she said she had two good reasons to fly over. Isn't it wonderful?"

"Yes. I suppose so." Eduard managed a smile, but the news had clearly made him realize that his condition was more serious than he had believed.

He yawned and sank deeper into his pillows, a twitching face muscle betraying a shaft of pain. "Thanks for everything," he said, as he turned his head slightly to fix his gaze on Peter's face. "And be careful. He may still be on the prowl."

Peter promised to be on his guard, then left.

A few hours later, Pauline arrived in Greene Street by taxi from Kennedy Airport.

Peter greeted her with a fond embrace. "Welcome to New York!"

"Thanks, Brother. I can't believe it!"

"Neither can I. Let me look at you." He held her at arm's length.

"How's Dad?" She had asked the decent, honest question, but her manner told him not to give her any bad news just yet.

"He's doing okay. Considering. You know. He was quite talkative today, actually."

"Talkative? That's a good sign! Right?"

"Of course. And he can't wait to see you."

"Oh, you told him." She pouted. "It was supposed to be a surprise. You spoiled it." She grinned and poked him in the ribs. "Hey, big brother, show me around. I want to see everything."

"First a drink?"

"*And* a drink."

Clara called back when they were having dinner. Same pasta and pesto sauce and green salad he'd planned for his dad two days earlier.

He told her in a few words what had happened, and that Pauline had arrived, "to see the show, basically." He played down the seriousness of Eduard's condition. "He'll be okay, I think. I just wanted you to be aware of what happened. No, no, no need to come over." He wasn't ready to cope with her, too. "Sure, you can tell Diedrich. He has a right to know. I'll keep you posted. Yes, it's pretty awful… I knew you'd say that. As if Chicago is any safer! Wait, Pauline wants to say hello. Talk to you soon."

Ten minutes later, Clara called again.

"Diedrich wants to fly down before school starts, to see the exhibition once again. He says the last visit was much too short. And he's worried about your dad, of course."

Peter said that would be fine, and suggested she put him on a plane in the morning. "I'll pick him up at LaGuardia." Pauline was pointing at herself. "Or maybe Pauline will. She's dying to see him!"

268

Pauline dismissed her brother's concerns about her jetlag and unfamiliarity with New York public transport by reminding him that she'd grown up while he was away. She would meet her nephew at LaGuardia and take him along to the hospital. And Peter could then take them to the exhibition the following day.

These practicalities out of the way, Peter told Pauline about Eduard's assassination theory.

"Let him believe it, Peter. He's always been a violence freak. It will put some spice back into his retired life."

"A violence freak? Because he took those war pictures?"

"I don't know, but he's always had a taste for it. War movies. Formula One, preferably with a pile-up. Even the evening news was better if it included an armed revolution somewhere or a good, bloody battle."

"I fail to see what that's got to do with his assassination scenario."

"Sensation, that's what. It makes a good story to tell back home. It'll make him look like a hero. That's why I say let him believe it. It will probably make him get well faster."

How wrong Pauline was, Peter thought, to believe that Eduard was motivated by anything as shallow as a thirst for violence. But she wouldn't understand his real reasons. The reasons Peter had only just begun to perceive, and which he thought would take the rest of his life to fully fathom.

"You may well be right," he said. "And why not? We all need our illusions to survive in this vale of tears."

He looked at Pauline, her smart-cut hair and stylish clothes. She smiled at him and he smiled back. He felt grateful having her for a sister, but this brief moment of happiness, unaccountably, made him acutely aware of his own unfathomable loneliness.

While they were getting ready for the night, Fran called to express her concern and to get a progress report. It was very early morning for her, and she was calling from their parents' home. After a few minutes, she put his mother on.

"There is something I want you to do for me, Peter," she said, sounding unusually clear and purposeful. "Your father is not the complaining type, but

I know he must hate that hospital food. Can you get him some good brown bread and Dutch cheese? Mature Gouda. They will allow that, won't they?"

Peter's impulse was to dismiss his mother's request as petty and uncalled for, but he controlled himself. "Sure, Mother, I can do that."

"And some ripe tomatoes if you can find them. Truss tomatoes. They have those in New York? He loves them, with the cheese and the bread. It's really his favorite food. I don't have to cook if I give him that."

"I'll see what I can do, Mother."

"And another thing. Tell him his paper called. They want him to do a full-page article on the birth of socialism in Holland. For their centennial edition in October. Right up his alley. Still plenty of time, of course, but he can start thinking about it in the hospital. That'll be good for him."

"Good idea. But why don't you tell him yourself? He's got a phone in his room."

"No, no, he can do without his wife's nagging for a while. I'll wait until he feels better. Until *he* wants to call *me*."

Peter laughed. He was surprised at his mother's acumen and caring. Somehow he had always taken her for granted, the way she moved about the half-dark house like a gray spectre, her days mapped out, resembling an unchanging bus route.

"You sure know the old fox, don't you?" he said affectionately.

"Enough to know when not to bother him." He thought he heard her chuckle. "Take it from me. A good wife knows how to make herself invisible."

He laughed again, a little too loudly, as if to drown out a flash memory of Clara. Was his mother's remark a veiled criticism of her always conspicuous daughter-in-law? No, his mother was not devious. Her criticisms, such as they were, had always been straightforward.

"I'll give him your message about the article. And I'll go and hunt for the groceries. Anything else?"

There was a pause. "Mother?"

"Tell him I'm taking care of the bills."

"The bills?"

"He always attends to them. You know, gas, electric, telephone. I don't want him to worry. Just tell him I'm taking care of the administration."

"Sure, Mother. I'll tell him." He felt a surge of loving warmth for her. Clearly, it was not the mundane words that had brought it on. The words were camouflage for deeper sentiments that were too private to name: the wife's affection and devotion to the husband. Her undying love.

But there was also buried in these simple words an echo of the eternal condition of women of her generation and before: her almost certain widow's fate. After a life of dependency on the husband she would one day be exposed, suddenly and irreversibly, to the realities of social and financial responsibility. His mother, with her reassuring talk about "paying the bills," had let it be known that, whatever happened, she was up to the task.

Peter marveled at her subtlety, his warm feelings tinged with a new respect. He thought with bitter sadness that Clara, with her own independent ambition in life, had been incapable of that kind of single-minded dedication. But then, theirs had been a different kind of marriage. A *modern* marriage, based on equality, in which such subservience had no part. Yet he couldn't help feeling that their bond, too, had been a strong one, and that it would have evolved into their own kind of happiness, if she—if *they*—had only let it.

# Chapter 35

The following morning Pauline took the subway to the airport and returned with Diedrich by taxi to Mt. Sinai Hospital where they had agreed to meet up with Peter. Before going in, Peter took them to a nearby café on Madison Avenue for a simple lunch.

Diedrich was subdued at the prospect of seeing his grandfather, whom he could only vaguely remember. He couldn't understand why anyone had wanted to harm him, and kept asking Peter for an explanation.

"There's no way to explain it, Son. There are bad people in this world, and your granddad had the misfortune to be targeted by one of them, someone out to get at his money. And because he resisted, he was…he got hurt…" His emotions were getting the better of him. He abruptly asked for the bill and said they'd better go.

At the hospital, he said that he wouldn't join them because it would be "too much" for the patient. He touched his son's head. "You go in there now, Son, with your auntie, and comfort your granddad. I'm going to take a walk in the park and see you in half an hour. Okay?"

Peter stepped out. It was another hot day, cooled somewhat by a soft, north-westerly breeze. Central Park at this level was full of family groups and running kids and nannies pushing baby carriages. Most of the people were African-American or Hispanic, evidence of Harlem's proximity, but there were many white faces mixed with the dark, including elderly or handicapped patients wheeled around by the usually dark-skinned nurses. Peter realized that African-Americans were still largely in roles of servitude, a notion he found profoundly disturbing.

It occurred to him that the heckler at the opening reception—the woman who had shouted, "Nothing has changed!"—might be right. Clearly, the "truth" often depended on who was talking.

Half an hour later, he was back at the hospital. It took another ten minutes before Pauline and Diedrich appeared. She had a frown of worry on her face.

"What's wrong?" he asked.

"I don't know, Peter. He's distracted. I don't really know if he was pleased to see us. One moment he's all lovey-dovey, patting my thighs and hugging Diedrich, and the next moment he hardly seems to notice us. It's not that he dozes off or anything, he just seems preoccupied with something else."

"Something else? What do you mean?" Peter asked, as they left the building and crossed into the park.

"Something to do with you. I think he wants to tell you something. He keeps saying, 'Peter has done it!' Even to Diedrich, he said, 'Your dad's done it!' But he looks more puzzled than pleased with what you've done."

"That I quit banking? Took up photography? That's three years ago."

"It's more than that. The stir you caused. The Harlem protest. The commotion. Your heroic speech. I told you he's a sensation nut!"

"Did he say all that?"

"No, but I think that's what he wants to talk to you about. It's my hunch."

Diedrich tried to get in a word.

"Yes, Son?"

"I think, Dad, that...I don't know, I think Granddad wants to know if..." He suddenly stopped to hug his father.

"Yes? What is it, Diedrich?"

"I think he wants to know if you, if you...love him!" He looked up tearfully at his own father, who could only hold him tight, as he gathered up Pauline with his other arm.

They stood there for a few long moments, not finding any words to add to what the boy had said. Then, to break the emotion, Peter diverted their attention to the chipmunks foraging under the trees. Here and there an early yellowed leaf broke the lush monotony of the late summer foliage.

"Let's take a walk around the park," he proposed. But Diedrich had other ideas.

"Can't we go to the gallery? I want to see your pictures again!"

Peter looked at Pauline. She looked at her watch and shook her head.

"We'll go tomorrow. It's too late today, and we're all a bit tired."

They spent the evening cooking, eating and playing Monopoly, which Diedrich won. It was past eleven when they finally turned in. It had been a long day.

They slept in and had a late brunch the following morning. By the time they reached the Magazine Gallery, it was early afternoon. A printed strip of paper with the words "Extended by popular demand" had been pasted across the poster at the entrance.

Peter wanted to introduce Pauline and Diedrich to Lunette, but he found her embroiled in a heated telephone conversation with, he thought, Bernard. So he showed Pauline and Diedrich some of the photos until they made it clear that they wanted to roam around on their own for a while.

As he drifted off in another direction his thoughts kept returning to Diedrich's feeling that "Granddad wants to know if you love him." So life, in the end, comes down to a need for reassurance, a reaffirmation of the unbroken bond between child and parent?

"Hey, are you there?" Pauline was trying to attract his attention.

"Sorry, vital reflections of the other kind." He noticed Diedrich gazing at a picture at the far end of the space.

"Just want to ask you a question. What were you thinking when you took the shot of the boy on the stairs, that one there, that image of no hope?"

Peter hesitated. "I don't remember. Maybe I was drawn to his grief, I guess. Because I empathized. Maybe I shot the scene to will the grief away."

"And then you display it on a wall. That's not empathy, that's exploitation. You're exploiting his grief."

"Wrong. I display the photo because the attempt at exorcism failed.

Because I'm actually powerless to do anything more than show the world that such grief exists. To…to rouse the conscience of the world. Exploitation is the furthest from my mind."

"So in the end you are a bystander. A silent observer."

"A *concerned* observer. There is a difference."

Pauline nodded. "I just wondered," she said, her confronting eagerness melting into a languid smile. Then she embraced him and kissed him on the cheek. "It's a fine exhibition, Peter. A really beautiful, moving exhibition." She seemed to swallow a tear away. "You are truly a great photographer, you know." Then she added playfully, "Just as I predicted."

"Thanks," said Peter. "Not great. Let's say serious."

"*And* great. I know about these things. I can tell when something has true worth."

This time it was Peter who smiled. His little sister had come a long way. He wondered where she'd learned her self-assured ways. Her insights were far from perfect, but there was a confidence, an urgency of intent and expression that betrayed considerable exposure to art and literature. When had she acquired that knowledge?

"You can tell when something has true worth? How? I often don't know the difference."

She gave him a "naughty you" look and then decided he wasn't teasing. "Oh, Peter, it's not a hard and fast thing. But I've discovered that I'm sometimes drawn to certain art in a hall, while all the rest leaves me cold. It's almost instantaneous, the attraction. I do a quick walk-around, and instinctively pick out the pieces that appeal to me. That I feel *drawn* to. Then I give them a thorough inspection. The rest I don't bother with."

"Ah, love at first sight, is it?"

"You make it sound banal. There's no love involved."

"Fascination then."

She looked at him askance. "Yeah. Kind of. But the word is inadequate."

Their eyes met. They both gave a brief, embarrassed laugh. It was one of those moments when he felt a deep bond with his sister. She was the only person with whom he could have a genuine understanding, a soul-to-soul subterranean communication.

Diedrich came running back. "Dad! The shot of the girl blowing soap bubbles! I helped you develop it!"

"You sure did! Remember why you liked it?"

"The girl. She looks so happy in her torn T-shirt. And the reflections in the bubbles, those faces!"

Pauline nodded. "That's also one of my favorites. Good illustration of the show's theme. Anyway, Brother," she said, "I really like your work. I love it. I want to take another look, together with the photographer this time, so I can ask all I want."

"Me too!" cried Diedrich.

They spent another half hour at the show, pausing at every picture, with Peter trying to respond to his sister's probing questions and his son's bursts of excitement.

As they were ready to leave Pauline said she wanted to take a stroll around the neighborhood by herself, "to get the feel of my brother's new environment."

Peter frowned. "You really want to do that? Alone?"

"You told me this part of town is safe. And I've got a map. So don't worry." She gave him a pat on the arm.

"All right then," agreed Peter, reluctantly. "But don't talk to strangers! Diedrich and I are going home to do some serious darkroom work, right, Son?" The boy smiled happily at his father.

Before Pauline ran off, Peter introduced her to Lunette, who still seemed upset by the telephone call.

"Hi, Pauline," she said. "I'm so sorry about your father. I'm sure he'll get well soon. I've heard so much about you!" *Rubbish*, thought Peter. He had never talked about his sister.

Lunette turned to Peter. "Bernard wants me to do the hanging for the next exhibition all by myself. He has to go to East Hampton, and the photographer, Victor Lamone, won't be returning from Paris until the day of the opening. It's unfair, don't you think?"

"I can help you," Peter said. He felt he owed Bernard something for the extension.

"Oh, no, I can't let you do that. What with your father in the hospital and all. No, I'll manage. I just think he's being unfair."

Pauline was getting impatient. "Nice meeting you, Lunette. Your problem sounds familiar! Good luck!" And to Peter, "I'll be back before dinner."

As they walked home, Diedrich wanted to know what kind of darkroom work they were going to do.

"Oh, a new project, about growing up, from baby to boy to young man." He paused for effect. "Also known as the Diedrich Series."

That hit home. "I know! I've already seen some of them!"

Back in the loft, there were two messages on the machine: One was from Clara to say she was thinking of coming over to see his father, and when would be convenient? The other was from Carlo and Tomoko inviting him over "for a bite, with your sister." He decided to wait with answering both.

They went straight into the darkroom and spent the rest of the afternoon there, under the red safelight, bent over the images slowly coming to life in the developer. Diedrich in his baby crib, as a toddler, in kindergarten, building a snowman, high on a swing, in school and at home, laughing and crying. To Peter, it was like reliving his old darkroom days, those long-ago times of intimacy with his dad, except now *he* was the dad. Fleeting thoughts of the old man in his hospital bed kept interfering with memories of the past and the innocent enthusiasm of Diedrich right next to him. Joy and sadness inextricably interwoven, the mystery of it all was more than he could handle. But he managed to conceal his emotions from the boy.

Once Pauline was back, the three of them went out for a simple meal at a neighborhood Italian restaurant. By ten o'clock, Diedrich was yawning, and Peter put him to bed.

"Sorry you have to fly back home tomorrow, Son. Pauline will take you to the airport, okay?"

"Sure, Dad. And you'll go and see Granddad tomorrow, won't you?" the boy asked.

"Of course I will."

Diedrich hugged his dad, said goodnight, and fell asleep.

Peter returned Clara's call and promised to call her again to fix a date for her visit after seeing Eduard the following day, "because he wants to be consulted first before every visit."

Next, he called Carlo to thank them for their kind thought. He said Pauline and he would, of course, be happy to come over once the situation had settled down a bit.

Then he opened a bottle of Meursault, fetched two glasses and joined Pauline for a quiet chat. He told her about the neighbors' invitation.

"How kind," she said. But right now she was more interested to hear how her brother coped, living alone in New York.

"Oh, I've learned to cook," he said.

"And what do you do for company? You know…"

"No… I admit it's lonely, but I've got to concentrate on my work. What about you?"

"Same thing, basically. No time for a serious affair, let alone marriage. And I love my freedom, I think."

He wanted to know more. "Am I prying?"

"I don't mind. But I don't know how to answer. You see, I do want a man. A permanent partner. It's easy enough to find a sexy hunk, or a stable executive with a big car, or even a pale brain with a Nobel in his future. But I want something different. A relationship that honors life. We've only one life to live, and I don't want to waste it. I can't say this to anyone else, but you, I think you understand, don't you? That I'm not just arrogant?"

"Not arrogant, no. Unrealistic, perhaps. What you're seeking is rare, and only available in short, unexpected little bursts, if at all." He thought of Laura. "There are no long-term leases available on happiness. If you try to organize your life around a model for everlasting bliss, you may end up an old maid." He hadn't wanted to come across so heavy-handed, but Pauline didn't seem to take it that way.

"I'm not looking for bliss. I'm looking for someone who can add the spice to my sugar, the helium to my balloon."

"Oh, you know how to fly without the help of someone else's gas."

"Only when I dream."

"Dream on then, little sister. But remember, even a man in a gray flannel suit may be able to lift you high, if you only let him."

# Chapter 36

After breakfast, Peter called the hospital and left a message that he would be there around noon.

Before Pauline left with Diedrich for LaGuardia, Peter took them to a grocery to get the bread and cheese and tomatoes his mother had asked for. At a nearby café, over coffee, they talked about Eduard, while Diedrich played with his Mattel Auto Race.

"You must let him speak his mind, Peter. Encourage him. He may not be able to later."

"I'm not sure I want to hear what's on his mind. He and I have never had a good talk."

"That's exactly why you should give him a chance. You'll regret it for the rest of your life if you don't. Remember what *he* told you yesterday?" she said, pointing at Diedrich.

Once he was alone, Peter lost no time getting to the hospital. Eduard was half-sitting up in bed, waiting for his son. Peter held up the shopping bag. "From Mother. Your favorite food. And she says not to worry. She's taking care of the bills."

"She's what? She's never paid a bill in her life!" Eduard rummaged half-heartedly inside the brown paper bag. "Can't have it yet, of course. I'm still on the drip."

"I know. I should have waited. But she insisted."

"Silly woman." But he smiled. "Paying the bills, eh?"

Only now Peter noticed the poster, complete with extension notice.

"Bernard brought it," Eduard said. "Very kind man. A bit of a show-off, but very kind of him to visit me."

"How so, show-off?" Peter felt some irritation that Bernard, who had never met his father, had decided to pay a visit without asking him first.

"Oh, he bragged about everything. His gallery, his magazine, his family, you."

"His family?" Peter didn't know anything about Bernard's family. And it wasn't really the subject he wanted to hear about.

"His two sons in college, his Alsatians, and his wife, in that order. His wife is a curator at the Whitney. But you know all that, of course."

"Yes. And what else? What did he have to say? About me?"

"That you were a…a…" He stopped and grimaced, and bent forward.

"Dad, what is it?" Eduard's face was contorted with pain. For a while he didn't answer. Then he straightened himself.

"Nothing. Must be the wound trying to heal. Contractions. Normal thing. Ah, this is better."

"Shall I call the doctor?"

"Oh, no, there's no need. You were asking… Yes, Bernard. He says you're sensational. A phenomenon. His words. You're a phenomenon because you turned your back on banking to become a daring lens man. And he called you a real pro. Are Americans always so gushing in their praise?"

His tone was almost mocking, but Peter could see he was struggling to suppress something, his "verdict" on his son's long-delayed career change, if not on the exhibition, which he had yet to see.

True, Eduard had specially flown over to New York to see the exhibition, but Peter wasn't at all certain that he was prepared to recant his earlier judgments about his son's photographic ambitions. After all, he had never recanted his socialist views either, in spite of overwhelming evidence of socialism's worldwide bankruptcy. He decided not to press the issue.

"Americans like to exaggerate, Dad. He was just being polite. Don't read too much into it."

His father now became obstinate. "How can you generalize like that? You're implying that all Americans are the same. Well, he seemed to mean it.

And his family came from Poland, he told me. That makes a difference, I'd think."

Peter's irritation now jumped to the surface. Irritation with both Bernard and his father.

"Okay, go and believe him then if it makes you happy. Believe that I'm the genius of the decade. It's the same to me."

Eduard looked at him in shock. "You mean you're indifferent to my opinion? That's what you're saying, aren't you? You are saying that I'm…"

Dr. Fenstein interrupted them. He was on his rounds, with a nurse in tow. "And how are we doing here?" he said as he came in, pushing the bedside trolley away and taking Eduard's pulse, all in one flowing movement. "Any pain?"

"Yes. But I can stand it," said the patient firmly.

"There's no need to play the hero. Just let the nurse know and she'll know what to do. Mmm, you're running a temperature. You'd better rest now, and we'll give you something to keep the fever down." He nodded to the nurse, and then perched on Eduard's bed.

"You're doing as well as can be expected under the circumstances, Mr. van Doorn," he said. "But we shouldn't underestimate the trauma you've suffered. It will take a while to get you out of here. Meanwhile, I advise you try to avoid excitement, and get plenty of rest." The doctor nodded to Peter. "I'd like to have a word with your son," he said. Peter followed him into the corridor.

"I'd advise you to keep your visits brief, for now. Until we have a firmer handle on his recovery. I don't like that fever. Could mean the wound got infected. I'll prescribe something for that. I think you'd better leave him now. You can visit him again tomorrow."

Peter told his father that he had to go, without giving a reason. But Eduard wasn't fooled.

"I know the doctor told you to. He's worried, and he's right. I don't feel good. But I want to tell you something, Peter. Don't worry, I take the responsibility. I've been wanting to tell you this for years. Sit down, and listen to me." Peter pulled up the chair and sat down. So this was it.

"Okay, Dad, I'm listening." He managed a wan smile.

"I want to tell you why I quit photography at the end of the war. You asked me that once, and I couldn't give you a truthful answer then. But I'll tell you now. The reason I quit is because I loved it too much. In those few war years, I'd developed such a passion for the camera, for aiming and shooting, it was close to an obsession. I think I saw it as a weapon, a weapon that could kill. When I took that shot in Arnhem, I was that German soldier plunging the bayonet into the enemy. Whose side I was on, whose side did the killing, that was irrelevant. It was the *moment* that counted for me, the photographic moment. It gave me a thrill to press the shutter at exactly the right moment.

"But I had a family waiting. So when the war was over, I made a decision. I decided to return to the family. And don't think that wasn't a hard decision to make. I had offers, and I enjoyed the freedom. But I placed morality above art, you might say. There is no objective merit in that. It was just my personal choice."

Eduard coughed repeatedly, but when Peter rose to comfort him, he shook his head.

"I'm okay," he said. "So I returned to my old life, though I didn't like the post-war politics. But that's another story. And then you took up photography, the very thing I'd given up. I encouraged you. I was happy working in that darkroom with you, seeing you come home with *my* old Leica hanging from your neck. You showed real promise.

"And then that awful incident. That man getting killed in the eye of your lens. And you, you forgetting to press the shutter. You...more interested in the...in the steaming soup and the woman's blue dress than in the instant of death. In the supreme...photographic moment! You failed me. It was an awful way to think, and ever since I've tried to find the words to apologize to you, but I couldn't. Because deep down that's what I felt. That you had failed me!" His cough came back.

"Dad, please!" But again, his concern was waved away.

"Let me continue! I even wondered if you had my genes. For if so, you would have shared my obsession and done the right thing! Of course this talk

284

of genes was ludicrous, even I knew that. I'd never had reason to distrust your mother. But that actually made it worse. You had the talent, but you squandered it. That's right! You *squandered* your talent.

"So I fixed you up with the bank. I was aghast that you accepted it so meekly. But that only confirmed my diagnosis. You didn't put up a fight. You hear me? *You didn't fight!* You…you…"

Eduard was flying into a rage, fists clenched, face flushed. He had another coughing fit, and he was clutching his side. Peter tried to calm him, but Eduard shook him off.

"Sorry. The past again. Actually, I knew I couldn't hold you responsible for what was really *my* problem. In the end, you were my son, and I wanted you to have a good life." He grabbed his son's hands. "You realized that, didn't you?"

"Yes, Dad, of course. That much I always knew," Peter said. He looked at his father, his earnestness and honesty, and he thought, so this is what his life has come down to: making peace with himself by coming clean with his son. By earning his son's respect.

That's what Clara had told him. Do the right thing, *or Diedrich will never respect you.* Eduard wanted to ensure his son's respect. Well, he need try no more. Peter's respect for him, severely shaken at times, was now fully restored. It pained him to see the straining figure before him, leaning sideways, holding his hands, beseeching him to believe what he was telling him.

"Thank you for telling me this, Dad. It helps me come to terms with my own life. But now you must rest and…"

"I'm not finished!" his father interjected.

"Tomorrow, Dad. You must get some sleep now. You know what the doctor said."

"Tomorrow I may be dead," he said with a sardonic smile. "I don't trust these amateurs here. No, I want you to hear me out. *Now.* That's all I ask of you."

"All right then. But try to keep it brief."

"It will take as long as it takes," Eduard said primly. "The most important part is what I have discovered here, this week, in New York."

"What have you discovered, Dad?"

"I will tell you in a minute. You see," he continued, in a low voice, "when I was a student, I discovered Marx. He had the answers! Equality was his goal, social revolution the means. I felt inspired and passionately committed. All my writing for the paper was colored by that passionate belief in salvation through socialism. Then the war came, and I had to escape. I took up photography because its message was universal and transcended language. It was a rational decision. But it became my second passion.

"Embracing passion had always been my way of dealing with life. It was also a physical necessity. Your mother could confirm that if she weren't so discrete..." He gave Peter a knowing look. "A good thing that there were so many equally passionate socialist young women around or your mother might have run away screaming!" Peter smiled, recalling the way his father had looked at the girls in the downtown café.

"Then came the decline of socialism and the 'liberations' of the sixties and seventies. They should have opened my eyes to the dangers of blind passion. But as a true believer, I blamed big business, right-wing politicians, America, the CIA, people's gullibility and stupidity in general. And I blamed you."

Peter stole a furtive glance at his watch. It was getting late. His father was not coming to the point.

"You hear me? I was blaming *you*!" his father repeated.

"I heard you. For what?"

"For compromising. For being bourgeois. For...for...taking life the easy way."

"The easy way? Do you have any idea..."

"I know! I *know*! That's what I'm getting at. You must let me finish."

"Dad, you're not well. We've got to wind this up so you can go to sleep."

"I'll sleep when I've unburdened my mind. Not a moment earlier!"

"Then tell me, Dad, what it is you've discovered in New York. I want to know."

286

"Very well. It's this: that following your dream, however enticing, is not a condition for a worthwhile life. But neither is the killing of that dream."

He waited for this declaration to sink in, for Peter to understand the depth of his discovery. It was slow in coming, as Peter tried to comprehend the implications of the confession. Had his father finally abandoned his stubborn prejudices? Was he saying that postponement of personal fulfilment was at least as valuable in life as yielding to a deep-felt passion—or to the resolute rejection of that passion for moral reasons? If that was the nature of his discovery, he was in fact telling his son that he, Peter, had lived his life right.

Peter felt his chest open up. He lifted his eyes and they met his father's. Yes, he thought that was his father's message. Without a word, he placed his arms around the ailing man and hugged him clumsily to his chest. His father's body felt hot. The fever must have gone up.

Eduard, embarrassed and uncomfortable, patted Peter on the back. "Now, now," he said, as he withdrew from the embrace, "it's not *that* earth shaking a discovery. All I'm really saying is, well done! You know my penchant for cloaking simple truths in elaborate formulas."

"But you haven't even seen my exhibition!"

"Oh, you're right! Well, it's irrelevant."

"Irrelevant? It's what you came to New York for, right? And it's been extended, for you!"

"No, no, by popular demand. Peter van Doorn, controversial photographer, showing in New York, by p-popular demand...Peter van Doorn..." His face, suddenly redder, seemed to be on fire, his eyes glazed and feverish. Peter got a cool towel and placed it on his forehead. Then he called the nurse.

"I just...woke up, here in my chair," he lied. "I think my father's temperature has gone up, don't you?" The nurse took the patient's temperature. Her face betrayed shock.

"Yes, I'll call the doctor. I thought you were gone long ago," she added in mild reprimand.

Eduard was getting delirious. His eyes were closed but he kept on

287

babbling. "Peter van Doorn, you better watch out, they're out to kill you. Pretty damn near killed me instead, right? You didn't know? That's why I'm here, in this rat hole…amateurs…trying to kill me too…made a mess of it…"

"It's all right, Dad. You're going to be all right. All you need is rest."

His father opened his eyes and lifted his head. His eyelids were swollen.

"You here, my boy? You should be working, shouldn't you? You're doing a fine job." He smiled and let his head fall back again. Then he opened them once more.

"Oh, I forgot. Tell your mother I'm all right with underwear. And socks. She always worries about my socks. Can't help it, I guess. And yes, yes, how's your son? What's his name?"

"Diedrich. Your grandson."

"Right! My grandson… Photo…photo…what do you call yourself?"

"Photographer. Like you were, Dad."

"No, no, I gave it up. You took it up! That's good, don't you think?"

"Very good, Dad."

"And my grandson…he must feel mighty proud of you. A photographer who…who…is wanted by the police." He frowned. "No, no, by the *people*. Don't get yourself killed now!" He wagged a warning finger in Peter's direction. "Let 'em kill me instead! Easy job." He smiled at his little joke, his eyes closed again, his face falling sideways against the pillow. "Easy job…"

The doctor, a different one from an hour ago, examined Eduard and decided his temperature was "far too high." They would need to run some tests.

"His heartbeat is strong, though, so I'd say there's no cause for immediate concern. I suggest you leave him to us now and call us in the morning for an update."

Peter thanked him and said goodnight to his father, who had dozed off and didn't reply.

Outside, the tension breaking, Peter choked away his tears. He felt responsible for the worsening of his father's condition, but immensely grateful for their talk, which he knew could only have come about under these dramatic circumstances.

Eduard's words of praise, his full *acceptance* of his son, had warmed his soul. He smiled in embarrassment as he realized that he had, after all, been waiting for this sign of his father's approval. But he knew the need for acceptance had been mutual, that Eduard had been in even greater need of Peter's respect and approval than Peter for his. At this stage in his life that had been, without a doubt, his father's single most important hope. And it had been realized.

In the Eyes of the Son

# Chapter 37

Eduard's condition rapidly worsened, the result of toxic poisoning caused by a rupture of his colon. The surgery attempt to save him failed. He died the following evening at 7:15 on the operating table.

Peter and Pauline, called to the hospital, were in the waiting room as their father passed away.

Dr. Fenstein was quick to point out that "excessive emotional strain apparently caused by lengthy relatives' visits" was a serious contributing factor in the death. Peter didn't react to the accusation, but knew it to be true. He did feel, though, that the hospital should have enforced its own rules and restrictions. But if they had, he thought ruefully, he wouldn't have had that restorative talk with his father, and Eduard might have died anyway.

They were waiting for the body to be moved to the morgue, where they could pay their last respects. Peter was holding Pauline's hand. She was distraught and quite at a loss to comprehend the abrupt turn of events.

"He wasn't an old man! He had a strong heart, the doctor said so himself. Why couldn't they save him, dammit!"

"Perhaps he was ready to die. He had lived his life, and he never was the same man since his retirement. The joy was gone. The glow in his eye. He'd lost it. But he did have some unfinished business."

"With you."

"Apparently. You were the one to realize that. And you urged me to listen to him. Your intuition was right, Pauline. You didn't know it when you flew over, but you had a crucial task to perform in New York. Father needed to make peace with himself before he..." Peter was overcome with sudden grief, and they embraced, brother and sister, seeking comfort in their sorrow, a sorrow that was enriched with gratitude for having helped their father in an unexpected way.

"I'm so sorry for Mother. I've robbed her of being at his death bed. And I've deprived Father, too. His place was by Mother, not in New York."

"His place was wherever he wanted to be, Peter," said Pauline, stroking her brother's hair. "Wherever he had to be. Perhaps there is no right place to die, only a right way."

"You think father died the right way? Stabbed by a Harlem hoodlum?"

"Not if you put it like that. But the point is that he died in peace and harmony with himself and his family, and that surely must be the right way. Most of all, he needed to know that you loved him. Just as Diedrich said."

Peter was grateful for her words. Such wisdom from her lips, such native insight. He embraced her again and whispered in her ear. "Thanks, Pauline. For seeing things clearly."

They followed a nurse down a long corridor. The cool hush of the morgue gripped them as they entered. *Another world*, thought Peter. *The other world, already.*

The nurse escorted them across the room, to a corner, where she opened a curtain. There, alone, lay Eduard van Doorn.

He had arrived only moments earlier, and his color hadn't completely drained from his face. His eyes were closed, but his mouth was curved in a faint smile. His whole appearance was one of repose and acceptance, not of agony. Peter knew now that his father had died in peace.

# Chapter 38

Peter and Pauline called their mother from the loft. There was a message on the machine when they entered. It was Mother. She had been unable to sleep and wondered if Father was all right. She had called his number at the hospital, but there was no answer. The time of the message was 7:10, five minutes before Eduard's death.

Peter didn't even have to wake her. She was waiting by the phone. She said she'd been expecting the bad news.

"He went peacefully, Mother."

"Did you have a good talk?" How did she know?

"Yes, an all-important talk. A life talk. There were no hard feelings left between us. Everything was cleared. I'm so grateful, and I believe he was, too."

"So he made his peace with you."

"Father was a good man, Mother. A wise man."

"He was a good husband. And a tyrant." He heard her swallow her tears. "I will miss him so."

Mother wanted Eduard back in Holland for the funeral. "So we can bury him properly, in Amsterdam."

"Of course, Mother. That's what we want, too. We'll bring him home."

"There's a plot reserved for him in the Zorgvlied Cemetery. You know that, don't you?"

"Yes, Mother, and that's where we'll take him. All together."

Before going to bed, Peter called Clara to break the news to her. She sounded wistful, as if the death of Peter's father also signified, in some way, the definitive end of her relationship with Peter. She said she would fly over to Holland for the burial, with Diedrich. "When's the funeral?"

"I'll let you know. It's swell of you to come, Clara. Thank you."

"I'm doing it for him, Peter. I liked your father. I think I understood him." Peter felt a twitch of the old resentment, but he didn't let on.

"Of course," he said, adding on second thought, "And at the end, he and I reached a deep understanding, too."

"I'm happy to hear that, Peter. But not really surprised. You gave him what he most wanted, after all."

"What I did was not intended as a gift to my father, Clara. Or to anyone else. But of course it pleased him to see me lead a…a different kind of life." There was a silence, and Peter feared that his choice of words had been unfortunate. "Professionally speaking," he added, a second or two too late.

"Yes, I can see that. Well, let me know when you've made the arrangements so I can take care of our bookings here. Sorry I can't be of any help, but you've Pauline with you."

Pauline proved indeed a great support. She handled the Holland side, while Peter made the necessary arrangements with the hospital and the airline. He also had to advise the Harlem police, which he decided to do in person. As the stabbing had now resulted in a death, they might want to upgrade their investigation.

He was right. Detective Sergeant Williamson said he would put another man on the case. "He'll be charged with manslaughter. I've a hunch we'll catch him."

"Why do you say that?"

"We've got a good description. Someone noticed a suspicious figure holding a rolled up T-shirt near the scene of the crime. The T-shirt may have concealed the weapon. Also, the money belt had fingerprints."

But Peter's mind was not on the police case. Perhaps his belief in justice was an abstraction, not tinged with desire for personal revenge. He was happy to leave the matter in the hands of the police. Besides, he had difficulty thinking of the assailant as "the killer." His father had, after all, survived the attack. His death had another cause, one in which he, the son, was heavily implicated.

He walked on. Everything was inextricably linked to everything else, he thought. But the linkage was only *activated* by some outside force, an act of violence, or an act of passion. His father was linked to his aggressor, and so was he, the son, without any act on his part. Yet they had nothing in common with this unknown assailant.

"Arbitrary," he said aloud. Life was arbitrary. He failed to see any grand purpose in it. It was meaningless to talk about "destiny" or "fate." What was not meaningless was to recognize the operation of cause and effect in human relations. His father's visit to New York had been triggered by his son's new venture into photography. One had clearly led to the other. But that Eduard's life had unexpectedly ended in New York was of no special significance, unless you embraced Eduard's assassination theory, which he didn't.

Eduard could have been attacked by a knife-wielding lunatic anywhere in the world. In the same way, Peter's reconciliation with his father had not been inevitable, and it could have occurred anywhere—or not at all. It might still have eluded them in New York had his sister not urged him to let his father speak his mind, or his son not sensed his granddad's need for his love.

The margins of truth and insight were indeed fearfully narrow. The chance to speak personally from the soul and be heard came perhaps only once in a lifetime, if at all.

Peter looked around him. Once again he found himself in Central Park. His chance for fulfilment of a different kind had occurred in New York, too. In terms of its soul-cleansing properties, it could be compared to what his father had experienced. The vibrations he was receiving here on the north lawn of the park, as he let his eyes rove about, were serene and life-giving.

It was a cool day for the time of the year. A cold air mass from Canada had brought a whiff of early autumn weather to New York. People were enjoying the respite from the heat. Figures were moving across the grass and under the trees, dogs and children were running about, a wheelchair pushed by a large, handsome black man with a shining face was coming up diagonally from the right, moving toward the center of his field of vision.

Suddenly, Peter was aware of a *design* before his eyes, a state of harmony between the constituent parts of the scene that hadn't been there moments earlier. The scene was framed by two tall trees whose clean, straight trunks and overhanging foliage served as a natural boundary of the composition. For a brief moment all was in equilibrium, the wheelchair in the middle right half with the crouched invalid in it and the powerful body of the attendant pushing it, providing a precise counterweight to the five or six frolicking children and their strolling mothers and nannies further away in the left half. A single dog, a large mongrel, leaping after a ball with its legs spread, provided a dynamic focus close to the center of the scene. The vision, so basic and yet so beautiful, frozen in time like a Seurat painting, excited him, and he knew that he must indeed have a special sensitivity to such matters. But he also knew that it might not last, that his chance for expressing his view of the world through photography had to be seized now, while it was alive inside him.

The following moment the scene had disintegrated into ordinariness, the separate elements once again in a state of flux and disorder, disparate, accidental. Peter turned away, chastened by the briefness of his vision, soberly directing his steps toward Mount Sinai Hospital, where he would meet up with Pauline.

She waved at him from a distance. He waved back. Soon she would be back in Amsterdam, and once the funeral was over, they wouldn't meet again for a long time. The thought was hard to bear. Her presence in New York had brought him face-to-face with his aloneness and temporarily banished it from his life. But this was no time for sentiment. He dashed across the intermittent 5th Avenue traffic to embrace her.

"Clara called. She and Diedrich will meet us at Schiphol," Pauline said cheerfully. "Oh, Peter, why did you two have to split up? Why can't you just kiss and mend?"

Peter hooked his arm into hers as they entered the building. "I've asked myself that question many times over. But I'm not getting any answers."

"I know," she said. "It's just the way things are."

He squeezed her hand. There was nothing more to say on the subject.

Upstairs, they made the final arrangements with the hospital for transporting Eduard's remains back to Holland. The flight had been booked for the following day. Pauline and Peter would travel with the body. They were to be met at Schiphol Airport by the Dutch funeral undertakers Pauline had hired. Mother and Fran and her family would be there, and so, now, would Clara and Diedrich. But no outsiders. Mother had insisted that it be family only.

There would be no church service; Eduard had always been adamant about that.

That night, their last together in New York, Peter took Pauline out to dinner at the River Café in Brooklyn. Afterwards, they stood on the deck, looking back in silence at the inexplicable nostalgia of the Manhattan skyline and the matching sentimental grandeur of Brooklyn Bridge.

Peter felt a stirring of impatience. The journey to Holland was looming as a daunting task, one he was proud and prepared to perform, but eager to get over with. He wanted to move on with his life. And his life *work*.

He thought of Laura, that single-minded artist in her two-room Amsterdam flat, bent over her photographs. He longed to see her again, to breathe the same air for a few hours, a day perhaps, and a night. He longed to hold her body, to touch it, to implant himself indelibly on her, and then to leave her without plan or promise, in freedom.

It was pointless to expect anything more permanent than that. Perhaps Laura was right to believe that their emotions would get in the way, that there was always a "price to pay," though he preferred to call it "consequences." Right now, he didn't think he could handle any more consequences for a while.

Pauline had been watching him stare across the river.

"You're having new ideas?" she asked. He thought her question concealed a world of understanding.

Peter smiled. He didn't know how much of his thinking he could share even with her. Some things were better left unsaid.

"The biggest idea I have is this. That, objectively speaking, life is without purpose. But having been cursed by evolution with self-awareness, we feel the urge to inject it with meaning. With a purpose. To make it liveable."

"And your purpose, Peter?"

Peter frowned. "I haven't worked it out. I'm bumbling along in search of the wisdom flower."

"You're not after capturing beauty? Celebrating it?"

"Of course I am. We all want *that*! But it's almost a luxury. There's something else, something deeper than celebration. Trying to understand the *whys* of life, of people's actions. And by illuminating them in the best way we can, perhaps help people to be *aware* of what they are doing, for better or for worse."

"And photography can provide that illumination?"

"I believe it can, sometimes. Because of the instant, unmediated effect photographs have on the human heart."

Pauline looked at her brother's face. He didn't look back. His eyes were on the Manhattan skyline. She hooked her arm into his. They walked along in silence.

Ten days later, Peter was back in New York. With his son.

Diedrich had kept mostly to himself in Holland. The boy was clearly moved by the burial ceremony which, in accordance with Eduard's wishes, was conducted without the help of clergy. Instead, as planned, Peter spoke words of remembrance, Pauline recited a poem she'd written, and Fran, flanked by Herman, read from her journal, ending with a God bless you. Peter's mother wished Eduard a tearful goodbye as she scattered a handful of earth on the descending coffin. As for Clara, her whispered "He was a wise man," was her way of expressing her feelings on this, her final farewell to Eduard and his family.

Diedrich, standing between his mother and father, held on to Peter's hand for much of the time. Afterwards, as they walked back, he found a moment with his father alone.

"Dad, I want to come back to New York with you!" He almost blurted it out. "I...I want to learn more about photography, and work in the darkroom

298

with you!"

Peter couldn't reply right away. The sense of family history repeating itself overwhelmed him.

"Well…but you…you've got to go back to school. You can't just…" He embraced the boy. "Let me talk to your mum, okay?"

"Because I really want to! You understand?"

"I understand."

Clara agreed to let Diedrich go back with Peter, for a week only. She'd call the headmaster, pleading the boy's sadness at his granddad's demise.

It turned out to be the most emotive period father and son had ever spent together. Peter relived those long-ago darkroom days with his own father as he watched Diedrich learn to handle the enlarger, and lifting the enlarged prints out of the basin. He recognized the boy's earnestness and was not surprised when Diedrich told him later in the week, over a simple lunch of bread, cheese and tomato, that he too wanted to become a photographer.

"We'll see," was Peter's response, but he knew that this time those words were not meant to discourage, and he smiled as he said them.

There was shouting in the street below and Diedrich rushed to the window. "Dad! Look, a fight! Quick, don't you want to go down with your camera?"

One glance and Peter knew what the commotion was all about. A serious brawl between two vagrants near an overflowing garbage can. *One black, the other Latino*, he thought. He had seen those two before. They were wrestling on the pavement now, and a flicker of steel suggested one had drawn a knife.

"Come!" he shouted as he grabbed his Leica. "But don't get too close!"

What happened next, Diedrich was unlikely to forget. His dad stepped out into the street and shouted at the fighting men to stop or he would take shots of their fight and send them to the police. Even Diedrich thought this was sheer bluff, but it worked. The men looked up and struggled to their feet, and after a few more shoves and punches left the scene, shouting obscenities at each other.

"You mean you didn't…" Diedrich asked incredulously.

Peter's smirk betrayed his secret before he revealed it. "I did, before I shouted. Two quick shots. Just in case."

"Wow! I want to see them!"

"Tomorrow," said Peter. "And after that, it's back to Chicago for you. Your school is waiting, Son, and I'll be waiting, and when it's vacation time, you can come back, and we'll work together, you and I, and we'll see what the future will bring."

They climbed the stairs, Peter's arm around his son's shoulders, which already felt strong and determined under his touch.

# About the Author

**Hans Brinckmann**, born in The Hague, suppressed his dream to embark on a career in writing and joined the Far Eastern staff training program of Amsterdam's Nationale Handelsbank fresh out of high school. He was assigned to the bank's Singapore branch, and then to the Kobe branch in Japan, eventually rising to Tokyo Branch Manager at age 29.

Always the "reluctant banker," he nevertheless continued to pursue his career, which eventually took him to New York, where he served as president of the Institute of Foreign Bankers, representing two hundred and forty banks, and as president of a Dutch-American foundation active in cultural exchange. In 1986, Queen Beatrix made him an Officer in the Order of Orange-Nassau for "cultural and professional achievement."

He retired from banking in 1988. Since then he has lived in London, Amsterdam, Sydney and Japan, developing his career as a journalist, lecturer, poet and writer of fiction and non-fiction prose. He has published two collections of short stories, a highly-acclaimed memoir, a post-war history of Japan and a book of poetry. Three of his books have been published in Japanese, in translations by Hiromi Mizoguchi. *In the Eyes of the Son* is his first novel.

In 2008, Brinckmann – together with his friend Ysbrand Rogge – held a month-long exhibition in Tokyo of photographs taken by them in Japan between 1951 and 1974, which drew 50,000 visitors. Brinckmann now lives in Fukuoka, Japan. He maintains two websites: www.habri.jp (bilingual English/Japanese) and www.habri.co.uk (English).

# Other Books by This Publisher

If you enjoyed *In the Eyes of the Son* consider these other fine works from Savant Books and Publications:

*Essay, Essay, Essay* by Yasuo Kobachi
*Aloha from Coffee Island* by Walter Miyanari
*Footprints, Smiles and Little White Lies* by Daniel S. Janik
*The Illustrated Middle Earth* by Daniel S. Janik
*Last and Final Harvest* by Daniel S. Janik
*A Whale's Tale* by Daniel S. Janik
*Tropic of California* by R. Page Kaufman
*Tropic of California* (the companion music CD) by R. Page Kaufman
*The Village Curtain* by Tony Tame
*Dare to Love in Oz* by William Maltese
*The Interzone* by Tatsuyuki Kobayashi
*Today I Am a Man* by Larry Rodness
*The Bahrain Conspiracy* by Bentley Gates
*Called Home* by Gloria Schumann
*Kanaka Blues* by Mike Farris
*First Breath* edited by Zachary M. Oliver
*Poor Rich* by Jean Blasiar
*Ammon's Horn* by Guerrino Amati
*The Jumper Chronicles* by W. C. Peever
*William Maltese's Flicker* by William Maltese
*My Unborn Child* by Orest Stocco
*Last Song of the Whales* by Four Arrows
*Perilous Panacea* by Ronald Klueh
*Falling but Fulfilled* by Zachary M. Oliver
*Mythical Voyage* by Robin Ymer
*Hello, Norma Jean* by Sue Dolleris
*Richer* by Jean Blasiar
*Manifest Intent* by Mike Farris
*Charlie No Face* by David B. Seaburn
*Number One Bestseller* by Brian Morley
*My Two Wives and Three Husbands* by S. Stanley Gordon
*In Dire Straits* by Jim Currie
*Wretched Land* by Mila Komarnisky
*Chan Kim* by Ilan Herman
*Who's Killing All the Lawyers?* by A. G. Hayes
*Ammon's Horn* by G. Amati
*Wavelengths* edited by Zachary M. Oliver

*Almost Paradise* by Laurie Hanan
*Communion* by Jean Blasiar and Jonathan Marcantoni
*The Oil Man* by Leon Puissegur
*Random Views of Asia from the Mid-Pacific* by William E. Sharp
*The Isla Vista Crucible* by Reilly Ridgell
*Blood Money* by Scott Mastro
*In the Himalayan Nights* by Anoop Chandola
*On My Behalf* by Helen Doan
*Traveler's Rest* by Jonathan Marcantoni
*Keys in the River* by Tendai Mwanaka
*Chimney Bluffs* by David B. Seaburn
*The Loons* by Sue Dolleris
*Light Surfer* by David Allan Williams
*The Judas List* by A. G. Hayes
*Path of the Templar - Book 2 of The Jumper Chronicles* by W. C. Peever
*The Desperate Cycle* by Tony Tame
*Shutterbug* by Buz Sawyer
*Blessed are the Peacekeepers* by Tom Donnelly/Mike Munger
*Purple Haze* by George B. Hudson
*The Turtle Dances* by Daniel S. Janik
*The Lazarus Conspiracies* by Richard Rose
*Imminent Danger* by A. G. Hayes
*Lullaby Moon* (CD) by Malia Elliott of Leon and Malia
*Volutions* edited by Suzanne Langford

Soon to be Released
*The Hanging of Dr. Hanson* by Bentley Gates
*Flight of Destiny* by Frances Powell
*Elaine of Corbenic* by Tima Z. Newman
*More More Time* by David B. Seaburn

http://www.savantbooksandpublications.com
http://www.savantbookstorehonolulu.com

www.ingramcontent.com/pod-product-compliance
Lightning Source LLC
Chambersburg PA
CBHW070919260626
47162CB00007B/2722